Mario Routi

Orizon

The Flame of the White Sun

Novel

LIVANI PUBLISHING ORGANISATION

Title: Orizon, The Flame of the White Sun
Genre: Fantasy Fiction
Author: Mario Routi, www.mariorouti.co.uk
Editor: Andrew Crofts

Translated from Greek to English: Eugenia Kollia
Edited by: Nick Austin

Published by: Livani Publishing Organisation, Crown House, 72 Hammersmith Road, Hammersmith, London, W14 8TH tel: 0207 559 3475, www.livani.co.uk
Distributed by: Gazelle UK, White Cross Mills, Hightown, Lancaster, LA1 4XS tel: 01524 68765, www.gazellebooks.co.uk
Print & Production: Livani Publishing Organisation
Art work, Design & Front Cover illustration: Track7 team: Thodoris Kyritsopoulos - Nektarios Chionis.
Pagemaking & Layout: Mercury

Promotion and Public Relations: Midas PR, www.midaspr.co.uk
Marketing Consultant: Alastair Giles, www.agile-ideas.com
Communication: The Y-club, www.y-club.com
Special Advisor: Nick Webb

1st Greek edition: October 2003
16th Greek edition: February 2006
1st edition in the U.K.: May 2006

ISBN: 960-14-1186-0

to my mother

CONTENTS

THE ABDUCTION

Rebecca put on her uniform, proudly attached her sword to her belt, and set out from her grandfather's house for the ceremony.

As she came out of the house she took a few deep breaths and looked up at the sky. A single white cloud sat calmly in the warmth of the sun, which had already completed most of its daily journey with only another couple of hours left before it could go to sleep.

Crossing the front yard to the stable, Rebecca noticed a large carriage drawn by four horses. A group of Orizon men were working on its rear right wheel.

"Are you Rebecca Newton?" one of them asked as she drew near.

"I am," she replied, smiling politely.

"Is your grandfather here? We need his help. Our carriage is broken and we're going to miss the ceremony."

Something about them made Rebecca uneasy. If they were on their way to the ceremony, why did they have no women or children with them? Her smile faded and her gaze grew wary.

"My grandfather's not here. Maybe I can help."

One of the Orizons made a grab for her. Although startled, Rebecca recovered in time to dodge him. He lost his balance and she landed a hard kick in his back as he fell past her. He shrieked in pain, clutching his waist and falling to the ground. The one who had spoken was now charging towards her. Leaping high in the air, Rebecca spun round, her foot making sharp contact with his throat, instantly immobilizing him. In those few seconds the remaining four had spread out a large net, which they cast with the skill of those Roman gladiators known as *retiarii* and Rebecca found herself entangled in it.

Her attackers pounced upon her like carnivorous beasts. She was floundering, lashing out at the burly men with her arms and legs. But the fight was futile as long as she was tangled up in the net.

As they brought her down she screamed for help, forcing them to gag her with a piece of hide as she kept fighting, trying to bite their fingers like a caged tiger. Her shouts turned to muffled growls once the gag was in place. One of them pulled his sword and, making a threatening gesture, snarled: "Shut up or I'll slaughter you like a chicken!"

All four of the attackers left standing were big men and their strength, coupled with the grip of the net, finally defeated Rebecca. She gave up her futile struggle. Despair filled her soul and a hundred questions rose into her mind. They roped and tied her inside the net and tossed her onto the floor of the carriage.

One of the men on the ground kept groaning, while the other stayed silent and motionless. When they lifted the first one he screamed with fear and pain. The other still made no sound. The men carefully laid both of their felled comrades beside her. Three of the men then climbed inside the carriage while the fourth went to the front to take the reins. As the vehicle lurched forward they quickly covered Rebecca and their two wounded colleagues with hides. As they clattered out of the yard they started to pick up speed.

Rebecca forced herself to keep calm. The ropes were tight and breathing was hard – it felt as if she were dying. Unable to use her arms to protect herself she was jolted and bumped painfully with every movement of the carriage. Her sword hilt was digging into her side. Trapped in a net! Now she knew how the poor fish must feel when they're hauled from the water alive.

The screams of the injured man filled the carriage; Rebecca guessed that she had broken his spine. She reckoned that the one she had struck in the throat was almost certainly dead. Her kung fu master had taught her to judge the effectiveness of each of her blows.

It was some time before one of her captors said: "We're far enough away. We can take off the Orizon clothes now."

Every excruciating hour of the journey seemed like a century to Rebecca as she was tossed back and forth. Snatches of conversation confirmed that the one they referred to as General Varta was dead and the other, General Bitho, was severely wounded. His screams faded when the pain became too great for him to bear and he passed into a merciful unconsciousness.

It was the first time that Rebecca had killed anyone; it was an unpleasant feeling. Even though it had been in self-defence she had nevertheless taken a life. She imagined General Varta's parents and the pain and distress they would feel if they were still alive; also his now fatherless children. If General Bitho had a spinal injury it meant he would be crippled for ever, confined to a wheelchair for the rest of his life. Disturbing thoughts roamed through her mind as she fought to control her own pain and fear. Her fate and her life had changed so abruptly and unexpectedly.

When Rebecca had stepped from her grandfather's house she had been thinking only of the excitement of the ceremony she was going to and of the enormity of the choice that she had made. Now she was a helpless captive, tied up and hidden from view. She could scarcely breathe; she couldn't see anything and had no idea where she was being taken or what fate lay in store for her.

It was as if the hours were riding inside the carriage, travelling with her, captured alongside her in the net, being dragged back so that each minute seemed like an hour and each hour like a year.

The pain grew gradually worse. If Rebecca's abductors intended to deliver her alive, they might well fail in their mission. In their hurry, they'd bound her so tightly that her circulation was impeded. Her legs began to stiffen, then her arms and finally she felt as if her whole body had become an alien object, lifeless. She knew that death would be upon her if the journey lasted much longer. All she could move, with great difficulty, were her fingers and toes, so she took courage from that. She dilated and flattened her nostrils, and wrinkled and relaxed her brow; these small actions were all indications of life and proof that her abductors had not yet succeeded in killing her.

Rebecca began to count how many movements she could make with her fingers, her toes, how many with her nose and her brow. It was like a game, an exercise that kept her conscious as the hours dragged past.

"Those horses go too slowly … If I was driving I would go faster," she kept thinking, hovering between life and death. *"I think I'll die. Death is sweet … I'll drive the horses … No … no … I don't want the riding crop …"*

Then Rebecca felt as though she'd been tied to the back wheel of the carriage, the one that they'd told her was broken. She felt she was spinning round and round with it. She soon felt dizzy. Her insides were churning and became mixed with her confused thoughts. She kept losing consciousness and then regaining it. She lost all sense of time. She heard creakings, other noises. She felt the wheels turning and then she lost herself once more in a strange chaos.

"The torture of the rack … I know … I have read … I won't tell those spies the secret … Never! I won't ever tell them that I'm Orizon … Never! Dad said I shouldn't … I'd rather die … Am I delirious? I mustn't …"

Rebecca groaned and almost fainted again.

"Why am I so stiff? Is my heart beating? It must be, since I can think ... But why do I feel so strange? Is death like this? If eternity is like this, it isn't nice … But … it may get better …"

Suddenly the wheel stopped. Rough hands bundled her in a large piece of hide.

"Have I talked? I haven't … I haven't given anything away … I'm sure of it!"

Someone slung Rebecca carelessly over their shoulder. She sensed that they were climbing up some stairs and it felt like they had taken only a few steps before she was dropped. As best she could, she braced herself to land on a hard floor but she hit something soft instead. Her limbs were numb and she had no strength left to struggle. The tight bindings had constricted her blood's circulation, she realized again. She heard people talking quietly but couldn't make out the words over the thumping in her ears. Then someone took away her covering.

As her captors pulled the hide wrap off her, Rebecca saw that she was in a large room, sprawled out on a couch. As they cut the ropes the blood rushed back painfully, causing her to take a sharp intake of breath. Still leaving her inside the net, they bound her legs more carefully. Once they were sure that she was securely trussed they pulled the net away and tied her hands behind her back. Managing to glance at her watch she saw that it was three in the morning. They'd been travelling for nearly nine hours. They took her sword away and helped her to sit upright. The pain in her limbs began to subside as her blood flowed more freely.

Rebecca looked around her. She seemed to be in a living room that was spacious but simple in style. The four men who had brought her there were standing around her and there was another man seated in an armchair opposite her.

"You may go now," the seated man told them. "See to Varta's funeral and have the doctors examine Bitho to see what they can do."

"Very well, Your Majesty," said one of the four. "Before we leave, please heed our advice. She is the most dangerous being we have ever encountered. You can't imagine how ferociously and skilfully she fought. We saw her, but we still can't believe it."

"I'll keep that in mind. Don't worry," he said.

The four men bowed slightly and left the room.

The man watched Rebecca calmly and smiled. He was sturdy and handsome and, even though he was seated, she could tell that he was tall. He had long, grey hair and a dark complexion, a small nose and a determined chin. Big black eyes shone out from below sparse eyebrows. The overall effect was friendly. He wore a black leather uniform and boots, and had a wide belt from which hung a huge sword in a scabbard.

"So this is King Turgoth," thought Rebecca.

"So you are the notorious Rebecca!" the tall man said, with a touch of admiration in his voice.

Turgoth stood up, walked silently to a corner of the room and returned with a knife. He came up so close to Rebecca that she caught the scent of his skin. With a few deft strokes he cut through the fibre rope that the men had so carefully used a few moments before to fasten her wrists. She noticed the veins on his hands, a prominent network of strong cordlike striations.

A terracotta jug and two cups stood on a small side table. Turgoth filled both cups with water. He placed the jug and one of the cups in front of her, taking the other cup with him back to his armchair.

"Drink some water," he said. "You must be thirsty."

Rebecca didn't move. She said nothing.

"What are you thinking? Have some water. It's no sin. A few sips of water won't put you in my debt."

Still no response.

"What have I done to make you sulk like this? If anything, I should be the one to bear a grudge. You've killed one of my generals and incapacitated another."

"It would have been better if they'd killed me," Rebecca said. "Abduction is one of the worst crimes. Don't you know that?"

"So, you *do* have a voice. Whether abduction is a crime or not depends on the reason for it."

"No," Rebecca insisted. "A crime is a crime. There aren't two sides to it. You must know, Turgoth, that your actions make you appear very low in my eyes. A man who acts like this does not deserve to rule a kingdom and have its fortune and future depend on him. Whatever your reason may be, whatever you expect to gain from me, your action cannot be justified. The purpose does not erase the crime."

She paused for a second. Turgoth said nothing, so she continued.

"For thousands of years on Earth there have been revolutions in which sovereign powers have been overthrown. Terrorists, thieves and blackmailers sometimes become prime ministers, dictators and governors as a result, controlling the lives of millions of people. When they plant their revolutionary bombs, they believe that they are blessed and justified. But they soon realize that the bombs of those who now want to overthrow *them* are criminal devices, so their opponents must be punished, imprisoned, exiled or executed. But whoever rises to power in this way is a criminal themself and their crimes cannot be erased simply because they lead them to power. I shouldn't have to tell you these things. You know history very well, Turgoth."

She could see Turgoth was stunned that she could argue so eloquently and boldly.

"Well said, Rebecca. You're right, of course. What you say is true, although I hope you don't think I came to power in such a manner."

Rebecca said nothing.

"When we were first divided, someone else was the king of Beast. He was killed about six hundred Earth years ago, at Lomani. There was no other immortal, so I was obliged to take responsibility for the Kingdom. I didn't usurp the throne. I would never have chosen such a role. I'd rather be a passenger or a crewman than a captain. I would rather play a minor role well than be the shining star. The whims of fate, however, dictated otherwise.

"But now I have a sacred purpose. All my efforts have been directed at gaining the same rights for my people as you Orizons have. Rightly or wrongly, the Mythical Gods granted the Flame exclusively to you. I don't know what the will of the Great Creator was. He probably never concerned Himself with this matter. But since that moment, only you have had the right to enjoy the privileges bestowed by the Flame. You never fall ill or grow old. The beauty and vitality of the Orizon women remain untouched while the beauty and vitality of our loveliest women are fleeting, just like those of women on Earth. The years stick like leeches, sucking away their freshness, first from the eyes and then from the body. Our women's skins become like the bark of a thousand-year-old trees, whereas the complexions of Orizon women remain like the petals of a lily. Youth fades away, old age arrives, and then comes death! The same applies to your men, too: none of them ever look more than fifty years old. Do you think this is fair, Rebecca? Shouldn't I fight with any weapons at my disposal to gain the same rights for my people? Do they not deserve that hope?"

"It's true that I didn't till now see any elderly people in Utopia. It's important to look young and be healthy until you die," Rebecca replied after a moment's thought. "Beauty, youth and good health are privileges that can also provide self-confidence. So, if things are as you say, then the discrimination between the Sharkans and the Orizons is not just."

"Well said again, Rebecca. I have lived for thousands of years, yet, I still can't explain the foolhardy decision of the Gods to divide us into two camps, not the various criteria that they used," Turgoth pressed on. "But the point is that ever since the division we have lost both the Flame and the right to travel to Earth and strive for its good. We are considered evil and useless. Is that just?"

He took a sip of water, aware that he had allowed his passions to take over. "But to make life bearable, we have to get used to living hand in hand with this injustice. Is that what you think?"

"Why have you abducted me?" Rebecca asked.

Turgoth raised his hands as if to confess his sins.

"I could have killed you. But I wanted to get to know you. I believe you are a talented person, with many fine qualities. You have a lot to offer, both to the Land of the White Sun and to the Earth. I had also heard that you were in doubt – concerning your decision, that is. I assume you made up your mind at the very last minute. I fear you made the wrong choice, despite your undoubted intelligence."

"But I *have* made up my mind," Rebecca said defiantly. "And it's final. So you had better kill me and get it over with."

"It's not so simple. I want us to talk things over. In the end, if you think that what I say is wrong I'll hand you the sword so that you can kill me. I give you my word!"

Rising from his seat, Turgoth drew his sword and placed it with the knife in the far corner of the room. Picking up Rebecca's sword he brought it back to her and cut through the ropes round her legs. Taking the tip of the blade in his hand he brought the hilt close to her chest, staring intently into her eyes.

Rebecca lowered her head, refusing to look at him.

"Rebecca, look into my eyes. If you believe that I'm lying or that we are enemies and must kill each other, then grab the sword and kill me. Take it. I'm not bluffing."

Rebecca kept her gaze cast down and made no attempt to take the sword. Turgoth did not move for a full minute. Then he left the sword beside her on the couch and returned to his chair.

"All right: you won't take it and you don't want to kill me. At least drink some water."

Rebecca remembered the lion in Kenya. She thought that she was now the lion and Turgoth was in her shoes. She couldn't hold back her tears and some of them rolled down her cheeks, dripping into the water. She lifted the cup and drank. It tasted good.

Turgoth noticed them and he too was moved. Without

a word he stood up and left her alone to compose herself, to gather her thoughts.

She was alone with the Leader of Beast. Just a little while ago she could have killed him in a second, had she wanted to. It was a lot to take in.

Rebecca looked around the room. It was similar to their living room in Utopia: spacious, simple and practical. The ordinariness of the room heightened the extraordinariness of the situation.

She thought of Turgoth's warm and expressive eyes. They seemed to emit a strange radiance, penetrating and exploring her thoughts. It was as if he could read everything that she was thinking, anticipating her words. It was like having a spy inside her head browsing through her mind, page by page. That was why she had turned her gaze from his, breaking off their unspoken conversation for fear of what might be said.

At the same time Rebecca felt that she also knew what Turgoth was going to say before he spoke. She had even predicted what he had done with the sword. It was as if they could sit silently opposite one another, just looking into each other's eyes, and be able to conduct a complete and meaningful conversation. In a way it had been an enjoyable game and she wasn't sure why she had put such an abrupt stop to it. Now that he had given her a chance to gather her thoughts, though, she decided to go ahead with it, following wherever it might lead.

Standing up, she took a few steps to stretch her aching legs. At last! After nine hours she was walking again. An open door led through to a library and her curiosity got the better of her. The shelves of books stretched from floor to ceiling and she recognized many of the titles. She had even read some of them and it was like coming across old friends. She cocked her head to one side to read the spines, occasionally pulling a volume out with her finger to examine it more closely, lost for a few moments in her own world of memories and thoughts.

When Turgoth returned he brought with him a large bowl of fruit and a jug of juice. They resumed their seats, she on the couch and he in his armchair.

"You've got a lot of books," Rebecca said, gesturing towards the library.

"I read a lot. We all do in the Land of the White Sun. It's one of the greatest pleasures. Cultivation is as essential to the mind and spirit as food is to the body."

"It was Cicero who said that, wasn't it?"

"Indeed." Turgoth smiled, pleased that she had recognized the quotation. "That's the meaning of life for me. I'm always thirsty for knowledge and I refuse to allow my thoughts ever to take a rest."

"I noticed that you have several editions of Homer's *Iliad* and *Odyssey*."

He nodded. "Those of us who travelled back and forth after Earth's destruction became interested in Homer's endeavours. He combined elements of life and mythology from before the destruction with things that he saw in his own time, after the restoration of life. I've been reading his works for thousands of years and I'll continue to do so as long as I live. He's inexhaustible. His zest and passion set my own imagination free. It's like listening to music. And music heals wounds!"

They fell into silence for a while.

"King Turgoth," Rebecca said eventually, staring him straight in the eyes, "how did you know about my decision in Utopia?"

Turgoth was surprised that she had used his title. He wondered whether she had deliberately meant to use it or whether it had just slipped out. He clasped his hands and cracked his knuckles as he considered his reply.

"I'm aware of everything important that goes on in Utopia. You can always find hypocrites, traitors and spies, even there."

Rebecca was shocked. A spy in Utopia? A traitor?

"Who is this traitor?" she blurted.

The king smiled. "If I told you that, then I would be a traitor too. I don't approve of treachery, but if such people bring me useful information for my people I will listen to them."

"I'm going to die anyway, so why won't you tell me?"

"Don't insist, Rebecca. It can't be done." Turgoth seemed irritated by her persistence.

"Is there just one or are there many?"

"There is only one. Don't ask any more."

They fell silent again.

"I don't understand," Rebecca suddenly burst out. "Why can't we live peacefully and enjoy God's bounty? Why do we have to fight? We can see when we travel around that the universe works in harmony and we gaze in awe at its perfection. Why can't we be the same? "

Turgoth thought for a while before answering.

"The Orizons have failed on Earth. For thousands of years they've achieved nothing. Earth's society is like a storm-tossed vessel. The prow is lavishly decorated with gilded wooden carvings, but below decks the galley slaves are in chains, parched and starving, their bodies scarred by the lash. Values are corrupted, rotten even before they're born, like ships that have sunk before they've left port. Most people don't apply them in that shallow, disorganized society. Happiness is just a couple of brush strokes on the huge painting of each person's life. All that exists is short-term self-interest. The planet will be destroyed once more and we'll have to start all over again."

Rebecca said nothing, knowing that Turgoth hadn't finished. After a few moments he leaned forward, speaking slowly as if anxious for her to understand the lessons he was giving her.

"We all have a coercive life contract, but none of us signed it. We were not present when it was drawn up and we weren't asked for our views on it. Only our parents, delighted by their newborns – as if they'd been given toys to play with – were present in front of the notary. Even worse, they handed us a ticket and a stamped passport and forced us to embark on a trip to death. The moment we were born, we were also condemned to death. You see, we are unfairly dealt with before we even come into existence.

"And the people of Beast continue to be treated unfairly, all through their lives."

Turgoth sat back in his chair, staring at her, watching to see the effect of his words.

Rebecca nodded thoughtfully for a while before speaking. "When the division took place in the Land of the White Sun, why did you choose to come to Beast?"

"We all have a right to be what we already are, or to strive to become what we want to be. It never crossed my mind that those who chose Beast would be deprived of the Flame.

"I've always been a rebellious creature. I like to think for myself. The procedure I follow is: Think, Choose, Believe, Express, Try, Fulfil. I didn't choose the road travelled by most people. I never followed the footsteps of others. More: never did I step into them. I blazed my own trail and traced new roads, regardless of the hardships along the way. I always chose to swim against the flow of the river, like a salmon, no matter how turbulent the current might be. I took care to avoid stumbling or being ambushed or falling into traps. From time to time I would rest and look back to see how far I'd come, and what I had been through to get there. I'd see how I'd drawn my course, what I'd left behind, what I'd lost on the way and what I'd gained. I made my own reckoning and evaluation. Then I would draw a few deep breaths, take courage from God and continue my lonely route towards the inaccessible mountaintops with their countless eagles' nests. I never went back to correct my mistakes. *'What's done is done. Just keep going and don't make the same mistakes again,'* I said to myself and in this way I benefited a lot from my mistakes and misadventures."

Turgoth paused, waiting to see if Rebecca would interrupt. When she didn't he continued: "I used to climb this tree which stood on the shore of my favourite lake. I would sit there in the branches with the birds for company and we would chat. We noticed the tree's twin planted upside down in the water and were enchanted by its colours and the way it rippled whenever the lake quivered under the kisses of the wind. I used to tell the birds that I was going to search among the dense foliage to find the fish and keep them company; that I would learn their dialect so that I could talk to them too. Then I would dive in. But whenever I did, the tree would disappear.

"I preferred listening to monotonous cicadas rather than to the varied, heady, melodious song of the nightingale. Of course, I listened to the nightingale too – I loved to hear it – but I was a true devotee of the cicada. I preferred the elephant that slept standing to the other animals that lay down to sleep. I favoured the wild, stormy sea, perhaps because its rhythms matched my soul's. I rejected the cream and gnawed hungrily at the scraps.

"I always believed that if I ever had to face the hangman

I wouldn't let him put the rope round my neck. I would do it myself to humiliate him and all those he represented. To everyone else it doesn't matter who fastens the noose, but it matters greatly for your own honour, your dignity and your history. Of course, the real point is not to end up on the gallows in the first place.

"So when the division began and most people wanted to stay in Utopia in order to side with the forces of Good, I chose the other path and came to Beast. I came here because I wanted to follow a different path, not because I am unclean or evil."

"What you just said about putting the rope around your own neck really impressed me. It reminded me of Napoleon when he grabbed the crown from the Pope and named himself Emperor."

"Well ... that's not quite the same, Rebecca. A crown is a different thing to a rope."

"Although I'm not as experienced as you, Your Majesty, I do believe that they are very alike."

Turgoth's surprise grew. He thought for a moment, closed his eyes and opened them again. Then he said: "You're probably right. Maybe it is the same thing. The responsibilities that the crown holds can choke you or guide you to the hangman."

"Anyway, what exactly happened at the division?" Rebecca asked.

Turgoth sighed. "The truth is that we were at each other's throats. We were fighting over silly things for no reason. We had everything we needed and lived a perfect life. We had our differences, certainly, but we had no wars or killing. The Mythical Gods supposedly became exasperated with our squabbling, although I suspect that was just a pretext. I think they had already decided to abandon us. Gods, kings, governors and politicians have always wanted to live separately, at a distance from common mortals. They reckon they're better off that way. So they gathered us all together and said: *'We are tired of your quarrelling. We are leaving, going to the Second Parallel Dimension. You will be divided into two kingdoms. Each of you can choose to which one you want to belong, so as to put an end to all your strife.'*

"They caused chaos, just as rulers and politicians constantly do on Earth. So either the Gods lost their minds, or there was a great conspiracy. That is how the division happened. It was only later that we rebels discovered we had lost the Flame! The chosen ones had grasped it.

"It's strange to think that the wars began because of the Flame, effectively abolishing immortality. If there had been no war after the split there would not have been a single death, since all the inhabitants of the Land of the White Sun were immortal. Eventually the battles destroyed all the immortal Sharkans – except for me – and many Porths and Cyclopes too. Utopia also sustained heavy casualties among the immortals and the Mythical creatures.

"For thousands of years I've tried to understand why humanity keeps starting wars, tried to work out the underlying causes. The oddest thing of all is that people actually want to participate. Those who volunteer to fight need their heads examined, what with their delusions of gallantry and self-sacrifice. Mercenaries are totally incomprehensible. Are they heroes or murderers?"

Turgoth paused, then asked Rebecca: "Do you want anything to eat?"

"No." Rebecca shook her head.

He rose and poured some juice, sipping it with obvious pleasure as he returned to his armchair. He sat down comfortably, crossed one leg over the other, let out a deep sigh and continued:

"Lord Life is authorized to travel to the Second Parallel Dimension to talk with the Mythical Gods. I have no such right. In the beginning, when I first took over the leadership of Beast, we used to travel together. On one of our visits, while we were eating dainty morsels and drinking rare wine with the Gods, I asked why the Creator had made some things on Earth the wrong way round. They almost choked. They stopped stuffing the faces and telling racy stories and demanded that I explain myself.

"I said, '*The Creator leaves the Earth bare and uncovered to shiver in the icy winter. In spring, when it is warm and no protection is needed, he dresses her up, clothing her in colourful dresses. In the summer he undresses her again. Her skin is scorched and cracked from the heat. He should have attired her warmly in winter, covered her lightly in summer and left her bare during spring to enjoy both the cool breeze and the sweet warmth. Only in autumn is she properly half-naked; the only part of the year that's right. Then the people till the soil, digging and hoeing it. The Earth is glad when they scratch her back, massage and tickle her. She breathes deeply and unites with the seeds.*'

"Well, their eyes bulged and they gulped whole jugs of wine to recover, but I kept going:

'*What is the use of sly poisonous snakes, crafty scorpions, sickly obstinate mosquitoes and filthy, irritating flies? Or of wild stormy seas that drown fishermen and sailors? Why are people born cursed with lifelong disabilities? Why do epidemics and diseases exist? And if He severely punishes humans with murderous earthquakes, violent floods, hailstorms, hot-tempered typhoons, thunderbolts and volcanic eruptions, what have the innocent animals and plants that die with them done to deserve this fate? And why does He send the rising and falling waves to drown thousands of innocent children? What is the point of rain at sea when huge expanses of land suffer chronic catastrophic drought? It's as if God used his watering can on the oceans while neglecting plants and animals. It makes people resort to litanies and sacrifices, pleading with their Gods. And why, in order to survive, must one living creature devour another, so that life can only continue through death?'*

"As I spoke, their jaws dropped like those of bulldogs waiting for the signal to pounce and mangle me. But I felt lightened, like a pregnant woman who gives birth when the foetus has come to term and she can't keep it in any longer. What they heard had been growing in me for a long time. It had swollen up, almost choking me, and I finally brought it forth with all the pain of childbirth.

"There was uproar. The Gods were furious! They cursed me and forbade me to visit them again without permission. I was disgraced and banished! I could see that the Mythical Gods of Egypt wanted to support me, but they didn't dare. Like the rest of them, when it comes to it they prefer to sit safely on their thrones and have a good time. Why should they make a fuss and risk losing their sweet euphoria?

"Since then, I have to tell Lord Life if I need to see the Mythical Gods, and he will take me to them only if permission is granted in advance.

"I have no wish at all to see them ever again, but in the interests of the people of Beast I must. I don't want them to disinherit my people because of my angry tongue. I can't bear the Mythical Gods, with their stale and rusty supercilious wit, their autocratic irascible ways and their sterility of spirit. I particularly can't bear their idleness. I believe that they should be genuine and truly involved. I want them to be infallible compasses, putting things right, not posing and acting important just because they are Gods. I want them to *care*. Most of all, I wish they'd resurrect all the great values and meanings of life from the mud and let them loose in the world.

"Whenever I visit them, I try to adopt Lord Life's affability and composure. Armed with those desirable qualities I try to find a way to communicate with the Gods. I behave with fine manners that don't suit me at all, and with a pretended politeness that chokes me. I explain to them that our fighting for the Flame is cruel. But they see me as a parasite. They believe I'm grumpy, ungainly, quarrelsome and ill-fated. They listen with deaf ears and stare silently with their stern bulging eyes, keeping their mouths sealed. They won't get involved, believing that we should solve the problem on our own. But we cannot resolve much simpler problems, so how can we solve the issue of the Flame?

"Sometimes, despite their apparent apathy, I believe that I can see jealousy in their eyes. As if they were in Hell while I am in Paradise. Maybe I'm imagining it. Who knows? In any case, I confront them stoically. I'm not a hustler, nor can I bargain with them. Even after thousands of years, I haven't learned how to hide my feelings.

"Although I am the only one who speaks, they make me stand in front of them still, as if I am supposed to sing the National Anthem. They try to humiliate me and make me feel like a small schoolboy in the presence of a teacher, or like a private soldier facing a general. But as I talk to them I rub the grass with my boots, as I would rub their faces in the dirt. I do of course recognize that I am talking to clever foxes and experienced operators, and that's why I try my best. But they keep looking at me with their disgusted expressions, like they're eating rotten food. They make me feel like the kid in the Dickens tale, the one who tried to wish Scrooge a Merry Christmas. And so the result is always the same: zero!"

They were both silent for a few minutes as Rebecca tried to take in everything she was hearing. Eventually she spoke.

"Through love, music, song, dance and the other arts, you can touch happiness and pave the way to that objective. But you have turned your back on the poetic approach to life. You chose to take up arms and kill in order to get the Flame. So, why do you wage war?"

"I've told you: I'm vehemently opposed to war, but I inherited an obligation over which much blood has been shed. A great injustice has been done to my people. Put your mind and your heart in the position of the Sharkans for a moment, Rebecca, and see how they feel. Who could tolerate it? Ours is probably the most justifiable war ever to be waged in this universe."

Rebecca looked deep into his eyes.

"Tell me honestly, King Turgoth, if you won the next Lomani and got the Flame, would you share it with the people of Utopia?"

"You must know that my subjects, and above all my generals, don't all think as I do. I don't want to shift the blame onto others, because I'm the leader of Beast. I don't need any excuses. But my people have been fighting and dying for this Flame for generations and for thousands of Earth years. So if they regain it once more at the cost of their own blood, I doubt if they will be willing to share it. If I ordered them to do so they would consider me a traitor. He who betrays the people he governs is the worst traitor of all."

"That happens almost every day on Earth," Rebecca said. Turgoth shrugged as if that merely proved his point.

"I hold Lord Life in high regard. He has a sharp mind, a rare impressive character and an organizational talent. Eloquent, always coherent and imposing – but also at heart a roughneck, an old man of the world, like myself. I believe that he faces the same problems I do. I'm sure he sees the injustice of it all. But he's aware that if he dares to share the Flame with us his people will consider him a traitor and Utopia will flare up, even though they've had the Flame to themselves for so many years. They've suffered casualties in the conflicts as well. So, Rebecca, I can never promise that if we get the Flame we shall share it with the citizens of Utopia. That is the truth."

"You've answered honestly. No one wants to lose what they have, especially if blood has been shed to keep it. Likewise, no one wants to share what they have acquired, especially if they've had to fight to obtain it. These are eternal truths.

"If a man sacrifices himself for an idea, then his children or his parents, perhaps even his close friends and companions often become fanatics in support of his views, whether they were correct or not. Sometimes they can spread that fanaticism and build entire religions on it. So hatred is spread and perpetuated. Everything I have read and heard tells me that happens all the time on Earth, in every revolution and every political and ideological confrontation. Of course, nobody ever admits that they've taken part in something like that."

Turgoth nodded thoughtfully, his stare boring into her eyes.

"So, in the end, what is Good and what is Evil, Rebecca? Why are *we* the evil ones? Why should it not be you Orizons, you who refuse to share the Flame?"

"There are many cases on Earth of seemingly insoluble problems, like that of the Flame. It's not right, but it happens."

"But is it right for the just people of Utopia – who call themselves good – to allow such injustice and create such a potential conflict?"

"Not being evil is not enough. We should not sit round doing nothing. We must actively try to do good."

"Are you saying that you Orizons are always striving for good and that we are constantly working towards evil?"

Rebecca opened her mouth to reply but Turgoth held up his hand to stop her.

"Our hands are tied. What else can we do? You can go to Earth and at least make an effort. We can't. But those efforts are still not enough. The bread that people eat on Earth is still stained with blood, as it has always been. Countless people have never known laughter and countless more are dried up from weeping. So far you have achieved absolutely nothing. Society is in a coma.

"You have the Flame as well. What do we have? Always remember this: the greatest, the worst, the only inexorable and invincible enemy for all mortals is time. On Beast, life comes and life goes at an extraordinary pace. When you are a child each day passes slowly, but as you grow older the years go by like the wind. People are kids only for a while, but they are elders for even less. It's the same for all mortals, living on borrowed time, which the lender can take back whenever he wishes. The basic meaning of their lives is that whatever lives must die! And they will never learn what death is. When they taste death, they will feel nothing. Life's death is certain, but death's life is unknown …

"My people suffer from illnesses and die natural deaths, regardless of Lomani. Children are born with defects and suffer throughout their lives. Some need transplants to stay alive and organs will be taken from those who are killed. How ironic!

"You see the innocent eyes of children looking around, carefree and seemingly unconcerned. But if you paid closer attention, you would see that they are sending you a message: '*We're in your hands and in your minds. It's up to you what kind of life and society you deliver us to.*' Here in Beast we give them over to disease, the nightmare of war and futility. On Earth, in addition to all that, we burden them with all the tribulations of the world.

"I cannot delay old age for them, make overwhelming illnesses disappear or stop death.

"You can't hide age! We feel it, and everyone else sees it. The older people of Beast drag their years along on tired legs. They cannot lift them, because each step they take feels like they are lifting the ground too. The fear of sickness and death overwhelms them. They get tired of being frightened!

"Nature and the Creator ought to allow mortals to retain a basic level of dignity rather than allowing them to become withered, rotten ruins, unable to look after themselves because of old age or sickness. Right up to the time that their lives end they should be strong, healthy, beautiful and intelligent, with all their senses unimpaired. They should die with dignity, rather than desolate, powerless, disgraced, tortured, miserable, piteous and aching.

"A dead person has nothing to lose. All those years are spent for that second of doom – a life of struggle for a moment of death. We live and die in hope. Why should the people of Beast keep on fighting? We consider families to be the most important part of the social network and we give them our full support. There are no divisions or great disputes among us. We cope as best we can with the weaknesses that Nature has bestowed upon us but, unlike you, we no longer have the energy of the Flame with which to overcome them. So we try to live as well as possible, without bothering the others. But we do want to help the Earth. That is especially true for me. It's my homeland and I still feel that I belong there. Here I feel like a refugee."

"King Turgoth, I agree with almost everything you say. Life is short, and each moment of it is valuable. But I also believe that for mortals there is no present. There is only the past and the future. These are two real concepts that constantly change. The past grows with every millionth of a second that passes while the future shrinks accordingly. You take a breath and, even before you exhale, it is in the past. The present is a tireless labourer with a spade who keeps on digging out life from the future and shovelling it back into the past.

"Of course immortality is a great temptation. An immortal, such as you, has a fixed past, present and future – as long as he isn't killed. A mortal has no present and his future – his life, that is – constantly diminishes."

Turgoth's eyes filled with tears.

"Rebecca, you have touched me deeply. You have been thinking about things that I too have pondered for years and that trouble me greatly. But you also speak of things that I've never thought about before, even though I am thousands of years older than you. You amaze me.

"I am Egyptian. When I was young, before the destruction, I learned about the religion of my land. I was told that I should always do good and not die in sin, because the Gods held a pair of scales where they weighed up the good deeds and bad deeds of our lives. If the scales didn't tip towards the side of the good deeds, I would have trouble in eternal life. I wasn't concerned about a passport to Paradise but about spiritual serenity. That was the reason I always had a pair of scales in my guts, night and day. At first it leaned towards the wrong side, because I committed many sins, and then I would try to make the scales balance. I would try to find something good to put quickly on the other side, so that I could ease my conscience.

"I had this war going on inside me all the time, my better nature and my instincts constantly leading me along different paths. Life is full of Homer's seductive sirens and we are not all as clever or as strong as Ulysses. The Trojan Horse is no more; and Ulysses was cunning enough to tie himself to the mast or hide in the hold in order to escape. I, being the street dog that I am, would plunge straight into temptation, taking the mast with me.

"When it rained and the wind blew strongly, I used to go out in the streets. I felt the water from the sky washing away my sins, as though I was being baptized. I would walk until the storm had finished, no matter how long it lasted. Then I felt pure, clean and innocent. But afterwards I returned once more to the passions and the needs of my fickle life, and to the sins. When I talk about sins, Rebecca, I mean foolish things. I didn't kill or rape anyone or steal. But I wanted to live and you are only alive if you feel, dream, search and want! I was hungry for everything. Even when I was asleep I would fight to keep my senses alert.

"I didn't believe the Gods could possibly get so angry so easily. They wouldn't torment or threaten anyone, I believed. Nor could they be so vengeful as to punish. Could they have created hell? Our priests told us that God was testing us. I didn't believe that, either. I don't think God tempts people to see what they will do and how they will react. It's impossible and meaningless, because He already knows how each of us will react. If He didn't know this, He wouldn't be God."

Turgoth sipped his juice, forgetting for a moment why they were there together.

"In those days I had a childish insolence," he admitted. "I was trying to apply independent rules, tactics and principles. I soon discovered that many letters were missing from the alphabet. I was starting with the solutions and then seeking out the problems. I had my own exclusive code to follow and I was trying to improve it constantly. I wanted to sort out what I *could* do, what I *wanted* to do, what I *had* to do, and what I *shouldn't* do. But I always loved imperfection more than the formal ideals.

"I disagreed with the Creator on many issues. I would have preferred trees to put forth their fruit first – so that people could eat their fill – and then produce their flowers. Because if the wind gets rough and blows them away, or winter returns and freezes them, there will be no fruit. Since He was omnipotent, I reckoned that He could easily have reversed the order, so that we could enjoy the substance first and the beauty afterwards.

"I hammered the symbols like a maniac, so that I could give them the shape I desired most, just like the blacksmith treats his iron in the fire.

"I'm sure that my rough character irritated the divine establishment. I had many conflicts with them because I wouldn't fit into their warped mould. I would become angry and I continually breached their entrenched religious and ideological positions. I would shout that the intellect needs freedom. It can't live in cells, caves, under crofts or in labyrinths. But they were closing my mouth with a muzzle, which I chewed like gum and spat in their faces.

"I preached each day: *'I am rich! I'm the richest person on Earth. I have my own sunrise and my own sunset. I have my own Golden Friend. Every day, without exception, I'm waiting for him to show up. I never miss a sunrise. I smile at him and he smiles back. He fills me with joy and optimism. And before he hides, every sunset, both of us talk and review the day that has just passed. I tell him what I met and what I thought on Earth, while he talks of the most important things that he's witnessed from the sky. Neither have I ever missed a sundown. Can you all hear me? Not one sundown have I ever missed! Even if the day was cloudy!*

"One day, when I was still a child, I said to my mother: '*I learned at school today that the Earth is round. So, mother, I thought that the sky has a good foundation, the Earth, on which it stands. But the Earth has no such basis. It is suspended in the air. I saw its picture in a book today. It has nothing at all to support it. So I choose to live in the sky. I want to live there, to have a strong foundation beneath me and not be on Earth, dangling in the air. Otherwise I'll eat my heart out. In my mind, mother, I cannot build a bridge from the Earth to the sky. I'd rather sail through the clouds than be tossed by the waves with the broken masts and torn sails of wrecked ships. Let the wind seize me and raise me up to the stars. Then I can find peace. There are exquisite gardens of colourful corals in the depths of the sea. Beautiful flowers and plants on Earth. I want to plant flowers among the stars from the souls and minds of the people, to water them and tend them according to the instructions of God. The Creator needs volunteer gardeners! Mother, my soul has already escaped from my body and is in heaven. I feel the breath of God caressing me and redeeming me.*'

"My mother didn't understand me at all. She became frantic! I was her dear son. '*Farah, our neighbour, has sacrificed to the Gods and turned your head,*' she said. Then she cursed the poor woman ten times and all the curses worked.

"She recounted everything I'd told her to her stingy brother with his misshapen body. He had been a scrap dealer but had managed to prosper and had raised himself to the trade of pedlar. My uncle, like the good relative he was, told her that I was loony and that he would prove it to her. So he called me into her presence and, despite her grief, commanded: *'Go to the top of the hill, my child, to check whether I'm coming back from the other village on my camel.'* I left immediately, running like a rabbit, and he looked triumphantly at his crushed sister, the hump on his back shaking with the strain of suppressing his giggles. After a while, I returned and reported to him, in front of my mother: *'You are not coming yet, uncle. Did anything happen to you along the way? Should I tell my mother?'*

"As soon as I said that, she grabbed me and took me to see a priestess who performed various kinds of sorcery to help me 'recover.' She looked carefully at my eyes and forehead. Then she spat on me again and again to will away the bad spirits and read my fate on my palms and on the soles of my feet. Finally she concluded that luck was on my side. That I could touch soil and it would turn into gold. The only thing that my mother had to do was give me her blessing. From that moment on, day and night, my mother never stopped blessing me. But nothing went well in my life. I would touch gold and it would turn to soil. I felt pathetic and defeated by life itself.

"Usually, when a storm subsides a rainbow emerges, its peaceful colours like a divine bow, touching the chords of the soul and inspiring optimistic feelings in the beholder. But after my tempests the rainbow was always as black as tar, the boiling pitch of hell. It would close slowly to become a loop. My sadness derived from the sense of failure that cut my soul to shreds.

"I couldn't piece my soul back together. It had been fragmented by the distorted feelings of that sensitive stage of adolescence. I felt as if the flowers sprouting inside me were being plucked, leaving just thorns and bloody spots. What a blow! I felt that I could never fit in. I had no more courage or weapons with which to resist. My shield had broken and so had my spear. The pain drained my heart and left my soul bare. What could I do with a dry heart and a frozen soul?

"Alas! I couldn't find any instructors who would teach me courage. So, as a victim of a crashed society, why should I follow its bizarre rules?

"I used to go to funerals and stare at the dead. They all looked alike. I tried to think my way inside them, to see, to learn, to understand how they felt. Whether their souls were still there or had gone elsewhere. Maybe a soul would be orphaned, like mine, and the two spirits would become friends and play together like homeless dogs. The dead would answer many of my questions."

Rebecca gave him a strange look. She felt troubled and thought that the king was teasing her.

"But how can this be? Can the dead talk?" she asked, obviously confused.

"Of course they can talk! They emphasize to us the nothingness of life. They urge us to be humble. They advise us not to go to war, telling us that all that matters is to love each other and not to hurt anyone. The dead keep shouting: *'Do only good!'*"

"Now I understand what you mean. But I've never observed the dead, so I haven't had that experience."

"During the period when I was studying them, the moment each night when I closed my eyes and tried to sleep I felt as though I was being buried alive. I would be shut up in the painted sarcophagus and could hear the soil falling on the lid from the spades of the gravediggers. I'd gasp and leap up, terrified. Then I'd stay awake for a week.

"Although I knew how extreme and inhospitable the Sahara was, one evening I went off into the desert. I walked barefoot, listening to the sound of the sand as it ground beneath the soles of my feet. I was so confused; I wondered whether I was sleepwalking. A light breeze sprang up and the music of the desert began. I pondered on the sickly functioning of society and how it would inevitably lead to decay. I mused on the concealment and distortion of the truth, the lack of cultivation of the mind and soul and on the many meaningless deaths and barbaric tortures that were occurring in the purgatories of various religions. Pain everywhere! Extreme pain.

"I walked a long way. The sun found me among the carcasses of camels. I didn't know where I was. As the hot moaning simoom blew, it brought a sandstorm. The sweeping khamsin raged for days and sand filled my eyes and choked me. I was exhausted and parched. My lips and tongue withered; they were covered with lacerations. I was constantly haunted by mirages and visions."

Rebecca wanted to tell him that she'd experienced similar feelings during her torturous nine-hour trip to Beast. But she decided not to interrupt.

"Just before I passed out I thought I was caught in quicksand, sinking very slowly. I raised my hands, trying to grasp the air, but the sand was already filling my mouth and nostrils as I yelled. After that … nothing.

"The Bedouins who rescued me said that I hadn't been buried, but even so was half dead. If they hadn't found me the Saharan furnace would have baked another tasty morsel for the birds of prey. When I came round I was in a tent. A face as wizened as a prune was leaning over me. The eyes, full of anxiety, held within them the sun, the sand and the sky of the desert. He was the Lord of the Oasis. Standing beside him, his daughter Haruma was looking at me anxiously too. Heavens, what sweet eyes she had, and a moonlit face like an evening primrose. I fell instantly in love.

"They kept me there until I recovered. I learned about the way they lived, their manners, customs, dances and a few of their songs. Hospitality is one of the Bedouins' great virtues, along with courage, generosity, dignity, independence, forgiveness and knowing how to enjoy themselves.

"Once we had got to know each other better, Haruma's father confided in me that had they known that she and I were going to meet one day, neither he nor his daughter would have given their word that she would marry her cousin who lived at another oasis. He had realized that Haruma felt the same for me as I did for her. We were attracted to each other by a powerful magnetism, but the previous promise the family had made stood between us.

"My senses stirred every time she looked at me. Our gazes would become locked in unseen exchanges of passion, our trembling lips meeting in invisible, ardent kisses. If you had looked into my heart you would have seen hers shining inside it; if you had looked into hers you would have seen my heart throbbing. They became one, with a beat that sent the life-giving blood coursing through us both. At night we slept opposite each other in the Bedouin's round tent, our feet edging outside the covers, the soles touching till morning. It was the most intense contact I've ever had …

"I wanted to stay there for ever, grateful even to have embraced her shadow. But they told me that she was going to move to the other oasis and start a family when she was wed. I never fell in love again, although I did cherish the wife whom I later married very much and cared for her tenderly.

"Shortly before Haruma's wedding, I collected my bits and pieces and my weary heart and returned to my village like the proverbial black sheep. Whenever the moon was full, I would go to my tree, dipping my thoughts into the silvery lake and drawing Haruma's face on the moon. The stars recognized her at once. In their delight they all ran swiftly to write her name in capital letters beneath the full lunar orb.

"Then the lake would fill with love. The tree, my faithful friend, would embrace me. And my companions, the birds, would awaken from their sweet dreams to dance and sing.

"I flicked through the pictures I had taken during those days and which I had sorted carefully in my mind. I showed them to the birds and the tree by the light of the crying moon. The branches folded in like an umbrella so that all the leaves could see and hear every detail. In my nostalgia, I described each image to them.

"Now, thousands of years later, even though it was my first and only love, my memories have not faded. In my heart is a corner with sand, palm trees and sky, and in it sleeps Haruma. On rare occasions she wakes up, dances and weeps, though with a smile. And I gaze at her as though she were a many-faceted work of art. When the hair at one's temples turns grey, the eyes grow wiser. They contain more affection, warmth, tenderness and, most of all, need. The good things that *should* come early are in fact late to arrive.

"In moments of weakness you get closer to yourself and discover some interesting new aspects. So, as my end approached, I gathered up what was left of me, went back to my mother and asked her only to curse me. No blessings. Her blessings didn't work on me. I asked her to curse me to die very old; never become rich; never own anything of my own but the bare necessities with which to live. My mother's curses were effective."

Turgoth fell silent, lost in his own memories.

"So what happened next?" Rebecca prompted him.

Turgoth looked up, startled, as if he had forgotten that she was there. "When the Earth was destroyed, I was chosen by the Mythical Gods and brought to the Land of the White Sun. They made me immortal. I became invulnerable to a natural death and will leave this life only if I am killed. Only then shall I peg out!

"When the Creator restored order to the planet, I was taken back and forth to help ensure that such things would never happen again, that the Earth would not be devastated as before. I went to my homeland. The religions there had become even stricter. But by then I was immortal and the threats did not concern me.

"The Pharaohs were egotistical, arrogant and vain, as powerful people usually are. For no good reason they built those huge pyramids with the sweat and blood of others, supposedly in order to gain immortality. Some other Orizons and myself used our technical know-how to help build the pyramids in the simplest way possible so as to alleviate the sufferings of the people who were working there. Most of them were slaves. If it were not for us using what was then very advanced technology, the Pharaohs would still be building and keeping the workers under the lash.

"One day I said to a Pharaoh who had filled Egypt with statues of himself: '*Why do you need so many statues? They'll be adorned with plenty of scornful bird-droppings for eternity.*

They are the only riches. When I die I'm going to ask the Gods to break up my soul into little pieces so that I can get inside birds.'

"He looked at me as if I were already a bird pooping on his head. He didn't send me away, though, because he wanted me to think well of him in case I really did become a bird in my next life. He didn't know that I was immortal. He was superstitious like fishermen are and, being Egyptian, he also believed in reincarnation. He summoned the priests immediately and asked them to perform ceremonies and offer sacrifices and do whatever else they deemed necessary. He told them to beg the god Osiris not to let me become a bird and to beg the rest of the Gods to make all birds disappear."

"I'd like to be a bird, too," whispered Rebecca.

"Let's not forget that the greatest achievements, the largest empires, the most powerful nations, all are eventually toppled and wrecked by human weaknesses."

"I agree." Rebecca nodded enthusiastically. "My parents often tell me about important families and large businesses with long traditions, which collapse because of some stupid human error or weakness."

"Anyway, Rebecca, I want you to know that I was no warrior. I was a man of the arts and of letters. By "letters", I mean history. I also designed and erected buildings – stadiums, theatres and temples. It was I, with a team of other experts, who supervised the construction of the houses and other buildings in Utopia and Beast.

"I was certainly no soldier, but after the division I was forced to fight. The first time I killed at Lomani I felt ill and troubled for days. What else could I do? If I didn't kill, I would myself be killed. This is the dilemma, the problem that thinking warriors always face, especially the novices. Little by little, I became tough in combat, killing many, so as to survive. The king noticed my progress, since I brought much death to the enemy, and he made me a general. When you kill during a war, not only do you not go to prison, but you get medals and a promotion."

Turgoth gave a scornful laugh and looked across at Rebecca, realizing that he had been rambling on for a long time. He wondered if she was as fascinated by an old man's thoughts and memories as she seemed. Rebecca had listened to all this with undivided attention. She was impressed as never before.

"King Turgoth, you are a learned historian and you know many things because you were alive when they happened. For me, it seems a tragedy to make statues of conquerors who butchered whole peoples, and to call them great men. I would accept making a statue of someone who has freed his people from an oppressive yoke; but to call someone great who has done exactly the opposite goes against my grain."

"I believe there are some intellects that shouldn't have died and others that should never have been born. The only areas that people should conquer are in the world of knowledge."

They remained silent for some time. They were thoughtful, like troubled judges before pronouncing a verdict.

After a few minutes Turgoth stood up and stretched.

"Take some fruit and let's go outside."

Sliding his sword back into its scabbard he led the way through to the garden. Rebecca was surprised to find that dawn had broken and the air was pleasantly cool. Having temporarily forgotten the danger she was in she was startled to find herself at such close quarters to the Sphinx that guarded the house.

"Wow!" she exclaimed, staring up at it. In Utopia she had

only seen the other Sphinx from afar, not realizing how huge these creatures were.

They strolled around the garden for a while, saying nothing, like Jean Valjean does with Cosette before they meet Marius. Rebecca thought that Turgoth might even take her hand with fatherly affection, just as Hugo's legendary hero does. When the king stopped and looked at her she immediately returned from the Parisian gardens and was surprised to see death in his eyes. She remembered that she was a prisoner, condemned to death in Turgoth's courtyard, even though she stood among beds filled with beautiful flowers. Without a word she lay down, stretching out and propping herself up on her left elbow. With the fingertips of her right hand she lightly caressed the flowers. Then she leaned over and started smelling the blooms one by one. Their fragrance sweetened her own breath. *"How strong are these soft, pliable, tender flowers that can pierce the hard earth like driven nails?"* she asked herself, wondering why she had not thought of it before.

Turgoth resumed speaking in sad, solemn tones, as if he was attending a relative's funeral.

"Rebecca, there are only three ways in which this can end for us. The first is that you remain in our camp and help us in our struggle to seize the Flame. Afterwards the two of us and anyone else wishing to follow will go to Earth and do our best to put things in order. I'm not asking you to fight against your own people, but you can help substantially, even without fighting."

He looked at her with raised eyebrows. But she remained silent, continuing to sniff the flowers as if she had heard nothing.

"The second possibility is for you to remain uninvolved. If you give me your word on this, you can go back to Utopia and refuse to take the Flame. I suspect that you are still unsure of what you want to do there anyway. You will go back to Earth, taking neither side. You would still be able to strive for the good of your planet and its inhabitants. I will trust you if you promise, as you trusted me by not taking your sword to kill me."

Turgoth paused again but still there was no reaction. The girl's courage and self-control were extraordinary.

"The third, alas, is for you to die. We must kill you. It is not in our interest to have you as an enemy in Lomani. You are too powerful in every way. Think carefully before giving me your answer. Take as much time as you need."

Rebecca kept gazing at the flowers, smelling them and fondling them with steady fingers, as if this were a last wish granted to her by her executioner. The first rays of daybreak were tenderly caressing the garden. The flowers changed colours as they welcomed the daughters of the sun. Turgoth looked at the shining orb as it rose majestically.

"King Turgoth, I'm sorry for the injustice done to the people of Beast. It is true that it took me until the very last minute to make up my mind about the Flame. It's too late now; I've made up my mind. When I declared my thoughts about the Flame, I was ready to face the consequences.

"So, like you, I don't want to be a traitor. I cannot accept the freedom that you're offering me because it would be like a dream that has been bought. I'm more than certain that, in my place, you would have done the same."

"Your decision breaks my heart, Rebecca. Alas, you must die!" Turgoth's voice seemed to come from far away, as if he were a ventriloquist.

He raised his head slightly to the sun and closed his eyes, as if praying. Rebecca's attention seemed to be still focused on the flowers. No one watching from a distance would have guessed what was passing between these two people who appeared to be enjoying the dawn in a beautiful garden.

"Although death has come before I really got to know life," Rebecca said, "I'm happy to think that I will die here among your flowers. When you cut off my head it will fall among them and I will be able to inhale their fragrance. What more can I ask for? Please, King Turgoth, if you hold me in as high regard as you say you do, do it now. Here!"

She bowed her head lower, stretching out her neck and lifting up her hair to make it easier for the king.

THE BIRTH

England, 1985. The twentieth century was now an old man. His days were drawing to a close. When he was born he couldn't have predicted the huge change that was just about to begin. As he grew older he watched in despair the world's technological development, but he couldn't react. His hair turned white faster while his soul was wounded by the wars, as well as by the radical changes that affected most of the inhabitants of Earth.

He only had a few more years to live. By now he had come to the conclusion that many of the inventions that had improved humanity's basic living conditions had also led to an overall deterioration in the quality of human life.

He could see that by meddling with the environment mankind had poisoned the air, the land and the sea. The hole in the ozone layer and the greenhouse effect bore witness to the devastation being wrought on the harmony of the planet and the lives of its inhabitants.

When he discovered that the once-beneficial rays of the sun had been transformed into cancer-causing killers, he would grasp his hair and pull it in despair, as if it was his own fault.

With a feeling of deep hurt, he witnessed glaciers shattering like glass and icebergs melting like butter, threatening thousand of wildlife species, such as penguins and polar bears, with premature extinction. A quarter of all mammals and one in eight species of birds had become endangered.

He burst into tears the moment he found out that the Eskimo population was under equal threat and had embarked on a futile legal battle to save itself.

Being old now, the century knew that the harmony between humans and nature had crashed for good. That, he thought, was the worst and most dangerous of all wars. A war of self-destruction!

Scientists kept producing inventions that only made things worse, while the majority of the world's population continued to live in a state of ignorance and indifference.

The only thing that offered him some comfort were those who tried their best to save the Earth, such as the ecologists, the animal-lovers and, of course, the Orizons.

"Will they make it?" thought the tired old century, who wished to see at least a small improvement before he shut his eyes for good.

The Newtons were living an apparently ordinary life in a pleasant detached house with a nice garden, in the countryside outside London. On the surface they seemed no different from most of their neighbours.

Had anyone cared to penetrate their privacy they would have discovered that Julius Newton was a high-ranking official in British Intelligence. Tall, powerfully built, with thick black hair and green eyes that seemed to pierce like X-rays, he was an imposing presence, a man of determination.

His wife Adriana had kept her shapely figure, in spite of her advanced state of pregnancy. Her thick brown hair reached down almost to her waist. Her large blue-grey eyes struck a contrast with her olive complexion and the peaceful lines of her face were reminiscent of the beautifully sculpted bust of an ancient Greek goddess. Despite the pregnancy, she was still carrying out her professional duties as a UN staff member.

The Newtons avoided close friendships and did little socializing. They kept themselves to themselves. Nobody who came upon them would have found any hint that they were different or that they had special powers. Always friendly, never arrogant, they simply radiated an air of true goodness and deep love.

On the morning of the day when the Newtons' first child was born, Julius was putting on his necktie while his wife studied the computer screen.

"It looks as if things will go well," she said, half to him and half to herself.

"There are grounds for hope," Julius agreed. "I should be able to give our visitors this evening at least *some* good news."

He kissed his wife lightly on both cheeks and on her distended belly and left for London. He drove carefully as always, aware of how many thousands of people each year were killed or left disabled by thoughtless speeding drivers.

The summer was riding its chariot, having for a passenger the sun. The three great horses who pulled it across the sky were well fed.

The countryside that slipped past the car window was resting after the great birth of spring, recuperating in preparation for its ritual mating with the rain, the sun and the seeds that people sowed or that the wind spread. Like a caring mother, it would then start again on the cycle that fed the whole world. It would adorn the Earth with flowers and scent the air with pollen, like a fine cook filling her house with the delicious aromas of lovingly prepared food.

Julius marvelled at the daily changes in nature, watching the harmonious seasons alternating like cheerful fellow-workers changing shifts. He knew that the Earth could produce more than enough to feed generously every person and creature on its surface. It just needed to be protected and cultivated effectively, and then the produce needed to be distributed fairly. Julius's aim was to bring all this about peacefully and with justice.

As he approached the train station he looked sadly at the tangle of flyovers and slip roads that carried the endless daily streams of cars. For thousands of years the gentle green hills of this area had been covered with only trees, grass and flowers. Hares, young deer and other wild animals had roamed freely and peacefully.

But mighty bulldozers had come again and again to areas where once families had picnicked in idyllic surroundings, and they had scoured the ground bare and laid it flat. The soil could not breathe any more through its asphalt mask. Then the unruly cars came in greater and greater numbers, their poisonous exhaust fumes drowning out the last traces of Nature's fragrance. In just a few decades the peaceful sounds of the landscape gave way to a cacophony of internal combustion engines and screeching rubber.

The moment Julius reached his office the phone calls started. Casual-sounding conversations that would affect the lives of millions of innocent people began.

Julius was among those working to avert the evil, struggling to convince the parties involved of the need to prevent the disaster.

His ultimate hatred was for war. Civil war especially is so terrible. Friends, neighbours, fellow workers, people who've grown up together, fighting and killing each other. Children who are one day playing with one another turning into soldiers and cutting the throats of their former playmates. Even members of the same family end up turning on one another.

Always patient and restrained, always optimistic, Julius left his office earlier than usual that afternoon in order to attend the most important event in his life: He was going to become a father!

Adriana welcomed Julius home with a warm kiss that she had been saving up all day.

"You managed to get away early."

"How could I do otherwise?" he replied, smiling and offering her a bunch of flowers.

To prepare themselves for the night's events, Julius placed one of his favourite classical records on the turntable. With a deep sigh, he stretched out on the sofa to enjoy Mozart's tender melody.

"So, Adriana," he said once they were sitting down to dinner. "Have you decided at last on a name for our daughter?"

"Aren't you going to help me?"

" I'd rather you decide all by yourself."

"All right, then. I suggest that we call her Rebecca."

Julius pursed his lips and thought for a few seconds, savouring the name like a mouthful of good wine.

"Yes," he said eventually. "It's a good choice. Rebecca it will be."

"Let's have some rest before our visitors arrive," Adriana said, glancing at her watch. "We've still got five hours. There's plenty of time."

"I'll be up in a minute."

As his wife made her way to the bedroom, Julius went out onto the veranda and sat in an easy chair. Leaning back, he looked up at the darkening sky. The stars were lighting up, one by one at first, then in twos, and finally in clusters. God was turning on the cosmic switches in the familiar sequence. It seemed to Julius as if there were more stars than ever before. The solemn sounds of the night brought him a deep inner peace. Under the baton of the Creator, the melody of Nature's symphonic orchestra spread through him. A cool, light breeze caressed his face and ruffled his hair as he looked up at the stars, immersing himself in their divine embroidery. Exquisite feelings swelled in his soul.

In a few hours everything would change and nothing would ever be the same for him again. Life as a parent would become more beautiful, taking on new meaning and new responsibilities. The child would have priority now. From this night on, before doing anything else they would have to take into consideration whether their actions might have a negative effect on Rebecca. Helping to form a child's character was a difficult, serious and sensitive process with deep moral implications.

For Julius and Adriana there had been the added responsibility of deciding whether they would give their daughter the necessary background, so that at the age of fifteen she would be able to decide her own course and, if she so wished, choose the difficult path. Julius believed that they had made the right choice.

His mind still heavy with thought, he finally went upstairs to get some rest in preparation for what was to come.

A few hours later Julius rose from the bed and drove to the nearby woods. Among the dense trees was a clearing, which was the reason they had chosen to live where they did. He parked his car and got out.

He looked at his watch. In a minute it would be two o'clock. He stood still, looking up at the sky. Exactly on time he saw a small luminous blue ring among the stars. Within seconds it had grown larger and a crystal sphere had descended into the clearing. The beam of blue light that had been shining from its circumference was extinguished as Julius walked quickly towards it. The sphere stood on four crystal legs about ten feet high. A hatch opened in its belly and a set of crystal steps descended to the ground. More pale blue light spilled out from the interior, softly illuminating the steps and the ground around them. A thin sheet of material emerged from the top of the sphere, spreading out to cover it like a veil. Made from the fibres of a plant that could adapt to its surroundings like a chameleon it rendered both the sphere and itself invisible within seconds. Julius stepped under the veil and stood at the bottom of the steps as the passengers alighted.

The first to descend was a shapely woman of average height. She wore close-fitting white leather shorts. Her top was of the same material and had a blue sun emblazoned on it. Her knee-high boots were made of blue leather, as was her wide belt, which had a white crystal sun symbol on its buckle. She had a striking face and an olive complexion. Her shining black eyes were large, her nose delicate, her ears small and her full lips like a half-opened rosebud. Her long black hair was glorious, glistening as though painted by a great artist. Even in the blue light of the sphere it seemed as though black flames played within her tresses. She came down the steps with the grace of a gazelle and the self-assurance of a lioness, looking no more than twenty-five years old. She embraced Julius who courteously brought her right hand to his lips.

"Welcome, Princess Felicia," he said in Ancient Greek.

"I'm so glad to see you, Julius. How is Adriana?" she enquired in the same language.

"She is very well and eagerly awaiting us," he answered.

A tall, slim man had followed the princess down the steps. Although his hair was snowy white, he looked no older than fifty. He had an open, likeable face and his blue eyes suggested a formidable inner strength. He wore a long white hand-woven robe in the style of the Ancient Greeks, and leather sandals. On the chest of his robe was a blue leather sun symbol. The two men embraced.

"Doctor Afterland, I've missed you," Julius said with obvious sincerity.

"I've missed you too, Julius, and I'm thankful that such an important and pleasant event should be the cause for our reunion."

The last person to descend the steps was a strapping giant of a figure over eight feet tall: a creature whose hairy, manlike body supported the head of a bull. Two small horns sprouted from the sides of his broad brow. Although his face was not human, its expression was gentle, his small eyes twinkling with the innocence of a child. He was Bull the Minotaur, pilot of the crystal sphere. He was dressed in a white leather sleeveless vest bearing a blue leather sun emblem on the chest. His boots too were made of blue leather. Instead of trousers he wore a short white leather skirt like that of a Roman gladiator. On the left and right of his blue leather belt hung two daggers, while in his hand a crystal lantern emitted a bright blue flame.

As soon as Bull reached the ground he passed the lantern to Felicia and held out his hand towards Julius, who shook it warmly.

"Julius, may the daughter who will be born tonight always bring you joy," the Minotaur boomed.

"Thank you, my dear Bull. Thank you."

Bull returned up the steps as the other three came out from under the veil. They crossed the clearing to the car. Felicia and Afterland sat in the back as Julius climbed behind the wheel.

Julius drew the car up in front of the house. A smiling Adriana was already waiting for them at the door.

Felicia passed the crystal lantern with the Flame to Afterland and the two women embraced. Their eyes filled with tears. Then it was the doctor's turn to kiss his hostess's hand.

"You look so well," he said, his good-natured face shining with pleasure at the sight of an old friend.

Adriana and Afterland went straight to the bedroom where Adriana had already prepared a large bowl of lukewarm water and had laid out clean towels. Felicia and Julius sat in the living room and discussed several matters.

Their quiet conversation was interrupted by the cries of a baby as the door opened and the doctor asked the princess to go through. Carefully holding the lantern with the Flame, she entered the bedroom and watched as Doctor Afterland made the final cut. Then she brought the Flame close, and placed it carefully on the severed umbilical cord of the newborn baby.

The crying ceased the moment the Flame entered the child's body through the cord, making it glow blue. After a moment the baby's belly began to glow with the same power. This lasted for about two minutes before Felicia withdrew the Flame while the doctor expertly knotted the cord. The princess returned to the living room and gave Julius a satisfied smile.

"Your daughter is beautiful," she said proudly. "A true Orizon girl!"

Julius felt his heart lift. Two minutes later the bedroom door opened and Adriana came towards them carrying Rebecca. She was followed by Afterland. Julius stroked his daughter's small head and kissed his wife.

"Thank you," he said.

"What have you decided to call her?" the princess asked.

"Rebecca," replied Adriana.

Felicia touched the blue Flame to the baby's nostrils and spoke in a deep solemn voice: "I name thee Rebecca!"

The baby seemed to inhale the Flame with a sigh of pleasure.

"The time has come to say goodbye," the princess told them.

Julius drove the visitors back to the woods where Bull was waiting for them at the bottom of the sphere's steps. He took the crystal lantern from the princess. Julius kissed her hand once more, embraced Afterland and shook hands with Bull.

At the top of the steps Felicia turned and waved to Julius before disappearing from sight, followed by her travelling companions. As the steps retracted and the hatch closed, the veil drew back. For an instant the blue ring was visible round the circumference of the ball before it disappeared into the sky within a split second.

On his way home Julius's mind was filled with thoughts of his new daughter, trying to guess what her decision would be when she reached the age of fifteen.

REBECCA

By the time the old century passed away, feeling disappointed and guilty, much had changed.

During the fifteen years since Rebecca's birth, Earth had deteriorated more than at any time since life had first existed on the planet. Many big cities felt like gas chambers and in the worst of them the inhabitants took to wearing masks to protect themselves from the noxious gases.

The harmony of Nature and life was reaching breaking point as the seasons mutated and fell into disarray. Spring and autumn were assimilated by their neighbours. Hot summers and harsh winters followed so closely on one another's heels that the trees were deceived into blossoming out of season. The fruit they bore became sickly or tasteless.

Terrible frosts, catastrophic floods, storms and unbearable heatwaves swept the planet and the scientists warned that things could only get worse if mankind didn't change its behaviour. Their repeated recommendations and warnings were to no avail. They predicted the total extinction of the human race if nothing was done to stop the harmful interventions of man.

Yet people not only continued with their destructive ways, they even started to meddle in the creation of life itself. They played God, manufacturing cloned animals and unheard-of monstrosities. They learned how to predetermine what gender of child a couple would bear, as well as its height, the colour of its eyes, the level of its intelligence and what diseases might torture it.

Some spread panic with talk of mad cows, while they should actually have admitted that they were the ones going crazy.

Almost everyone had seen the threats looming for years. However, they were apathetic, as if it did not concern them. They were actually proud of the huge tomatoes they produced and the outsize cows they raised. But when the nightmarish results of their activities started to rise up, they panicked. By then much of the damage had become irreversible.

Rebecca's parents never had to pressure her into doing well at anything. They encouraged her to spend every moment she wasn't at school learning special skills like riding, fencing, archery, javelin throwing and the Chinese martial art of kung fu.

It was no surprise to them that she was good at all of them, or that she was always happy to spend extra hours practising. Despite her modesty at school she was unable to hide her extraordinary physical talents and everyone talked about her as a future Olympic champion.

It was in the kung fu classes, however, that she really amazed all the experts. A martial art both of defence and of attack, kung fu had been conceived many centuries before at the Chinese temple of Shaolin. Rebecca's parents enrolled her at the school of Grand Master William Cheung, whose students could be found teaching the martial art all over the world. Cheung regularly visited the schools to monitor them and observe the students' progress. He was the man who had urged the famous Bruce Lee to take up kung fu and he had been Lee's first instructor.

From the very first class Rebecca made an impression with her quick adaptation, the speed with which she absorbed the lessons and the skill with which she performed the exercises. When William Cheung was in England he taught her himself, instantly recognizing her great talent. She combined the agility of an acrobat with the strength and aggression of a warrior. She took off like a rocket, hitting her target and landing as if she were made of rubber in a split second. She moved with such speed that it was almost impossible for anyone to strike her, even with a bullet. She deployed the butterfly swords so expertly and so quickly that the human eye could not follow her movements. At fifteen she was just one level below her instructor.

Rebecca's mind developed at the same startling rate as her body. During her childhood Julius spoke to her in English and Adriana addressed her in Ancient Greek, so that she would be fluent in both languages.

She loved music and dancing, playing the guitar and singing. And she loved to think.

She enjoyed theatre in all its forms, especially operas and musicals.

Rebecca felt that theatre could enter more deeply and meaningfully into the problems of society and life. Something that cinema couldn't so easily accomplish. In a theatre, the live actor can "touch" the audience. He can unite them and fascinate them. He can hold their hands, like a grandfather holds his grandchild's, taking them for a ride and making them happy; showing them new things and teaching them what life really means. He does, however, risk getting booed. In ancient theatre, besides booing, the audience would throw rotten fruit and vegetables at the actors if they disliked what they saw. In a cinema the actor is in no danger. The worst that can happen is that the audience will leave.

What Rebecca liked best, though, was painting. It was the kind of creativity that caused her feelings to overflow. She used to talk to her canvases while she worked on them, feeling as though she was imparting to them pieces of her own soul.

Her themes combined a realism of expression with a romantic dimension. She loved the tension and the effort it took to combine these qualities. She used colours with great sensitivity and an explosive dynamism.

She tried to make close friends with Nature, to get to know its secrets and the infinite poetry it contained, so that she could represent it properly in her paintings. She worked intently to use light correctly and in her own authentic manner.

For the most part Rebecca painted landscapes and animals, subjects connected with Nature, in which she emphasized man's intervention. She adored the colours of all flowers, preferring to paint those that grew wild because they'd been planted and cared for only by God.

She played with as many animals as she could and never harmed them. She was careful not to touch butterflies in case she damaged their delicate wings, simply admiring them in the garden or out in the countryside where they shared their beauty with the flowers and the leaves of the trees. She could not bear to see birds singing in cages as if they were being forced back into the egg. She loved watching them fly free, enchanting her with their graceful flight and playful antics. It was as if she understood their language and all the important messages they were sending from their feathered throats.

All this went into Rebecca's art. Every time she finished a picture she would fetch her guitar, sit in front of the canvas and compose a song that the subject had inspired, bringing the images to life. Birds, animals, flowers, mountains, rivers and seas would dance before her eyes. Delighted, she would enter the picture herself to celebrate with them. At such moments she felt as if her paintings were her newborn babies.

Her great love of nature came partly from her parents. Neither of them would ever harm an ant, preferring to feed them on crumbs so they would be less troubled and tired while they worked. They contributed to animal welfare and environmental organizations, concerned about the diminishing number of species. They believed that the planet grew poorer with every loss.

"Never forget," Rebecca's father would tell her, "that animals love those who love them. They can sense it instantly because of our aura."

Rebecca had travelled widely for one so young. When travelling she would take every opportunity to visit archaeological sites or museums and attend cultural events or art exhibitions.

She studied the magical world of mythology and became an expert on the subject. Most of all she enjoyed Greek mythology.

She also read books and watched films about extraterrestrial beings, spaceships, life on other planets.

These interests, however, did not come about entirely by accident. Rebecca's parents had carefully cultivated them, always whetting her appetite to explore, to read and to question things, while at the same time being careful not to put pressure on her or violate her greatest right: her freedom!

When Rebecca turned thirteen they began to talk to her more openly, telling her that all the theories about aliens and space might not be pure fantasy, that some of them just might contain a grain of truth. They gave her articles to read on the subject of flying-saucer sightings. They gradually fed her with the idea that there was life somewhere in space and that the Earth was visited from time to time by beings from other places.

"There are people living on Earth who are attempting to prevent its destruction," they explained, going on to talk about some of the unpleasant things that kept happening on Earth and how difficult it was to prevent a disastrous outcome. They spoke of ecological organizations and their efforts to improve the quality of life.

As time passed, Rebecca realized how hard Julius and Adriana worked at trying to prevent anything that might harm or take lives, pollute the planet, degrade living conditions and lead humankind to self-destruction. She saw them happy when something good was achieved and upset when anything brought trouble and pain to humankind or had a deleterious effect on nature.

"These holidays," Rebecca's parents asked her one day, "would you like to visit your grandparents in South Africa? You would have to travel by yourself, though, because we're too busy to take a trip at the moment."

Rebecca was ecstatic. She hugged them and kissed them and jumped up and down. She adored her mother's parents, who had visited several times over the years.

Martha and Paul Flery had been living in South Africa for many years and worked for the protection of African wildlife. Martha, who always looked about fifty, was beautiful and in extraordinary shape for her age, while her husband looked no more than sixty. Rebecca knew that they must be older but they were both so healthy and energetic, their happy faces always brimming with love.

Rebecca had grandparents on her father's side, too: Lisa and Tony Newton. They had visited only twice in her life. The first time she had been too young to remember; the second was when she was ten and they had stayed for a month.

"We live a long way away," they explained when she asked why they didn't come more often. "It's difficult for us to travel." Only recently had she started to wonder just *where* they lived.

When Rebecca landed in Cape Town her maternal grandparents wept for joy, throwing their arms around her and covering her with kisses. On the way to their home from the airport they showered her with questions, occasionally interrupting their own flow to point out passing sights.

They lived in the country, far from the city, in a simple bungalow with a big garden and many trees.

In the following days Rebecca soaked up the country's atmosphere. Having read about its history, its development and its immense problems, she was now able to see it all first-hand. It felt as if she had lived there for many centuries. Her grandparents were pleased to see how she took in everything that went on around her. They talked day and night sleeping little, excited by her company and her endless questions.

"Rebecca," her grandfather said one night as they sat together in the garden, "tomorrow we're flying to Kenya. It's a beautiful country; we're certain you'll love it. We'll begin our tour in the countryside, where you'll be able to see the wildlife."

"A safari?" She could hardly contain her excitement.

"Yes." Her grandfather nodded sagely. "There is some controversy about these excursions. Some say that they should be banned because they disturb the animals, while others say that through such expeditions people become more aware of wild animals and learn to love them in their natural surroundings. The visitors realize they shouldn't kill the animals or capture them and make them live in unnatural conditions.

"Your grandmother and I have dedicated the greater part of our lives to the protection of wildlife and the environment."

"Our greatest problem hasn't been professional hunters," Rebecca's grandmother joined in, "but those who kill for sport. It completely mystifies me how it's possible for kings, nobles, honoured citizens, humanists, ideologues, heroes of all types and scientists to kill lions and other animals so shamelessly. How can intelligent and sensitive people pose for photographs while standing proudly next to their innocent victims? Such people have made our jobs very hard."

"So, Rebecca," her grandfather said, "tomorrow you will be able to form your own opinion."

At Nairobi airport a local driver picked them up in a jeep and drove them many miles to a picturesque lodge standing amid lush vegetation. Chimpanzees played in the trees, letting out strange cries of welcome as they swung from branch to branch.

At dawn the following day Rebecca and her grandparents were ready to begin sightseeing. They travelled with all their luggage, intending to spend the next night at a different lodge. The driver sat alone at the front, and the rear of the cab had wire-mesh windows. The roof was raised on four small poles, providing shade and fresh air, while the seats were angled so that all the passengers had a good view.

The driver maintained radio communication with other drivers and with park wardens. Sometimes he would stop the jeep and turn off the engine, signalling the tourists to stay silent for fear of frightening the animals away. During the day Rebecca saw several herds of zebra and antelope, an elephant herd and some leopards.

That night as they ate at their lodge a tall Kenyan man dressed in a white robe approached their table, bowing to Martha. Paul stood up and the two men embraced.

"I'm glad to see you, Thomas," Paul said, patting him on the back. "I've missed you."

"Welcome, my friend. I heard you were here. Enjoy your dinner. After your meal, I'll be waiting on the veranda for you. There is something I want to discuss."

"A lot of the Africans I've met have been tall and handsome," Rebecca said once Thomas had left. "But he was really impressive."

"He's a descendant of the renowned Masai tribe," Paul explained. "Apart from his work for the protection of wildlife, Thomas is very involved in the affairs of his tribe. They are an exceptionally interesting people."

Once their meal was over, Rebecca, Paul and Martha strolled out to the veranda. When Thomas saw them, he rose courteously and offered them comfortable seats. At first they talked about the progress of the tourist season and the threats facing the gorilla and chimpanzee populations from the Ebola virus.

"You said you had something important to tell us," Paul said after a while.

Thomas sighed and nodded. "Three days ago, in the Masai Mara region, just before dawn, two poachers killed an elephant that had become separated from its herd. As they were trying to cut off its tusks, it seems that they noticed a lioness with her two cubs, watching them. The poachers panicked and unleashed a burst of gunfire while running for their truck. They drove away but the sound of the shots brought park wardens to the scene. We surrounded the area and cut them off.

"Sadly, they had killed the lioness and both her cubs. We tried to get close, but an enraged lion had arrived by then. He must have been the father. The closest we could get was about five hundred yards. For three days the lion hasn't left the dead cubs' side. We have him under constant observation. He won't even go to a waterhole about a mile away to drink. He has not eaten anything, either. It seems that he's decided to stay close to his family. If he goes on like this without food and water he'll die too. We want to save him but we don't know what to do."

"It's too late to do anything tonight," Paul said. "We'll all set off early in the morning. Bring some helpers, medicine, food, water and anything else that we might need."

"Everything will be ready," Thomas assured him. "I'll leave you now to get some rest and we'll meet in the morning. I'm very sorry Rebecca had to hear about such a sad event during her visit here."

Rebecca stood up politely as Thomas was leaving, and then she slumped back into her armchair, devastated. She couldn't believe that such atrocious acts against animals were still committed. Gloomy thoughts overwhelmed her that night as she lay in her bed.

Three jeeps set out in the morning. Thomas had brought five more people to join the party. It took four hours of hard driving to reach the spot. They stopped the cars at some distance and got out to watch through binoculars.

After focusing the lenses, Rebecca could see the two cubs, lying motionless, resting on the belly of their dead mother. Beside them sat the lion, moving only his head and tail. Everyone talked at once, making suggestions about what they should do, while Rebecca stood aside, silent and thoughtful. Then, looking boldly at her grandfather, she said:

"Grandpa, I want to go to him. I'll take food and water. Don't worry: he won't harm me."

Both her grandparents listened to her without surprise, smiling proudly.

Paul nodded his agreement.

"Prepare a water can," he told Thomas. "And put some smoked meat into a bag, along with a knife, a small pickaxe and a small spade. We'll get them as close to the lion as we can. Then Rebecca will have to carry them the rest of the way."

The others stared at him as if he was mad.

"What are you saying, Paul?" gasped Thomas. "He'll kill her. No one can get close to a hungry lion. How can you even suggest such a thing?"

"Prepare the things as I've asked," Paul said firmly. "Rebecca will be fine."

"I can't take the risk," Thomas said. "I will be prosecuted by the police if anything happens to her."

"Her grandmother and I will share the responsibility. Nobody is going to blame you for anything. If you are afraid, leave the provisions with us and go."

The men hung their heads and shuffled their feet furtively. How could they leave a young girl and two old people in the middle of nowhere with an angry lion? Reluctantly they did as Paul had requested.

Paul took the water can and slung the bag over his shoulder and, together with Martha and Rebecca, started walking towards the lion. When they were about two hundred yards from the animal they stopped. Paul put down the can and the bag, hugged Rebecca and kissed her. Martha did the same. Then they moved away, looking back from time to time at their granddaughter as she hitched the bag over her shoulder, picked up the water can and slowly but steadily walked towards the lion. It watched her approach.

The lion was lying right behind the body of the lioness, embracing her with his right foreleg. Rebecca was shocked to see that tears were flowing from his eyes, streaking the fur on his cheeks. She knew that animals never cried. Yet this one was feeling such pain that he had gone against Nature itself.

The lion's embrace of its dead mate reminded Rebecca of a movie that she'd seen: *Notre Dame de Paris*. In the film, some wicked people had killed the hunchback Quasimodo's beloved, the beautiful gypsy girl Esmeralda, again for no reason. They had thrown her dead body into a basement, where Quasimodo found her. He lay beside her, gazing at her tenderly, stroking her hair and weeping. Then he embraced her, staying like that for days and nights until he too died of thirst, hunger and love. Many years later people who had gone down into the basement by chance stumbled upon two skeletons lying side by side in an embrace.

Rebecca sat down beside the lion and began to caress his head and mane. For a while he didn't seem to know how to react but eventually he turned and looked at her with his sad eyes, as if to ask: "*Why are some people so evil? Why have they killed my family? What did they do to them?*"

"There are people who are good and people who are evil," she said as she continued to stroke him. "But you should know that most people love you. You can be found in most peoples' houses in paintings, statues and curios that are made in your likeness. Children play with toy lions, sleeping with them in their arms. You set an example to humans. When we want to praise a man for his bravery and strength, we say that he had the courage of a lion."

The lion seemed to be listening to her carefully and from time to time he used his tail to swish away the flies that were trying to land on the dead bodies. The sun was scorching and the heat was becoming unbearable. Rebecca took off her baseball cap to let the breeze cool her head, putting it back on quickly when she felt the full heat of the sun.

She got up, took out the knife, went to a nearby tree and cut off a leafy branch. She went back and sat close to the lion again, using the branch as a switch to help him keep away the flies.

"Don't tire yourself. Let me do it for you," she said.

Gently, she laid her head on his body.

After a while, she said: "Now, please drink some water. I'll drink some after you."

She took off her cap and filled it with water, bringing it close to the lion's parched mouth. He did not react.

Rebecca tilted the cap and let a few drops trickle onto his lips. But the lion clamped his mouth firmly shut and turned his head away in clear refusal. It was as if he was saying: *"I don't want it. Don't push me. I want to die. What do I have to live for? My mate and my cubs have been killed. I am all alone!"*

His eyes filled with tears of pain and despair again. Rebecca carefully poured the water back into the can without drinking a single drop herself, even though her throat and mouth were dry.

"All right. Since you don't want to, we won't drink," she said softly. She lay down once more and put her head lightly on the lion's side again, stroking him tenderly but remaining silent to give him time to think things over.

Night fell swiftly, the vanguard of stars appearing proudly in the sky.

Rebecca started to sing ...

Her soft voice carried across the plain to the camp that her grandparents had pitched to protect themselves from the sun. Unable now to see Rebecca and the lion in the dark, they listened instead.

Later, around the campfire, Paul told the others that he didn't want anyone else to know what was going on. He didn't want the media or any other inquisitive people showing up. If the news spread, things could become awkward for Rebecca. The very fact that she had got so close to the lion and stayed with him for hours was a scoop that would most certainly be broadcast around the globe if the media were tipped off.

"She would be hounded for the rest of her life," Paul said. "Please respect this wish of mine. Don't tell anyone about this and don't take any photographs. When this is over, no matter what the outcome, only we will know what happened. What is important is the result. If the lion is saved, we will have succeeded in our aim and we won't need to do anything else."

They all listened attentively and assured him that they would respect Rebecca's privacy. Apart from anything else, none of them was sure whether anyone would believe them if they did tell of what they had seen that day.

The night wore on and Rebecca kept singing. Once more she tried to give the lion some water but to no avail. She didn't insist but she didn't take anything to eat or drink herself either.

"All right," she said, "You don't want to drink, but won't you at least get some sleep? You're exhausted."

Listening to the nocturnal hum of the landscape Rebecca

sensed the frenzy that was churning inside her new friend's head and heart. Through the mingled voices of a hundred different creatures she sensed the presence of watching hyenas and other scavengers, attracted by the smell of the carcasses, biding their time under the cover of darkness until they would be able to eat their fill. The lion's presence kept them at a safe distance, but she could hear their impatient whimpering as they waited for him to die as well. Every animal had its own survival strategy.

The night passed without either of them sleeping a wink.

The moment dawn broke, Rebecca's grandparents were searching with their binoculars and found Rebecca and the lion still in the same positions.

Rebecca was struggling to stay awake, her eyelids heavy and her eyes burning as if filled with hot sand. She splashed some water on them. Then she stood up and stretched, walking around in an attempt to stop herself from falling asleep.

Every minute seemed to pass more slowly than the last, every hour becoming an eternity in the unbearable heat as the suffocating smell of the carcasses rose into Rebecca's nostrils, threatening to stifle her.

She thought how much easier it would have been if the lions had been shot a few yards further on, where the foliage of a clump of trees would have protected them from the scorching sun. She wondered if she could pull the bodies into the shade but she decided against it. The lion might not understand what she was doing, and she wasn't sure that the corpses wouldn't disintegrate now.

Rebecca felt ashamed of these notions. *"I must be getting ill to have such thoughts,"* she said to herself.

She kept trying to persuade the lion to drink but he stubbornly kept his mouth shut. At one point she took out her handkerchief, dipped it into the water and pressed it against his brow. He watched her with resigned eyes and even seemed to like it. She kept applying the compresses as the heat of the sun increased.

Rebecca's lips were cracking like dry plaster. She wanted to tell the lion that she was thirsty, that she had reached the end of her tether, but she forced herself to keep her thoughts to herself. She didn't want him to think she was using her own suffering to pressure him. Somehow she managed to survive another day, although she could feel the strength ebbing from her.

As night approached, the lion's weeping and his movements faltered. Rebecca feared that he was nearing the end. If she couldn't persuade him to take some water they would both be dead by the next morning.

"You must drink, you must eat and sleep. You can't go on for six days without food and especially without water. Do you want us to die together? I've brought along some meat. We can share it. I know you prefer fresh game, but I think you'll like what I've got. It's clean and tasty."

Rebecca opened her bag, took the knife and cut off a portion of smoked meat, bringing it close to his mouth.

The lion turned his head away once again and she put the meat back into the bag, lying down next to him, mustering all her strength to keep stroking him.

Every so often her eyelids would close with exhaustion and she would have to shake her head to wake herself up. Huge menacing black birds of prey started circling above them, apparently poised to swoop down and tear them apart. Rebecca jumped up, terrified. "*I must be seeing things from lack of sleep,*" she thought. The adrenalin fought the sleepiness back and the vision of the birds disappeared.

Rebecca knew that members of the big cat family are used to staying up all night to hunt and to sleeping during the day, but she also knew that they rarely stayed awake for more than five consecutive hours. She couldn't understand how the lion was managing to defy Nature.

All through the second night he didn't take his eyes off her, just watched her, as if wondering whether there could possibly be a person who would decide to die together with an animal, while others were willing to kill for no reason.

As she returned his gaze, Rebecca thought that despite his obvious exhaustion she could see sparks flickering in his sad eyes.

By morning they were both in a wretched state. Rebecca stood up but with great difficulty, taking a few unsteady steps to try to shake the numbness out of her legs. It felt as if they didn't belong to her and she had to concentrate hard in order to stay upright. It was as though her whole body had doubled its weight overnight.

The lion kept on watching her.

After a while she sat close to him once more and looked him straight in the eye, mustering the last of her strength. "Every day humans, who are not as strong as you, lose children, wives, husbands, parents, beloved ones, but we don't give up. We struggle to keep going. Parents raise a child minute by minute, day by day, year by year, and then suddenly this child may be brought home dead, killed without reason or wasted by illness. But the parents go on living, as well as the grandparents who might be a hundred years old. Sometimes, after a devastating earthquake, a rescue team finds a very old woman alive while her children, grandchildren and great-grandchildren have perished. It's an immense injustice, which people find very hard to swallow. There's no logic in it. The natural cycle is reversed. Yet they survive. A few people kill themselves or go mad with grief when they lose someone they love, but most of them overcome it, even though the pain and sadness stay with them for the rest of their lives. Will you, the personification of natural strength, let your life go like this? Will you knuckle under to your misfortune without a fight?"

Rebecca thought she saw a minute change in the lion's expression, as if he was pondering her words.

"I must be imagining it," she thought *"I'm probably hallucinating again from lack of sleep."* But she took heart and went on:

"During our life, we sometimes feel like lions and sometimes like sparrows. Your mother teaches you from the first weeks of your life how to claim your food. She brings the prey in her teeth, but she doesn't feed it to you. She clenches it tight in her jaws, so that you and your siblings have to struggle to seize it from her. Each cub has to fight to get its share. If you don't, you die of hunger. After a while she hunts down small animals, wounds them and hides them. Then she leads you there and lets you kill and eat them while she watches without intervening. It's all important and necessary training to help you survive. Before you get to know the world, you learn how to be lions, not sparrows.

"A sparrow is a most likeable bird. It has to search a lot to find food, especially during a heavy winter when it shivers both with cold and with the chill of uncertainty. It never knows in the morning whether it will still be alive by nightfall. It's aware that its future is uncertain. The same is true for us humans. Every day we work hard for our daily bread. We don't know whether we shall be successful or what the next day will bring. Just like the sparrow looking for crumbs in the cold, we humans struggle to feed our families. The children and the younger generations feel a cold uncertainty about their studies and their futures. And then, all of a sudden, we feel like lions. We acquire great strength. We strive against adversity and we defeat it. We find courage to face the future with all its hardships. And this happens as if both you and the sparrow live inside us. So you, our shining example, can't disappoint us by giving up like this."

For the first time in hours the lion averted his eyes from Rebecca's gaze as if ashamed, or so it seemed to her. She softened her tone a little.

"I know humans get support and courage from their gods and religions, but don't you feel my love? Can't you lean on me a little and let me support you? As well as on all the other people I've told you about who admire and love you? You're young, beautiful and strong. You have our support and so many reasons to go on living."

The lion raised his head and looked at her.

"Sometimes humans go on hunger strikes too. We become angry about some grave injustice done to us or to our fellows and so we revolt. Sometimes, though, we're duped and we rebel without realizing that we've fallen victim to the mean interests of other people. Maybe you are on a hunger strike, not only because you've lost your family but also because humans have been mistreating animals for such a long time. You are the king of beasts and it is your right to protest on behalf of all the other animals. For hundreds of thousands of years, while you ruled your kingdom, things were in balance. In the last hundred years this balance has been disrupted and many species face extinction because of human intervention."

The lion let out a low growl, as if to express his agreement.

Finally, after almost three days, Rebecca had heard his voice. She felt her courage lift.

"I'm sure you understand. I give you my word of honour that I will dedicate my life to freeing all the animals from every circus in the world. I don't know whether I'll succeed, but I will try."

The lion growled again and Rebecca filled her cap with water once more. As she lifted it the lion opened his mouth and she poured a few drops of the water onto his parched tongue. Tears of joy and relief rose in her eyes.

Rebecca did not let the lion drink too much at once, pouring the rest of the water on his head to cool him off. Then she sipped a little herself and washed her own dry, burned face.

"I don't know what is the right thing to do about zoos," she said, settling down against him once more. "If they didn't exist, millions of children would never see many kinds of animals. Not all of them can afford to travel far to see you in the wild. By visiting zoos they show that they love and appreciate you. If zoos were closed down, children would lose all contact with animals. They would see you only in books or on screens."

The lion turned and propped himself up on his forelegs. Rebecca poured more water into her cap once more and offered it to him. This time he drank it all and she hugged him and kissed him on the head. Then she drank too. She took out the meat and placed it in front of him, keeping for herself the piece that she had cut the day before. She began to eat her portion slowly, washing it down with more water. At first the lion watched her, and then he began to eat too as she stroked his back. After a while she felt that she was regaining her strength. The sun wasn't too high yet and a gentle breeze started to blow.

Using the pickaxe and spade Rebecca tried to cover the dead

bodies with earth and stones. The lion paced in circles around her, like a warden. It was a harder job than she'd imagined it would be and every now and then she stopped to drink some water and eat a few morsels of meat. In two hours she had succeeded in covering the corpses lightly, enough to protect them from birds of prey and hyenas for a while.

She sat down to rest. The lion lay beside her and rested his head on her legs. She told him that soon her friends would cover his lioness and the cubs better, in a deeper grave. And she told him that this grave would remain there for ever and they would tend it.

"Now I'm going back to join my friends and family, and you'll go back to your kingdom. We'll both work to make things better."

Rebecca got up, picked up the bag with the tools and set out towards the waiting party. The lion strode by her side. A short distance from her grandparents' camp she knelt down, flinging her arms round the lion's neck.

"Thank you for escorting me here," she said and kissed him again and again. "I'll miss you," she whispered. "I'll be thinking of you. I love you. From the warmth of your breath, I feel that you love me too. I promise to come and see you again. You have my word that we'll meet again soon and I'll stay longer. Please go now – and thank you."

Rebecca disengaged herself and the lion turned and padded slowly away as she knelt in the dirt, watching. After a few yards he stopped and turned back as if he didn't want to leave her. He gazed at her for a few seconds before turning round again and, breaking into a run, he disappeared into the scrub.

The others ran to Rebecca with cries of joy. Her grandparents remained calm but their pride and satisfaction were obvious as they hugged her and kissed her.

"Can we bury the dead bodies properly?" Rebecca asked. "I know you're all tired but I promised the lion we would."

"Don't worry. Some of us will stay behind and take care of everything," Thomas assured her. "It will all be properly done."

Reassured, Rebecca climbed wearily into the jeep and instantly fell asleep in the arms of her grandfather. She was still asleep when they arrived back at the lodge, so they carried her straight to bed. She slept for the next two days, only waking twice for drinks of water. By the time she finally woke, it was time for her to fly back to London. She and her grandparents agreed that she would return to Africa soon.

THE GREAT SECRET

The school year was coming to an end and one evening Julius told Rebecca that he was leaving on an important trip. He had to deliver a report on several projects he was handling. The trip would also give him an opportunity to visit his own parents, Lisa and Tony Newton.

"I'm leaving at midnight," he said, "and I would like you and your mother to come and see me off."

Shortly before midnight, Adriana was waiting at the wheel of the car as Julius and Rebecca got in. Within minutes they had reached the woods, where they all got out of the car. Julius kissed his wife a loving goodbye and then embraced his daughter tenderly, lifting her up and holding her tight against his chest, spinning round and making her laugh.

Putting her down, he waved to both of them and walked into the woods. Rebecca watched him go in puzzled silence before getting back into the car with her mother.

"How can he leave the woods, Mum?" she asked as the car moved off.

"He has his ways, darling," her mother answered, smiling enigmatically.

The following day many of the newspapers carried a curious story about two pilots reporting sightings of a huge blue flying object falling to Earth at tremendous speed, yet their aircraft radar had detected nothing. They had expected to see an explosion when the object hit the ground, but nothing had happened. It had simply disappeared, swallowed up in darkness.

Several car drivers had confirmed the report, adding that the "flying saucer" had plummeted into the same woods that Julius had disappeared into. The police and the fire brigade had been called out to the area but no trace of anything unusual was found and the authorities attributed the sighting to some unidentified atmospheric phenomenon.

Adriana deliberately left the newspapers open on the kitchen table where Rebecca was bound to see them. Because she was already interested in UFOs it wasn't hard to catch her attention, and it was only after she had been reading for a few minutes that she recognized the description of the woods. She looked up at her mother, wanting to ask questions but unsure where to begin.

Her mother's warm gaze seemed to be answering her unasked questions: *'Yes, love, it's true. What you think is really happening. Your father has left in the object that they saw coming to Earth.'*

"That particular UFO ..." Adriana said after a moment. "It wasn't seen leaving because it takes off at such incredible speed that it becomes invisible to the human eye. It takes only a fraction of a second from take-off until it leaves the Earth's atmosphere. However, when it enters the Earth's atmosphere, it slows down a little and that's why it's sometimes visible."

Rebecca still didn't say a word. She was lost in her own thoughts.

Ten days later Adriana and Rebecca went back to the woods to pick Julius up. Rebecca said nothing all the way home.

"Did you see grandpa and grandma?" she asked her father when they were safely back in the house with cups of tea.

"Certainly. They send you their greetings. They miss you a lot, but they're happy at the thought of seeing you soon."

"What? Are they coming here?" Rebecca asked excitedly.

Her father took a few sips of tea. "Rebecca, for the last two years your mother and I have been trying to prepare you to accept the things that you have to learn as easily as possible. No matter how well prepared you are, however, some of the things you're going to hear will seem unbelievable to you at first. Do you feel ready to hear what I have to say?"

"I feel fine," Rebecca said, consumed with curiosity.

"This summer, when you turn fifteen, you're going to begin a new life. You've been adequately prepared for this new life, whose ultimate course you alone will choose. For our part we had to decide whether you would be given powers at birth that would enable you later to make good decisions for yourself.

"We had to choose before you were born because at the moment of your birth you had to receive the Flame of the White Sun, which is the accumulated energy of the universe. Whoever has this energy never falls ill. That's why up till now you have never had any of the common children's ailments that your friends at school fell prey to.

"We who have this Flame are called Orizons. Our race matures slightly faster than other people do and we come of age at fifteen. That's the reason many people have commented on your maturity. You also have more strength and stamina than other girls of your age. That's why you excel at sport and your other activities.

"In addition to maturity, you possess other powers. First of all, because of the energy inside you, you only love; you never hate. You love everybody, including all animals. Animals reciprocate your love, that's why your grandparents let you go to that lion. They knew he would never harm you."

"How many of us are there?" Rebecca asked.

"About a thousand Orizons are active on Earth, all of them working to save the planet and to do good. We aspire to drive out evil from humanity so that love and goodness prevail. Good always comes under attack. Our job is to serve Good and support it.

"Orizons have characters made of steel and are devoid of jealousy, envy, malice, selfishness, avarice and arrogance. They aren't greedy. They're satisfied with the simple things in life, the bare necessities. They lack nothing of what's needed for the healthy enjoyment of life's beauty.

"We Orizons firmly believe that the family is the foundation of society. In our families we try to live as close together as possible; to eat, talk and have fun together. When Orizons have children, they never separate. Children are always wounded by a divorce, no matter what age they are. If a spouse is killed the other can marry again if they so wish.

"Unfortunately, as you have seen for yourself, the family institution is in decline here on Earth. People divorce without giving it much thought. Even when they live in the same house, they rarely spend time together. Children eat at fast-food outlets while their parents have working lunches or eat out with friends. Respect is rare. We have to try and change all that because the outcome isn't pleasant.

"Orizons don't get angry or quarrel with each other. We don't speak ill of anyone. Our homes are always calm and peaceful. We don't answer back, but simply express our opinions. We have understanding and good sense. Orizons don't use flattery, but we do give praise when it is due. We don't criticize the short-comings of others. We don't fight back if people mistreat us. We don't accuse others or swear or strike out at anyone. We avoid giving advice even to our own children. We simply offer information. We don't oppress anyone. We always show respect towards one another and especially towards our elders. We never smoke. We don't drink alcohol, except for a glass of wine with a meal occasionally.

"Our land is in the First Parallel Dimension of the universe and it is called the Land of the White Sun. I won't answer all your questions today. There are others whose job it is to tell you more. Your mother and I will tell you the basics that you need to know before you leave."

"Leave?" Rebecca asked her eyes wide. "Am I going to this land?"

"As soon as school closes, you'll travel to your true homeland. Your grandparents will be waiting for you there. They and others will teach you what you need to know, until the time comes for you to decide about your future. The trip to our land will be pleasant."

"Like a plane journey?" Rebecca asked, remembering the reports of the flying saucer.

"Much more comfortable," Julius assured her. "You'll be travelling with other Orizons of your own age from other countries on Earth, who'll be visiting their homeland for the first time as well. You'll speak to each other in Ancient Greek. All Orizons speak Ancient Greek. It is the language spoken in the Land of the White Sun."

Rebecca was listening attentively. It felt almost as if she had been expecting something like this all her life, as though she had had a premonition.

"In the Land of the White Sun there are powers of Good but there are also powers of Evil. The powers of Evil want to seize the Flame so as to have the same advantages as the Orizons and be able to travel to Earth. But if they come to Earth and join forces with the evil ones here, the situation will grow even worse. We have to defend the Flame, which is the source of our power and our energy, the power of Good."

"So we have to fight?" Rebecca asked.

"The Orizons never kill except in self-defence. They never initiate war, but they must fight to defend and preserve the Flame because the powers of Good derive all their energy from it. From time to time war breaks out in the Land of the White Sun. We call it 'Lomani'. Unlike on Earth, though, wars are fought with simple means. The weapons used are swords, spears, bows and arrows. That's why you've been trained to use them since you were young. Lomani is a kind of battle where only courage and good training count. There are no weapons of mass destruction as there are on Earth.

"Here what counts is not training and courage but weaponry. Pressing a remote-control button kills thousands of soldiers. Their courage and their months or years of hard training are rendered useless. Snipers and concealed landmines put an end to bravery. Heroes are killed before they even go into battle. The rattling fire of a single machine-gun can wipe out entire companies.

"Beyond a certain point, only technology seems to count on Earth. In the Land of the White Sun, however, we use equivalent weapons.

"Until you finish your education here on Earth, you'll be going to our land every summer to train. Not just for war, but to get to know our way of life there. You'll be like a migrating bird.

"The existence of the Orizons has been a well-kept secret for thousands of years. If it is ever found out it will be a disaster for Earth. Our efforts and our network will be rendered useless.

"Rebecca, the Orizons never lie but, if they must, they can hide the truth. Never forget that. It is not necessary to speak the whole truth, but what you say aloud must be true.

"Well, that's enough for you to take in for one day. There'll be time to talk again before you leave. We'd better get some rest now."

"Dad," said Rebecca, "what about my promise to the lion? I told him that I would dedicate my life to freeing all the animals from circuses. I also promised to go and see him again ..."

Julius raised his hand to calm her. "Don't worry. It won't be difficult to keep your promise to the lion. All Orizons take an active interest in the protection of animals and in helping them lead a natural life. And you know your grandparents are responsible for this matter in South-East Africa. Whatever happens, you will be able to devote as much time as you wish to accomplishing your goal. All of us will be on your side. Everything will work out right, you'll see."

They went to bed, but Rebecca scarcely slept at all. It was hard for her to absorb the news that she and her family were not ordinary humans. She tried to imagine what the Land of the White Sun was like. Her mind teemed with a thousand thoughts.

As the days passed Rebecca's parents took every opportunity to answer her questions while pointing out that she would learn much more when she reached her homeland. They told her that thousands of years before, humans had wiped out life on Earth by meddling with Nature. Then the Creator had set things in order and life flourished once more. They also said that instead of learning from history, mankind continued to repeat the same mistakes on an even larger scale.

When the day of Rebecca's departure arrived, Adriana packed only a few clothes for her.

"You'll wear different clothes there," she explained.

Even when it was time to leave the house, her parents were as calm as ever.

"Rebecca," Julius said, noticing that she was listening to him just as she had when she was a little girl and he was reading bedtime stories to her, "in a while we'll set out for the woods. The sphere will come for you at midnight. Bull the Minotaur is the pilot. Bull is one of the nicest creatures. He loves everyone but most of all he loves children and young people. He is their protector – their hero! Another fifteen children of your age will be travelling with you, so no doubt tomorrow the newspapers will be reporting multiple sightings of flying saucers. Well, let them do so ... We don't really care." He smiled ruefully. "Our Lord's daughter, Princess Felicia, will be waiting for you there, and after a few procedures you'll go to your grandparents' home. Don't worry. Everything will go well, and you'll be back soon. But come on – it's time to go."

On the dot of twelve, standing in the woods with her parents, an excited Rebecca saw the blue ring hurtling towards Earth. Once it had landed and the steps had come down, her parents moved forward with her. Rebecca's heart pounded against her ribcage. Bull was already waiting, his hand outstretched towards his passenger.

The fairy tale had now become an extremely realistic cinema movie, and Rebecca had an important role in it!

"Rebecca, you look exactly as I imagined you would. You combine the beauty of your mother and grandmothers. You glow! But come, we must take off now. We have many things to talk about during the journey and even more when we reach our destination. You'll get tired of the sound of my voice."

Rebecca and her parents bid each other a quick farewell and Bull politely helped her up the steps, which then retracted. The hatch closed and Rebecca found herself in a large circular cabin. Everything was made of crystal. There was a cockpit for the pilot and about thirty crystal seats with comfortable leather cushions. The other children who were already there all looked in her direction as Bull went straight to the cockpit.

"This is Rebecca," Bull announced and they all stood to greet her. Within seconds the ship had taken off and the Earth was dwindling on the screens, turning into a speck and then disappearing.

There were fifteen other children, five girls and ten boys. Rebecca tried to fit their names to their faces as they all clamoured to shake her hand and introduce themselves.

"My name is Pedro," the first boy said, extending his hand. "I live in Brazil." His tawny skin looked like velvet and his large, ash-coloured eyes seemed to flicker with sparks. His hair was fairly long and he was tall for his age.

"I'm José, from Mexico," said the next boy. He was a little shorter than Pedro, with broad shoulders and a muscular athletic body. He too was dark-skinned, with a strange nose that looked like the beak of a tortoise. His eyes were the colour of honey and his untamed hair covered his entire forehead.

"My name's Lee," said the next. "My family and I live in China."

His cheerful eyes seemed to smile even more than his lips. His fingers were long and wiry, like pincers.

"Louise," said a pleasant black girl, giving Rebecca a hug. "I live in New Orleans with my parents."

Louise had full purple lips, expressive eyes and long hair pulled back into a ponytail. She was tall with shapely legs and hips. She reminded Rebecca of an antelope.

A charming blonde girl raised her hand in greeting. "Hi, Rebecca. My name's Susan. I live with my parents in Canada." Her glossy fair locks, dark red lips and snow-white skin made her stand out from the others.

"I'm Nargis and I live in India with my mother and grandmother," said another girl, squeezing Rebecca's hands. She had a sweet face and a slim, delicate body.

"My name's Bill and I live in Washington," said a tall athletic boy who had a strongly masculine face to which his freckles gave an extra charm. He gave her a warm handshake.

"I'm Rashid and I'm from Egypt." Rashid's expression was cheerful and attractive. He had a large, well-shaped nose and dark curly hair.

"Sergei's my name and I live in Russia." Sergei was built like a giant, with a bull's thick neck. He had short reddish-blond hair, a ruddy complexion and impressive blue eyes. His handshake was warm.

"My name is Tamina and I live in Japan."

Tamina was sweet and elegant, with a face like a pale moon. She put her arms round Rebecca and kissed her.

"I'm Abu and I live in South Africa," said a tall sturdy black boy. As he smiled he flashed a set of shining white teeth. He shook her hand with both of his. Although he was still young, his looks reminded Rebecca of Thomas.

"I'm Tiki, from Tahiti. Tiki shook hands with her, with a slight bow of his head. He had a strong body, wheat-coloured skin and a good-natured expression.

"My name's Jabal and I live in Saudi Arabia."

Jabal had a jolly face, a pleasant manner about him, and his movements were graceful. His shiny skin had a dark ashen colour.

"And I'm Carlos. I come from Spain." Carlos shook hands and bowed. He was tall and dark, with long hair and green eyes. He had a clear, beaming face. Rebecca noticed that his neat chin had a nice dimple. He flashed a smile and two more dimples formed in his cheeks.

"I'm Samantha and I live in Australia with my parents," said a tall, striking girl with bushy hair. Her turquoise eyes looked like crystal globes filled with clear sea water; her eyelashes fluttered like butterfly wings. Her beauty was dazzling.

"Hi." Rebecca stood back to get her breath. "My name is Rebecca and I live in England and I'm very much afraid it is going to take me a little while to remember everyone's names."

They all laughed and talked at once as they settled themselves down in their seats again. Having set the sphere on its course, Bull left the pilot's seat and joined them.

"So, how are you doing, children?" he asked. "As you've guessed, I'm Bull the Minotaur. I would like to thank every one of you for being so prompt. We were able to collect you all in less than sixty Earth minutes from all over the planet. We spent longer going up and down the steps than we did moving between destinations.

"Your parents have given you a general outline of what lies ahead for you. And you will learn much more once we arrive. But let me just tell you a few things. Now that we've left Earth, things have changed; time and distance don't matter any more. Right now we're not travelling in time or space. To travel in space one needs many Earth years, centuries even, to cross short distances."

Bull paced back and forth among them as he spoke. Rebecca

thought that his smile mixed all the optimism of a sunrise with the sweetness of a sunset. It was the most likeable face she had ever encountered.

"You will now learn a few important things about space travel and aliens. In space, there are more dimensions than those we know. There are parallel dimensions, meaning parallel worlds. I don't know how many. I only know two: the First Parallel Dimension, where we're now heading, and the Second Parallel Dimension – about which we'll talk more later.

"Creatures can travel between these parallel dimensions. Scientists don't know that yet. Only the Gods, the Mythical Creatures and the Orizons have that knowledge. Nobody can travel there in space, because the distances are too huge.

"Once we are out of Earth's atmosphere, we first leave its magnetism. Then we develop tremendous speed, even faster than light. That way, we stop travelling in time and space. Without understanding it, we enter the First Parallel Dimension of the Universe. There we shall see something marvellous: our land. The Land of the White Sun!"

"We thought the spaceships that we'd been hearing about for so long were flying saucers," said Rashid.

Bull's smile grew wider.

"It's true that some people think beings from other planets visit Earth in flying saucers. But we're the only ones who come: there's nobody else. People who have seen the blue beam encircling our sphere might *think* that they've seen a flying saucer. The light is the accumulated energy of the Flame of the White Sun. This energy reacts with water and generates the amounts of energy needed to power the sphere. In the Land of the White Sun, we use water to produce all the energy we need. There's no life on other planets. If the Creator had wanted humankind to live elsewhere, He would have created life there, too. Earth is all they have.

"So why do people travel in space and try to explore it and the planets, if there is no life there?" asked Nargis.

"Because humans meddle in things that they should leave alone," Bull said cheerfully. "Wasting money and energy, instead of trying to improve the quality of life on their own planet. The vast amounts they spend on the space race could be used to save and improve many lives on Earth if it was spent properly. They should simplify their lives instead of trying to conquer the universe, especially as their efforts are all in vain. They cannot find happiness, peace or health in their own backyards and yet they expect to triumph over the universe.

"Even if life did exist on other planets, exploring them wouldn't benefit people on Earth. Distances are so vast that it would take thousands of Earth years to make a single trip to a planet where the human race might be able to survive. So it's impossible."

Bull's face became serious. "Children, the Earth is wounded, suffering, bleeding. Its inhabitants are being killed, falling sick, starving and dying for no good reason! Skeletal children search for food among the rubbish. They die of starvation. Some, irrespective of age, choose to be captured and imprisoned just to find a shelter to spend the winter and put food in their bellies."

The children listened to Bull attentively, nodding their heads in agreement. It was hard to imagine that they were actually talking about space travel with someone who piloted a spaceship.

"I always thought that spacecraft were a different shape from this one so they could cover vast distances more rapidly," said Samantha.

"The Creator, however, made all the planets spherical, Samantha," Bull said. "They travel in space for billions of years and cover unimaginable distances. So the sphere is the right shape. Yet the space scientists on Earth haven't even considered such a simple thing."

Bull's sweet face beamed at them. He was never happier than when he was among children, watching their hungry young minds soaking up knowledge.

"Do you know what the fastest thing is?" he asked. "Light is like a snail compared to it. Can anyone tell me?"

They all thought hard. They'd been taught that light was the fastest traveller in the universe, so what was Bull talking about? They remained silent, looking a little anxious, like school children that haven't done their homework.

"Well," Bull boomed, "to put you out of your misery, let me tell you that human thought is the quickest thing in the universe. You can recall places you have visited, however far away they may be, instantly. You can see pictures, landscapes and people you have met. Imagine that you travelled to the remotest planet in the universe, which light would take thousands of Earth years to reach. When you finally returned, you would be able to send your thoughts there in less than a tenth of a second. Billions of miles in just a tenth of a second! Of course, if you try to do it now, you will only visit it in your imagination. Your thoughts, however, can provide real images of every place you have ever visited. So you possess the fastest thing in the universe inside your heads!"

The children relaxed and laughed, happy to think that they had such power. They were excited by the images that Bull's teachings conjured up in their imaginations.

Then Tamina spoke, changing the subject.

"This crystal spacecraft must cost an amazing amount of money," she said.

"It costs precisely nothing," Bull answered.

"How come?" asked a chorus of voices.

"Money is not used anywhere in the Land of the White Sun. Money is one of the worst human inventions: the principal cause of war and the corrupter of human conscience. Each one of us has all he needs without money and no one claims anything. Nature provides all the things we need to live well and happily. What do we need a purse for? This sounds strange to you now, but you'll soon see it for yourselves.

"We are all self-sufficient! Self-sufficiency provides the greatest riches of all. If we happen to need something that we cannot obtain by ourselves, anyone who can help us does so voluntarily and gladly. There's no trade-off. There's no obligation and there are no ulterior motives. Everything is clean and pure. Self-interest plays no part; if I give you something, you don't have to give me something else in return.

"We don't buy the sweat and toil of others. We don't want others to polish our boots, or wash and iron our clothes. We take pride in producing our own food and we never pay someone to cook it for us. Nor do we sell ourselves."

The look of astonishment on Samantha's face was mirrored on those of several of the other children.

"You mean people who work for someone else are selling themselves?" she asked.

"Yes, that's exactly what I mean. What's more, it's not even an auction for the highest bidder; it's more like selling to the lowest bidder. Money dictates people's freedom. But with society structured as it is on Earth, things can't operate any differently at the moment. Most people on Earth look like overloaded freighters being tossed about by storms, don't you think?"

One or two of the children nodded, their faces screwed up

in thought as they tried to understand everything the Minotaur was telling them.

"No matter how much make-up they use, the mess, the misery and the alienation of society cannot be covered."

"I'm still not sure whether we sell ourselves by working for others," insisted Samantha. "But maybe it's better for us to get to know the Land of the White Sun first and analyse it afterwards."

"I agree," said Bull. "You will see that the Creator provides the food for us. We have to do very little, whereas on Earth most people have to get it themselves, suffering day and night in all sorts of sweatshops – with blood, sweat and compromises. Some even have to demean themselves by begging. Our life is simple and beautiful and our people do not need money. Money cultivates bad habits and leads to many other unpleasant things.

"The only luxuries we have in our land are intellectual. We're greedy for cultivation through books, discussion, companionship, art, sport, entertainment and any satisfaction that we get from participating in worthwhile creative activities. People on Earth sacrifice the best years of their lives to insipid interests. By the time they realize, it's too late for them to do anything about it."

Although Bull spoke calmly and clearly, there was no mistaking the passion of his words.

"Bull." Sergei raised his hand to be heard. "My parents told me that unfortunately there are wars between Good and Evil in our homeland. They said you'd give us more information on the subject."

"You've studied all the mythologies of the Earth. The things you've read are not fairy tales, though they have been distorted considerably. Historical pranks and travesties occurred, making the darkness even blacker. Many years ago, human activity destroyed life on Earth. The planet was flooded and became a polluted watery wasteland. Even before that happened, however, all the Mythical Gods had decided to abandon Earth. They took with them the creatures and beings that made up the mythical world of the time, as well as people from all the races on the planet. They also took with them specimens of every animal species. We were transferred to the Land of the White Sun, which is in the First Parallel Dimension. We have lived there now for countless years.

"When the great Creator restored the Earth once more, He made it as beautiful as it had been before man destroyed it. Life started all over again. Every animal species and many people from every race returned to Earth. Life and the human and animal populations developed normally again.

"The Gods of mythology, the mythical creatures and a number of people called Orizons, who came from all the races of the world, together with several pairs from all the animal species, remained in the Land of the White Sun.

"Alas, humans soon got up to their old tricks again on Earth. So the Gods decided to send Orizons to the planet to help save it and prevent a second catastrophe. The Orizons were sent because they have no evil in them.

"But back in the Land of the White Sun the Orizons and the mythical creatures began to quarrel. The Mythical Gods grew fed up with their complaints and they decided to move to the Second Parallel Dimension and live there for all eternity. The demigods and heroes of the so-called mythological world went with them to this Dimension. The place they live in is called the Elysian Fields. The paradise of the Elysian Fields is a combination of all the best things to be found in the paradises of every religion on Earth. In the Second Parallel Dimension there is no war, discord or evil. Everything is perfect.

"Before departing from the First Parallel Dimension where our Land is, the Mythical Gods divided the inhabitants into two camps. Those who believe in Good and struggle for it to prevail and those who oppose it. The Gods entrusted the Flame of the White Sun to the powers of Good. It was their job to use and protect it.

"Your families, the Orizons, belong to the camp of Good together with some mythological creatures such as the Amazons, the Centaurs, Glory the Sphinx, Pegasus, Leiko – son of the demigod Hercules – and myself. The Orizons who chose the other camp were called Sharkans. The mythical creatures that joined the Sharkans were the Porths, the Cyclopes and Calphie, who is *their* Sphinx. There are also two Medusas who take no sides and live by themselves in the forest."

Bull could see from the looks of intense concentration on the children's faces that they were having trouble memorising everything he was saying.

"Don't worry," he said. "This will all become clear once we reach our destination – just bear with me. I am the first cousin of the Minotaur, who lived on the island of Crete. But he chose the path of Evil and that's why he was slain by the Greek hero Theseus. The forces of Good settled in Utopia and the forces of Evil in the area called Beast.

"The Mythical Gods appointed Lord Life to govern the powers of Good in the Land of the White Sun. The Gods entrusted the Land to him because he is wise, careful, patient, considerate and above all just. His flawless ethos played a significant role in their choice; so did his courage, simplicity and modesty. He is not conceited and he never puts himself above the others. He strictly maintains the integrity of his character. His almost infallible instinct usually helps him to make the right decisions. He enjoys the esteem of all the inhabitants of the Land of the White Sun.

"When his daughter Princess Felicia grew up and he realized that she had the required abilities, he assigned to her the army command. He himself withdrew from these duties and now he mainly deals with matters on Earth, guiding the Orizons who operate there. Perhaps, at some time in the future, the Gods will let Lord Life rest among them by taking him to live out eternity in the Elysian Fields.

"In our land, the powers of Evil are under Turgoth's command. He is very skilful and has many talents. His aim is to seize the Flame of the White Sun so that the powers of Evil obtain more energy and, most of all, can visit Earth in order to help Evil reign supreme. In answer to your question, that's why there are wars in our country.

"Ours is a fairy-tale land, the like of which you've never seen. It's our homeland, the homeland of your parents and grandparents. In our land there is no crime, so there are no courts. There are some basic rules that are obeyed by all, even by the powers of Evil. For instance, our forces only take defensive action; they never initiate a war and the powers of Evil always warn us before they are about to start one. Neither side ever takes prisoners of war. When the battles are over, each side collects its dead and wounded. We call this war Lomani."

Bull rose and went over to a table on which there were three big clay pitchers and seventeen cups. He filled the cups with water.

"Now that we have arrived in our land, let's make a toast."

"What, have we arrived already?" they all said at once.

"Of course we have," answered Bull, laughing.

"But we've only just left," said Louise in wonder.

"Yes, and we've already landed on automatic pilot. We haven't been travelling through space; we've changed Dimension."

Moved and amazed, the children picked up their cups and raised them towards Bull's.

"Welcome to your homeland," he boomed. "Your home: the Land of the White Sun!"

IN THE LAND OF THE WHITE SUN

The children collected their bags and descended the crystal steps. Rebecca looked around, wide-eyed in amazement. The spaceship had landed on an area covered with vivid green grass, like a football pitch on Earth. There were two similar ships parked nearby and an open carriage with two snowy-white horses champing at the bit.

"Okay, children, climb into the carriage," Bull called out to them. "This place is the Highlow Cosmodrome. As you can see, it's small and simple and it's inside the Fortress of Utopia. Now we'll head for the open-air theatre, where all the important functions take place. Princess Felicia is waiting for us there, together with your relatives. It's not far. Enjoy the ride."

The children clambered into the wooden carriage, sinking into the soft leather seats while Bull climbed up proudly into the coachman's seat, taking the reins and spurring the horses into a trot. Rebecca was impressed that Bull was a coachman as well as a spaceship pilot, humbly bridging past, present and future, epochs separated by long time-spans and tremendous differences in technology. From a point close to the beginnings of mankind and on to where man has always dreamed of reaching, travelling through the Universe in a spaceship.

The carriage rattled out of the cosmodrome onto a road covered with the same immaculate grass as the landing field. Elegant avenues of trees stretched as far as the eye could see. Monkeys swung through their branches, reminding Rebecca of the lodge in Kenya. Brilliantly coloured parrots and other tropical birds flew round the carriage in a squawking guard of honour. Deer and other wild animals grazed and ran fearlessly along the road and among the trees, as if they were playing children's games like tag or hide-and-seek. Simple single-storey structures of all sizes were dotted around the landscape.

They passed other horse-drawn vehicles and many riders. Everyone looked happy and healthy and Rebecca was struck by the fact that she didn't see any elderly people as she would have done in a street this size on Earth.

"Here we are," Bull said, drawing the horses up and jumping down a few seconds later.

Rebecca noticed several smaller carriages and horses already resting in the shade. She and the other children got out and followed Bull up some steps and through an arched gateway into what looked like an ancient Roman theatre. Tiers of seats rose up all around in the shape of a horseshoe. The seats above the gateway were different to the others, designed to fit Centaurs. The ground was once again covered with grass.

A stage had been raised at the far end and beyond it stood a short tree with a thick trunk and sparse branches bearing thin foliage. On the platform, in a bamboo chair next to the tree, sat Princess Felicia, dressed in the same uniform that she had worn for Rebecca's birth. Opposite her were seated the children's relatives and those who would be responsible for their training. A Centaur sat in the last row. Sixteen seats in the first row stood empty, evidently reserved for the children.

Several Orizons stood in front of the tiers of seats on both sides, playing harps, flutes, violins and other instruments. Their music filled the theatre, creating a celebratory atmosphere and making the children feel welcome.

Bull led the procession towards the princess. As she stood up the music stopped and the musicians sat down.

"Welcome to your homeland," Felicia said, her voice clear and warm. She asked each of the children their names in turn, embracing and kissing them one by one.

After the greetings, Bull led the children to the empty chairs and took his own seat next to the princess. They sat down and the princess began to speak to the assembled crowd.

"I trust you've had a good journey, although I'm sure that you are all feeling a little anxious and strange at the moment. If it wasn't for the fact that you each have the Flame of the White Sun within you, such a dramatic experience might well have caused you to lose your minds. No ordinary human mind can absorb such extraordinary changes, especially when they take place so suddenly."

Felicia paused as a ripple of agreement ran through the crowd of onlookers. She looked each of the children straight in the eye, emphasizing every one of her words.

"However, we are Orizons! You will soon adjust and understand that what is happening to you is not a dream. We are all going to get to know each other well. We shall work together for the good of our land as well as that of the Earth, which has been your home until now."

As she spoke she walked along their row of seats, making each child feel as if she was talking only to them.

"Your training begins tomorrow. Here in the Fortress we have classrooms and practice grounds. You will have lessons for eight hours every day. Your tuition will be completed over three summer periods.

"The war here – a type of conflict which, as you know, is called Lomani – may break out at any moment. We must protect our Flame. It gives us great strength and with this strength we fight for Good to prevail. You, however, are not permitted to take part in Lomani until you have finished your training. Only then will you be adequately prepared to fight if the need arises.

"At your homes, you will learn the customs of our land and you'll see how simple and easy life can be."

Felicia turned round and pointed to the end of the stage. "Do you see how the Flame burns on that hillock? The positive energy of the universe is concentrated there. We will always protect it and will never let it be taken away. That place is sacred to us and is protected by the Sphinx."

Rebecca looked to the end of the stage where the ground rose, forming a hillock. At its peak shone the blue Flame, rising from a large crystal plate which stood on a square crystal base. Beside this base sat a Sphinx. It was the first time that Rebecca had seen such a huge creature.

"From your upbringings and with the Flame you already have inside you," the princess continued, "you have begun to develop good sense and wisdom. We all gain wisdom from experience and profound observation of what goes on around us. And it leads us to make careful choices in our daily lives.

"Great philosophers go beneath the surface to explore things in depth, tirelessly seeking knowledge and interpreting what they discover for others to understand. Some of their opinions are helpful and we can apply them in everyday life. But usually they are expressed in such an obscure manner that few can understand them.

"In our view, real wisdom is that which everybody can understand and from which they can reap benefits by putting theory into practice. Hidden meanings, locked up in trunks and perceived only by the refined keyholders, are worthless.

"We Orizons discuss things, telling one another what we know and believe, and we find these dialogues fruitful. We all have the spark of philosophical reasoning inside us because of the Flame and our upbringing.

"Among the many gifts the great Creator has given us in this wonderful land is the Wise Tree of Knowledge. It is the Tree that you see here." Felicia turned and walked over to the tree at the centre of the stage.

"The Wise Tree of Knowledge suggests solutions to many serious problems. It teaches us, using simple words so that everybody can understand it. Today, on your first day in this land, you will have the good fortune to hear it and talk to it." She stroked the tree's trunk affectionately and it moved slightly.

Now that she was looking closely, Rebecca noticed that just above the middle of the trunk was the outline of a mouth, a nose and two large, expressive eyes. She couldn't help but smile at the friendly look on the wrinkled old face.

"Let's hear what it has to tell us, then," said the princess.

The Wise Tree blinked, looked at its spellbound audience and smiled. "Thank you, Your Highness, for your kind words. Our princess is truly wise – and modest, too. Modesty, after all, is a sign of wisdom." The Tree paused briefly, cleared its throat and continued in a deep, husky voice. "I bid you welcome, dear children. I am always glad to talk with people and especially with young people. Youths and elders can agree in many fields, when they want to. If you want to say something or ask a question, do please stand up.

"Let's begin by talking about the greatest of the gifts that the Creator has given to all creatures: freedom. We should all be completely free. It may sound simple, but it isn't. There is a thin line linking us to absolute freedom, a line that we should never break. Our absolute freedom extends only as long as we don't hurt others. But we shouldn't allow our freedom to hurt ourselves either.

"To achieve great things, we must take a good look at ourselves from the outside and face our inner selves humbly, without conceit or arrogance. We must try to see ourselves as others do, observing ourselves fairly, without bias. Once we have succeeded in taking this first crucial step and have discovered our mistakes, we shall know what we have to do in order to improve. And we cannot do it just once. We must judge ourselves objectively all the time.

"Then comes the second step. We have to look deep inside ourselves, searching every nook and cranny to know who we really are. We have to become friends with ourselves and find ways to mend any misunderstandings. But to do this we need to enter with courage, with pure and unbiased intentions, with our eyes wide open like those of scouts and not closed like those of moles. This is the most difficult step but it will help us to know when to claim our rights and how to meet our obligations. By searching within ourselves we can try to create a harmonious balance of the senses, the spirit and the heart, bringing them together in a fruitful union leading to inner peace. That in turn will become a positive force for benefiting those others around us."

As Samantha stood up, the Tree stopped talking and all eyes turned to the Australian girl.

"What if we get frightened by knowing ourselves?" she asked. "If we despair and become disappointed, what do we do then?"

"Good point! Yes, it is possible that may happen. You might be surprised by the new acquaintance, even if everything is right. But you still need to know where you stand, what you want and what you expect from life, which of your inner weaknesses you can improve upon and which you can eradicate."

The answer did not seem to satisfy Samantha completely. But she sat down again anyway, feeling that she had made her point.

"I want you to pay close attention to what I tell you now, because you'll have to make some important decisions. Remember that when one tries, one always faces the prospect of failure or defeat. In our situation, because of the wars, we also face the risk of death. If you do nothing, you will never fail or be defeated. You'll be a mere spectator, indifferent to everything. You'll never feel the joy of victory and success. But you will never have the painful feeling of defeat or face the danger of being killed, either. It is therefore a matter of choosing how much excitement you want in your life; how it will become meaningful, and how much you feel the need to take risks."

The Tree stopped, gave its branches a shake, sighed and declaimed loudly:

"Without struggle there is neither victory nor defeat; so think carefully when the time comes for you to choose."

Having made everyone sit up, it continued in a softer tone.

"The Creator has given us everything in abundance. But we cannot enjoy it all without giving anything back. Our contribution is not limited to material things. If we look at buds with love, they will bloom into beautiful flowers. If we tenderly caress flowers the air will suddenly be filled with their perfume. If we ignore beautiful roses they will wilt; their leaves will fall off because they'll feel useless. Plants are alive, you see, and highly sensitive. So we should behave accordingly towards them. We should treat them lovingly.

"We should also treat the people around us affectionately. We should be close to our parents, our mate and our children; if we are indifferent towards them, they too will wilt. We should try to touch their souls. Then they will open for us their bolted gates. Remember these things I've told you today, no matter how many years go by. Is there anyone who wants to ask me a question?"

No one spoke, all of them were lost in their own thoughts.

"Having said enough for our first session I want to conclude for today. But I'll always be available. Come to me whenever you want to talk."

"Thank you, Wise Tree," Felicia said, rising from her seat. "Now, children, it's time to present to you my key colleagues. You all know Bull the Minotaur, and you'll have a chance to get to know him better as the days go by. This is Doctor Afterland, who attended the birth of each one of you."

Doctor Afterland stood up, walked over to the children and shook hands with them, one by one.

"Welcome to our land," he said. "We'll have several classes together. We do not have dates here because they do not interest us. We do follow the dates of Earth, however, so that we can communicate and work with the Orizons living there. Here we only have hours. The sun always rises at six in the morning and sets at eight in the evening. Please adjust your watches by the theatre clock," he said and pointed to a huge clock at the top of the horseshoe tiers. "As you can see, it's eleven o'clock in the Land of the White Sun.

"Our lessons together will include basic medicine, social studies and sex education. Our first class will be tomorrow morning at nine. The building where we'll have our lessons is next to the martial-arts training facilities. Your relatives will show it to you today."

The doctor turned and went back to his seat and the princess stepped forward again. .

"Now I would like to present General Claudia to you. She is the leader of the Amazons."

A striking woman with firm breasts and symmetric curves stood up to greet the children. She was wearing tight shorts, a brown leather top and boots. Her carefully dressed hair reached her waist. Her eyes were the colour of an unripe olive. It was difficult to tell her age from her smooth, pleasant face. Her whole appearance radiated strength, her movements showing all the confidence of a mythical warrior with an added feminine grace.

"Welcome to our beautiful land," she said, after greeting each of the children. "I know you're already trained in the rudiments of archery but I will take you to the next stage, combining it with riding. I will see you tomorrow after your lesson with Doctor Afterland,"

"Next you'll meet the leader of the Centaurs, General Hunter," Felicia announced.

"Together we will learn how to use the javelin, the spear and the shield," the Centaur told them. " I will see you tomorrow. Welcomc to our land."

"Finally, our Commander-in-Chief, Field Marshal Foster."

A tall virile man got up to greet the children. He had thick blond hair and dark skin; his whole appearance was imposing, even awe-inspiring. He wore the uniform of white leather shorts and tunic with the blue sun symbol on it, and blue leather boots. Round his waist was a blue belt from which hung a crystal sword and scabbard.

"In my lessons you will learn how to use the sword and how to fight. I know you can all fence but you will find out that the proper use of the sword during battle is something quite different. Your training will be hard, but it will prove useful in the future. We begin tomorrow. Welcome to our wonderful land."

"Now," Felicia said, "greet your relatives and then the feast will begin. We are all going to dance a lot."

As the children hugged and kissed their relatives, many cheeks were streaked with tears of joy. Two massive tables, laden with an assortment of fruits and juices, were brought in and placed in front of the stage, and the musicians began to play again.

As the dancing got going the spirits of the crowd rose even higher. Even the musicians were dancing as they played and the Wise Tree clapped its branches in time to the music.

After dancing with Field Marshal Foster and Doctor Afterland the princess went over to the Tree, hugged its trunk and swayed with it. The Tree embraced her with its lower branches and stroked her hair, moving in time with the music.

When the clock struck twelve the music stopped and Felicia stood in front of the Tree.

"Your relatives will show you the main buildings inside the Fortress. Then you can go home."

Lisa and Tony Newton left the theatre with Rebecca between them and headed for their carriage, to which a beautiful black horse was harnessed. They all sat in front and Tony took the reins.

Rebecca hadn't seen them for five years and they hadn't changed at all, not in the slightest. They looked as if the passage of time hadn't touched their faces in any way. If anything, they looked younger. It made Rebecca glad, but it also puzzled her.

They drove first to the buildings where Rebecca would attend formal lessons. There they showed her the facilities for practical training. Next door stood a massive armoury.

"In here are all the weapons we need for war," her grandfather explained. "In our homes we only have the swords we carry and a few javelins."

Next they saw the schools, the library, the administrative building with Felicia's house, the stables, indoor and outdoor theatres, the printing house, museums, halls for cultural events and the music schools.

"We always have concerts of all kinds of music. Sometimes we too participate. Your grandma is an excellent violin and cello player."

"What do you play, Grandpa?"

"I usually play the saxophone and a few other wind instruments. We also have dance competitions and lots more. For all age groups and all tastes. We have the best dancers in rock 'n' roll, waltz, Argentine tango, even break dance. We often have parties in our houses as well. It's all about warm, human contact."

"Stop filling the girl's head with it all," Lisa scolded him, with a smile. "She's going to be working far too hard to begin with to attend all thc cultural events."

Near the training buildings and gyms was the house of Bull the Minotaur, single-storey like all the others and set among various activity areas: children's playgrounds, and basketball, volleyball and tennis courts.

"Bull has a very big house," Rebecca remarked.

"He needs big rooms where children can gather," her grandmother explained. "He teaches them games; they organize activities and put on exhibitions, plays and other shows. Bull spends all day with the children."

Next to the playgrounds was the largest building Rebecca had ever seen.

"What is that building?"

"It's our Orphanage," said her grandmother. "We have two hundred and forty-two Orphans under the age of fifteen in Utopia, and eighty-seven of them live in the Orphanage. There are Orizons, Amazons and Centaurs. Everyone in Utopia knows them by their first names. All of us have adopted all of them. The same thing should happen on Earth. Adoption is a noble act.

"So, Rebecca, their living conditions are excellent. Lots of talented teachers volunteer to nurture them from their very first steps until they grow up, become independent and can live on their own. Some of the Orphans remain there voluntarily when they grow up and help the others. They study and become the most useful teachers because they know the needs of Orphans better than anyone."

"Bull is in charge of training and of education in general in Utopia," said her grandfather. "He has studied every text on Earth to do with education and what influences it – philosophy, culture, history, ways of life and the structure of the family. When drawing his own conclusions, he took into account the intense feeling for Nature that must be combined with so-called prevailing logic. He separates education into areas such as upbringing, basic learning, general education, culture, humanism and participation in public affairs.

"These are accepted only to the point where they don't suffocate the personality and freedom of the individual. We need to allow for individual variations from one person to another. We must never go to extremes but always find the golden ratio for each child.

"We accept that the most important role in upbringing is

that of the family and primarily of the mother, and that the family environment is the foundation of happiness. But for the Orphans the corresponding role is played by the Orphanage. And this is where the state of Utopia has a huge responsibility.

"Bull monitors and approves the content of the books that are recommended by teachers, and continually enriches them with everything helpful and necessary that arises from new discoveries being made on Earth.

"We believe that education is not only for children and young people: it goes on for life.

"We don't allow children to be used as guinea pigs; their upbringing goes hand in hand with human development. Knowledge must be passed on in a positive and healthy manner that makes it easy to put across properly. The innate abilities of each child must be cultivated and children should be stimulated to think, understand and form their own opinions.

"An axe can't mould a student. Delicate art tools are needed to carve and create the masterpiece that is a child.

"We believe children learn best from playing, especially at an early age, and that it helps them learn how to experiment, understand, dare, reflect, create and find solutions on their own. It helps them sort out their inclinations and talents, familiarise themselves with the world around them and get used to a normal healthy life and collective work.

"In our view, entertainment, learning, physical education and artistic activities such as dance, music, painting, writing songs, and working with various materials such as clay, wood and marble, as well as outdoor excursions, are the basic elements of a proper upbringing. Parents and teachers must be encouraging and should intervene carefully."

"Orizon children who live here," said Rebecca's grandmother, "start to go to school at the age of seven and their schooling lasts for eight consecutive years. They have lessons for four hours a day, and the rest of the day is free. So they don't need holidays as they do on Earth.

"The important thing is that they learn the essentials very well at school and they don't have any homework. They learn mathematics, physics, chemistry, Earth geography and of course history, mythology and how to write compositions. Finally, apart from Ancient Greek, which is their native tongue, they all learn English and the language of the race they come from. So if they ever have to go to Earth, they won't have any difficulty communicating and this, together with their knowledge, will enable them to adjust easily and make a contribution."

"Who teaches all these subjects?" asked Rebecca.

"There are teachers here who have taught at the most prestigious universities on Earth," her grandfather replied. "I'm a physicist myself, Rebecca, and I could teach there if I wanted to; if the need arises, I shall. Now there are younger volunteers, who gladly teach the subject."

"We understand the purpose of training and education," interposed her grandmother: "As your grandfather explained, we ascribe greater importance to cultures which may effectively cover any gaps in education, though the reverse does not apply. Training and education, which are superficial, can never replace culture.

"Pupils in our schools don't learn the same lesson ten times over. They learn it only once, at the right time and the right age. They learn easily, even about the construction and operation of a spaceship. And they learn how all the harmful contraptions on Earth function. This saves time and children make the most of their time at school."

All the buildings inside the Fortress were one storey high and were made of wood and stone. Everywhere the streets were covered with the same perfect turf. The many parks were planted with countless trees and flowers. Next they visited the sports grounds. They saw the great stadium where football games and track events took place.

"All the teams and sports are mixed," said her grandfather. "With the Flame, Orizon men and women are equally strong.

"From time to time we also organize Olympic Games in which the powers of Evil participate. We want to keep in touch in this way, in the hope of promoting goodwill and stopping the wars. Sport can reconcile even sworn enemies. Communication between enemies can sometimes soften hearts.

"We have rowing competitions on the lake and surfing contests in the sea. Most of the sports played on Earth were started off here thousands of years ago."

After two hours they finally left the high Fortress walls.

"These corridors and stairs lead up to the battlements," her grandfather explained. "There is an agreement that has been honoured for thousands of Earth years. When the powers of Evil plan to attack, they send a messenger to alert us. We prepare at once and draw up our forces according to our defence plans. During the war, we never take prisoners and we never strike our enemy in the back. This agreement has always been honoured, too."

As their carriage approached a great door, it swung open. It looked impregnable to Rebecca as they drove through.

"This forest ahead is known as Domus. It is where many battles have taken place. Some parts of Domus are also used as training and exercise grounds. The area around the Fortress is deemed to be a battle zone and the enemy has the right to use it when attacking. But beyond that point the land belongs to Utopia, where the houses of the Orizons, Amazons and Centaurs are. The enemy never goes there and never touches either the non-combatants or their belongings. The forest of Domus is immense and it is neutral ground, used by everybody. Every species of animal is represented there, without exception – even every kind of dinosaur!

"Now we're heading home and when we get there I'll show you the map of the Land of the White Sun so that you can get your bearings. Each Orizon family has about twelve acres of land where, apart from the house, there are stables for the animals, orchards with various kinds of fruit trees and fields where we grow what we like. We all have plenty of water that comes down from Mount Thunder and is channelled by the principle of connected vessels to all the houses and wherever else it is needed. The pipes are made of clay so that water quality is never affected.

"As you can see, each house stands more or less in the middle of its plot of land, and on a slightly raised artificial platform. Any water used in the house is then directed to the rest of the land through an irrigation system that utilizes clay, sand and plant fibres. In these ways we irrigate all our fields but we don't create the need to discharge dirty or used water into our lakes and seas."

"Do people build their own houses?" Rebecca asked.

"With the assistance of volunteers," answered her grandfather. "We help one another build houses, and we do so with pleasure. The same applies to all the other jobs such as manufacturing weapons, building furniture, and, working at the printing house and the forge, as well as the cleaning and upkeep of all the facilities in the Fortress.

"We have about two hundred empty houses. Couples who get married and start a family get a house and cultivate its land. Until such time the fields surrounding the vacant houses are left untilled; vegetation and fruit trees grow wild. Anyone can help themselves to fruit and nuts, but that rarely happens because everyone has more than enough land of their own to live on comfortably. Everything here is simple and easy, unlike Earth where, in order to build their houses, people mix the soil with sweat and blood instead of water and lime.

"There are beautiful beaches, but no farms are close to the sea or have a view of it. No farm has an advantage over another because they are all in similar locations."

"Do the Amazons and Centaurs have the same kind of houses?" Rebecca asked.

"Yes, except that the Centaurs have bigger doors because of their size."

There were no fences or gates on the family's farm, just a line of bushes to mark the boundary of their plot. Rebecca and her grandparents passed the stables, the hen-coops and the barns to reach the house, parking the carriage in a small shed made of wood and thatched with fibres.

As they made their way to the house, Rebecca turned and looked at the satisfied horse drinking water cheerfully. "*I wonder: what is it thinking*?"

Rebecca felt deeply moved to be finally visiting her grandparents' house, the home where her father had been born and brought up. It was simple in design and had many large comfortable rooms. Everything was made of stone and wood.

"This is our workroom," her grandmother said, leading her into the biggest room. "All the Orizon houses have one."

They showed her the loom on which they wove cotton, wool

or plant fibres to make clothes and bedcovers and the equipment that they used to make clay utensils and works of art. There was a kiln where they baked their clay artefacts. Next to it was another worktop for painting.

They also showed Rebecca where they processed hides and coloured them with flower and vegetable dyes. They used these natural colourings for dyeing cloth, too. And there was a woodcarving bench where they made useful household items and many works of art.

Rebecca studied everything intently, particularly the works of art. The uniquely shaped clay pieces were painted in beautiful colours and decorated with eye-catching scenes. The woodcarvings also showed great imagination and painstaking execution of detail. It was obvious that the artworks were the product of two artists with very different characters and styles.

"I see that both of you are artists," she said.

"Your grandmother has no equal in colour composition and painting," Tony Newton said proudly. "And she's just as talented at woodcarving."

"We work on some pieces together. Art unites!" her grandmother said, smiling. "Art should only be practised to give spiritual and intellectual satisfaction to the artist and those relishing it. The artist's inner self is reflected in his work. I'm certain you feel that too, Rebecca, when you paint."

Rebecca nodded, flattered to find that her grandmother knew about her hobbies.

"Observing art, we feel the mind and soul of the artist permeating us. Art provides the soul with strong wings and it flies to touch our senses. Sadly, when art becomes a mere profession it loses its greatness."

They moved to another part of the room.

"Here," said Rebecca's grandfather, "we have our water-operated energy source. It's very simple, easy and safe. Look, there's a container full of water. The liquid then flows slowly through this crystal pipe, producing energy that is distributed throughout the house for lighting, heating and whatever else we need. This is how we heat the kiln in which we bake the clay.

"This power source provides light in every room from the crystals that you see on the ceiling, light which you can regulate by turning a switch. This energy doesn't kill as electricity does nor does it burn fuel or pollute."

After giving her the tour of the house and explaining its basic functions, Rebecca's grandmother put her arm round her shoulders.

"Your grandfather, like many Orizons, is an expert in energy production and the operation of such equipment. Now let's try on the clothes and boots that we've made for you."

"How did you know my size?"

"Your father brought a sample of your clothing on his last visit. I think they'll fit you well. But if they need alteration we can do it today. Why don't you go to your room now and get ready? Then we'll meet for dinner. You needn't hurry."

As Rebecca put her few items away in the wardrobe in her room she found the rail already crowded with clothes made of processed leather and cloth. After taking a long bath she got dressed and went to the living room where her grandparents were waiting for her. They sat at the table and Rebecca gave them all the latest news about her parents. When the meal was over, her grandfather stood up.

"Let's go and choose you a horse, Rebecca," he said.

There were four horses in the stable: one white, one grey, one dark and one light chestnut.

"All four of them are wonderful horses," Tony told her. "Whichever you choose will become a loyal companion."

Rebecca took her time, stroking each one in turn and kissing them between the eyes.

"I like all four of them, Grandpa," she said eventually. "Does it matter if I don't choose one but ride them in turn? If it's all right with you I'd prefer not to have one all to myself."

Her grandparents hugged her, touched.

Back in the living room, Rebecca noticed a raised semi circular platform next to the fireplace. It was covered in white leather and there was a polygonal crystal on the ceiling above it.

"What's that?" she asked.

"It's the three-dimensional projection area," her grandmother replied. "It's something like television on Earth which, unfortunately, emits dangerous radiation. We have three-dimensional projection instead, which is completely harmless. The building from which it is broadcast is inside the Fortress. There's only one station and one programme, which is on from eight in the morning until ten at night. The station usually broadcasts documentaries, but it also shows various events such as sports broadcasts, news – mainly from Earth – as well as films.

"From the station itself we communicate with three different locations on Earth, sending and receiving messages, mainly to help us schedule the flights of our spaceships. In other words, when we want to transmit something to Earth, we send it to those secret stations that immediately relay it where it's needed. Do you want to see?"

Rebecca nodded eagerly. Her grandmother went towards the raised platform and turned a switch. Pictures immediately flooded from the crystal on the ceiling. The raised platform was filled with images of birds, trees and a river full of fish. A voice talked about the life cycle of salmon. It was as if the scene was right there in the room. Everything was so vivid – it seemed as if the river would flood the house. Rebecca stood up and went closer. After looking at the scene from all angles, she put her hand in a brook, as if she wanted to drink some water. Immediately, the projection dissolved beneath her fingers. Above and around them, however, it continued uninterrupted.

"It's marvellous. It's unbelievable. Unbelievable!"

"This system has been in operation for thousands of Earth years here," Lisa said, "but it has remained educational, extremely useful and, of course entertaining. It is not used for propaganda or deception or for promoting anyone's interests. A careful selection of Earth programmes is made by a panel of Orizons who live on Earth and we broadcast only the ones that are both entertaining and informative. It's not like most of the television on Earth, undermining so many moral values and principles. We could see all the programmes shown on Earth if we wanted to, of course; our station is capable of it. But we've chosen to run it like this.

"Three-dimensional projection has another use, too. The princess can use it if she wants to send a message to any house or group of dwelling so. She simply goes to the station and chooses to whom her message will be broadcast. Immediately a red lamp on our roof flashes and a small siren goes off. That's how we know there's a message and we turn on the projector."

"Now," said Rebecca's grandfather, "it's time for me to give you your sword. You'll get the rest of your weapons at the armoury."

He went into the workshop and came back with a crystal sword sheathed in a blue leather scabbard.

"Your grandmother and I hope that this sword will protect you. It's made of a kind of crystal that will never break."

Rebecca unsheathed the sword and looked at it closely. There was an "R" engraved on the hilt. She made a few passes in the air with the blade before returning it to its scabbard.

"I'm used to a fencing sword but I think I can soon get accustomed to it," she said. "Where do you find this crystal?"

"It comes from Mount Thunder. We mine it there and bring it to the Fortress to be processed at our special workshop. It's the most durable material in our world," replied her grandfather.

As she lay in bed later that night, Rebecca couldn't believe that it was only twelve hours since she had left Earth. It felt more like ten years. However hard she tried, she couldn't work out where in the Universe she was, how many thousands or millions of light years away from Earth, after a journey that had lasted no more than half an hour. She thought how everyone she had met so far had such calm peaceful faces and how they seemed to radiate love, completely different to the faces she was used to seeing on the streets of Earth. There everyone seemed burdened with problems. She wondered why she hadn't seen any old people at all.

As she drifted towards sleep, she became confused about what was real and what were her dreams.

When Rebecca woke up in the morning there was no one around so she went outside, barefoot and with her long white nightgown trailing along the ground. The birds had been waiting for her and the moment she appeared their monotonous chirruping exploded into a melodic contest, accompanied by acrobatic displays as they swooped around her. They had come to welcome the beautiful young new resident of the house and impress her with their skills.

Marvelling at the spectacular concert threatening to engulf her, Rebecca flung her arms wide lovingly as if to embrace them all. The just-awakened sun shone with happiness as it saw the white vision, her arms outstretched.

She found her grandparents exercising with their swords and javelins, running and wrestling together. She couldn't believe her eyes. They were like young children, supple and strong. When they became aware of her, they stopped and walked over.

"Did you sleep well, dear?" her grandmother asked.

"Very well; I feel rested," she answered, but she looked puzzled.

"We exercise every day, Rebecca." Her grandfather chuckled at her expression. "We must always be fit and ready to fight. At regular intervals we all exercise together, as though we are really at war. We never forget that we must always be ready to defend the Flame of Good, the Flame of the White Sun."

After breakfast her grandfather rode with her until the Fortress came into view.

Rebecca was now dressed in white leather, with blue boots on her feet and a blue belt, from which hung her sword in its scabbard, around her slender waist. She looked splendid on the horse, her hair waving in the breeze.

Pedro, Sergei, Samantha and Louise were already waiting outside the training building when she arrived and they chatted about their first impressions of their homeland. One by one the others arrived, all wearing the same colours and carrying almost identical swords.

At nine o'clock on the dot, Doctor Afterland opened the

training building's doors and invited them into a spacious room that contained about fifty desks and comfortable seats. There was a blackboard and a teacher's desk, just like schools on Earth.

"Good morning, everyone," the doctor said as they found their seats. "I wish you all a successful beginning. In my classes you'll learn in the next three terms how to help in the war against Evil, mainly on Earth. All the knowledge that you acquire must be perfectly thorough. A little knowledge is always a dangerous thing. It is better to know nothing about a subject than to know half of it.

"We must be fully prepared when we offer our services. Otherwise we'll have nothing worthwhile to offer. All our sweat and effort will be useless, just as if we'd harvested wheat before its time: green wheat-spikes produce no flour as I'm sure you already know.

"A good education is not enough on its own. If we are to apply successfully what we've learned, we should actively love what we do. Otherwise we're doomed to failure. You must think very carefully before making your ultimate decision. If you're not absolutely positive that a certain path is right for you, that you like it and want to take it, then don't opt for it.

"You'll learn how to survive anywhere, under any circumstances, without any supplies, completely on your own; something like the Earth hero called Rambo. You'll be trained how to find food to survive even if it comes from the roots of wild plants.

"On Earth, with the help of your families, you will gradually learn the proficient use of all the weapons to be found on the planet. This will begin after your three terms of training here, when you will have come of age according to the laws of Earth.

You will all become expert pilots of all kinds of aircraft, captains of all kinds of ships, both for war and peace, as well as nuclear submarines and tanks. When new models are constructed, you'll learn how to use them if it's deemed necessary. It goes without saying, of course, that you'll all be taught here how to fly our spaceships in the future.

"Some of you may decide to become doctors. Medicine is the most sensitive, complex and difficult profession. One plus one doesn't always make two in medicine. Doctors must combine great knowledge with dedication and diligence. They must be intelligent, highly responsible, meticulous and precise in what they do. They have to work with extreme caution and provide exemplary care. Additionally, surgeons and doctors applying invasive diagnostic techniques need great skill.

"We shall also spend a lot of time studying the problem of drugs. Drugs are the worst plague on Earth. Drugs kill, and they ruin lives. They turn people into spineless, dependent beings with no minds of their own, no heart or feelings, unable to function properly in society. You'll learn how to help drug addicts.

"You must know that there will be no quackery, and above all there are no witches or witchcraft. No mediums or astrologers. You'll learn how to deal with those human inventions that have been created by twisted and greedy minds. So when you are on Earth you can help save those unfortunate people who are misled by such swindlers who take advantage of other people's weakness and pain.

"There are at least seven thousand Orizons altogether and almost a thousand of them live on Earth. There are also two thousand Amazons and two thousand Centaurs. The powers of Evil consist of ten thousand Sharkans, three thousand Porths and two thousand Cyclopes. The Centaurs, Cyclopes, Porths, Sphinxes, Leiko and Bull the Minotaur are mythical creatures and cannot die a natural death; they can only be killed.

"We have a Sphinx called Glory and the powers of Evil have one called Calphie. The Sphinxes are the strongest creatures in the Land of the White Sun. They have lion's paws with sharp claws and immense power. They are twice as big as the largest elephant and have great wings whose tips will kill anything they touch. They don't participate in Lomani. Sphinxes never sleep. Our Sphinx always guards the Flame, while Calphie guards Turgoth's house.

"The next-strongest creatures after the Sphinxes are Bull the Minotaur and Leiko, the son of Hercules, who lives with Lord Life. Next come the Cyclopes, the Porths and the Centaurs. Bull is not only exceedingly strong, but he can also throw his dagger from a great distance and strike anything he aims at.

"Among other mythical creatures there is also Pegasus, the winged horse that stays with Lord Life. Then there are Stheno and Euryale, the two Gorgon sisters of Medusa who, as you know, was beheaded by Perseus the son of Zeus. They don't belong to either camp and they live in Domus forest. When the Gods asked these mythical creatures to choose sides they decided to remain neutral. As you already know from your mythology lessons, Gorgons are terrible monsters with serpents instead of hair. They also have huge teeth, very strong copper arms and golden wings. Anyone who happens to look into their eyes turns to stone and can't move. But the Gorgons don't disturb or harm anyone here, not even animals. If you happen to meet them in the forest, though, it is better not to look into their eyes.

"We know that the Centaurs were a savage tribe that did many wicked things on Earth. But when they moved to this land they chose to take the side of Good, and now they are in our camp. The Creator, wanting to reward them for their decision, created female Centaurs so that they could reproduce.

"Something similar happened to the Amazons, who were divided on Earth. That is, there were good and bad Amazons. Once here, they immediately chose the side of Good. So the Creator rewarded them likewise. He permitted marriages between them and male Orizons so that their race wouldn't become extinct. Not a few male Orizons are married to Amazons. In those cases if the child born to them is a girl she becomes an Amazon; if he is a boy he becomes an Orizon.

"To stand out in battle, we Orizons wear white leather clothes, blue boots and blue belts. The Orizon uniform has a blue-sun emblem emblazoned on the chest. The Amazons wear brown leather clothes and boots. The Sharkans wear black leather clothes and boots while the Porths and Cyclopes wear green."

Samantha raised her hand. "Why is our emblem a blue sun and not a white sun, like the name of our land?"

"The Mythical Gods called it the Land of the White Sun. When the separation occurred we used the colour of the Flame in our emblem to emphasize its power."

Doctor Afterland's lesson lasted two hours. Then the children went out to the training ground where General Claudia was waiting for them. She had an exquisitely carved bow over her shoulder and a beautifully decorated blue and white leather quiver.

"I know you've all studied archery for several years," she said. "But learning a sport is not the same as preparing for war. Until you make your decision, you'll focus on how to aim properly and hit your target, whether you are on horseback or on foot.

Later, when you have made your decision, we'll go on to a more difficult task, which is how to avoid the enemy's arrows.

"Regardless of what you already know, today we will begin from scratch. That is, how to hold the bow, how to place an arrow and how to stretch the bowstring. These are stages that will take you some time to learn."

During a break in the two-hour lesson the children talked about the decision they were going to have to make. Everyone kept talking about it. What exactly did they all mean?

Hunter the Centaur came out of the armoury holding a selection of javelins, which he propped up in a corner as the children surrounded him.

"We're going to spend quite a lot of time together. You'll learn how to use the spear, the javelin and the shield. We'll begin with the javelin, which we must be able to use both on foot and on horseback. The spear is used only on horseback. After some time, each of you will find where your talent lies and which weapon you can handle better in battle.

"You all know that throwing the javelin is not only a matter of strength but also of speed and of skill. It's a difficult combination and that's why it needs lots of practice."

By the end of another two hours the children were raving about the general of the Centaurs.

After the break, Field Marshal Foster appeared, every imperious stride that he took demonstrating his supreme confidence. The sun shone on his untidy but luxuriant hair, making it look like bushes moving in the wind. His look was serious and searching and it pierced all of them.

"I see you all have your swords. I've brought the helmets and the breastplates that will protect you completely until you make your decision."

Again someone was talking about their decision. But none of them had the courage to show their ignorance and ask what he meant.

The Field Marshal gave them sixteen crystal breastplates that had fibre tapes at the sides to fasten them. The helmets were made of crystal too, with only a small opening to breathe through.

"Put on your breastplates and helmets," he ordered. His voice was sharp now.

Soon everybody was ready. Foster drew his sword.

"Draw your swords and attack me. Try to hurt me," he ordered.

The children froze, turning pale, their feet rooted to the spot. No matter how good the Field Marshal was, they were sixteen strong, nimble children and, above all, talented fencers. Some of them had even won honourable distinctions for their expertise back on Earth.

The Field Marshal became angry. "Why are you all standing there looking at me? I gave you an order and orders are to be obeyed at once. Come on, attack me – strike to kill. That's an order."

Samantha found the courage to speak.

"With all due respect, Field Marshal, what you're asking of us is too difficult. I'll accept fighting with you one to one, but I don't feel right about all of us attacking you at once. I believe that if we do it, it won't be fair."

"All right, Samantha. Come here on your own and fight. But you must really try to kill me. That's an order, as I said. Come on, then."

Samantha approached the Field Marshal, moving cautiously like a leopard getting ready to strike. And she suddenly found herself without her sword. In one brilliant move, faster than the eye could see, the Field Marshal had disarmed her. Samantha hung her head in shame, not knowing what to say.

"I'm so … sorry, Field Marshal," she stuttered. "Please kill me. I feel deeply humiliated. I didn't even manage to touch my blade to yours …"

"No, Samantha, no! Orizons must never cry when in pain. Don't compare your training on Earth with our kind of training. Defeating the powers of Evil for thousands of Earth years has made us Orizons different. That's why I wanted all of you to attack me; it wasn't for me to show off. The first thing to learn is discipline.

"You must, within three summer terms, become so good that I'll find it difficult to face even one of you. You must believe it. As you know, Orizons never lie. I'm sure that you will become as good as I am, even better, though it may seem unbelievable to you now. Until then, however, you need blind obedience, hard training and self-discipline.

"As you can see, I'm wearing no protective gear, no breastplate or helmet. Pick up your sword, Samantha. I order you all now to attack me and try to kill me."

Samantha bent down, retrieved her sword and joined the others. All together, they charged at Foster, shouting their blood-curdling war cries.

In less than a minute all sixteen were disarmed and had been tapped on the helmet the moment Foster had taken the swords from their hands. In theory he had killed them all.

"First, you must all learn how to hold your swords so that the enemy won't be able to disarm you," he said.

For two hours Foster worked with them tirelessly, demonstrating how they could hone their skills. He really was an exceptional teacher.

When the lesson was over the children mounted their horses and rode home, tired but also happy with what they had learned that day. But something about the incident with Foster was bothering Rebecca. She was completely certain that if she hadn't wanted him to Foster wouldn't have been able to take her sword. She had been ninth in line when he'd attacked her. She knew that she could have both kept her sword and fought against him but in a split-second judgement she had decided to let her sword fall, not wanting to stand out too much from the others. She did not believe that she would have actually defeated Foster, but she was certain that she could have put up a fight and surely made things difficult for him, giving the others an opportunity to wound him while his attention was taken up with handling her. Rebecca decided to mention her doubts to no one.

THE DECISION

The children found the next twenty-four days exhausting. But it was also exhilarating to acquire so much new knowledge. There was no distinction between tasks for males and those for females.

During this time the children also got to know each other better. In the evenings they would meet or visit each other's houses. Strong bonds of love, companionship and solidarity grew between them.

Bull was usually part of the group. When he was with them he acted as if he were their age, talking about anything and everything. He was a good friend as well as an invaluable teacher. He observed their individual progress closely, advised them and boosted their morale and confidence; he taught them games to help them relax. One evening before going to bed, he said with feeling:

"It's easy to parrot the alphabet; but the important thing is to learn each letter individually, out of order, without forgetting a single one of the others.

"We depend on Orizons to save the Earth and its people. You'll spin the cloth of life, weave precious dreams and then strive to make them all come true. You'll embroider emotions and stitch up wounds.

"The mind must always fly freely, like a proud eagle: with

strength, rhythm, confidence, a clear target and a successful result!"

Within a few days of the children's arrival it became obvious to all the teachers that Rebecca's skills far surpassed those of the others, even though they could see that she was holding herself back.

One day Doctor Afterland decided to bring up the subject with Princess Felicia.

"She reminds me of you when you were a student. In fact, I'd say that she's even better than you at some things. I can also see that she's holding back deliberately and won't let all her skills show – though I may be mistaken."

The princess smiled, pleased with his words. "I agree. I believe she will become a legend. Of course, it all depends on her decision and which path she chooses to follow. I too think that she isn't showing all her abilities. I don't know whether she's doing it consciously or not."

"Time will tell," said Doctor Afterland.

As the days went by, Princess Felicia watched the classes and the children's progress closely. On the twenty-fifth day of training, she assembled them in her living room and told them that she was completely satisfied with their progress.

"For five days, starting tomorrow, I'll be working with you too. I'm going to teach you something enjoyable and relaxing."

The children looked at her expectantly.

"I'm going to teach you how to fly. Not like Superman or other human fairy tales. You'll learn to fly the same way you swim. Slowly. It's not for use in war, purely for pleasure."

"Will we be able to fly when we go back to Earth?" Samantha asked.

"No, gravity there is different. Tomorrow, after classes, we'll go to the lake and make a start. On a more serious note: you've been training for some time now and you have a good idea of the kind of difficulties that you are going to face. Now you can receive the Flame again and its power will stay with you, in your soul, for the rest of your life. But for us to go ahead with this procedure, you and only you have to choose which path you want to follow. This is the decision that we have all been talking about so much, the one that is so important.

"One of the paths open to you is to return to Earth, forget everything, and live a normal life which will probably be happy and peaceful. You won't face wars or dangers beyond those encountered by all humans; nor will you have to endure the heavy obligations and the struggle against Evil that the Orizons have to cope with.

"But if you decide to follow the other path and remain Orizons, your life will immediately become full of dangers and great hardship. When the powers of Good need you, you will have to fight with all your might.

"You may live for a long time here in our land and fight continuously. You may even be killed on your first day in battle. You may never go back to Earth if you are needed here, or you may be going back and forth as needs dictate. While on Earth, you will have to fight against Evil all the time with all your strength.

"By the end of the next five days, once you have finished your flying lessons, you must have reached your decision. You must do so without outside influence. You mustn't talk about it among yourselves, nor discuss it with your relatives or with anybody else. The decision must be all yours and it must be made carefully after serious consideration. Any questions?"

José rose from his seat. "Princess, I have already made my decision while you were talking, because I'm prepared ..."

"Please sit down, José." Felicia cut him short. "I asked if you had any questions; not if you had already made up your mind. Whatever your decision is, put it aside for the moment and think about it very seriously and calmly; dispassionately and wisely. A decision is like an eel – easy to catch but hard to hold on to. That certainly cannot be the case for us.

"Whatever you decide, you cannot ever change your mind in the future. If you take the Flame again to remain an Orizon, you cannot reverse your decision later. And if you decide to live like ordinary people now, you cannot change that resolution afterwards. There is no shame in deciding to live your lives as non-combatants. With your experiences and the Good that is inside you already, you can still offer much both to yourselves and to others. Don't think that anyone will criticize you if you decide not to go on. Whatever decision you reach will earn you the same respect. We won't talk about this subject again for five days, at which time I'll hear your decisions."

Rebecca put it to the back of her mind, excited by the prospect of learning how to fly. Like many people she had always longed to be able to fly, and she often dreamed of it. She had read that the great writer Leo Tolstoy had jumped out of his window once, believing that he could fly. It was the world's good fortune that he had survived to write his masterpieces.

The next day the children rode with Felicia to the lake in the Domus forest. They dismounted and sat on the grass to talk.

"Whenever you fly," Felicia told them, "you must be above water. Then, if you get tired or if something goes wrong, you will have a soft landing and can swim to safety. For the first two days of training you will attach palm leaves to your arms and legs to help you. Gradually you'll be able to take them off.

"You have to believe that you can do this. Having faith in our abilities is the most important thing when trying to achieve difficult goals. You need self-confidence! Understand that we all have enormous powers sleeping within us, skills that we don't even know about. We can achieve incredible things when we unleash those powers. The Flame will help us to concentrate those powers and make the most of them. That's why Orizons are different. With the power of the Flame and our own belief we can overcome gravity in the Land of the White Sun and fly."

The princess led them to the edge of the beautiful lake and pointed to the clean water, "It deepens abruptly; so even if you fall in as soon as you take off, there's no danger of hurting yourselves."

Taking off her boots, Felicia strode towards a stand of palm trees. Swiftly climbing the first tree she came to she sliced off four fronds with her sword. She took the same amount from each tree until she had enough, never taking enough leaves from any one tree to weaken it. She then cut off some fibres from a tree which had plenty to spare, using them to attach the palm fronds to each child's arms and legs.

"Okay," she said when they were all ready. "Watch me. First we bend our knees and bring our bodies down close to the ground. We raise our arms in the air. Then we straighten our legs sharply and bring our raised arms down to our sides like birds. While doing this you must firmly believe that you are going to fly.

"As you lift off the ground, don't try to go straight up vertically but lean forward and gain altitude gradually. Watch me now. I'm going to show you how I move my arms and legs. Move your legs the same way you do when you swim with flippers, and flap your arms like birds flap their wings. Gradually you'll learn to move your arms in other ways too, like doing the crawl or the breaststroke when swimming. We'll do that when you learn to fly without the leaves."

Felicia bent her knees, then rose with slow, graceful movements. The children watched in astonishment. It was like being in a dream. The princess lifted gently off the ground, circled once over the water and returned. As her feet touched the ground, she bent her legs again and landed softly.

"Don't try to land on the ground yet. Fall into the water and then swim out. You'll just go home with wet clothes, that's all. Don't be disappointed if you don't get far today. By tomorrow you'll be able to do so much better. Now, who wants to try first?"

Louise stepped forward. "I'll have a try."

Felicia walked with the girl to the edge of the water, helping her get into the right position for take-off. Louise straightened her legs and sprang up into the air, like a diver launching herself from a springboard, slanting her body slightly and swooping over the water for a few seconds before falling into the lake. Felicia and the other children cheered and clapped their hands.

With a few strokes Louise reached the side of the lake and José and Sergei helped her out.

"It was wonderful. Wonderful! I can't believe it," she kept saying as she skipped around, water pouring off her.

One by one they all tried it, with varying degrees of success and a great deal of laughter. By the time dusk fell they didn't want to go back. It was the best experience of their lives so far and it had taken their minds off the decision they each had to make, even if only for a few hours.

On the way home they all felt the dilemma of that imminent decision weighing down on them again. But over the next four days they all learned how to fly as skilfully as Felicia, which lifted their spirits and helped make the burden bearable.

When the final night arrived Rebecca found that she couldn't sleep. She took her guitar and went outside, walking around the grounds of her grandparents' home with a million thoughts churning round in her head. From time to time she would stop to sing and play softly to herself. No matter how hard she thought, she just couldn't see what the right decision might be.

Her parents weighed on her mind. If they hadn't taken the decision they had at the time of her birth, she wouldn't be facing this dilemma now. She wouldn't have known anything at all about the Orizons, the Land of the White Sun or the Flame. She didn't blame them: she just wanted to understand why they had done it, why they had wanted to put her on a path which might lead to her being killed in a war.

Was that what they had had to do? Maybe it had been the right thing to do. Yet Rebecca might lose her life in the very first battle in this foreign land. Here war was unavoidable. Sooner or later it would happen and continue to happen. So the odds of her being killed were significant. Were her parents so heartless, then? She felt very confused.

Her grandparents understood her soul-searching. They had been through that themselves once. They left her alone with her thoughts. Rebecca went to the horses. She stroked and talked to them, and then she went to the hen-coop. She liked the image of proud horses with strong legs grazing peacefully together with powerless, unprepossessing hens.

The hens were asleep. "*Who knows if hens have dreams?*

And why do they have wings since they can't fly?" she wondered. She sat down on the grass, watching them.

Rebecca shook herself out of her reverie. She must concentrate on the decision. It was close to midnight when she finally stood up and walked briskly towards the house.

She went indoors, took off her nightdress and put on her leather uniform before returning to the stables and mounting a horse bareback. Bending over its neck and holding onto its mane, she galloped off, as fast as the wind.

Soon she was at the Fortress Gate. The guard recognized her. "What are you doing here at this time of the night?"

"I'm going to see the Wise Tree."

The Gate opened and when she reached the theatre she jumped off the horse. She ran to the Tree and sat cross-legged in front of it.

"Having trouble sleeping?" the Tree asked. "I can understand that."

"I often wonder why the Creator made human beings with weaknesses," Rebecca said, the words tumbling out. "Why He created both good and evil people and not just the good. Why is there jealousy and envy?"

The Wise Tree lowered one of its branches and scratched its nose. "If He had made all beings the same, with the same intelligence and the same feelings, then they wouldn't be living creatures with a soul and a mind – they'd be machines. The Creator is not a factory owner, producing standardized products. If He ordered all people to think the same, then He would have to dispense with any notion of freedom of action and thought. Life would be terribly boring, empty and indifferent. If everybody were good or bad, there wouldn't be any means of comparison, no way to distinguish Good from Evil.

"Everything has been created according to the unique wisdom that only the Creator possesses. Everybody has everything – but in different quantities. Certain factors influence one's development. As human beings grow up, they question, mature, change and evolve. They feel satisfied when, after an inner struggle and free choice, they make progress towards something better. But they may often choose paths that don't lead towards Good. That's why they seek something else after a while. People are not just what they are born but also what they become.

"When people are born, Good and Evil are both inside them. They coexist. They both develop and there is an ongoing battle between them for predominance. People decide which path to follow according to their intelligence, their morals and the influences to which they are subjected. The Creator doesn't interfere or try to influence that choice. He has given complete freedom to people's spirits and ideas and He never punishes, regardless of the choice that each person makes. Everyone is completely free and has every right to choose as they wish."

"But people often cannot tell Good from Evil. They get confused. Each person might give a different interpretation to the same action or behaviour. There are so many criteria for judging what is good or not."

"That's very true. In many cases people cannot differentiate between Good and Evil. Something that is bad in the eyes of some people may be neutral or even good in the eyes of others. There are also many things that are difficult to classify as either Good or Evil.

"But do you not think this is another proof of the greatness of Creation and the wisdom of its Maker? Is it not proof of our freedom of thought and action? As people go through their lives, they can learn if they want to. They discover what is useful, what affects everyone's life positively and also what is the right thing to do. 'Right' doesn't mean what is good for each individual person's interests but what is generally beneficial.

"When people have a comfortable life, they don't care about what is going on in the next house or the next country. They're indifferent to the misery and pain surrounding them. Not only do they not care, they actually feel happy when they see someone else being ruined. They are jealous and envious, so they want to be the only ones living well and standing out from the crowd.

"There's something odd that I've noticed during my short life: the very same people who show great strength and humanity, may suddenly become weak hearted, cruel and inhuman. I've never been able to explain it. I've read books, seen films, heard stories based on real events; concentration camps, torture, exile, forced labour in terrible conditions, mass murders. I've witnessed heartless behaviour from people who have been transformed into monsters, and then become humane again. They listen to beautiful music whereas once they listened to people screaming like frightened animals. They killed with the same hands they now use to caress young children. They play with instruments of torture at the same time as with musical instruments. I just can't understand it."

"It's such a pity that all these things happen. So Orizons must fight to put an end to that. They must show people how to live together in friendship and love; in search of spiritual truths; with clear hearts and minds; free from ill and petty thoughts. The Orizons' consciences have wings that can spread everywhere. They must spread the wings of love to cover the whole world."

Rebecca stood up and embraced the Tree. "But how can love

exist alongside the sword, blood, war and death? Is there no other way?"

Without waiting to hear the answer, she ran to her horse, mounting it in a single leap and riding away, through the gates and on to the edge of the lake. As soon as she arrived she jumped from the panting steed and lay on the grass by the shore. The horse lowered its head over her, blowing air on her face.

"I'm so sorry!" Rebecca said, scratching it between its ears. "I forgot to thank you. You were so good. You ran marvellously."

Satisfied, the horse neighed and went to the lake to drink. Rebecca lay back again and put her hands behind her head, enjoying the soft breath of the wind which carried the essence of Nature's fragrance to her. Many of the stars above were nesting among the foliage of the tall trees like Christmas lights. Only the snowflakes were missing.

As her thoughts roamed, the lake was still: everything around her was calm and soothing. The cicadas continued their concert and then Nature's romantic troubadour, the nightingale, began its melody.

"*It must be wonderful to be a bird*," Rebecca thought.

She got up and stripped down to her underwear. Then she bent her knees, lifted her arms, sprang up and flew, her mind filling with joy and tranquillity. The nightingale stopped singing to watch. It was in ecstasy, enjoying the girl's unique aura. Its beak opened wide, making it impossible for it to trill. It had woken up early, not having slept much, and on discovering the strange night visitor in its neighbourhood, it had begun its serenade before dawn. It felt like the luckiest bird in the world, like the first living creature in the universe to witness such an extraordinary sight. Rebecca's flowing hair made her look like a fairy playing under the stars as she skimmed her chest and belly across the surface of the water before rising up into the air again, turning her body slowly, her movements full of grace, harmony, rhythm and suppleness, expressing all the peace and pleasure that she felt.

"If only I had my guitar with me," she thought. "I would be able to enjoy myself even more."

The thoughts made her feel guilty. Here she was enjoying a privilege that no one on Earth had, something she had been dreaming about for years, and all she could do was wish for more. She felt greedy and wondered what else she might have wanted if she had not been an Orizon. Dropping gently into the lake she swam to the side.

Lying once more on the bank, Rebecca continued to look at the stars. Then she realized there was something that she missed very much. She had been in the Land of the White Sun for thirty days and she hadn't noticed until now that there was no moon. But now she realized its presence was vital to her. For all those years on Earth, the moon had kept her company without her being aware of it.

"*When you live with something all the time, you don't care about it very much. You don't appreciate it. But if you lose it, then you realize how much you miss it,*" she thought.

Pulling her clothes back on, Rebecca galloped back to the Fortress. When she arrived at the Gate the guard looked surprised but didn't ask her any questions. She went and sat in front of the Wise Tree once more.

"Do you know what the moon is?" she asked.

"I'm sorry, I don't."

"You're lucky, because you would miss it terribly if you did."

"What is it?"

"It's a heavenly body, like the sun. It's just the right size, neither too large nor too small. The sun is countless times bigger but from Earth they look almost the same size in the sky."

"And what does this moon do?" asked the Tree.

"To tell you the truth," Rebecca said after a moment, "I've never thought about what it does, exactly. But today I realized that it kept me company and soothed my soul. When I was younger, it used to come through my window and lie on my bed from time to time. I used to hug it and sleep with it in my arms.

"I've often painted the scene, with a small child asleep in the moon's embrace. I tried to portray in his face the bliss that I felt. Now I feel I need it. I miss it a lot. It's a pleasant friend, because it talks to you only when you want it to. So, to answer your question, I think the moon keeps people company, especially when they're otherwise alone. It's an undemanding friend because it talks only when asked. Moonlight can warm people's hearts. I think it can arouse their emotions, too. It is a source of love, peace and comfort. Those who look at it are bathed in its immense tenderness; they are moonlight-adorned.

"But I think it's also a tease. Sometimes it disappears for a few days so that we miss it. Then it appears like a sliver in the sky and grows bigger every night. When it becomes a half-moon, it stands upright. But sometimes it lies on its back. Then the weather changes and scolds it for taking a rest.

"One night a month it grows to its full size and we call it a full moon. On that night people are filled with happiness and peace floods their souls. After that, it gets smaller every night until it disappears completely. The moon promenades through the sky by night and the sun passes through it by day, but there are also times when they are both in the sky together. Luckily, the sun never gets angry about this intrusion or sends the moon away. When it appears at night, it paints the lakes and the seas with silver."

"Indeed it is a tease, as you say. It sounds like a child's toy to me," said the Tree.

"Yes! When I was small I thought it was a shiny toy hanging from invisible threads. During the day I thought God hid it in his sack, together with the stars. At night, after scattering the stars across the sky in handfuls, he would hold the threads in his fingers and take the moon for a walk.

"When I go back to Earth, as soon as I see the moon I'll take it in my arms, stroke it and pull its little nose."

"What! Does it have a nose, too?" asked the Tree, surprised.

"Of course it does! It has a nose, eyes and a smile. Just like you."

"Like me? I have a mouth. I don't smile often, though. I mainly talk."

"The moon only smiles. But its destiny is different from yours ... Perhaps I'm wrong ... Maybe there are similarities in some aspects ..."

"No wonder you miss it. I wish I had a moon like that to keep me company, especially at night. The nights pass slowly. I think and think and think ... and dawn is sometimes so slow in coming," said the Wise Tree sadly. "In my loneliness I often have to trisect myself: my trunk, my branches and my leaves. We start talking together. We discuss our good points and our flaws. Loneliness comes to so many people. So we must be prepared and get used to living with it.

"I do think, however, that there are people who feel even lonelier when they are with others. Yes, this can happen too. But we all need friends. Friendship is a kind of connection where you say what you want and listen to what your friends want to say. If these two are in balance then a friendship thrives, otherwise it is lost.

"True friendship is rare, Rebecca. Not only in youth but throughout life. We all have our faults. Only someone who talks to you about them frankly, while hiding them from others and praising your virtues, is worth having as a friend. You need to be careful, because a false friend is worse than the worst enemy.

"Always remember: the sneakiest and most dangerous enemy is someone you can't recognize as such, because he is hiding his feelings and intentions."

Bodyguards and the most trusted people killed or betrayed their bosses, relatives and dear friends would betray or even murder those closest to them. *"Trusted people betray us, because we tell them our secrets,"* Rebecca thought.

Then she addressed the Wise Tree again.

"I'll come and keep you company some nights," she said. "We can talk. I'll read books to you. A book is the most loyal friend. And there are many great authors!"

"An author writes the books from which children learn how to read. That's the only kind of book I've ever heard of," said the Tree.

"People who write school books are also called authors. An author who writes stories – novels, fiction – observes many things and then cultivates and develops them in his imagination. Then he puts together soul and spirit and, after preparing this kind of communion, he spreads it on paper, constructing worlds, creating people and shaping their characters. He weds his pen and together they create whatever beings he fancies. He guides the thoughts and actions of his creations. He makes them happy or unhappy, in love or lonely, rich or poor, good or bad. At one moment he makes them immature children and then he turns them into grown-up, mature, philosophizing thinkers or into superficial wayfarers walking through eternity.

"He can make them look like lucky well-fed dogs that are taken out to play, wearing an expensive collar around their neck. Or he could transform them to sick and hungry homeless mongrels that desperately dig through garbage to get a bite.

"He starts and ends wars, storms and other disasters. He causes his characters to fall ill and then heals them or lets them die. He can kill them, too. But he can also bring them back to life, and develop a new religion!"

The Wise Tree listened in amazement. "So an author is like a God, able to do so many things?"

"An author is not a God but he or she can be wise like you. On Earth, the authors of antiquity said many wise things, setting them down for posterity."

"Where?"

"On stone, marble, clay tablets and wood, on papyruses and parchments and later in books too. All modern writers and poets repeat almost the same things those ancient scholars said. This doesn't necessarily mean that they copy them. No idea is conceived by a single mind only, but by many, maybe even thousands. But everyone writes in his or her own style. They put the characters whom their imagination has created into a book and it becomes a novel. Poetry is difficult. In just a few verses poets can convey profound, constructive and precious meanings. Strong poetry stirs the soul and its beauty is overwhelming.

"Some books are pleasant to read and others seem boring. But opinions depend on who reads the volumes concerned, what they prefer and *why* they read. Personally, I like to read something pleasant which also teaches something useful. A great book is one that you open with pleasure and close with profit.

"Books add value to life. And whatever gives value is precious. Books are like springs: you can drink from them to satisfy your thirst and bathe in them to feel refreshed. But some springs are poisonous and dangerous. We need to know which ones to choose!

"I dearly love books. When I hold them in my hands it's like embracing the heroes inside them. Sometimes I feel that I'm embracing the writer too. Often, in the evening, when I'm reading I fall asleep with the book on top of me. Then it's as if we were all asleep together.

"An author speaks to you through his heroes. Some kind of relationship is – or should be developed between the reader and the heroes. The fantasy is spread before you and you travel to unknown and magical worlds of dreams or reality. Sometimes what you read may not impress you. You may get tired or even annoyed with what you read. Then you shut the book and put it into a grave.

"Many great authors who do provide reading pleasure also have the habit of leaving some important and inner meanings of what they write unrevealed, and let their readers discover them. They're like the philosophers whom the princess was talking about the first day we were here."

"Well, that's okay, as long as the readers don't misinterpret those meanings. But, Rebecca, I'm impressed by what you've taught me today. I wonder how I didn't realize for so many years that such books existed, and that I could get into them. But it's never too late! Will you teach me how to read so that I can do it all by myself?"

"All right, I will. Though you can't turn the pages," Rebecca teased. "Perhaps I won't miss the moon so much when I'm with you."

It was almost daybreak before she finally stood up, said goodbye to the Tree and left.

She trotted home at a leisurely pace while the roosters tried to stir their dreaming hens.

When she arrived home her grandparents had already started their morning exercises. They greeted her lovingly but asked no questions. She went to her room, had a bath, put on a clean uniform and had breakfast. Then she saddled another horse and left for her training session.

After class, all the children went over to Bull's house. They had three hours free before they were due to assemble at the theatre where they were all to announce their final decisions. Bull had laid a table with all kinds of delicacies and he had planned games to pass the hours until it was time to go to the theatre.

They left a little before six o'clock, the children riding on horseback and Bull driving the carriage that had brought them from the Highlow Cosmodrome exactly one month earlier. When they got to the theatre, Bull told them to get into the carriage. When everybody was on board, he sat down with them.

"Each one of you will go in alone, in the same order that I collected you from Earth. I'll escort you. As soon as one finishes, I'll come back to fetch the next. No one going in should know what the preceding ones have decided. All right, then – Nargis, you're first."

Nargis and Bull stepped down from the carriage and went in. Felicia, Afterland, the Generals and the children's relatives were gathered there already. There were no musicians this time. Nargis stepped onto the platform and approached the princess, who rose to embrace and kissed her.

"Nargis, it is time for you to tell us your decision."

Nargis looked at Princess Felicia and all the others. She remained silent for a while. Then she bowed her head. "I'm very sorry, but I don't want to take the Flame and remain an Orizon. I prefer to be on Earth."

The princess beamed. "My dear Nargis, don't be at all sorry and don't be upset. We respect your decision. We understand that you're thinking of your mother and grandmother on Earth who lost their husbands here in the Lomani. You will return to Earth tonight. Now take your seat."

Bull left to fetch the second child. The next fourteen children all decided to remain Orizons. Finally, it was Rebecca's turn. She too received a hug and kiss from Felicia.

"Princess, Doctor Afterland, dear Bull, honoured Generals and instructors," Rebecca said. "Even at this very moment of decision I am not sure what is the right thing for me and which is the correct action to take. I have been thinking hard these past five days and nights but I haven't come to a conclusion. My heart has overruled my mind."

She remained silent for a few seconds, her mind racing. Then she took a deep breath and continued, with a sigh:

"Right now, then, I decide to remain an Orizon and accept the Flame. As I take this path, I promise to work with all my powers and knowledge to become a worthy Orizon, whether on Earth or in the Land of the White Sun. I love Earth more than the Land of the White Sun. I consider Earth to be my true homeland. I think it will stay that way. It won't change even if I spend the rest of my life here. But I'll fight with all my strength and I'm willing to be killed in order to protect the Flame of the White Sun. Thank you all so much."

Tears began to flow from the eyes of the Wise Tree and a murmur of amazement rustled through the gathered crowd of

Orizons, who had been living for so many years in the Land of the White Sun but had never seen the Wise Tree cry. Rebecca went over and hugged it.

It whispered in her ear: "I want you to introduce me to the moon."

As soon as Rebecca took her seat, Princess Felicia gave all the children a loving look. "Only Nargis has decided not to be an Orizon any more and so tonight she will be going back to Earth. We believe that her decision is absolutely correct. Tomorrow at the same time the great ceremony will take place. All the inhabitants of Utopia will be present, as well as my father and mother. Once you have received the Flame there'll be a big party with dancers and shows and singing. Tomorrow there won't be any training; you can rest and prepare yourselves mentally to receive the Flame. Goodbye."

Everybody rose and the children hugged and kissed each other and their relatives. Nargis was feeling rather awkward because she was the only one to have decided differently from the others. But everyone treated her well and gradually her spirits recovered. While they were kissing her goodbye, the other children did not act as if they were trying to cheer her up or to understand her, but simply as if her decision was something natural and absolutely right.

After all her restless nights Rebecca slept late the next day. It was about two o'clock when the Newtons received an important visitor: Field Marshal Foster. They welcomed him and sat down together in the living room. They could hear Rebecca playing the guitar in her room as they talked.

"Is that Rebecca playing?" the Field Marshal asked as he finally stood up to leave.

"Yes," said her grandmother, "she loves it."

"Thank you very much," Foster said as they took him to the door. "I'll be expecting you."

After lunch, Rebecca noticed her grandparents getting ready to leave. "Isn't it a bit early to be getting ready?"

"We're leaving earlier because we have a job to attend to with the Field Marshal. You should come along to the theatre at the appointed time."

"Okay." Rebecca was disappointed that they would not be going as a family, but the Field Marshall was far too important a person to question. She went out for a walk around the grounds, still trying to grasp fully the new future that was taking shape in front of her. She walked for some time, stroked the farm animals, caressed the plants, smelled the flowers, heard the birds sing and absorbed Nature's soothing presence. Then she went back to her room to get ready.

By six o'clock the gigantic theatre was filled. The Sphinx descended from the small hillock and sat just behind the Wise Tree so that she too could watch the ceremony. The crowd cheered as the pure white winged horse Pegasus appeared in the sky, carrying Lord Life and Lady Danae. They flew low around the theatre stands and greeted all the people of Utopia, who applauded happily.

Pegasus landed behind the Wise Tree near the Sphinx and Felicia ran to embrace her parents as they alighted from the winged steed. They stepped onto the platform and sat in the waiting armchairs.

Bull the Minotaur rose from his seat and walked over to Felicia, bending close to her ear: "Rebecca is missing. She hasn't arrived yet."

"Let's wait a few minutes longer. Meanwhile, go and ask her grandparents, please."

"Your granddaughter is late," Bull whispered to Tony and Lisa. "Didn't you leave together?"

"No," Tony replied. "She was going to come on her own. Don't worry, Bull, she'll be here."

As the minutes passed Rebecca's grandparents began to worry. Everyone was whispering their concerns. Some thought that she might have regretted her decision and was ashamed to admit it.

Felicia told her parents how worthy Rebecca was, how she was potentially the best warrior in Orizon history.

"She's absolutely ready to fight. Even Foster finds it hard to beat her. And that's after only one month's training."

When half an hour had gone by, Lord Life and Felicia decided to begin the ceremony without Rebecca. It was the first time that such a thing had happened in the Land of the White Sun and it made everyone feel flustered and uncomfortable.

Princess Felicia rose and gave the signal. The music ceased and silence fell. "Dear citizens of Utopia, we are all gathered here today to perform the ceremony of the Flame which takes place every three Earth years. One of the children who began her training has decided to go back to Earth, while the rest have decided to become Orizons and fight against Evil. Unfortunately, one of them, Rebecca Newton, hasn't arrived yet. We must proceed, however."

The theatre had perfect acoustics and her voice could be heard clearly in every corner. On a small table next to her seat was the crystal lantern that contained the blue Flame. Felicia held it between her palms and raised it high.

"This Flame will now enter the new Orizons. They will become like all of us. Let the children come now, in turn."

Sergei stood up. He was deeply touched. He went to Felicia and knelt down in front of her. She placed the Flame under Sergei's nostrils and he inhaled it for almost two minutes.

When Felicia took the Flame away and Sergei stood up the whole auditorium began to shout and cheer. The Wise Tree clapped its branches; Pegasus and the Sphinx flapped their wings.

One by one, the children received the Flame to the same rapturous reception. But still Rebecca had not appeared. Princess Felicia put the lantern with the Flame back onto the small table.

"Now you, the new Orizons, will learn the great secret that all we Orizons have kept for thousands of Earth years. We didn't tell you before you received the Flame because we did not want to influence your decision."

She looked at them, one by one, straight in the eye, and continued:

"From this moment on, you are immortal! You will live for ever, unless you are killed. This is our great secret. Orizons never grow old. They always retain the same vitality, the same strength and the same energy. So there comes a time when children look almost the same age as their parents and grandparents. This complicates the Orizons' activities on Earth, because the people around them must not become aware of their unique endowment.

"That's why senior Orizons who live on Earth use artificial means such as hair dye to look older. When the time comes for an Orizon to leave Earth and come here to live for eternity, we arrange fictitious deaths or, in rare circumstances, mysterious disappearances. That's why newspapers on Earth sometimes report that various people, mainly scientists, disappear and some people surmise that they have been abducted by aliens. As you can understand now, that seemingly fantastic notion comes rather close to the truth.

"If the need arises, Orizons can return to Earth under other names, taking up different posts and living in different countries, according to Lord Life's orders, so as to combat Evil and protect the planet. You'll find out more about all this from your relatives. You have seen what it means to keep a secret and that it can be kept for ever if you behave properly. Now I would like to ask the Wise Tree to say a few words about the secrets that you may have to keep during your lives."

All this time the Wise Tree had been looking worried and sad. It kept glancing at the theatre entrance, expecting to see Rebecca. Nevertheless, it began to speak:

"It is very pleasant to see more Orizons joining the forces of Good today. You have become immortal and you will live for ever if, of course, you don't get killed. In any case, we are not concerned with time here as people are on Earth. A minute there may seem like eternity and a whole year may seem like a single minute. People who live for five decades or more don't understand how they have grown old."

The Tree paused, glanced at the theatre entrance again and went on:

"It is highly significant that this secret has been kept for thousands of Earth years. It is also essential to understand that you must loyally keep any secret you have. We often feel the urge to discuss our secrets with a friend or with someone we love. This is a grave error that no Orizon must ever make.

"The moment when someone else knows our secret it is no longer a secret because then it is sure to leak out. That is absolutely certain. If we, whom it concerns, cannot keep the secret to ourselves, how can we expect another person to keep it when they have no reason to do so?

"If you feel the need to disclose your secret to unburden yourself, then find a complete stranger who doesn't know you at all, who won't find out who you are and whom you will never see again. If that's impossible, tell your secret to the plants, the flowers and trees. If you are on Earth, tell it to the moon. Although I don't know the moon, I am sure it is a very trustworthy and good companion at times like these. I bid you farewell and I wish you every success in your struggle against Evil."

Princess Felicia thanked the Tree and spoke again:

"Now our celebration begins. First of all, we'll see traditional dancing by various groups and tribes, reminding us of the first years of life on Earth before coming all the way up to the present. We're going to dance and celebrate, so have fun."

Some Orizons dressed in magnificent traditional Aztec costumes and holding musical instruments rose from their seats and came down the tiers to the front to perform.

Tony and Lisa Newton came over to the platform and approached the Lord and the Lady. Then Rebecca's grandfather turned to the princess:

"We ask permission to go home to see what has happened to Rebecca ..."

"Of course you may go. We shall be waiting for your news," she said, while Lord Life nodded his head in agreement.

When the Newtons arrived home they couldn't find Rebecca anywhere. Everything was in order and they could tell that she must have dressed in her formal uniform and had her sword with her. They went to the stables and saw that none of the horses were missing. They searched the farm, calling out her name, but in vain. No answer came.

"Where can she have gone?" asked Lisa.

"I don't know," Tony said, putting his arm around his wife's shoulders to comfort both of them. "There's no chance that she regretted her decision. She had been on edge until the moment she made it but she calmed down after that. She slept, she talked easily and all her reactions were normal. She didn't give any indication that she was at all concerned. We must report back."

The Newtons returned to the theatre where the party was in full swing and found Felicia dancing with Bull. The princess and the Minotaur stopped as soon as they saw Rebecca's grandparents and moved to a secluded spot to talk.

About two hours later the party ended and the theatre began to empty. Only Felicia, Afterland, Bull, Foster, the other Generals and the Newtons remained.

"We must search," announced Bull.

"Where shall we begin?" wondered Foster uneasily. "I hope she is on her own somewhere, thinking. A sudden illness is out of question since she still has the flame inside her to protect her. Nothing serious could have happened to her. I suggest that we wait until morning. If she hasn't appeared by then we should discuss what action to take."

"I'm going to start looking now," Bull said and the others agreed. Even Foster eventually followed.

BULL THE MINOTAUR

Two days and nights went by and still Rebecca was nowhere to be found. Some suggested that she might have gone to the lake or the sea to fly and that something had happened to her there. But she had not taken a horse and she would have had to walk for at least two hours to reach the lake and twice as long to reach the sea. Nevertheless, both the lake and the seashore were thoroughly searched.

In order to fly she would certainly have taken off her sword, even if she had kept her clothes on. It would have been left on the shore, but there was no sign of it there.

Foster still believed that she must be hiding somewhere, probably too embarrassed to show her face because she had gone back on her decision.

"I'm not saying that Rebecca was afraid," he said at one of the Generals' meetings. "She's fearless and very strong. But she came forward without having reached a decision until that moment. She appeared to be in two minds. She had to take a stand because she couldn't do otherwise. Later, when she thought it over, maybe she regretted her decision. We shouldn't worry. She's fit, tough and can survive under difficult conditions. I believe that in two to three days she'll reappear and ask to go back to Earth."

Despite his assessment of the situation Foster had searched for Rebecca as diligently as anyone else.

"If she had wanted to be alone to think, she would have taken her guitar along with her," Tony said to Lisa as they racked their brains for a plausible explanation.

"I agree. Something's wrong. Something else is going on. But what?"

On the second day, Tony and Felicia told Rebecca's parents what had happened. Bull was asked to fetch them from Earth.

So, on the third day after Rebecca's disappearance, Julius and Adriana arrived in the Land of the White Sun. They all went to Princess Felicia's house for a meeting with Lord Life.

"Rebecca was upset," Tony Newton explained to his son and daughter-in-law. "On the last night she stayed out and came back at the crack of dawn. She couldn't have slept a wink. But once she announced her decision she relaxed completely. She gave us no reason to suspect that she might be regretting it."

Most of the others present were now inclined to believe that Rebecca had changed her mind – they could see no other explanation. But Bull, her grandparents and her parents were adamant.

"I know Rebecca very well," Julius said. "Once she decided, she wouldn't change her mind. But if she did I'm certain that she would have told you before receiving the Flame. Something else has happened, for sure."

Bull was pacing up and down, his lower lip almost touching his nostrils. He was snorting as if he had just run a marathon.

"I fear that forces from the Land of Beast have harmed her," he said.

Field Marshal Foster sprang out of his seat. "What are you suggesting, Bull? For thousands of Earth years they have kept to the rules. They have never broken a single agreement, even during battle. You know that! Why would they suddenly violate the agreement? Why would they do such a terrible thing?"

The atmosphere in the room suddenly grew tense and gloomy.

"Field Marshal Foster," Bull replied darkly, "there's no reason to lose our tempers. Of all the explanations we've been discussing, only two are possible. The first is that Rebecca has changed her mind and is too ashamed to come forward. The second is that the forces of Beast have harmed her. My instincts and my knowledge of Rebecca tell me that the first explanation is out of the question. Rebecca would never have left her relatives in such an agony of worry and suspense, not for a minute."

Lord Life looked at Bull and Foster. "Sit down – and calm down, too," he said. "You're both right. It's true that for thousands of years the powers of Evil haven't violated the agreements. So why should they do so now? Yet Bull's viewpoint is reasonable too. I don't know Rebecca. You all speak of her in glowing terms. You say that her abilities may even surpass Felicia's. The fact that she made her decision at the very last moment raises the possibility that she's weaker than you all seem to think she is. On the other hand, it shows that she thought it over deeply. That's a positive factor. Moreover, her words showed great courage, sincerity and commitment. All these qualities add up to an exceptional personality that would not retract a decision easily. And even if she did, I believe that she would have told someone in authority. She wouldn't have let her relatives undergo a minute of anxiety. This is the most important thing to note."

He turned towards Felicia.

"Send a messenger to Turgoth. Tell him that I want a meeting with him tomorrow at the Castle. Let him set the time. Both of us will go with Julius and Bull," he said. The wrinkles had deepened in his forehead. He stroked his beard as he continued. "As of tomorrow we'll call off the search and continue with the children's training. Utopia must return to its normal pace. Whatever has happened to Rebecca has happened. I believe that we'll soon find out exactly what took place. I want our forces to be ready. There must be sentries at the Fortress and everyone must be on full alert."

Bull rose from his seat again. "Venerable Lord, excuse me for interfering but I'm afraid it would be a grave mistake to proceed in this way."

"Sit down, Bull, and explain yourself," Lord Life said mildly.

"If we suspect that Turgoth had something to do with Rebecca's disappearance he must be caught off guard. If we send a messenger to inform him of our wish to hold the meeting tomorrow, he'll have time to prepare. In my opinion, we should go to the Castle unexpectedly and *demand* a meeting. We may be able to draw some conclusions from the way he reacts. Will he receive us at once? Will he find excuses to delay? How will he respond when he suddenly sees us?"

"Sound thinking, Bull! We'll set out right away. Have the horses saddled. I'll leave Pegasus here so that we can all go together. Field Marshal Foster, Claudia, Hunter, Doctor Afterland: you all know very well what to do if anything happens to us."

Lord Life's voice was full of power and he seemed ready for action.

Bull ran to prepare the horses while Julius rode fast to his father's house and went straight up to Rebecca's room. He looked at her guitar and stroked her clothes before taking a quick shower. Then he donned a uniform and buckled on sword.

The four chosen horses were ready to go by the time he returned, and Princess Felicia was dressed in combat gear. Bull's horse was taller and more powerful than the others, in order to carry his weight. As always, Lord Life was wearing his uniform, his sword and the white leather cloak with the blue-sun symbol emblazoned on the back. Bull did not take a sword but added two more daggers to his belt.

After five hours of hard riding they reached the Castle of Beast. The great Gate was closed but the sentry on the tower saw them and called out, asking what they wanted.

"I am Lord Life, and I ride with my daughter, the Princess Felicia, Bull the Minotaur and another Orizon. I want to see King Turgoth," announced the Orizon leader.

"Lord Life, I'll let you in. You know the way to the king's house. If you don't find him there, the Sphinx will inform you where he might be." The black-clad guard opened the Gate for them to ride through.

When they entered the courtyard of Turgoth's house the Sphinx rose apprehensively.

"Calphie, we want to see the King," Lord Life declared.

"I will inform him at once," she said.

Taking up a baton with her massive forepaw, she struck a gong that hung from a wooden pole of the balcony. Immediately a servant with a shaven head answered. He wore a black tunic like the guard on the gate.

"Zengo, inform the King that Lord Life is here and wants to see him," ordered Calphie.

The servant went back inside and reappeared a few minutes later with Turgoth himself.

"What a surprise this is!" Turgoth came down the steps, grinning. "I can't believe my eyes. Dismount from your horses and come on in." He turned to his servant. "Zengo, look after the horses. They must be worn out."

Turgoth ushered them in with the gestures of a good host,

even touching Bull lightly on the back as they came into a spacious living room and sat down. A tall, skinny servant, also dressed in a black tunic, stood waiting, bowing slightly. His head was shaven too; from his ears dangled two long earrings and his eyes were hidden deep in their sockets.

"Mirko, bring some water for our visitors and tell Lydia to prepare a meal for everyone." Turgoth beamed at Lord Life. "It is the first time you've ever visited without announcing your arrival, Lord Life. It must be something serious. Have you decided to give us some of the Flame?"

"I'm in no mood for jokes, Turgoth. A trainee Orizon has disappeared: Rebecca Newton is her name. Her father Julius is here with us. Such a thing has never happened before."

"How can I be of help?" Turgoth asked.

"Hear me now, Turgoth. You've never given us any reason to doubt you because you have never broken any of our rules. In fact, I distinctly remember that you severely punished a Cyclopes because he had violated a minor rule during a game. But since there are beings that do not respect the agreements, as they should, maybe some of your own people have harmed Rebecca without your knowledge. So would you please call your generals and ask them if they know anything about this matter?"

"Gladly. Although I believe that if such a thing had happened I would have been informed immediately. What can it have to do with us if a girl has gone missing? Where did it happen?"

"We don't know exactly what happened. She was at home, she got dressed to come to the Fortress and then she disappeared. She left without a horse."

"How many days is it since she went missing?" asked Turgoth.

"Today is the third day," answered Lord Life.

"Very well, then. While we have something to eat I'll send for as many of my generals as we can find."

"Thank you for your kind hospitality, Turgoth, but none of us has an appetite."

"I'd really like to feed you, but I can't insist. I'll send word for the generals of the Porths, Cyclopes and the Sharkans to come," Turgoth said. "In two hours most of them will be here. I think it would be better if I saw them in private in the conference hall. But if you wish, Lord Life, we can see them together."

"No, it's better for you to see them and talk to them alone. But remember – if they really have broken any rules they might try to keep it a secret, even from you."

While they all waited they talked about various matters concerning the Earth. The atmosphere was oppressive and their words came out with difficulty, like an interrogation. Turgoth gave no sign that just forty-eight hours earlier Rebecca had been trussed up in this very room.

Two hours later Turgoth was informed that the generals were awaiting him in the conference room. He left at once but was not gone for long.

"Unfortunately, no one knows anything," he said as he returned. "Most of them came; only a few are absent. I explained the gravity of the situation to them. I asked them to investigate it as best they could and gather any information. I'm truly sorry."

Lord Life and the others rose from their seats.

"Thank you again for your goodwill and hospitality. If you have any news, good or bad, please let us know at once," Lord Life said as he headed for the door, followed by the others.

When they had ridden some distance and the Castle had disappeared from view, Bull signalled to them to stop.

"Lord Life, I wish to stay behind. There's something I don't like about this. It seemed to me that the sentry at the Gate was expecting us. And Turgoth didn't know when Rebecca disappeared, yet he asked how many days she had been missing. Rebecca could have gone missing last night. Why did he use the word 'days'? I may be exaggerating, but my intuition tells me that something's up."

"All right, Bull. Stay and do whatever you think is best. ," said Lord Life.

Once he was on his own, Bull rode into the forest, searching for a while until he found some special trees that had long fibres. He cut enough of them to weave a sturdy rope about ten yards long. He pulled a hook from the saddle, attaching it to one end of the rope, and tested it. Satisfied, he lay down and slept.

Bull woke at dusk, mounted his horse and headed cautiously towards the Castle. When he was within half a mile he tethered the horse and waited for full darkness to fall.

Around the Castle was a war-zone clearing. The front of the clearing, where the Gate stood, faced Domus Forest where Bull was hiding. The other sides of the war zone bordered on the farms and houses of Beast's inhabitants. The only sentry Bull had seen so far was on the Gate tower.

At midnight, when everything seemed quiet, he moved to the left through the forest. He was going to risk crossing the half-mile of the clearing at the side, hoping that no one would notice him. The sky was clear and the stars shone as brightly as the lights of a chandelier.

Bull took the rope that he had made and crept towards the Fortress. It seemed to take for ever but eventually he reached the walls, straightened up, twirled the rope with the hook at its end a few times above his head and hurled it over the battlements. The hook caught straight away. He tugged on it a couple of times to test its strength and then climbed like a leopard.

At the top he paused and looked around. There was complete silence. He dropped the free end of the rope down the other side of the wall and shinned down it, moving as silently as any cat burglar. He was inside. He took out one of his daggers and cut off the excess rope, attaching it to his belt. He headed for Turgoth's house.

Bull's greatest problem was Calphie the Sphinx. He knew that she never slept and that she had a keen sense of smell. If Calphie became aware of Bull's presence she would kill him, easily. He headed towards the stables, knowing that Zengo's house was close by.

Bull slithered like a snake for the last few yards to Zengo's front door. He stopped and listened attentively, looking all around. Then he stooped and crept beneath the window, glancing inside briefly. It was pitch black. He went back to the door, opened it cautiously and entered. As his eyes adjusted to the darkness he could see that he was in a living room. There were three closed doors and one that had been left ajar. Going to the open door, he found a kitchen with a large dining room next to it. Inside the first closed door two children were sleeping in separate beds. He opened the next door and saw another two children asleep. Now he was sure that Zengo and his wife Lydia would be in the next room. He closed the first two doors silently and then just as carefully opened the final door. He could hear the couple's rhythmic breathing. He closed the door softly behind him, stood still for a moment, then pounced on the sleeping pair, straddling both of them. With his left hand he covered the woman's mouth while with his right he pressed one of his daggers to Zengo's throat. The couple's eyes opened in fear, shock and confusion.

"Don't make a sound or I'll slit your throats," Bull hissed.

The menace in his voice froze them and they shook like leaves beneath him. Bull pressed the knife harder against Zengo's throat.

"I'm no Orizon, Zengo, you know that. I'll carve you up into little pieces, you and your wife and your children too. I know that Rebecca was brought here and I know too that you played a big part in her abduction. The only way you'll stay alive is if you help me get her out."

Zengo's throat began to bleed where Bull's blade had punctured the skin.

"Don't kill me! It's not my fault! Rebecca isn't here. She may be dead," he gasped.

Bull lessened the pressure of his knife against Zengo's neck.

"I'm getting off you now but if you let out as much as a squeak you'll both be dead in a second – and your children will be next. I give you my word. And you know I always keep my promises." The couple had no doubt that he meant what he was saying.

Bull got off them and they took deep breaths to try to calm their shuddering.

"Sit up. Careful, now – don't try any tricks."

They got up cautiously and sat on the bed, still trembling.

"Tell me exactly what happened. And no lies!" Bull ordered them.

"They brought her here one evening. I heard that she'd killed someone. She was with the king all night. She wasn't here in the morning. They either killed her or hid her. The next day the king was very upset – he was nervous and moody. I don't know anything else, Mr Bull, sir, I swear. Please don't hurt us."

Bull tried to think coherently, but a rage kept threatening to overcome him at the thought of Rebecca lying dead somewhere. He wanted to kill Zengo and his wife, but he forced himself to stay calm.

"If Rebecca is dead, nobody involved in her abduction and murder will be left alive. I'll slaughter the lot of you. You killed a girl, a child."

Bull was transformed. He was no longer lovable Bull, the children's best friend. He was Bull the Minotaur, cousin of the terrible Minotaur of Crete. The couple felt death reaching out for them.

"I di-didn't say that she's dead for sure, Mr Bull, sir. I don't know what happened but whatever did it's not our fault," Zengo and his wife both burst into tears.

"Have pity on us; we're not to blame."

"Shut up! If you wake the children, I'll slit all your throats," hissed Bull.

He tried to think calmly. "Has Turgoth been away at all these past few days?"

"No, I wasn't aware of him leaving. He hasn't even left his house," Zengo replied.

"Could he have hidden Rebecca inside the house?"

"No, that's impossible. There aren't any secret hiding places in the house. My wife here, Lydia – she cooks and takes care of the king – as well as Mirko and myself haven't seen or heard a thing. I'm absolutely sure that Rebecca isn't in the house. She may be at some other place in the Castle. We have so many buildings. But, even so, we would have got wind of something. She must be outside the Castle because he asked for a carriage and sent me to notify some of the generals."

This small sliver of hope cleared Bull's mind.

"You must help me find a way to capture that filthy liar Turgoth. I can't beat the Sphinx. She could kill me as easily as I can kill all of you. You must find a way to remove her from her post so that I can get to the king."

"But how can I make her leave her post, Mr Bull, sir? I can't think of a way. She never leaves it," Zengo whined.

"The Sphinx must know that Rebecca was brought here, and that she was taken from the house, dead or alive. She watches everything, day and night, doesn't she?"

"Yes, she does," answered the Sharkan, desperately searching inside himself for some courage.

"The Sphinx saw us coming here today. She must know that we're searching for Rebecca. If you tell her that you've noticed five or six Orizons near your house she'll come with you to investigate. Distract her by taking her here and there to search. Delay her for as long as possible. I'll get Turgoth and leave through the reception hall at the back of the house so you won't see me while you're searching. I need at least five minutes, ten at the most.

"I'm taking your wife with me. If you make the smallest mistake, I'll kill her. So go and play your trick on the Sphinx."

The three of them crept out like escaping prisoners. Bull and Lydia hid behind the bushes deep in the garden and watched anxiously as Zengo spoke to the Sphinx. After what seemed like an age, the Sphinx rose and moved towards the stables, accompanying Zengo. Immediately Bull and Lydia ran towards the house, entering through the reception hall and reaching the room where Turgoth was sleeping.

Lydia, a short, plump woman with huge eyes and a small beaky nose, began to hope that she might survive. She knew that Bull kept his word and she believed he would treat them well now that they'd helped him.

Bull took out his knife and cut a piece from the hem of Lydia's long nightgown. Then he kissed her on the forehead.

"Thank you both for your help. I'm sorry I frightened you but I couldn't do otherwise. Pray that I will find Rebecca alive because, if I don't, nobody will escape from me. As soon as you see me capture Turgoth and leave, go quickly back to your room so that no one can suspect you of being involved."

Bull opened Turgoth's door and crept in. Turgoth was asleep. Bull dealt him a heavy blow on the head, carefully calculated to knock him out without killing him. He opened Turgoth's mouth and stuffed the scrap of Lydia's nightgown into it, tying a short length of rope tightly round the king's neck and up over his teeth to hold the cloth firmly in place. Using another piece of rope, he tied Turgoth's hands behind his back. Then Bull picked the king up, slung him over his shoulder like a poacher carrying off a slain deer, left the house and vanished into the darkness.

As Bull raced to the spot where he had left the rope hanging, Turgoth came round, finding himself helpless to do anything but emit grunts of protest.

"Shut up, Turgoth, or I'll tear you apart!" Bull hissed, dropping him to the ground and giving him another blow to the head.

He freed Turgoth's hands briefly before tying them up again in front of him. Looping the newly limp king's arms over his own head. Bull swung Turgoth onto his back like a haversack and began to climb the rope. Once on the ground outside the Castle walls Bull hauled Turgoth off his back, slung him to the ground and bound his feet. Then he began to crawl slowly, pulling Turgoth behind him, like a carnivorous beast dragging its prey back to its lair. It was a laborious business and by the time they reached the edge of the forest Turgoth was recovering consciousness again. Bull once more freed the king's hands, pulled them behind him again and bound them to his waist, leaving the rope dangling. Then he freed Turgoth's feet.

"You murderer!" Bull snarled in his face. "I'll tear out your innards and wind them round your neck! Come on! Get up and walk before I kill you!"

Turgoth stumbled forward on the end of Bull's rope like a dog. Even though he was a big man he looked like a child compared with the giant Minotaur. His long black nightshirt was now dirty and ripped to shreds, his skin grazed and bleeding. From time to time Bull was unable to resist the temptation to kick his prisoner, humiliating the king still further. Once they were among the trees, Bull stopped to catch his breath.

"Sit down," he commanded, kicking Turgoth's legs out from under him.

Bull removed the gag, kneeling opposite the king.

"Now speak! Where have you hidden Rebecca? You hypocrite! You thought we believed you, didn't you? You thought we didn't know that you had her in your house that first night. Do you take us for idiots? Don't you know that we have spies?"

Bull was bluffing, like a good poker player. He gave the king no chance to deny the accusations.

"Go on – speak, then! I've been patient for too long already!"

"What can I tell you?" Turgoth replied. "Rebecca is dead."

"You murdered her! You slaughtered a young girl! Do kings slay children?"

"Of course! That's what powerful leaders do every day on Earth," Turgoth spat back.

"But this isn't Earth. We have principles here. Murderer!" Bull was shouting wildly now, his tear-filled eyes blazing with rage and grief.

"Rebecca is not a child," Turgoth argued. "She killed one of my best generals. Don't look on her as a child, Bull. Don't think that – *aah!*"

Bull's dagger had flashed down and hacked off the king's right ear.

"I'll cut you up, piece by piece."

Blood pumped from the wound as Bull dangled the severed ear in front of Turgoth's eyes.

"Now eat it, you punk," he ordered him.

The king closed his mouth tight but Bull's hands were like an industrial-strength jack, prising his jaws open and pushing the ear into his mouth.

"Chew it, you filthy piece of garbage," cried the Minotaur.

Blood smeared across Turgoth's lips and cheeks as he struggled to escape. The moment Bull let go, Turgoth spat the ear back out. Furious, Bull grabbed the king's left ear by the tip and pressed the dagger against it.

"Don't!" cried Turgoth. "Stop! I'll take you to where Rebecca is. She may still be alive."

Bull sprang up, pulling the king to his feet by the scruff of his neck like a slaughtered fatling to be hung on a hook.

"Which way do we go?"

"To Mount Thunder."

Bull threw Turgoth up onto the horse's back and untied his hands so that he could grip the animal's mane. Then Bull mounted behind the king and spurred the horse into a gallop.

They had ridden for about an hour when Turgoth shouted to Bull to stop.

"I've changed my mind. I won't take you anywhere. What do I have to gain? You're just going to kill me in the end, anyway – especially if Rebecca is dead. I would rather die now, with some dignity. So kill me and get it over with."

"There will be no dignity for you," Bull replied. "First I'll cut off your other ear, then your nose and then your tongue. I shall dismember you piece by piece. You won't get out of my clutches that easily."

"Is that so? And you, Bull, are the one who is supposed to be on the side of Good, while I'm on the side of Evil? I'm not afraid. Do as you please and let's get it over with."

Turgoth made a move to dismount. But Bull held him back, worried that the king meant what he said. If he couldn't change Turgoth's mind, Rebecca would be lost for ever. Bull tried to calm him down.

"Turgoth, you know that I keep my word and that I'm not a hypocrite – unlike you. If we find Rebecca, I'll let you go free. All you'll be missing is an ear. Think about what you've done and maybe you'll mend your ways and stop the wars. That would restore your lost dignity."

"If I take you to the place where Rebecca is, I'll have betrayed my people. Do you understand that, Bull? What am I to say to them, to those who believe in me? To those who always fight by my side?" Turgoth thought for a moment and Bull forced himself to wait. "All right. Let's keep going and we'll see. But let me tell you, Bull, I don't care about my life. You have shamed me, dragging me along like a dog. You've reduced my dignity to shreds, treating me like I was the lowest thing in the Universe, just garbage.

"If I agree to your demands, I'll only be doing it for Rebecca. I've come to like that girl. I think she has a great deal to offer the world, and not only in the Lomani. I believe that in a few years she will become a great leader.

"I've been thinking about her these past few days as if she were my own daughter. That's why I'm so sad. Those who have her may already have killed her if she resisted them. Which she might well have done: after all, she murdered General Varta and seriously wounded General Bitho.

"I once had a wife who was immortal, but she was killed in the Lomani. I never remarried because I didn't want to see my next wife withering away, like a flower that hasn't been watered, while I remained unchanged. I couldn't bear to see her becoming a sick old woman, suffering after a stroke, or ill with Alzheimer's disease.

"I never wanted a family with kids, because they impose such a huge responsibility. Besides, I couldn't know their point of view before bringing them to life. I practically live like the hermit monks of medieval Earth. I've been thinking of retiring if I don't succeed in taking the Flame on my next attack. I don't care what people will think of me when I'm gone, especially after earthworms have eaten my flesh.

"I've lived for thousands of Earth years. I see Sharkans being born, growing up, striving and, all too soon, growing old. Their whole life is like a single day of ours. In the end they die. It's a great injustice. Why do you think I fight like a madman during the Lomani? I pray that I'll get killed if I don't win, every single time. That way I might find redemption. But then I think that if I die in battle I won't accomplish my aim – that's why I fight so hard. So, Bull, don't think you can make me fearful for my life. I don't care if you kill me. I'm tired of living. Fed up! My desire is to die in Egypt. It draws me like the Sargasso Sea draws the eels before they die."

For a fleeting second Bull felt sorry for Turgoth. His heart softened. He wouldn't like to be in this king's position. Nor in any other king's position, either. He believed that he who wears the crown sleeps uneasily. He knew that Turgoth fought like a lion in the Lomani, always taking the lead, retreating only when he was sure that he was going to lose the battle and that his soldiers would die pointlessly.

"Why did you kidnap Rebecca?"

"All the sources told me that she would prove a dangerous foe, even stronger than Princess Felicia herself. She might even surpass Lord Life's war skills. So, we've had it! That was all I needed to know. For the good of my people, Rebecca had to die before receiving the Flame again.

"I had heard that she had wavered until the very last moment. I hoped that if I explained the truth to her from my perspective, before she received the Flame, she might change sides or, at the very least, decide to remain neutral."

"Where did you get such detailed information?" Bull growled.

"Come on, Bull – don't be naive. I have spies! Just like you ..."

"Spies in *Utopia*?" Bull couldn't conceive of such a thing. But how else could Turgoth have known that Rebecca had stayed undecided until the very last minute? The Minotaur remained silent, his mind spinning as he tried to guess who the traitor was.

Turgoth continued: "As I was saying, Bull, when I met her and talked with her for a whole night she impressed me. I was shocked. She fired my thoughts! I realized that it would be a pity for such a creature to die. Whichever camp she's in, she'll only fight for what is truly good.

"But I couldn't possibly reveal my thoughts to my generals. None of them understand the deeper meaning of life. Nor can they evaluate situations properly. They are obsessed with the injustice that we suffer and they are completely ruled by jealousy. They would be incapable of grasping the usefulness of talented people such as Rebecca.

"I believe I have as much self-knowledge as any of you. I want Rebecca to live but I don't want to be a traitor to my companions and subjects. I'm certain that as soon as Rebecca is mature and ready she will fix many of the mistakes on Earth. The Mythical Gods made so many errors when life returned to Earth, like placing only a few tribes on the vast plains of America. It wasn't fair for such a small number of people to inhabit such an enormous expanse of land. But their destruction by the invaders who came later was an atrocious crime and the division of the land that followed was legalized theft.

"The Orizons proved unable to stop so many horrors – conquests, butchery, colonization, wars, the murderous Inquisition, the slave trade. During these dark ages, people were bound in chains and sold like vegetables. Men wielding swords and axes cut off heads like gardeners pruning bushes. They strung people up like carcasses in a butcher's shop. They shot them as if for target practice. Only a few years ago, the Hebrews were sprayed with poison gas, as if they were mosquitoes, and after they'd been killed they burned like firewood.

"Murderous times arrive on horseback. Cannons, pistols, rifles, fighter planes and missiles slaughter innocent people while they dream, pray, breastfeed and make love. Orizons observe all these atrocities, washing their hands just as Pontius Pilate did.

"Many more mistakes and crimes might have taken place had they not been present, and there were important people who left behind magnificent achievements.

"My homeland, Egypt, had a tradition," Turgoth continued. "An advanced civilization, wonderful religions, an artistic background and intellectual heritage. Then came the storm! Conquerors imposed their own religions against the people's wishes. They enslaved and degraded the country. They quenched its fire. Its extraordinary people are now plagued by a thousand tribulations.

"The women in Egypt used to enjoy equal status with men. There was mutual respect and appreciation, as there is among the citizens of the Land of the White Sun.

"Women are the force that energizes, refines, and beautifies the world, Nature and life itself.

"I have put my ear to women's breasts and heard their hearts beating. Then I lay down on the ground and did the same with the Earth. They both had the same beat and told me the same things: '*We have uteruses. We are mothers!*'

"A man's character can be revealed from the way he treats women. I believe Rebecca will give women their rightful place, neither higher than men nor lower. She'll put right many things – if she's still alive, that is."

Turgoth tried to swivel his head and look the Minotaur directly in the eyes.

Bull didn't return the look. Instead, he asked: "Is this the right way, Turgoth?"

THE EXECUTION

Turgoth opened his eyes and looked down at Rebecca as she lay among the flowers with her head bowed, waiting for him to execute her.

"I'll never forget you for as long as I live," he told her. "You're very brave and very genuine. I'm sorry you've made this decision, but if I were you I'd probably have done the same. Alas, you must die and it gives me great pain. I wish you'd just lie to me. I think that if each of us had the Flame we could save Earth."

Turgoth bent down and helped Rebecca up. Already she seemed to be in another world as they walked towards the house, moving like puppets whose strings were pulled by children.

"Ask Zengo to come at once," Turgoth told Calphie the Sphinx.

As they went inside, the king took off his sword and left it in the corner again.

"I'll wait on the veranda for Zengo. I must give him instructions," he said and went back outside, leaving Rebecca alone.

She sat and looked at her sword lying next to her. She could reach out and touch it. Had Turgoth left her there all alone on purpose so that she could grab it and then kill him? During their discussions it had been as if there was a truce between them. But once the situation had been clarified they were at war again and now she had every right to defend her freedom and her life, didn't she?

Rebecca kept looking at her sword and the open front door. A few minutes earlier she'd believed that she was already as good as dead. She wondered where she found such calm and composure. She guessed it must come from the power of the Flame.

If she killed Turgoth while Calphie was away on an errand she stood a good chance of escaping alive. Turgoth was unarmed. She could easily kill him either with her sword or with a kung fu blow. But perhaps Turgoth believed that there was still a truce between them and that was why he had left her free.

Time was running out! If she didn't act immediately her last chance would be gone. Rebecca gripped her sword firmly and stood up, feeling determined. A battle raged inside her between her conscience and her sense of duty – her responsibility to protect the Flame and her life.

She took a few steps ... Then her conscience won. Rebecca turned, put aside her sword and sat back down. She felt relaxed, as if she had just got rid of the greatest burden of all. She heard footsteps and voices. Turgoth entered the living room and slumped into his armchair. He looked like a prisoner wrongly sentenced to death who, although he had been granted a favour, refused to accept it.

"The generals of the Porths will soon be here for you. They're the ones who will execute you." Turgoth paused, struggling with internal battles of his own. "Why didn't you kill me and free me from all my dilemmas and my troubled conscience? It would have taken you only a few seconds. You would have become a heroine by relieving the forces of Good of me, their Satan."

Rebecca did not answer. She was almost in a state of ecstasy: *"He left me alone with my sword on purpose. I guessed right. He sent the Sphinx, away too! What kind of creature is he? If he is evil, then who is good? Oh, God, what a mess."*

They both sat in silence. Then Turgoth got up.

"Stand up, please, Rebecca, I have to tie you up," he said. His voice sounded faint, as if it came from the bottom of a deep well.

Rebecca obeyed. Turgoth picked up a piece of rope from the floor.

"Put your hands behind you, please."

He tied her hands securely but carefully, so as not to hurt her. But from the pain on his face one could tell that it was he who felt pain. He felt as if he had bound his own heart with barbed wire.

"Do you think there is a place in between God and humans?" Rebecca asked. "Are there spirits among us?"

"In my opinion, such things don't exist. They are an invention of religion. How did they suddenly appear out of nowhere? Thousands of years passed and all of a sudden evil spirits and similar idiocies appeared in the holy books of certain religions.

"They are the inventions of deceivers who mislead and take advantage of people, charlatans who create cults and conduct ceremonies in their lairs. They even make sacrifices and commit other crimes. They all maintain that spirits and demons exist and influence our lives and the lives of others. They ordain that their followers should use them for their own good, as well as to harm others.

"At the same time other religions claim to fight against these evil spirits. But in fact both sides are dealing with something that doesn't exist. Evil and Good are relevant and existing notions, but the so-called spirits are dangerous unfounded fabrications.

"With imagination and faith anyone can see whatever they wish, whatever suits them. Invisible things supposedly become visible. Many think that they witness miracles and they support their views with fanaticism and powerful arguments, deceiving thousands. An invisible world with alleged supernatural powers is created; for the faithful, this is more true than the visible world and reality itself.

"Mediums, parapsychologists, astrologers, self-proclaimed witches and other frauds lead – *mis*lead – the gullible. They are predators, with people as their prey. Sometimes, due to luck, human's own powers of self-deception, and autosuggestion, they get results and – in the eyes of the naive – they receive the credit for accomplishments that are not theirs. Legends, phantoms, spirits, vampires, devils and demons – all lies – acquire followers among those who are drawn to the mysterious and the unknown ...

"Meanwhile, the forces of Evil on Earth want to destroy all religions and all governments and eventually replace them with their own super-government. It already exists today, although it is invisible. And with it would come their own super-religion.

"We in Beast have never said that people should give up their religions or their Gods. Religions offer a great support to people, as long as they aren't taken to extremes. Zealotry is the most dangerous thing in existence.

"I respect all religions, but the holy books of Earth's religions resemble each other in many ways, almost as if they had copied one another. That is logical, since all creeds aim to help people. But it isn't good for people to have to barter all the time for the benefits of religion, and for the faithful to become objects of exploitation.

"In my opinion, whichever faith the people on Earth espouse they should not have to keep paying tolls to the retired Gods to get into paradise. Sacrifices, offerings, fund-raising and donations are man-made functions. It isn't right, in my view, for so many churches to be built practically side by side on Earth. Churches should be austere and their construction should not cost as much as a small town. In some cases, a single temple costs as much as a hospital. What do Gods want with gold furnishings and palaces? I don't think that helps develop religion."

"King Turgoth, the churches are the trustees of faith, tradition and certain principles. I do agree, though, that their buildings should be simple and austere."

"Are we obliged to beg and bribe the Gods to do what they should? As people lift their arms to heaven and pray, they expect the Creator to toss presents into their open arms. People who belong to the powerful religions are always told that the Kingdom of God is coming. Yet all they see coming is hell on Earth.

"Rebecca, I feel truly bad about tying your hands," Turgoth said, changing the subject. "But your executioners will be here soon. There's something you should know before they come – a secret we have all been keeping from you. But I can't keep it any longer. It's choking me! Orizons who receive the Flame at your age become immortal. That's why you saw no elderly people in Utopia."

"What are you saying? I don't understand ... Who is immortal? Surely only the mythical creatures, the Mythical Gods and you who lived on Earth before the great destruction are immortal. I don't understand what you mean."

"If you had attended the Flame ceremony you would have been told. It's the great secret that the Orizons have kept for thousands of Earth years. After taking the Flame you would never die unless you were killed. You aren't told about it before you make your decision so that you won't be influenced."

"*So my parents chose this path to give me the chance of becoming immortal,*" thought Rebecca, feeling a wave of relief. She could see now that they had made the right decision for her. She was glad to think that her parents and grandparents were immortal. She turned her gaze towards Turgoth again.

"I see now why you feel so strongly about the injustice done to your people," she said. "If I had known the full truth I wouldn't have made the decision that I did. Truly, King Turgoth, I too would have turned evil if I had experienced this injustice. It's unbelievable that the Sharkans are mortals while the Orizons bask in immortality. Thank you for telling me. You've helped me resolve some dilemmas of my own ..."

They heard voices and footsteps outside. Three Porths entered the living room. They were giants, more than six and a half feet tall and more or less humanoid in shape. But they had dark green skin, thick tails covered with scales, small red eyes and large sharp yellow teeth. They had black nails and pointed protuberant ears. Great swords swung from their belts and they were dressed in green leather. As soon as they entered they bowed to Turgoth and one of them said:

"King Turgoth, we are ready and waiting for your final orders."

"Rebecca," Turgoth said, "this is General Sam who is accompanied by General Max and General Tom. They and another two generals command the Porths. You will be leaving with them shortly."

The king motioned to them to go with him to the adjoining room so that he could give them their instructions. When they returned one of them grabbed Rebecca's legs and held them fast while the others tied them securely. The Porth who was holding her slung her over his shoulder as casually as he would a jacket, while another one picked up her sword. They carried her to a closed carriage drawn by four horses which was waiting next to Calphie the Sphinx, laying her on the floor and covering her with a hide as before. Two of them sat inside with her. The third one got in front, took the reins and the carriage rattled out of the Castle and into the forest of Domus.

"Where are we going?" Rebecca asked.

"We are on our way to Mount Thunder to kill you," answered General Sam, who seemed to be the Porths' leader.

"Why go so far? Why don't you kill me here and be done with it?"

"The king's orders," General Sam replied in a tone suggesting that he was in no mood for conversation.

After nearly four hours they reached a deserted house. One of them put Rebecca back over his shoulder, carrying her to the house's living room and throwing her onto a couch. The last Porth to enter held her sword in his hands.

"See this? This is what we're going to kill you with: your own sword. That's the order we've been given."

"I need to use the bathroom," Rebecca said.

The Porths conferred as if they had to solve the greatest problem in the world. They whispered and appeared to disagree. Finally, all three of them approached her.

"Don't try anything funny because otherwise you've had it," said Tom.

Rebecca looked at them angrily. "Are we going to play games with threats now? You're going to kill me anyway."

"All right, all right," said the one called Sam. "No need to get angry. You can go to the bathroom but as we want you to. You're a dangerous creature. You've harmed two of our Sharkan generals, one of them fatally."

They rebound one of Rebecca's hands behind her back, leaving the other one free, and loosened the rope around her legs enough for her to hobble. One of the Porths went outside to guard the toilet window while the other two stood guard outside the door.

As she shuffled back to the living room, Rebecca saw that the house had many bedrooms. She watched as the Porths carried in some food parcels, stacking them away in the kitchen.

"Why did you bring all this?" she asked. "Are you planning to stay here a long time?"

"Curiosity killed the cat," retorted General Sam. "Now go and choose your bedroom. We'll have to board up the window to prevent you from escaping."

"You choose one for me," replied Rebecca. "I'm fed up with you. You push and pull me this way and that like a sack of potatoes and you mess me around for no reason at all. Why are you wasting your valuable time? Kill me and get it over with."

The Porths, taken aback by her courage, chose a bedroom and boarded up the window both inside and out to make it impossible for her to escape. They ushered her in and tied the door handle to another door so that she wouldn't be able open it.

"Call us if you need anything," General Sam told her.

Rebecca lay down on the bed. As long as she was bound there was no chance of escaping. She knew that she could pass from life to death at any time, as easily as taking a drink of water. She thought about her family, about the anguish that they would be feeling at her disappearance, and fell into an exhausted sleep filled with nightmares.

Rebecca woke up drenched in perspiration with no idea of how long she had slept. She was very thirsty. She struggled up off the bed and shuffled to the door. She tried the handle but the rope only allowed it to open a few inches. Hearing the movement the Porths rushed out of the living room.

"Where do you think you're going?" she heard a gruff voice booming out. "Didn't we tell you to call us?"

"I forgot," Rebecca said as they untied the door. "I'm still half-asleep. Why are you shouting, as if I were strangling you?"

"Night has fallen. You've been asleep for many hours." Sam said.

She went with them to the living room. "Well, dear generals, if you are not going to kill me now you must give me something to eat. You should also tell me what plans you have for me. Don't you think it's reasonable for me to know what my fate is to be?"

"You can eat but we're not telling you anything until tomorrow morning," General Sam told her.

"That's unreasonable. I've been a prisoner for more than twenty-four hours. Do you consider it right to keep me in suspense, you three experienced generals?"

"We're following orders," said General Max. "And, being generals, we have to follow them to the letter. We cannot tell you anything. Eat and go back to bed."

Rebecca ate and then went to the bedroom. This time the Porths tied her to the bed.

She thought about King Turgoth. He was certainly the most interesting creature she had ever met. His experience, the observations of thousands of years, and the changes he had witnessed in his life gave him a distinctive charm. Many of his mature and honestly expressed observations kept coming back into her head.

Rebecca eventually drifted off to sleep. When she woke the next morning she shouted for the Porths. General Tom opened the door and stared in at her.

"You're awake! Did you sleep well?" he asked.

"Not even slaves are bound like this," she complained.

In the living room a fine breakfast was laid out, with many delicacies and fruits and they all sat down to eat.

"It looks like the last meal for a condemned woman," Rebecca commented.

When they'd finished eating, General Sam looked at his comrades and then at the young Orizon.

"Rebecca, we have orders to tell you what is about to happen. The king told us to ask you, twenty-four hours after we picked you up, if you'd had second thoughts and had decided to cooperate. If your answer is negative then we are to ask you once more tomorrow morning. If your answer is still negative then we are to repeat the question the following morning at daybreak. If you have not changed your mind by then we'll execute you when the first rays of the sun appear. Those are our orders. Do you have anything to say?"

"Thank you for telling me of your plans at last. When you see the king, thank him on my behalf for giving me time to think. He is very wise and he acts prudently. He tries to explore all avenues for the good of his people. But I'm not going to change my mind. So don't bother asking me again tomorrow or the day after tomorrow. Just go ahead and execute me."

Rebecca did not sound like someone about to die, more like a schoolgirl about to go on an excursion. The Porths were left confused and puzzled.

"We are obliged to ask you again tomorrow morning and the day after tomorrow. Otherwise we wouldn't be following our orders," insisted General Tom.

Rebecca found it hard to tell the Porths apart. They looked and behaved so much alike, as if they were made from the same patterned cloth. She wondered how it was that they didn't get mixed up themselves.

"Have you any children? Have you got families?" she asked later.

"We have families and children are very much part of them," General Tom replied. "Our women can give birth once every five hundred Earth years. I have three children, General Sam has two and so has General Max. We also have grandchildren, great-grandchildren and great-great-grandchildren."

"Why do you fight wars? After all, you're immortal: you don't fall ill and you don't need the Flame."

The Porths exchanged puzzled looks and said nothing. They'd never thought about it before. Rebecca watched them and waited patiently. General Sam motioned to the other two. They got up and went outside.

She could hear them muttering and arguing for nearly two hours before they returned. General Sam cleared his throat before speaking for all of them.

"After holding a strategic conference and having examined the matter from all possible angles, we have to reply that we don't know why we fight, since there is no benefit for us and we are under no obligation to do so. Although we Porths are very clever creatures, this has never occurred to us. But we fight with all our might to bring the Flame to Beast, just like our first king told us to do."

Rebecca looked at each one of them in turn, like a stern schoolteacher, and said:

"So you think it's right for you, your families and your children to be killed for no reason whatsoever? It's unbelievable! On Earth too they kill each other but there is always some kind of pretext used to justify these wars, even if the real reason is camouflaged."

The Porths listened carefully. They looked unhappy. Changing tack, Rebecca asked them about their children and grandchildren; their lives were genuinely interesting to such an eager student of life as she was.

They were obviously not very bright creatures, despite their claim to be clever, and she wondered how they had ever made the rank of general. Then she remembered that on Earth too there were people in high-ranking positions who lacked intelligence but on whom thousands of lives depended.

"You go to war for the sake of other people's interests." Rebecca returned to the subject the next day. "They send you to kill and be killed. But if you stayed neutral who would harm you? If you tell King Turgoth that you don't want to fight any more for Sharkan interests, I believe that he will understand. Then you can live in peace. Tell the Cyclopes the same thing. Why do they go to war? So, the day after tomorrow, after you have executed me, go to Turgoth. You must struggle for peace and for your rights."

The generals looked at her without replying.

The second day passed in much the same way. But on the third day, as dawn approached, the Porths got up and prepared themselves to carry out the king's orders to the letter. If Rebecca persisted in her decision, they would have to kill her at the exact moment when the sun began to rise.

When they entered her room she was still asleep. They were amazed that anyone could sleep so soundly at such a moment.

"Perhaps she has decided to compromise," General Tom suggested. "Maybe that has allowed her to sleep."

When they woke Rebecca she opened her eyes and smiled at them as if she had been enjoying the most pleasant dream.

"What time is it?" she asked. "I'm still sleepy."

"What did I tell you?" said General Tom happily. "Look! The girl is relaxed and wants to sleep. She has such a sweet smile, too ..."

Their expressions were transformed from those of the bloodthirsty, warlike generals of the past. Their faces softened and kind, like those of happy children, they looked like creatures whom no one would have recognised.

The previous night they had discussed Rebecca's words for hours and had decided that as soon as they had followed their orders and returned to Beast they would talk to the other two Porth generals. Then they would go to see the king. They would tell him that they wouldn't go to war again but would live in peace with their families. They were sure that the other generals would join them in this decision once they'd thought about it.

"If you want to go back to sleep, go ahead," said Sam sweetly. "You must have reached the right decision."

"No, my worthy generals," Rebecca said. "I cannot make any other decisions. But it's true that I'm still sleepy. However, if you have orders to kill me before sunrise, let's get it over with." She closed her eyes as she spoke. "It would have been better if you'd killed me without waking me up, so that I wouldn't have felt anything."

Realizing that nothing had changed, the Porths became agitated and confused. They sat on the bed speechless, their hands clutching their cheeks, looking as if they all had toothache. Then General Sam leaped up suddenly.

"The sun is going to rise," he cried. "We have to kill her."

"How shall we kill her?" General Max asked, his eyes swivelling in panic. "All three of us together?"

"The king told us to execute her with her own sword," General Sam reminded him. "Straight through the heart, so we can't do it together. Who's going to kill her? Does either of you want to?"

None of them spoke but all of them were horribly aware that time was passing.

"I've got it!" General Sam said triumphantly. "We'll cast lots – quickly, though, because it's getting late. If the sun rises, we'll have disobeyed our orders."

So they cast lots and the duty fell to General Max. He went to fetch Rebecca's sword, walking as if he was going to his own execution.

Rebecca looked round the room and then at the two remaining Porths.

"I'll blindfold you so you won't see Max put the blade through your heart," General Tom said.

"I don't mind that, general. But I'd rather die outdoors, close to Nature and looking at the trees, than in this room, looking at four lifeless walls. Can you take me outside?"

"Sure. Why not? We'll take you outside," General Max said as he came back into the room.

They cut the ropes from Rebecca's feet, allowing her to stand up. They walked outside, surrounding her, unsure how to behave, their movements awkward.

"Oh, no!" cried General Sam. "We've disobeyed our orders. The sun is already rising."

Their faces were a picture of dismay. Never in their lives had they disobeyed an order or allowed any of their subordinates to do so. General Sam had actually executed subordinates who had committed such an offence. The other two generals said nothing but they looked equally unhappy.

Rebecca looked up at the sky and breathed deeply. She saw an isolated old oak standing close to the house and walked towards it. The Porths followed her as though hypnotized.

"Do you too happen to speak?" she asked the tree when she reached it. But it did not answer. She leaned her back against it and felt it shudder. It seemed to her that it touched her very tenderly, as if it was caressing her, giving her courage.

Rebecca noticed a couple of woodcocks playing in the air just above the treetops. They seemed to be showering in the fresh sunbeams, making themselves clean and beautiful. Their morning calls were the prelude to their mating dance. She felt jealous of their freedom and the feeling started to tear her apart.

General Max raised the sword slightly as he approached her. His legs were shaking. Her vision blurred as her gaze left the amorous pair of birds and fixed on the crystal blade, which her grandfather had made and had given to her for her protection. She watched it coming close to her heart. An ice-cold current flowed through her veins, making her shudder.

Rebecca longed for the pleasures of her past: for the lion, her paintings, her music. "I shall never see the moon again," she whispered.

She looked up at the sky again but the woodcocks had disappeared.

"Generals of the Porths," she said, "for the first time I feel something that must be fear. I'm too cowardly to look at the sword as it penetrates me. I'm sorry, but could you please blindfold me?"

General Max stopped in his tracks and General Tom trudged back to the house to fetch something with which to blindfold her. Rebecca looked at the sky again. The sun had risen completely now, sleepless and upset by a nightmare. It opened its eyes, and as soon as it saw Rebecca it realized that its bad dream had come true. It looked at her as if to say: "*It's your fault that you're going to die, not mine. You will never get to enjoy life, like the woodcocks. You can change everything in an instant if you want to. Decide!*"

Resisting her first and final temptation, Rebecca shouted out loudly:

"No, no! Leave it. I don't need the blindfold. Just kill me!"

All the forest heard her, including the two woodcocks that were hidden now but were snuggling up to one another.

Rebecca thrust her chest forward to receive the blow bravely. General Max raised the sword again and resumed his approach as the sun went pale and the sky turned yellow. The girl's vision grew cloudy and time seemed to freeze. Her mouth was dry and she struggled to breathe. She could hear her pulse pounding like a drum.

A horse charged out of the forest, carrying Death himself in his flowing black robe. It seemed as though Death was being held by Bull from behind. Bull leaped from the horse, followed by the cloaked figure.

Bull let out a loud war cry which could be heard all the way to the skies and ran towards them. The Porths drew their weapons and General Max threw Rebecca's sword onto the ground. Bull pulled out four daggers and immediately hurled three at the Porths.

Death yelled, "No ... no ... no!" and fell to his knees. He slumped forward and held his head between his hands. Then he just watched, although his empty eyes saw nothing.

With each 'no' a dagger flew into the throat of one of the Porths, bringing them toppling to the ground where they writhed and died. Bull ran to Rebecca, cutting the ropes round her wrists and taking her into his arms. He held her tight, spinning her round and round and kissing her joyfully, crying with great heart-rending sobs.

"You're alive. Alive! I can't believe it."

When Bull eventually put her down and she saw that the Porths were dead, Rebecca picked up her sword and replaced it in its scabbard. Death was still crumpled on the floor with his head in his hands. Then she recognized him. Bull took her by the hand and they walked towards Turgoth.

"King Turgoth, let's go into the house for a while to recover," Bull said, surprising Rebecca with his respectful tone.

Turgoth rose and walked with them, talking to himself. "A king's duty is to die for his homeland. It's too great an honour to leave it for someone else to do. What shall I tell their children? What shall I tell their families? What shall I tell my people? We've lost four generals and another one is crippled for life. I've betrayed my people. I'm guilty and there is nothing to alleviate my guilt. I'm losing my mind."

Both Rebecca and Bull understood what he meant. As they sat him down, Rebecca noticed that Turgoth had a large wound encrusted with dry blood where his left ear had once been.

"Bull," Turgoth moaned, "you should have thrown your fourth dagger at me. Put an end to my misery. How can I go back and face my people after what I've done? I can't become a chameleon and a trickster. I have to tell the truth."

"The truth is that I abducted you and cut off your ear."

Then Bull turned to Rebecca.

"You should know that it wasn't me who saved you; it was the king. That's the truth. I'm sure you'll remember it for the rest of your life."

Rebecca looked at Turgoth but did not speak. She was still very confused.

Turgoth's head was bowed. Eventually he said: "This house belonged to our first king. He built it a short while before he was killed. He used to come here from time to time to rest. I rarely use it. Have something to eat if you wish. We must see to your horse, Bull. It needs a rest so that it can carry you back. I'd give you the carriage but I need it to carry the dead bodies. I'd rather you left your daggers in them where they are, Bull. I want to take them like that for the people to see."

Turgoth wandered off to a bedroom in search of a uniform. When he came back, he and Bull took care of Bull's horse, harnessed the other horses to the carriage and laid the dead bodies carefully inside it. Then they went back to the living room where Rebecca had been waiting for them.

Turgoth was thoughtful and looked sad. "If my people still accept me as their leader after all this I'm going to prepare my forces better than ever before and attack Utopia. If I'm defeated again, I'll resign."

Rebecca knew from the look in his eyes that when he said 'resign' Turgoth meant that if he lost the battle he would ensure that he was killed.

"Give your attention to the Earth," the king told her. "Read, seek and ask questions. You'll find that all that I've told you is true. I'm a historian. I'm well aware that the facts are constantly being distorted to serve other people's ulterior motives."

"Yes, that's true," Bull said. "Prehistory most of all. Those times are shrouded in complete darkness for humans, exciting their imaginations and filling them with inaccuracies. They have misjudged the eras by several thousands of years. They can't explain even simple things. They can't understand how pyramids exist in separate parts of the Earth, all of them built at a time when communication between the continents was supposedly impossible. How are they to know that the people who had lived then would soon return to Earth?"

Turgoth nodded approvingly: "Everybody talks about the Great Flood even though they don't know when, how or why it happened. Isn't that so, Bull?"

"Yes. People have no idea, Rebecca." said Bull and the expression on his face became childlike once more, something that pleased the young Orizon. Bull sat down and went on: "Historians often become storytellers. History is one of the most distorted of disciplines, as the king knows better than me. But if you look deep enough you will discover the truth."

"We who are older, Bull, know that all people have some jealousy, hatred and desire for revenge in their make-up. If Rebecca can to some extent suppress those passions and limit their growth, then she will be successful on Earth. This is the basis on which to construct a solution to the rest of the problems," Turgoth said.

"That's right," said Bull. "You must not allow those negative impulses to flourish, Rebecca. It is an onerous and difficult task that you face. To succeed you should minimise the differences among people, differences which those in power create deliberately."

"Do you really believe that I can achieve so much on Earth? It seems to me too much and too complicated. I feel too small and powerless to achieve what you tell me."

Turgoth looked at Bull and then at Rebecca.

"We in Beast – apart from the problem with the Flame – have a good life. We have everything that Nature provides. We read, we entertain ourselves, we love, we enjoy art. We are content.

"That's how people should live on Earth. You must take the Flame so as to live in eternity. You must strive to light people's hearts with love, understanding, patience, humanity. Don't you agree, Bull, that she is capable of it?

"I trust Rebecca, too," answered Bull. "She should be able to keep jealousy, hatred and the wish for revenge at bay. She will fight for it. Put Earth in order, Rebecca, and then try to maintain it. If, as the king says, you are able to nullify the causes that make evil grow among people, then everything will turn out well."

"Apart from the problems with every individuals" said Turgoth, "the biggest difficulty is the group of people who control everything and promote social inequalities.

"All the world's riches, Rebecca, are in the hands of a few powerful families. Wars never stop and the young, the old and especially the innocent – children, mainly – are killed. The Orizons know very well who makes wars happen and why.

"After careful planning, the powerful ones prepared a vaccine for what is called variously: Freedom, Democracy, Justice, Equality, Solidarity. They injected all the people on Earth while they knew very well that only after death do people achieve true equality. The world was divided in two big camps: Right and Left."

"That is, people in the right and people in the wrong," said Bull sarcastically. "Each side considers the other to be responsible for what they are going through."

"That's what I think, too," Rebecca interrupted.

Turgoth nodded in agreement and added: "Propaganda that violates the people's brains creates hatred, jealousy and a passion for vengeance. Social strife is a satanic plan that bears fruit. It creates fanaticism.

"Mass psychology has been analysed intensively so as to ascertain the best methods – which are then applied. Bloody revolutions are provoked that result in pain, misery, unhappiness and, of course, death. All those impressive-sounding but actually false theories bring confusion. Like Gods, they divide the world, both socially and politically. They give to people's hearts and minds counterfeit hopes and enthusiasm for impossible conquests. They provide false and utopian guidelines to generations of people."

A little diffidently, Rebecca added her opinion:

"I think they deliberately take advantage, mixing religion and politics and exploiting them according to their own selfish interests. All those victims of fanaticism pick up flags and rush out chanting slogans, cheering, hating, fighting, destroying, sabotaging and creating chaos. It is the younger people who usually act like this, according to my father. They're deluded into believing that what they do is right and proper. That's why they sacrifice themselves, go to prison, kill and get killed. They keep sucking the manufactured sweets they've been given by those who sacrifice them. My father has always told me to be wary of such arguments."

"Most people are not aware that they have become instruments in the hands of the people in power and in this way they serve the same purpose as their opponents," said Turgoth. "Maybe a few are aware of it but they are powerless to do anything. And if they dare to express their opinions they become objects of ridicule from both sides."

"I think that internal strife, discord, violence, hatred, fanaticism and chaos exist for no rhyme or reason," said Rebecca, "and, most of all, to no positive, meaningful effect."

Bull stood up and gripped the only dagger he had left, looking as if he wanted to kill all the human predators responsible. He drew his knife and hurled it against a door so hard that it almost passed through it. He then sat down, much calmer.

As he went on to speak, Turgoth thought again that it would have been better if he had been the target. He looked angry too.

"The Orizons have remained mere spectators and, though they know who is to blame, they do nothing about it. They observe the international chessboard and the world leaders who move the pawns," sighed Turgoth sadly.

Bull jumped up once more.

"There is no chessboard, King Turgoth, there is no such game – because there are no opponents. For a true game to be played at least two opponents are needed. But there's only one team and its members are the pre-ordained winners. They don't need to play chess or any other game and they never take any risks.

"As you know, King Turgoth, most of the rest of humanity are in effect prisoners because their spirits and their hearts are imprisoned. They've become robots, doing what they've been programmed to do, consciously or in ignorance, but always according to the plans of those powerful groups. The only 'opponents' are the divided prisoners themselves, Rebecca. When there is a plan for profit or experiment, they make them fight or kill each other. This terrible fact is very difficult to change."

They all fell silent, lost in thought. Then Turgoth rose and stood before Bull, who had sat down again.

"You may be right, Bull, about the chess."

Then he moved towards Rebecca and, looking at her, he connected with her mind, creating a kind of visual transfusion.

"I'm going to tell you what I foresee and what I believe about you, Rebecca. You've been born to win. You will play chess with them! You will become the opposing team, as Bull put it. I'm sure you're going to stand out. Even if you don't win the game,

I'm sure that you will make things difficult for them, these bloodsuckers who monopolize everything. You may force them to revise some of their one-sided plans. You may even have to govern the whole Earth. I can imagine that you do not care for such a thing but you must do it for the sake of Good. You must do it because you have both the charisma and the qualifications. You'll become a shining source of workable new ideas. What do you think, Bull?"

"I too believe that Rebecca can, when she grows up and matures, give much to the world," the Minotaur answered.

"I'm glad we're of the same opinion, Bull. For thousands of years philosophers, ideologues, sociologists and politicians as well as all religions have tried without success to define the nature of Good.

"Some link it to knowledge, values, logic and prudence, but all these are relative. That is to say, Rebecca, they believe that whoever knows a lot knows what Good is ..."

"It sounds preposterous," said Bull indignantly. "But unfortunately, Rebecca, what the king says is true."

"Many people maintain," Turgoth went on, "that the power of the word, good persuasive oratory, can convince people of what is Good. And this, regrettably, happens too often."

Turgoth continued to stand in front of Rebecca and to look at her with his penetrating stare.

"I believe," he said, "that there are limits to goodness, while Evil is endless. I also believe that at present goodness is powerless and hatred is invincible. Yet all this can change. You, Rebecca, can define Good with your heart and the Orizons will always follow you as well as all the forces of Good.

"With you at the helm, the hungry will eat, the thirsty will drink and the naked will be clothed. For those burning in the sun, you will be a protective shadow and the soft breeze that cools them."

Bull interrupted Turgoth. He rose, went to the door and pulled his dagger from the wood. He put it back in its sheath and stood next to Turgoth. He too looked at Rebecca.

"Rebecca, you must work for justice. They say that justice is blind. Well, then you must take the blindfold from her eyes. Judges must be alert and open-minded, healthy in body and mind, intelligent, well-read and hard-working. Above all, they must be conscientious, because conscience is the only just judge and, as Rousseau said, it is the voice of God in our soul ..."

"Excuse my interrupting you," said Rebecca, "but what you tell me seems a huge burden to me."

Turgoth kept looking her straight in the eye.

"Justice holds a pair of scales in her hands but judges have to be taught how to use them properly."

"How are they to do this, King Turgoth, since they don't have weights?" asked Bull thoughtfully. "They have to find weights. When the judge strikes the gavel to start the trial, it is as if he hits Justice on the head to disorientate her. So she stays confused during the whole process. When it is time to announce the verdict he pounds her on the head again and one last time at the end of the trial. Most of the time this last use of the gavel is the final blow to an already stupefied Justice."

"I agree with you, Bull," said Turgoth. "I think that no judge has ever asked for pardon even if any mistake that he's made has been proven. How can such a man sleep at night, I wonder? How many innocent people have been executed? How many have rotted in prison? How do the jurors feel when they discover that their verdict was wrong? As with judges, has there ever been a juror who has said that he was sorry?"

"Surely there are judges who shine like beacons in the chaos of darkness," said Bull and his eyes shone too. "But many of their colleagues – indeed, the system in general – try desperately to extinguish their flame."

"Yes, that is so," said Turgoth, his voice deepening. "For me, Rebecca, the combination and coexistence of the tragic with the comic represent the real state of the fleeting human life.

"I want you to know that I feel no remorse for giving the order for your kidnapping. I want Bull to know this, too. It was a political act. But I will regret till the day when I'm killed the lies that I told Lord Life when he came looking for you. It was the first time I ever told a lie."

The visual transfusion stopped as Turgoth stepped back. Bull took Rebecca's hand, helping her to rise.

"I may not see you again. I definitely don't want to meet you in Lomani. It would be very painful for me, and for you too, I think," Turgoth said.

He bent his head and kissed Rebecca's forehead. His eyes were full of tears. "I wish you ... good luck."

"Thank you, King Turgoth. I wish the same for you."

Rebecca stood on tiptoe and kissed the king's wet cheeks, tasting there the pain, love, affection, respect and admiration that he had been unable to hide.

As she and Bull rode away she turned to look back at Turgoth standing outside his house. He raised his hand and waved until they had disappeared. Rebecca was reminded of the lion in Kenya.

When they stopped later for a rest Bull explained what had happened when he had come to the house and seen her. "I couldn't assess the situation immediately," he confessed. "I saw you standing at the tree with your hands tied behind you and a

Porth with a sword near you. I couldn't take any risks. I hadn't expected to find you alive.

"Turgoth kept telling me that we had to hurry. He became anxious and misty-eyed as we drew close. He was torn between remorse for his people and his desire for your rescue. *"That girl must live,"* he kept on saying. When dawn came he lost heart. When the sun rose, although we were quite close to the house, he held his head in despair and said: *"Bull, we've lost her. Rebecca is dead for sure."* It was then that I too lost hope, because he spoke with such conviction and desperation. A few minutes later we reached the house."

"They had been ordered to execute me when the first rays of the sun became visible," Rebecca explained. "Because they were a few minutes late you were able save me."

Rebecca then told Bull all that Turgoth had done for her. Giving her three days to think, and before that, in his house, offering her the sword to kill him, and, later, leaving her alone, giving her a chance to grab the sword, murder him and escape.

"Tell me, Bull, don't you think the Sharkans should have the same privileges as the Orizons and that we should both share the Flame?"

Bull seemed thoughtful. Then he said:

"The right thing would be to share it. But that cannot be done now, not after so many wars and so much bloodshed. A bad beginning was made. The Mythical Gods shouldn't have imposed such discrimination."

"And you, Bull, why do you fight on our side in support of such an injustice since the Flame doesn't concern you?"

"I found myself on this side. I had to belong somewhere. I like what I do. I rarely fight in battle. The Creator decided that there should be no female Minotaurs and that I should not have

children. If I had my own children, I would not be so concerned with the souls and minds of the other children. What I do now is the best, the most interesting thing to do. Children are our hope."

"I lost my courage in the end," Rebecca said. "When I saw the sword coming towards me, I felt fear for the first time in my life as well as a craving for life. Maybe it was because of the birds and the sun. I soon recovered, though. Maybe it was Moira's hand that caused a delay of a few seconds, so you saved me. Have you ever been afraid?"

"Yes, I flinched once when I was on the Earth, thousands of years ago. It's a long story. I may tell it to you one day. Don't let it worry you that you were frightened. Remember that you're human. There are weaknesses that are shielded by the Flame, making you an Orizon. The Flame in you has weakened a little from so many unexpected adventures. That's why you all need a second dose at this age, a dose which will last for ever. It's like recharging a battery."

Then they talked about the traitor in Utopia and agreed to discuss it only with Princess Felicia. They decided, however, not to mention anything that would sully King Turgoth's reputation.

It was almost noon when they reached Rebecca's house. As soon as they heard Bull's horse, her parents and grandparents rushed outside, crying for joy. Rebecca jumped down from the horse and Bull galloped away. He wanted to leave the family alone and knew that their gratitude would embarrass him.

"We must get ready," Rebecca told them after a few moments, "because I'm going to meet Bull in an hour at the princess's house."

Soon the signal of the three-dimensional projection was

heard and Felicia appeared to announce the good news to the people of Utopia. She also informed them that the ceremony of the Flame for Rebecca would take place the following day at six and that a big celebration would follow.

The people started to come out of their houses onto the streets of the Fortress, cheering at the news that Rebecca had killed a Sharkan general and rendered another useless, and that Bull had killed three Porth generals. They saw it as a great victory for the forces of Good against Evil. Rebecca was already a heroine in Utopia.

That evening Rebecca road to the theatre and went straight to the Wise Tree of Knowledge. They embraced and she sat down.

"I heard the good news. Everyone is celebrating. I can imagine how you must be feeling after such an adventure. I was very unhappy. I thought I'd lost you and that now I'd never learn how to read books," the Tree teased.

"Do you believe it is justified for the forces of Beast to wage war against the people of Utopia?" Rebecca asked.

"No war is justified," the Tree said after a moment's thought. "Wars degrade values. Values and killings don't go together. Wars should be abolished."

"So, in your opinion, the war of Beast against Utopia is not justified?"

The Wise Tree did not answer.

"Think about it and I'll ask you again in a few days. Also, why are the people of Beast considered the bad ones? Why do we call them the powers of Evil and ourselves the powers of Good?"

"I promise you that I'll think hard and give you my honest opinion."

"Have these issues never troubled you before?"

"Sometimes we don't want to trouble ourselves with questions, nor search for answers, nor even think about certain subjects. There are some things in life that become established and we accept them without thought."

"You've answered all my queries. I don't need anything else."

Rebecca stood up, said goodnight and left.

The next day, Rebecca's Flame ceremony took place.

Lord Life arrived on Pegasus with his Lady, making his usual circle flying low over the theatre tiers. After inhaling the Flame, Rebecca announced:

"Thank you all for your great concern and for your many efforts to find me after my abduction. I want to thank you also for your demonstrations of love ever since I came back. I'd like to thank Bull the Minotaur in particular. He is the greatest protector of children and adolescents. All of us are his adopted children. Bull would certainly lay down his life for each and every child if the need ever arose, because he loves us very much. He believes that the future depends on the children.

"So we all must strive for a better future. A future without wars, without bloodshed and misery, both here and on the Earth. I promise, with the strength that the Flame gives me, to try not to disappoint Bull's hopes."

Felicia raised her hands to silence the roar of applause. She told Rebecca that she had become immortal and that she must keep this a secret for ever. Then the Tree repeated what it had told the other children about secrets.

A big party followed, after which Rebecca said farewell to her parents, who returned to Earth with Bull.

The following day she talked to her grandfather.

"Can you tell me, grandpa, why you went to Field Marshal Foster's on the day of my abduction and why we didn't all leave the house together?"

"Foster asked me to go and pick him up so that we could go to Claudia's house together. The energy system at her house was malfunctioning and she had asked for his help. Foster knows a bit about it but not as much as I do. He had tried to do a temporary repair job, but it had got much worse.

"We went there together and I had no serious difficulty in fixing the problem. Then we all left for the ceremony."

Rebecca listened in silence, wondering what the Field Marshal's real role might have been.

THE TREACHERY CONTINUES

The children entered a new phase as their war training became more difficult and more strenuous. In Claudia's classes they now had to learn how to avoid arrows or use their shields to deflect them. They began to use their bows, spears and javelins while on horseback.

Field Marshal Foster's classes were the most dangerous because they were about single combat. The students learned how to dodge lethal blows and how to manoeuvre and attack precisely, methodically and effectively. Foster used experienced Orizons as his assistants and they fought as fiercely as they did in Lomani.

Because Lomani was usually waged around the Fortress and in a certain part of Domus Forest, the children trained in the woods. They learned how to use trees and bushes for camouflage as well as how to set traps and how to avoid them. They would hide and make surprise attacks. A few days later they began to participate fully in the exercises that were organized for all the combatants of Utopia. Following Rebecca's abduction, group exercises became more frequent. Felicia was worried that Turgoth might start a war at any moment.

Felicia and all the other leaders were most perturbed because with Rebecca's abduction Turgoth had violated all the rules and treaties. They could no longer predict how he might behave, what his next move might be and whether he would strike again in a similarly devious manner.

But the days went by and nothing untoward happened. In ten days' time the first term of training would come to an end. The course would conclude with a two-day training exercise in Domus Forest, with no instructors present. Then the children would visit Lord Life's house where they were to stay for three nights. After that they would go back to Utopia and the following day they'd return to Earth.

In addition to her regular training, Rebecca had begged Bull to show her how to use the dagger. She had been impressed by its effectiveness as a weapon and wanted to become an expert with it.

Bull spent many afternoons giving her systematic instruction and Rebecca soon realized it would take many months, if not years, to get results. She and Bull kept talking about the traitor in their midst, speculating about who it might be. Bull told her to rule Foster out, assuring her that it must have been a coincidence that her grandparents had left earlier because of him.

"Foster is one of the most praiseworthy Orizons in the history of the Land of the White Sun," he said. "He's dedicated, fearless and brave. If you saw how he fights in Lomani you wouldn't believe your eyes. He's always at the front. He lost his wife in combat and then his only son, who was also a fine warrior.

"Even though he's a charming man and has had many marriage proposals, he has remained faithful to his wife's memory for hundreds of years. It's said that Claudia has been in love with him for a very long time, but Foster has kept to his decision to live without a wife and not have any more children. He will hold to this vow until the day he is killed.

"Rebecca, I firmly believe that Foster is above suspicion. Put the idea out of your mind!"

The day arrived for the children to set out for their two-day exercise in Domus Forest and their visit to Lord Life. They assembled early in the morning at the training ground. Each student's equipment consisted of a sword, a shield, a spear, a bow and a quiverful of arrows. Their instructors gave them their final directions and the schedules that they were to follow together and separately. It was emphasized that they should work without a leader.

"You are a powerful team," Field Marshal Foster told them. "You will have to act both as a group and as individuals. All of you have reached the same level of training. If the need arises, you must act as one body and one soul to help anyone in need. You must perform the exercises according to the rules you have learned. Follow to the letter the instructions in the programme. Study them as soon as you enter Domus Forest at the spot where we train to climb and fight among the trees.

"You will not work under the supervision or guidance of an instructor. There must not be any single combats among you. You will eat nothing and drink nothing, not even water, until you reach Lord Life's house. Good luck!"

The children left the Fortress on foot. Finding the appointed location, they read their orders carefully.

"We have to cover a considerable distance today," Sergei said. "We'll be going deep into the forest, which will be fascinating. We may even see a dinosaur, if we're lucky."

"At some point we separate and then each of us has a different path to follow," Abu said as he read through the schedules. "We all meet up again for the night. We'll have to be really careful when we enter the denser parts of the jungle. It may seem like fun at first, but a jungle always conceals great dangers. I grew up in similar surroundings – we must be extra careful not to get lost or have an accident."

"It might have been better," said Louise, "if in our first-ever instructorless exercise we stayed in pairs, especially at the point where in fact we each individually have to follow a different route. But our instructors must know what they're doing. So let's get on with it."

They began their first exercise by climbing the enormous trees and fighting a mock battle among the branches and hanging fibres, keeping only their swords and leaving the rest of their equipment on the ground.

The foliage of the tall trees was tightly intertwined, creating a green canopy that blocked out nearly all the view of the sky. The children swung from one tree to another, like Tarzan, fighting a simulated sword battle in the air. At certain points they would jump down to the ground and continue their pretend swordplay there. While they were high up, they had to hang from the fibre ropes, having been ordered to make no attempt to fly.

They presented a wonderful spectacle as their crystal swords flashed in the few bright rays of sunlight that filtered through the thick foliage. They looked like exotic blue and white birds in their uniforms as they leaped, fit and agile, from tree to tree. They were acrobat-warriors, fighting an invisible enemy in an imaginary war.

After an hour's battle they picked up their equipment and carried on with their journey, encountering species of animals and birds that they had never seen before.

The moment arrived for them to separate and follow different paths. In three hours' time they were to meet up at the place where they would camp for the night.

Rebecca followed the map showing her designated route and in a short while came across a river. Her orders stated that she was not to try to swim across with her uniform and equipment, as the waters were deep and turbulent. She had to find another way.

The only solution that she could think of was to build a small raft. Putting down her equipment, she ran back into the trees, using her sword to cut some fibres and sturdy branches. She carried them back to the river-bank as fast as she could, repeating the trip three times.

Rebecca used the thicker branches to construct the raft's main frame and the smaller ones to fill the spaces in between. An hour later the raft was ready. She carefully secured all her gear on it and placed her clothes and boots in her upturned shield. Then she pushed the raft into the water and, holding on to it with one hand, began to swim across the river.

Despite the strong current pulling her downstream, Rebecca steered the raft diagonally across to the opposite bank. She pulled it out and dressed quickly. Then she tried to pinpoint her exact location on the map. She hadn't drifted far off course but she had lost quite a bit of time. She now only had one hour left to reach the meeting point.

The sky filled up with warm colours, a melancholy beauty saluting the passing day that was passing by. Soon the night would take its brush and paint the heavens a uniform black. Rebecca watched the setting sun with a sense of devotion as it made its escape, exchanging silent promises with it that they would be together again the following day. The mountains lay slumbering as the departing sun blanketed them in deep purple. A few clouds, filled with grey and white down, scudded past as if trying to avoid being painted black. The birds were singing a victorious anthem for Rebecca, while the river blushed with reflected fading sunlight as if in embarrassment at having been defeated by the young Orizon. Then the birds swooped down to take their last sips of water for the day and bade Rebecca farewell, congratulating her once again on her victory, before flying off into the trees to give the last concert of the day before going to sleep. They would try to dream of God, to ask Him if they had done their duty that day too and if He was happy with them.

Rebecca entered a dense part of the forest filled with enormous trees of a kind she had never seen before. Their soft trunks were green with moss and they were shaped like huge umbrellas. She wondered if this might be the area where the dinosaurs roamed; there was certainly room for them beneath the high canopy and the ends of some of the long branches reached low enough, sometimes almost touching the ground, for tall herbivorous creatures to graze comfortably.

By the time Rebecca reached the meeting point night had fallen and several of the children were already resting there. Only four of them had not yet turned up. The same large trees and thick vegetation surrounded the spot where they were going to be spending the night. As the remaining children arrived they talked, bubbling with excitement, about their adventures along the way.

Their programme instructed them to choose sleeping places that were neither too close together nor too far apart. Having selected their spots and left their equipment they gathered again to talk. Proud of what they had achieved and exhausted by their efforts, they all soon decided to get some sleep.

As the children stood to go to their sleeping areas, a ferocious screaming noise made them spin round. Two gigantic, horrifying creatures burst from the trees, running straight at them.

"The Gorgons, the Gorgons!" Samantha shouted. "Don't look at them, anyone."

Covering their eyes Samantha, Louise, Susan, Tamina and Rebecca ran into the forest. After only a few yards they realized that the boys weren't with them.

"We need a leader," Samantha said. "One of us must take charge. I don't think the arrival of the Gorgons was in our instructors' plans."

"The Gorgons are neutral, aren't they?" asked Louise. "So maybe they had no intention of harming us –"

"It's no good discussing it," Samantha interrupted. "Do you agree that we need a leader?"

The other girls all nodded.

"I propose Rebecca."

The others agreed unanimously.

"We mustn't waste time," Rebecca said. "Let's go back cautiously and try to find out what's happened to the others. Stay well hidden and don't look into the Gorgons' eyes. Despite their awful shrieks they may wish us no harm."

The girls dropped to the ground and crawled as they had been taught during their training. Peering through the undergrowth they saw that all ten boys had been turned to stone, frozen into a variety of positions. The Gorgons appeared to be furious about something: their huge, sharp teeth protruded gruesomely from their mouths as they flapped their golden wings and flexed their bronze arms restlessly. The knots of serpents on their heads hissed, writhing in a frenzy of anger, their heads and tongues darting in all directions in search of something or someone to inject their venom into.

"There were five girls," the Gorgon called Stheno said. "How did they get away? I can't believe it. We have to find them."

"They probably ran back to Utopia to get reinforcements," her sister, Euryale, said. "Even if they've hidden somewhere, we won't find them easily. The forest is enormous and they're well trained. I suggest that we move these boys to our lair and wait. The girls may come back to look for them and then we can turn them to stone or tear them to pieces."

Without waiting for a reply she picked up two of the stone boys as if they were mannequins weighing next to nothing and ran off. Stheno grabbed two more with equal ease, holding them under her arms and following. They reappeared a few minutes later to scoop up four more.

"Don't move," Rebecca instructed the girls. "When they come to get the last two, I'll follow them. One of you will follow me from a distance, then another and then the others. We won't be together but we'll be able to look out for one another. If I give the signal, the first in line is to come close to me and the others will follow. Otherwise, keep your distance. Stay clear of the serpents, they're venomous: one bite means instant death."

When Euryale snatched up the last two boys Rebecca followed at a distance. The other girls brought up the rear as they'd been told. The Gorgon disappeared into a thick cluster of trees. Rebecca inched forward until she reached the clearing where the lair of the Gorgons lay. It was like a large room, with a natural roof of leaves and branches, the darkness lit by two torches. There were two gigantic beds, a table and two outsized chairs. Euryale was sitting while Stheno paced to and fro among the frozen boys.

"I think they're lying low and will come back to look for their friends. We must get them. We've promised all fifteen children," Stheno said.

"I don't know if we should be involved at all," Euryale muttered. "We could end up losing our neutrality if we're caught meddling. We've maintained it for such a long time, and we've had a good life as a result. This could bring trouble for us. The whole of Utopia will soon be searching for these children. They'll be outraged."

"I'm tired of being impartial," said Stheno. "I need some action. What do we do, day in and day out? Eat and sleep, that's all. I want to kill – and kill Orizons above all! I hate them so. We have made a deal now and we must carry out our side of it without fail. The Porth and Cyclopes generals, who told us about this meeting point, want to surprise Turgoth with this gift; and *we* want to live in Beast and have houses and TV sets." As she talked the serpents on her head stretched out and hissed viciously. "Our children are thirsty. They want to sink their teeth into something, to drink blood."

"But our lives are comfortable," her sister Euryale grumbled, obviously not convinced. "We lack nothing. Why do we want to live among others? We're independent here, accountable to no one. Now we'll be answerable to others, perhaps even under their control. What for? Just to live in a house and watch television?"

"Why? Doesn't that excite you?" asked Stheno, continuing her agitated pacing. "Television will keep us company. We'll be able to watch hatred, jealousy, wars and battles. We'll watch killings, rapes, deception and other evil things, day and night. All these things are treasure to us."

"But if the people of Utopia find us," Euryale sighed, "they might kill us. Then these children will return to life and we won't have gained anything. So I suppose that we no longer have any choice in the matter: we must find those girls and let the serpents bite them. Then we can rip them apart and devour them. That way we'll get something out of it and we'll have delivered on our promises to Evil."

Rebecca had heard enough and she crawled back to find the other girls. Once they felt they were far enough away to whisper she told them what she had heard and seen. The only thing that she kept to herself was her realization that the Gorgons must have been tipped off about the children's exact movements. It had shaken her, confirming the existence of a traitor in Utopia – and a high-ranking one, at that. She wasn't ready to think about that yet. Their priority now was to free the boys by killing the monsters.

"We should go back to Utopia for reinforcements," Tamina suggested.

"That would take a whole day," Samantha pointed out.

"I can see the sense in that," Rebecca said. "But I don't like the idea of leaving the boys for so long. We have no idea how they're feeling. They looked like marble statues on the outside but their hearts and minds may still be working. Greek mythology never described the feelings of people petrified by Medusa. They may be in terrible anguish and every minute could be torture for them.

"I think we have to rescue them ourselves. I need to take the Gorgons by surprise and kill them. I will use my shield to protect myself from the serpents. When Perseus decapitated their sister, the serpents were still small, but in the thousands of years since then they have grown enormous.

"The danger is that in watching the movements of the snakes I may accidentally look into the Gorgons' eyes and be turned to stone myself. As far as I can remember the serpents only perish if their Gorgon's head is cut off.

"If I kill them, we'll be able to continue with our schedule. If something goes wrong I should have enough time to glance into their eyes and turn to stone before they kill me or their serpents bite me. That way they won't be able to hurt me before you get back with reinforcements."

"But if you *don't* manage to get turned to stone," Samantha said, "they'll certainly kill you and tear you to pieces with their teeth."

"In either case," Rebecca said, "you must then do your duty and go back for help."

The girls tried for a while to make her change her mind. But Rebecca remained adamant.

"I've made my decision. If they turn me to stone, then, when you save me, I'll be able to tell you about the experience."

"Rebecca," Samantha said, "I trust you implicitly and you're our leader. But I need to come with you."

"All right," Rebecca said, willing to accept that she might need some help in the forthcoming battle. "Bring your spear and shield and let's go."

They went to the spot where she had overheard the Gorgons' conversation. Both of the monsters seemed to have gone to bed now, although the torches were still burning.

"You attack from the right and I'll approach from the left," Rebecca whispered. "We'll try to spear them in their throats. Then we'll kill the snakes with our swords so that we can cut off the Gorgons' heads."

"Shouldn't we aim for their hearts?" Samantha asked.

"Gorgons have no hearts."

The two girls took deep breaths and charged at the beds. Samantha thrust her spear right through Euryale's throat. The sleeping Gorgon writhed for a few seconds, her arms thrashing violently against her mattress, and then fell motionless. The serpents woke in a fury, flinging themselves at their attacker as she drew her sword and slashed wildly at their heads. They were very dangerous and Samantha had to calculate the distance accurately so that her sword arm wouldn't come close enough for the serpents to bite her. Although she was an expert swordswoman the serpents proved quicker than her. Her shield, though, proved adequate protection as the deadly creatures thrashed furiously against it.

Rebecca was not so lucky. Stheno was not asleep and reared up unexpectedly, her stare meeting Rebecca's startled gaze, turning her to stone instantly.

Meanwhile, the instant Euryale died the six boys she'd turned to stone returned to life. Five of them drew their swords and prepared to attack Stheno.

"Be careful, boys!" Samantha shouted as she continued slashing at the other Gorgon's snakes. "Don't look at her or you'll be turned to stone again."

As soon as Stheno got over the shock, she became furious when she saw her sister writhing and dying under the young Orizon's spear. She prepared to pounce on Samantha. Then she saw the boys rushing towards her.

Stheno was at least a metre taller than the boys. For a few seconds she dithered. Should she attack Samantha or deal with the approaching boys who were brandishing their swords?

Bill attacked first. Aiming at Stheno's throat, he struck her from the side, intending to cut off her head. But at that moment the surviving Gorgon twisted aside and the heavy blow fell against her bronze left arm. With a lightning movement, she grabbed Bill by his upper arms, immobilizing both him and his sword. She lifted him high like a piece of prey. He felt his feet leave the ground as the huge sharp teeth of the Gorgon closed greedily on his neck. He felt his death coming and he looked in despair at the fiery eyes of the monster as her teeth sank into his throat.

The five stunned boys looked on helplessly as Bill died. Samantha was unaware of all this because she was concentrating on Euryale's serpents.

Unexpectedly, the Gorgon dropped Bill with a scream of pain the moment her teeth began to sink into the young Orizon boy's neck – where they met hard stone instead of tender flesh. At the moment of his death, Bill had inadvertently looked into her eyes and had turned into marbled stone once more.

The sixth of the boys whom Euryale had turned to stone was Pedro. When he had changed back, he had not taken his sword out like the rest. Now, in a split second, he assessed the situation and understood what had happened. He tried to take Rebecca's spear, but it proved impossible because she was gripping it in her right hand that had turned to stone. He stepped quickly to the dead Euryale and pulled the spear from her throat, being careful to avoid the slashing fangs of the serpents.

He calculated the distance carefully. The moment Stheno threw Bill aside and prepared to attack the other boys, Pedro closed his eyes and bravely charged in the direction he had calculated, thrusting the spear that had killed her sister into the remaining Gorgon's throat with all his might.

Stheno's eyes bulged; she grasped the spear with both her hands and began to pull it out slowly. Blood gushed from her neck and ears, splashing down onto the ground. She shrieked like one possessed and her screams echoed through the forest as she vomited blood and green bile. She finally managed to dislodge the spear, snapping it in half like a matchstick, dementedly hitting her chest with it. At the same time she fell back on the bed. Her tongue stuck out like one of her serpent's. She convulsed, stretching her arms, legs, fingers and toes and lifting her head as she let out more blood-curdling shrieks. Her eyes looked as if they were going to pop out from their sockets. She opened and shut her mouth as if she wanted to bite off her own tongue. Finally her head turned to the side, touched the ground and did not move again.

The four boys whom she had turned to stone came back to life. So did Rebecca. Samantha, who finally understood what had happened, stopped trying to deal with Euryale's serpents and knelt by Bill's side. She put her sword and shield next to him and examined the neck of the marble Orizon. The marks of the Gorgon's teeth were clearly visible but she couldn't gauge the depth of the wound or if his throat had been fatally damaged.

Luckily, Bill began to come round. The first thing he saw was a pair of eyes – but these were blue like the sea. They looked nothing like the eyes of the monster he remembered seeing before he'd lost consciousness and they were looking at him anxiously.

"*I believe I'm alive*," he thought as he felt Samantha's fingers touch his neck lightly.

The rest of the children gathered around them and watched anxiously. When they saw Bill move their hopes rose.

Bill, with the help of Samantha, stood up slowly. Fortunately, he did not feel any ill effects and they soon realized that the bites in his throat would heal. The marks were sure to disappear within a few days. But if his being turned to stone had been delayed even by a tenth of a second, he would have had his head bitten clean off.

Everybody looked around in awe, finding it hard to take in everything that was happening so quickly. As soon as they had made sure that Bill was completely safe, the other boys drew their swords and tried again to kill the Gorgon's serpents.

But what they were attempting was too difficult. The serpents were many. They were also big and dangerous. Five of the boys were trying to kill the angry serpents on the head of one Gorgon and four were attacking those on the other's.

Samantha and Rebecca held shields, which helped both of them to watch the serpents' movements. But time passed and the boys had not killed even one snake even though they were constantly in mortal danger. Understandably, they were growing tired.

Then Abu sheathed his sword and boldly picked up the two torches that lit the area. He threw one of them on Euryale's face, sending her serpents rearing back in fear. Then Abu drew his sword and, with a well-calculated stroke, cut the Gorgon's head off. The serpents died instantly. He repeated the action with Stheno.

Abu picked up the torches again while the others stamped out the small fires that had flared up on the ground.

They all looked at each other without saying a word, trying to catch their breath. No matter how much strength the Flame had bestowed on them, such strange and perilous situations still affected them. At that moment, the other three girls entered the lair.

"We would have charged too, but we had other orders," they told the boys.

"Orders must always be obeyed," Rebecca said "Though if we see something change, then we can be flexible and act according to what we think best. We don't wear blinkers nor do we keep our minds in straitjackets like some Porth generals I have met. But you three acted completely correctly.

"Success is gained by prudence as well as valour. Our lives depended on the three of you. If you had joined us just now, we would have been in the hands of Moira, the goddess of fate and chance. She's the one who arranges our meetings with good or bad Luck, not ourselves. We must never leave anything to her. She has a two-faced head that spins uncontrollably. We can never be sure which of the two faces will stop and look at us: fortune or misfortune, angel or devil, sorrow or happiness, pain or joy. One bad encounter with her means the end of everything. Sometimes we think that we see the face of Luck staring at us, and then she sticks out her tongue and mocks us."

That night, as the children talked it over, their adventure began to seem unbelievable.

"How did it feel to be turned to stone?" the four girls who hadn't suffered like Rebecca and the boys kept asking.

Everybody who'd been afflicted insisted that they'd felt absolutely nothing and couldn't remember anything. It was as if they had suddenly gone into a dreamless sleep while standing and had woken up in the same position. The exception had been Bill's second encounter with a Gorgon, which had very nearly killed him.

The next day they followed their schedule as planned, approaching Lord Life's house just before dusk, wondering what new experiences lay ahead of them.

THE WINGED HORSE

Lord Life's farm lay on a small hill, surrounded by trees and undergrowth. The children arrived at the scheduled time, just as the sun was about to set. Once more it had done its duty. Now, tired but satisfied, it was going to bed, having painted the land with its rich palette. The birds, mesmerized by the sunset's fabulous colours, sang an intoxicated anthem.

At the entrance to the courtyard a tall, muscular, suntanned man awaited them. Bare from the waist up, he was wearing brown leather shorts and sandals. His hair and beard were thick, black and wavy. The colour of his large eyes matched the leather of his shorts.

"Welcome! You're right on time. I saw you from a distance. Lord Life and Lady Danae are waiting for you. I'm Leiko."

He beamed as he shook hands with each of the children. As they walked through the gardens towards the house they noticed many species of flowers that they'd never seen before.

Lord Life and Lady Danae stood up to welcome the children inside the house. For the first time Rebecca noticed how closely Felicia and Danae resembled one another. Danae was a slender, beautiful woman with black eyes, full lips and long wavy black hair. She was wearing a full-length white Grecian robe, which added to her appearance of grace and majesty.

Lord Life was also tall. His long hair was speckled with silver at the temples and the same effect could be seen in his beard. His green eyes radiated strength and wisdom.

"How was your journey?" he asked, smiling.

"It's a miracle that we're still alive," Jabal said.

The smiles vanished from the faces of the adults as Jabal gave them a detailed account of the Gorgons incident. When he had finished, Lord Life paced up and down angrily while Danae put her head in her hands and gazed at the floor, apparently lost in thought. Leiko's anger was boiling up, making him breathe hard like a steam engine. He bit his lips and clenched his fists as though he were choking a thousand enemies.

"It's unbelievable!" Lord Life said, "Just unbelievable ... Truly, it's a miracle that you escaped. They're extremely dangerous creatures. Something is terribly wrong here. Rebecca's abduction and this attack mean that things in the Land of the White Sun are getting worse. The rules are being violated, making the future uncertain.

"Go now and get ready. Then we'll all dine together. You must be tired and hungry. Lady Danae has prepared a meal that I'm sure you'll enjoy."

The children picked up their equipment and followed Danae as she showed them the two large dormitories where they would sleep. There were clean outer clothes for everyone, as well as pyjamas and sandals.

Feeling relaxed after their baths and dressed in comfortable simple tunics, the children returned to the living room an hour later and sat down around the dining table. Once they'd eaten, Lord Life gave them their timetable for the following day.

"We'll begin at seven in the morning. Before dawn, Leiko will fly on Pegasus to Utopia to inform Princess Felicia about the Gorgons. He'll be back in time for the start of our programme."

The children offered to help Lady Danae to clear the table and wash up.

"You're my guests," she said. "Leiko and I can take care of everything."

"But Orizons don't have servants, do they?" Samantha said, shocked.

"Leiko is not our servant." Lady Danae smiled at the thought. "A son of Hercules could never be a servant. Leiko lives with us because he loves us, Lord Life in particular. When the Heraclids – the descendants of Hercules – were in Attica, Eurystheus tried to annihilate them. Lord Life helped young Leiko and his mother, Deianeira, escape his wrath. Since then, Leiko has felt grateful to Lord Life and has wanted to be here with him.

"When the Mythical Gods, the Demigods and the Heroes left the Land of the White Sun to go to the Second Parallel Dimension, Leiko asked to stay with us. They gave their consent.

"But that's enough talking for tonight. Have a good night's sleep, children. We'll meet here again in the morning."

The following day, at precisely seven o'clock, they all assembled. As instructed, they were wearing loose-fitting trousers and shirts. Lord Life and Danae, dressed in the same style, led them out into the garden where Leiko was waiting, to an open grassy area with hurdles, ropes hanging from horizontal bars and a basketball court.

"Children," Lord Life said, "this morning's programme includes exercises and basketball. We'll then have breakfast and some time outdoors among the flowers."

Unable to contain himself a moment longer, Leiko burst into

activity, running, jumping the hurdles, hanging from the ropes, leaping to the ground and bouncing up again like a spring. Lord Life and Danae followed the same routine, performing the exercises with ease and skill. The children followed suit until, half an hour later, Lord Life signalled for them to stop.

They all moved on to the basketball court, forming into two teams of nine. There was no need for a referee. If someone committed a foul they would admit it themselves and the game would stop. Louise was captain of one team and Tamina of the other. Both of them had been in junior teams that always won championships in tournaments back home.

The game was exciting even though there were so many players. The children were surprised at how easily Lord Life and Danae scored three point shots. By contrast, Leiko was a poor shot but a powerful defender.

In spite of Lord Life's and Danae's high scores, Tamina's team won and gave a mighty cheer at the final whistle. Everyone in Louise's team promised that next time *they* would be the winners. They left the court arm in arm, all of them happy.

Over breakfast their spirits remained high as they relived the game, joking and teasing each other. Lord Life laughed as long and loud as anyone. Rebecca watched him and was impressed. She recognized his wisdom and humour, two of the greatest virtues for a leader. She knew that one of the hardest things in the world is to create a pleasant atmosphere and that it was a great skill to give joy through simple means, whereas it was always easy to create misery. It pleased her to see the other children so happy, even though half of them had lost the game.

Her father had once told her: "*To get to know a friend well, you have to watch how he behaves if he loses a game. A bad loser has problems. If you don't know how to lose, then you have to think about it and rectify whatever it is that makes you feel that way.*" So Rebecca always observed the behaviour of others when they were on a losing side and drew her own conclusions.

After breakfast the children and Lord Life went outside and wandered in the gardens, admiring the flowers.

"Although our irrigation system is good," Lord Life explained, "I also watered the beds early this morning, before the sun came out. It's important that we don't just water flowers when we feel like it, but when we *should*."

The children began asking questions about the names of the flowers and the seasons in which they bloomed. Lord Life appeared to enjoy answering all their queries, sitting on the grass among the flower beds.

"You can see how beautiful Nature is, children," he said, gesturing around them. "It delights both soul and spirit. The cause of such beauty is concealed, however, and we can't see it. The things we don't see are often more significant than those we do."

The children looked puzzled.

"With all due respect, sir, I don't understand what you mean," piped up Tiki.

"I have such fond memories of your homeland, Tiki. Polynesia is one of the most beautiful places on Earth. Even man has not yet done any great damage to its natural beauty. You must fight hard to keep the natural environment intact.

"What I mean is that we can't see the roots of the trees and flowers that surround us, yet they exist. And without them those trees and flowers wouldn't be there to be seen. So, which is more important for the flowers, their roots or their blossoms? When you look at the trees, which do you think is more important for them, their roots or the trunks and branches which carry the leaves and fruit? Of course, without the things that we see on the surface the roots have no meaning or value. They are like buried treasures. However, roots can exist without flowers or tree trunks or fruit; but nothing can exist without the roots. Roots are the pipes that carry the life. Like the mother who breastfeeds her babies.

"The same applies to us. The things that we don't see in a person are often more important than the things we do. So we must love the roots as well, because it is essentially they that generate the beauty we see. In the same way, we must also search for that which doesn't show in people and love it. We shouldn't stop at the surface, at what is visible and beautiful."

The children gazed around them in silence as they took in his words.

Having given them a moment to reflect, Lord Life continued.

"As we water the plants, we should sense the roots too and hear them rejoicing. They are the fairest things in nature. They distribute water and nutrients fairly to all parts of the plant."

Rebecca wondered how people on Earth could become more like roots. If that happened nearly all their problems would disappear.

"Roots are also the foundation, the support," Lord Life continued. "And they're very smart. They know how far and how deep to spread so as to support the plant. They go just as far as is necessary. No less, in case the plant is blown over by the wind, and no more, in case water and food are wasted and deprive the rest of the plant. People should establish their roots in the same way – their foundations, their support frames – so that storms won't sweep them away."

The group got up again and began to walk among the trees as Lord Life showed them some that bore strange fruit.

"These trees grafted themselves. They intertwined their branches. Though each of them already produced exceptional fruit, when they united they grew even tastier. Their flavours mingled and a new kind of food was produced, unique and rare in its taste. The same applies to people. Marriages, unions, collaborations, alliances and agreements frequently produce amazing results."

They came to a picturesque lake swarming with ducks, swans and other birds. A flock of flamingos took flight in a blaze of pink and Rebecca vowed to herself that she would remember the beautiful scene and turn it into a painting.

"We come here to swim," said Lord Life.

They reached the stables and Lord Life showed them the horses, saving the very best until last: Pegasus, the mythical flying horse. The children gazed in awe at his pure white coat and gigantic wings. He was much larger than normal horses but was still exquisite in every detail. They stroked him nervously as if afraid that they might damage such perfection.

"Do you feel like taking the children for a ride?" Lord Life asked Pegasus.

"With great pleasure, my lord," Pegasus replied. "You know how much I love children and how much I look forward to flying with them. I miss them greatly, especially since Princess Felicia grew up"

Lord Life led Pegasus out of the stable and the children followed, wide-eyed with excitement, their faces beaming. This was the best gift that any of them had ever received.

"We'll take each of you in turn," said Lord Life. "We'll fly together as far as the lake for you to get the hang of it. Then I'll dive into the water and you can continue on by yourselves. You'll fly for approximately ten minutes each. But you'll see a lot in those ten minutes because of Pegasus's speed – he's almost as fast as an airplane. So, who's going to be the first?"

"If nobody objects, I'll go first," said Lee after a few seconds. They all signalled their agreement.

"Have no fear at all," Pegasus reassured Lee. "You can't possibly fall off me, but even if you do I'll catch you. Besides, by now you all know how to fly."

Raising his wings, he rubbed them together in happy anticipation. Lord Life helped Lee climb up and then sat behind him.

"Where are the reins?" Lee asked.

"We don't need them," Lord Life assured him. He touched the soles of his feet to Pegasus's belly and the giant flying horse took off.

The other children clapped their hands and cheered happily.

Pegasus flapped his wings lightly and rhythmically, tenderly caressing the air. Lee felt exhilarated: his forelock fluttered in the wind like a Chinese war banner while Lord Life's hair streamed behind him like a silver-embroidered veil. Once they had reached the lake, Lord Life jumped off and Pegasus flew unhurriedly over the farm. Then he increased his speed and surged forward. It felt like a dream to Lee, something that he couldn't even have imagined three months earlier.

Pegasus varied his speed, almost grazing the tops of the trees with his hooves as he followed the course of the river, sometimes going so low that he splashed his legs in the water before climbing steeply into the clouds. From time to time sunbeams would shine through and illuminate his wings, making them reflect the light like sculpted gold flames. Throughout the flight he talked to Lee, telling him about the places they were flying over, such as the location of the Gorgons' lair.

"This is where you met my aunts, Euryale and Stheno."

"Your *aunts*?"

"My father is Poseidon, God of the seas, rivers and all water, and my mother was the Gorgon Medusa, their sister. I popped out of her head at the very moment when Perseus cut it off. Leiko told me about your great adventure and the danger you were in. You were lucky to escape with your lives."

In precisely ten minutes they returned to the lake and Pegasus landed next to Lord Life. Then Lord Life mounted once more and went to pick up the next child. Two and a half hours later the children had all had their turns, and had watched Lord Life flying on his own.

"As you can see," Lord Life told them, "even I, who have been flying for thousands of years, only do so when I can take to the air above the lake. Now, you've seen enough of me; let's see you flying for the last time before you depart. When you come down you can enjoy a refreshing swim in the lake with the swans, if you like."

Lord Life lay down, cushioned his head on his arms, and admired the children like an eagle watching its eaglets playing in the thermals around the family nest. They were the offspring of the White Sun! Its future and its hope. They were the green shoots that would become evergreen trees and would help goodness, rightness and justice prevail upon Earth, working to prevent the devastation of the planet. Lord Life was completely satisfied. He saw that they were skilful at flying, trained by the best.

Pegasus was sitting on his rump and from time to time he would clap his hooves together in enthusiastic applause.

"Well done, children. Well done!" he shouted gleefully at every well-executed move. He had a good word for all of them, calling each one by name and offering them advice. After all, he was the best-qualified creature in the Universe to judge and teach flying.

All the children landed at the lakeside, deciding against the swim. Lord Life kissed each one of them in turn.

"Congratulations. Well done! You were all excellent."

Pegasus, still sitting on his rump, then hugged each of them tenderly with his forelegs; his open wings moved gently, like delicately embroidered victory flags.

Back at the house the children bathed, put on their tunics again and went to the dining room. Lady Danae was a superb cook and they looked forward to every meal that she prepared. As they tucked into the delicacies she had laid out Danae implored Leiko to tell them the tale of the thunderbolts in his youth.

Leiko blushed, not liking to brag, one of the many virtues that his father Hercules had instilled in him.

"Come on, Leiko, don't be shy," Danae insisted. "It's good for the children to learn some facts."

Leiko put up his hands, pleading to be let off.

"Then I'll tell you the story myself, children," Danae laughed. "The goddess Hera hated Hercules and his children because Zeus had fallen in love with Alcmene and Hercules was their son. One day Hera purloined one of Zeus's thunderbolts and hurled it down onto the Forest of Mysteries, where the Heraclids were living. Hera wanted to kill them to get her revenge on Hercules. Leiko was then fifteen years old. He was the only one who saw the thunderbolt falling and ran to the rescue, catching it in mid-air like a lightning conductor before it could touch the ground and set light to the forest, killing all the inhabitants including the Heraclids. He was a great hero that day."

Leiko blushed more deeply, while the children gazed at him admiringly.

When the meal was over, Lord Life told them that they had an hour to walk in the garden and digest their food. They were to take their shields with them and meet in exactly one hour at the place where they had started their morning training. There they would do a new kind of training for four hours. At eight o'clock that evening they would assemble in the living room to talk.

The children chattered excitedly about everything they'd learned and all the experiences that they'd now had. In exactly an hour they had all gathered at the designated spot. Leiko was already there, holding his huge club, looking like pictures of Hercules the children had seen in books and films.

"Welcome," said Leiko. "Now you will learn how to deal with the Cyclopes and their terrible clubs. This will be the last lesson of this year's course. The club is a dangerous weapon, deadly in the hands of those who know how to use it. The Cyclopes definitely know how to use it effectively, as did my father and all the Heraclids. You know that the Cyclopes are gigantic, very strong and have only one eye in the middle of their foreheads. This is their weak point. They cannot see very well what's going on to their left and right.

"We will work on how to capitalize on their disadvantage, how to attack from the right angles so that they can't see you coming, and how to use your shields to protect yourselves from their terrible blows. Tomorrow, bring your swords so that you can learn how to attack as well.

"First of all, though, let's see how dangerous a club can be, even from a distance."

Leiko pointed to a pole driven into the grass that had a

basketball balanced on top of it. The pole was six and a half feet high and stood about thirty yards away. He flung the club, which spun through the air and hit the ball, knocking it off the pole. Leiko did not waste a single second. He ran, seized his club and the ball and returned to the astonished children.

"As you can see, anybody standing there would no longer be alive. The club would have brained him! His skull would have been split open like a watermelon and his grey matter would have looked like an omelette. All right. Let's start the lesson."

The training was arduous but the children were so enthralled watching Leiko in action that the four hours flashed by. He was truly a demigod, something supernatural.

Later, back in the living room, Lord Life listened to the children's their bubbling enthusiasm for a while before interrupting.

"Soon," he told them, "you'll be returning to Earth. After getting to know another world in a different dimension of the Universe, you'll have changed. You'll find yourselves looking even deeper into everything that happens around you. You've been trained here not only to protect the Flame but also to help humanity stay on the right path and to try and save the planet from destruction. This is your primary mission. I hope that we have no more wars here and that it won't prove necessary for you to fight, so that you can use all your powers and all your knowledge on Earth.

"Each one of you will choose which road to follow; what – and whether – you want to study; which profession to follow. But, whatever you choose, your basic aim is for Good to prevail, because you are Orizons. You might decide to help tackle the serious, uncontrolled problem of drugs. They can destroy people, turning them into weak-willed and dependent beings.

Addicts become dangerous when deprived of their deadly habits and commit atrocious crimes to get their fixes. They all need your help!

"You can also help people to avoid being misled by the sort of extremist socio-political and religious movements that will destroy their lives and their futures. Fight fanaticism!

"Or you could help reduce air pollution and stop the destruction of the environment. Human life on Earth has developed in such a way that society depends on the energy produced by fossil fuels. If the planet was left without this energy for a day, everything would collapse and nothing would work. Half the population would be at risk of dying from famine, thirst, heat or cold. That's what humanity has been reduced to. Here, as you've seen, we don't need any kind of fossil-fuel energy. We can still live comfortably, even if we don't have artificial light at night.

"Remember that, just as we have kept the secret of the Orizons for thousands of years, it is your turn now to do the same. When there is no alternative and we are in danger of being exposed, we retreat. We organize fictitious disappearances, or one of our people supposedly dies and the inventions that they've been working on are never completed. Great scientists whose names you learned at school or have read about are Orizons. They left the Earth following my instructions and they are now here in the Land of the White Sun – or if they went back they used different names to start again.

"Orizons are like the rocks on the shore: no matter how hard the stormy waves try to swallow them, they cannot do so.

"As you grow up and choose your own paths, keep on trying to help. Keep us informed and we'll give you guidance whenever you need it. Is there anything you would like to ask?"

"In our countries," Susan piped up, "we believe in the religions they have there. Each nation claims that theirs is the only true God and the only true religion. They all say the same thing. They kill each other for it. Who should we support? Who is the best and more powerful God? What is right?"

"That's a very good question, Susan. We respect all religions and all the Gods of the world," Lord Life replied. "It's regrettable that each religion claims to be infallible. But we respect this too. It is their right to believe this.

"What we have to strive for with all our might is to stop people from killing each other in the name of the God they believe in. Many bloodthirsty warriors have been proclaimed Gods, prophets, saints, protectors and priests by the followers of different religions. Many crimes have been perpetrated in the name of different religions' claims to uniqueness. Much blood has been shed in the names of many religions' Gods.

"We are a loving group, children. We have the Flame inside us, but we belong to different religions. There are no disagreements among us and no problems. It is quite possible for the same to happen on Earth."

Carlos asked permission to speak and Lord Life nodded his assent.

"The representatives of all the religions have become stricter than their founders. I wonder why, in many of the churches I visited when travelling, the image of the Almighty painted in the dome has such a severe gaze. Our God is full of kindness and love. I don't think it's right for iconographers to paint Him in such a way that He is almost frightening. The church should attract the faithful, who are entitled to feel the affection of the Almighty."

"Religion is a support to most people on Earth," said lord

Life. "We must be careful: we mustn't dash a man's hopes if we cannot give him new ones. We should always bear this in mind. People have an inner need for communication with their God and their saints. They want to talk to them and ask for their help in solving their problems. These are important spiritual cravings and are essential to those who feel them. Most people feel better when they experience such emotions in their churches with their priests. So it is good for those who feel such needs to go to church. But they shouldn't have to pay an entrance fee to do so, and you know what I mean by this. I don't believe that God needs offerings and gifts in order to help anyone who is in need of His help.

"In my opinion, God don't just have a specific address. He is everywhere and not only in churches and monasteries. This is what I believe and what I think all Orizons believe. God is in houses, trains, gyms, streets and football fields. He is even in taverns, in a group of friends. He is anywhere that people unwind and relax after a day or a week of hard work. God is in the fisherman's boat, down in the mine in the bowels of the wounded Earth, close by the shepherd who tends to his herd. He is in every school, with the teachers and their students. He is in the shade of the trees.

"He is simple, hospitable, accessible. He always carries a large nest under His arm and if you are cold He puts you in it to warm you. If you are too hot, the nest will cool you. Whenever I need Him, children, I can feel Him come. He puts me on His lap. He caresses me as if I was a small child. He talks to me and consoles me. It sounds strange to you, doesn't it? God putting on His lap an old man like me, who's lived for thousands of years. Yet He does so when we need Him. We're always like little children. That's the way God sees us and takes care of us.

When our burdens are too heavy for us to carry, we ask for His help. He takes our burdens upon Himself. He makes our load lighter."

Everyone felt a lifting of their spirits as they listened to Lord Life's words. His face had a glow to it as he spoke but at the same time his expression was calm and peaceful, as if he could feel the presence of God at that moment. He pointed out that the children's parents had been well trained and could guide them wisely whenever they had questions and problems.

"Distortions emerge in all religions, created by twisted people who know how to charm others. You should avoid such individuals. They're dangerous. They can sway people who have no inner balance or strong foundations and hence are easy victims. People who feel a great void inside themselves and who seek some kind of meaning are always vulnerable to predators.

"People can meet their basic needs on their own. They can fill up their emptiness and find their own feet. They can address their God by themselves without the need of any intermediaries. Gods only exist because people so wish. The same is true of heaven and hell. If people don't want them, then they don't exist.

"Alas! Within all religions, from time to time, evil people have set up cults that have many followers.

"Explain to people that there are some fruits that we can eat whole, others that we must first peel, and others still of which we may only eat a part.

"When we're bombarded by so many obscure messages and find it hard to make careful choices immediately, we sort them out and store them away for a while. Later, when we feel more clear-headed, we take them out again and ruminate over them. Then we calmly choose what is best and right."

"Lord Life," Bill said, his face grave. "Many people have questions about our existence. Where do we come from? Where are we going and what will become of us? What shall we tell them?"

"There are many unsolved mysteries, but the greatest of them is the mystery of life. We Orizons do not search for answers. Feeling the greatness of Nature and its Creator, we know how difficult it is for our minds to conceive of something so immense. There are so many times when God tells us: *'Thus far and no further!'* The wisdom of Nature is infinite and eternal. Everything around and inside us is an incomprehensible miracle. No one can ever explain anything with absolute certainty.

"Myriads of mammals constantly migrate, covering inconceivable distances to find nutrition, clean water and ideal climatic conditions. They accurately predict floods, droughts and the change of seasons, adjusting their routes accordingly.

"Even though they're scattered in small herds, at some point they communicate with one another and all meet up. They make their rendezvous as punctually as if they were wearing high-precision watches. They become one huge herd and then migration begins. Then they split into smaller groups again and enjoy the abundance of Nature. Eventually, inexplicably, they all meet up once more and return to their starting point.

"Migratory birds cover even greater distances, crossing from one continent to another, following precise routes. They return to their old nests or build new ones and stay in smaller flocks. Suddenly, one day, they all assemble. Who gives the signal? Nobody knows. They fly in large formations over great oceans and return to their old hideouts. The slightest mistakes could wipe out whole species, but it never happens.

"Then there is the miracle of the beehive. When scout-bees

return to it, there are guards at the entrance to check whether the nectar they bring is free from pesticides and other dangerous chemical substances. Only then do they permit the bees to enter. They act like Saint Peter at the Pearly Gates of the Christian Paradise, not allowing sinners in. People are not so clever, which is why tons of narcotics pass daily through seaports and airports and across borders.

"Whose mind can explain all this? The wisdom of Nature is infinite and eternal. So Orizons don't question these things. We think about simple, pleasant matters. About what is tangible and necessary for true peace. We believe in love, in goodness. We revel in Nature and live in harmony with it. We are God's creatures. We cannot possibly answer such questions. That is His job. The knowledge that we acquire should bring us pleasure, not lead us into impasses.

"Some scientists use serious arguments to try and prove that God exists. Others try to prove that life stems from chemical reactions, that evolution is a continuing process or that we are made from stardust. They're content to make do with general positions and questions that make an impression. They lead some people towards religion but not others.

"The answer to science is that man has two ears, two eyes, one nose and one mouth, and they're in the right place so that he can hear and see keenly, and can smell while he eats."

Samantha blushed slightly but spoke up in a firm voice, her turquoise eyes flashing.

"Indeed, my lord, the designs of the bodily organs to which we owe our senses are remarkable. But every time we eat we run the risk of choking on a morsel of food if God doesn't put his finger down our throat and unblock it. And our hearts work on electrical energy, the source of which science is hard put to explain. Mortals are in danger of dying at any moment from a sudden power cut – unless they wear pacemakers, a human invention. Every day, when they wake up, people thank God that their hearts did not stop beating during the night. If the smallest pipe gets blocked, people get strokes or heart attacks. A nerve breaks and they are handicapped for life. And humans have plenty of nerves. Thousands of people die of an allergic reaction because they've been stung by the wonderful bee. Life is just a breath away from death."

"If it had not all been wisely and properly planned," Lord Life replied, "every species of animal would have become extinct. The great questions about life will remain unanswered for ever. The mystery of life and death will always remain just that: a mystery!

"Two thousand and four years before the destruction of the Earth, in a picturesque seaside village, a six-year-old boy looked up at the August moon and asked his father: '*Where are your grandparents*?' And he replied: '*In the sky.*' The boy looked at us all with his innocent but sad eyes and said: '*I think that when we go to the sky we'll all be like we were before we were born. We won't laugh or think or feel anything.*'

"Maybe that is the answer to all our questions about where we come from and where we are going. Don't look too deep or too high. Happiness is to be found in attainable things; in what is simple and easy!"

"Is the Land of the White Sun a round planet like the Earth?" asked Carlos.

"We don't know anything about that," Lord Life answered, "and we don't want to know. We have everything: mountains, sea, lakes, rivers, trees, fruit, animals, the sky with the sun and stars. What do we care if the Land of the White Sun is round or flat?

"What did people gain from discovering that the world was round? It would be better if they didn't know its shape but kept it pure.

"This is not a planet like Earth. It is a Parallel Dimension and we can't explore it. As we travel from the Dimension of the Universe towards our own, we enter this Land, without seeing anything else. I believe that not even the Mythical Gods know anything more, even though they now inhabit the Second Parallel Dimension.

"Knowledge is like medicine. If people take a little at a time it may do them some good. But if they take it all at once, they may die or go mad.

"What I'm interested in is stopping the wars on Earth, eliminating misery and saving the planet from destruction. Fishermen cast their nets in hope. They haul them in with anticipation. They are never disheartened with their catch, which is sometimes large and sometimes small. They keep at it for their whole lives. This is how we should feel in our quest for the rule of Good."

Rebecca wanted to ask Lord Life why he allowed the great injustice against the Sharkans, but she respected his hospitality and said nothing. She felt that such a discussion should not take place in front of the others.

After breakfast on the following day, the children wandered around the farm again with Lady Danae, all of them delighted by her wisdom and her simple ways. She talked about family values and principles: how couples should behave towards one another, how parents should treat their children (and vice versa) so that families should be happy and have solid foundations.

"The evolution of contemporary society on Earth is breaking

up the core of that very society, the family unit," she told them, sadly.

She showed them her vegetable garden.

"What are the secrets that make your cooking so tasty?" Susan asked.

"Whatever I use," Danae replied, "I have raised myself. Plants are living organisms, including the ones that we eat. They know that this is their destiny. So when you plant them yourself and watch over them as they grow, with love and nurturing, they're tastier than the produce that most people buy on Earth, which comes from an anonymous grower and goes to anonymous buyers and is then eaten by anonymous customers. Everything is important in life. But it isn't just the flavour that we enjoy when we eat these vegetables: we also feel satisfied because we have produced them ourselves.

"The same thing happens in a few places on Earth where people haven't abandoned their land to move to the concrete cities to eat tasteless, dangerous manufactured products.

"During this aeon, people on Earth have left the natural life of the provinces and have gathered in suffocating cities. They've built blocks of flats and towering steel skyscrapers, so high that even birds gasp for breath as they fly to the top. People crowd together in these cages, one on top of another, but they often don't even exchange greetings with their next-door neighbours. Yet in their most private moments they are separated from their neighbours only by a thin brick. A few years ago Lord Life and I went to a big city in America and I could hear the people next door snoring.

"People scorn living in the provinces, tilling fields, tending orchards and rearing animals. They're proud to live in cities and become architects, lawyers, scientists or civil servants, because it gives them a feeling of security. They don't understand that life will go on without architects or lawyers, but without crops and livestock everyone will starve to death. Being a farmer is one of the most useful and necessary occupations. Those who tend the land should feel proud."

Having shown them everything, Lady Danae led the children back to the house.

"Now we're all going to cook together some of the dishes that you have come to know during your stay in our Land. Each of you will prepare something different."

Lunch turned out to be varied, interesting and amusing. Each child's creation was greeted with caustic comments as well as much laughter and praise. Like her husband, Lady Danae was an excellent hostess, creating a happy atmosphere by saying the right things at the right time.

In the afternoon the children had four more hours of training with Leiko, in which he taught them how to use their swords effectively against the Cyclopes.

That night, after dinner, Lord Life told them that the way back to Utopia the next day would be faster than the route they had followed during their training.

"In about five hours, you'll be back in Utopia. Leiko will follow you on Pegasus."

The girls went to bed early and Rebecca immediately fell asleep, only to be woken a few hours later by a dream. She tossed and turned in bed but couldn't get back to sleep. According to her watch, it was almost midnight. Since she didn't seem to be able to sleep, she decided to take a stroll in the garden. She didn't bother changing out of her pyjamas.

The night was dark. Many clouds were trying to play hide-

and-seek with the stars. Rebecca walked among the trees. From time to time she would sit on the grass. She remembered what Pegasus had said to her when they'd been flying over the Gorgons' lair.

"*We have to be tough and ready when something difficult happens. You suddenly went from your school desk to another world that not even the most vivid imagination could have conjured up. You were held captive and you fought, wounded and killed others. You were turned to stone. You kept going back and forth between life and death, like a wrongly addressed letter. It has been a lot for someone of your age and even with the Flame I wonder how you coped.*"

"*Today I heard you complain about your life becoming routine,*" Rebecca had replied. "*You looked really bored. But then you were filled with joy and you looked very happy.*"

"*When Lord Life took part in the Lomani I was busy fighting alongside him. But for the past few years I've had almost nothing to do. I rarely take him to Utopia. Luckily, the Orizon trainees come here and I take them on rides. If only you knew how much I looked forward to your visit!*"

"*Do you really prefer to fight rather than enjoy Nature and the peaceful life? Besides, you can fly whenever you feel like it. Lord Life wouldn't stop you.*"

"*Flying alone isn't worth it. I need company. I'm a horse, too, but there is no mate for me. Even if you can do the best things in the world it isn't worth it if you're alone. War is one of the worst things in the world but at least it is an emotional outlet. Even the worst things are sometimes better than nothing at all. I reminisce about the good years on Earth. Heroes used my abilities in great feats, like Bellerophon who killed the Chimera with me. I need action, adventure, suspense.*"

As Rebecca approached the lake, lost in thought, she heard voices and saw the boys gathered on the shore with Leiko.

"Well, hello," said Leiko.

"We couldn't sleep," Bill told her. "So we went to Leiko's house and then we all decided to come here. We flew a bit and had a swim."

"I'll leave you to your conversation," Rebecca said. "I think I'll visit Pegasus. Is that all right, Leiko?"

"You can go anywhere you wish. But you cannot fly on Pegasus without Lord Life's permission."

"I don't want to fly, I only want to continue the conversation we were having earlier."

Rebecca said goodnight and walked on towards the stables, surprised to find that the door was standing open.

"If he's asleep, I won't wake him," she thought.

She peeped in cautiously. Pegasus was lying down. At first she thought he was asleep, but she knew that, with rare exceptions, horses don't lie down when they sleep. His body seemed to be in a strange position but it was too dark to see clearly. Rebecca plucked up her courage and tiptoed in. As she got close she saw that Pegasus's eyes were wide open but unblinking and his head was covered in blood. As her eyes accustomed to the gloom she saw that his wings had been smashed out of shape.

Rebecca felt faint. She couldn't believe that Pegasus, with whom she had been flying the day before, had been reduced to this. He was dead! Dead and crushed. Her stomach knotted tightly and she fell to her knees. A strange dizziness threatened to overcome her. This was something that she hadn't felt before, not even when she had expected the Porth generals to execute her. She put her hands on the floor and felt the still-warm blood. She began to shiver with the horror of it. Her pyjamas soaked up the red liquid, which stained her knees. She felt as if she was bleeding herself, as if all this blood was gushing from her own heart. Although she'd been told that the Orizons didn't cry when they felt pain, hot tears still ran down her face. The Flame, it seemed, was unable to combat such grief effectively.

Rebecca opened her mouth to call for help, but nobody would have heard her. She couldn't understand how such a thing could have happened. Her brain was buzzing. In her confusion, only one coherent thought kept whispering despairingly in her mind: *"Someone hit the Mythical Horse and killed it."*

Who had done it? Such a ruthless killing suggested that all of them were in danger. Rebecca mustered her courage and crawled to the stable door as if she herself had been wounded. Once there, she grabbed the door jamb and with a huge effort she pulled herself up.

"The Flame is working," she thought and left the stable like a sleepwalker. She moved slowly towards the lake like a wounded waif wandering uncertainly in the night. As her courage grew and her strength returned, her steps quickened and soon she was running.

The boys and Leiko were sitting and talking quietly, exactly as she had left them. Some of them saw Rebecca coming and jumped to their feet.

"What's wrong?" Leiko asked.

"Someone's killed Pegasus," Rebecca said in a hard, flat voice before diving into the lake to wash away the blood.

Her courage was back. She felt a hundred per cent Orizon.

For a few seconds there was confusion. Everybody spoke at once, trying to take in Rebecca's words.

Then Leiko and the boys rushed toward the stables.

Rebecca followed them, dripping wet. She called after them but they didn't pay any attention. She kept thinking of the other girls who were sleeping, as well as of Lady Danae and Lord Life. Confusion reigned as she kept shouting at the boys to forget Pegasus and run back to the house. Finally they stopped running.

"What are you shouting, Rebecca?" José asked.

"We should warn Lord Life and Lady Danae and wake the girls," she said. "Something terrible is going on. Pegasus is dead now – we must see to the living."

As they all turned and ran towards the house huge flames rose up into the night, stopping them in their tracks. They were coming from the direction of Leiko's house, about five hundred yards from Lord Life's abode. Now they knew that something terrible was happening and they ran on even faster, shouting warnings at the tops of their voices.

Leiko rushed to find Lord Life and Lady Danae while the others went to the girls' room.

"Just get your swords and shields," Rebecca shouted at them as they were jerked from their sleep. "Don't bother changing – we must all get out. Right now! Once we're outside run to the trees."

Moving fast but without panic they were outside within a minute, following Rebecca's lead and racing to the trees. They had already accepted her as their leader and obeyed her without question. As they ducked behind the thick trunks they saw a large group of Cyclopes and Porths closing in on the house, brandishing swords, clubs and flaming torches.

The attackers separated into four groups and surrounded the house, one group on each side. Some broke the windowpanes and threw their torches in, while others set fires against the walls. The house, old and made entirely of wood, had caught fire easily and was already burning like a huge bonfire.

Five minutes later the children still had no idea what had happened to Lord Life, Lady Danae and Leiko, none of whom had appeared at either of the doors. The Porths and Cyclopes stood around the blazing house, waiting to attack anyone who ran out. Anyone who stayed inside would soon be burned to death.

Suddenly they burst out through the kitchen door. Lady Danae and Lord Life were armed with swords and shields while Leiko wielded his club.

A party of five Cyclopes and five Porths fell upon them. Three of the enemy fell quickly. The Cyclopes and the Porths standing guard on the other sides of the house did not leave their posts, even though they realized what was happening. They had orders not to move and to keep the whole exterior of the house under surveillance in case any trainee Orizons escaped. They had no idea that the children were already outside, watching them.

"We'll move as far to the right as we can," Rebecca told the others, "behind the trees. Then we'll attack. As soon as the other groups realize that we're already out of the house they'll all charge. We must kill the first seven as quickly as possible. We'll be in a tough position but we're sure to overcome them. Attack without war cries so that the other groups don't notice us immediately."

By the time the children charged there were only six opponents still standing, three Cyclopes and three Porths. Lady Danae, seeing the rescue party coming, was distracted for a second and a Cyclopes's club struck her an almighty blow on the head. Lord Life saw her sink to the ground but he kept on fighting. The children killed the remaining six aggressors in less than a minute.

The other Porths and Cyclopes rushed towards the victors before they'd had a chance to catch their breath. Now it was seventeen against thirty and the battle became fierce.

Lord Life was enraged. Whenever he could he glanced at the slumped Danae, desperate to go to her aid. The children used their shields to protect themselves from the blows of the clubs. Their training, their courage, their sense of injustice and, most of all, the Flame gave them strength and spirit. Six more enemies fell, sapping the morale of those left and encouraging the Orizons.

More of the enemy fell and soon they were seventeen against nineteen: seven Porths and twelve Cyclopes. When Lord Life killed another Porth, making the numbers almost even, the enemy became agitated.

"We must leave," a Porth bellowed.

His comrades began to retreat, followed by the Cyclopes. Lord Life, Leiko and the Orizons did not pursue them, obeying the laws of war in the Land of the White Sun.

The attackers from Beast had been so sure of their victory. The operation had been carefully planned. A powerful strike force had been organized. Twenty of the best Porths and twenty of the best Cyclopes had been chosen. Some of them had suggested that more were needed but that proposal had been considered shameful since there were only fifteen children and three adults in the house. Now the attackers would have to think of some excuses to justify their disgrace.

LORD LIFE

As their foes left, Lord Life sheathed his sword, dropped his shield and knelt next to Danae. Fifteen terrible minutes had passed since she had been hit. The children watched as he touched her body in different places in search of a heartbeat. Then he lifted her and walked away without a word. Everyone realized that Lady Danae was dead.

Lord Life laid her down on the grass under a tree and sat silently beside her. The others moved away from the heat of the burning house, putting aside their swords and shields and sitting at a respectful distance, all struggling to come to terms with what had happened.

If this was so hard for Lord Life and Leiko, who had thousands of years' experience of war, bloodshed and death, how could the fifteen-year-old children grasp it? As Pegasus had pointed out to Rebecca, just a few days ago they had been going to school in another world.

Nobody spoke. But for the loss of Lady Danae it would have been a minor battle. The death of Pegasus had saddened them all, but the loss of Danae was a blow that shook them to their souls. They stared at their bloodstained swords, none of them able to count how many foes each of them had killed or wounded.

They had often spoken about how they would feel at the moment they would have to kill. They had discussed it even more than they had spoken about the possibility of their own deaths. Now it had happened. Could it really have been that easy? Had the horror of losing Lady Danae diminished the emotional impact of the blood drying on their own swords? Or was it their training and the Flame inside them that had made them so calm?

Sergei kept touching his left arm and seemed to be suffering. Leiko went to him.

"Are you in pain, Sergei? Are you hurt?" he asked, examining the boy's arm and shoulder carefully.

Sergei yelped. "I was hit by a club," he said. "Luckily it missed my head. It didn't hurt much at the time."

Leiko probed the arm again and moved it slightly.

"You're lucky. Nothing's broken. It will be painful for a week or so. You must be patient."

After some time, Lord Life stood up and trudged towards the children and Leiko, who all rose to their feet. The spark in his eyes had died and his gaze was like a cloudy winter evening.

"Leiko," he said, "take Pegasus and Lady Danae and fly to Utopia. Leave her in front of the Wise Tree, then wake Felicia and tell her the tragic news. Be gentle with her. She may be the leader of the Orizons in Utopia, but her mother's death will be a terrible blow.

"Tell her to raise a general alarm for everyone to prepare for war. I think the Sharkans are going to attack. They expected to kill us all today, which would have lowered the morale of the people of Utopia in advance of any battle. That would have given the powers of Evil a great advantage. If war hasn't already started, Turgoth may think twice when he hears that we're still alive. Their own morale will have taken a blow once they hear that so many Cyclopes and Porths were unable to defeat us. The children and I will set out on foot and in a few hours we'll reach the Fortress. We'll take the five horses that we have here."

Leiko spoke without raising his gaze from the ground.

"Lord Life, it seems that Pegasus too is dead. They killed him first, then torched my house before coming here."

Lord Life said nothing. As he ran towards the stables the others scrambled to retrieve their swords and shields and follow him. When they arrived they found that Rebecca had been right – and that all the other horses had been clubbed to death as well.

The children saw the tears welling up in Lord Life's eyes as he struggled to suppress his sobbing. They were shocked to see such an emotional reaction from the Leader of the Orizons.

"They were completely defenceless," he said in a broken voice, his lips quivering like leaves in a cold north wind. "We must leave out water and food for the rest of the animals."

Once that had been done they returned to Danae.

"We'll make a stretcher from branches," Lord Life said, his voice growing steadier. "We leave at once."

They worked by the light of the burning house as the last of the walls crumbled to ashes. Lord Life found his wife's sword. As he bent to pick it up, he heard a groan and a fallen Cyclopes stirred. His head was bloody and his eye was shut tight. Lord Life knelt down close and touched him lightly.

The Cyclopes whispered and Lord Life leaned in closer to hear.

"Water… water… a little water."

His voice sounded distant, as though it was coming from another world.

"Leiko … Leiko!" Lord Life called out. "Bring some water. Someone is alive."

As Leiko and the children ran over they felt the scorching heat of the fire.

"He must have been unconscious and he's just coming to," Lord Life said. "He's badly wounded. His skull is crushed. Bring me some water, Leiko. The hen house is closest. Fetch a bucket and something to pour water into and help him drink. Make haste, please!"

Leiko sped off. The children looked on in amazement. Despite all that had happened, Lord Life was helping a Cyclopes! And now he was about to give him water to drink!

"Children, please help me move him further away, near Danae. It's too hot here."

With only half their hearts in the job, Bill, Jabal, José and Carlos lifted the fallen Cyclopes.

"Easy, easy, children. Steady!" Lord Life kept saying while holding the Cyclopes's head with both hands, as if it were a newborn baby.

They put him down close to Danae and Lord Life knelt at his side again.

"He's losing a lot of blood. We must stop the bleeding," he said "Go to a Porth and get me his vest. Let's see what we can do. If you can find a knife on one of the dead, bring that too."

For a few seconds no one obeyed. Then Rashid and Abu headed reluctantly back to the bodies. They took a vest from one of them and found a knife. By the time they returned, Leiko had brought a wooden bucket and a deep clay bowl that was used for chicken feed.

The Cyclopes groaned every now and then, slipping in and out of consciousness. Lord Life cut a piece of leather from the vest and used it as a compress. He dipped it into the water and then put it to the Cyclopes's lips. He also cleaned his wounded head. Blood was pouring from a gash in the Cyclopes's temple and from his ear. The wound was deep and ugly. The Cyclopes's eye remained shut.

Lord Life picked up the bowl and tried to give him a little water to drink. The Cyclopes sipped a few drops with difficulty but most of the liquid spilled onto the ground.

"Leiko, help me make a bandage out of the vest and try to stop the bleeding."

Leiko squatted down on his heels too. All of the children knew that it must have been Leiko who had inflicted this terrible wound on the Cyclopes with his club. Now he was tending to him, trying to save his life, and he seemed to be doing it as wholeheartedly as Lord Life and not like them, who deep inside wished that the Cyclopes would die.

They cut the vest into strips, made a bandage and tied it round the Cyclopes's head. The children recognized the way that Doctor Afterland had taught them to bandage wounds. Lord Life gave the Cyclopes more water to drink.

"What do you think, Leiko?" he asked.

"It looks bad; quite bad."

The Cyclopes opened his eye and looked at Lord Life intently.

"Lord Life ... Lord Life ... thank you – Lord Life, I killed your wife ..."

His voice was low but steady.

Lord Life did not react at all, as though he heard nothing. But everyone else had heard.

"Leiko," he said. "We'll fix up another stretcher. As long as he's alive we'll carry him. We'll take some water with us. If he dies, we'll leave him behind. Watch over him. "Then he turned to the children. "You'll get tired, but we must take the Cyclopes along with us, as long as he's alive. You can take it in turns. He's very heavy so four of you will carry him at a time.

"Don't look at me like that. The battle is over. He's no longer our enemy. He's a creature of the Land of the White Sun; he's in a hard spot and we must help him. We must never be cruel! We must show some compassion. Can't you hear him bleating?"

Nobody spoke. Soon the second stretcher was ready; it was bigger and stronger than the first one. The Cyclopes was going to be a terrible weight and the children secretly hoped that he would die and they would be able to leave him behind.

Lord Life placed Lady Danae's sword on her body. Before they left they drenched the glowing embers of the burning houses to ensure that the fire didn't spread. When every spark was extinguished Lord Life walked to the end of the stretcher where his wife's head lay, turned his back, knelt, took hold of the stretcher and lifted it carefully while Leiko took the other end.

The children ran and tried to help.

"No," Lord Life told them, feeling a need to be with his wife all the way on the final journey. "I must carry her to Utopia. Those of you who wish to take turns with Leiko may do so."

He lifted the stretcher, gripping it tightly to keep it safe, as if he was holding his whole world, his whole being.

So it was that they set out for Utopia. Everyone took turns apart from Sergei, who was in too much pain. They did it for the Queen of Utopia, the gracious hostess they'd met only two days earlier, who had treated them so warmly and tenderly. She had embraced them all, like a mother hen sheltering her chicks. They all believed that they were the reason she was dead.

Those who carried Danae put their swords and shields on the Cyclopes's stretcher because they had no scabbards. They were dressed only in their bloodstained pyjamas.

As Lord Life walked he reminisced, his thoughts wandering the Universe: the galaxies; the solar system; the Earth, eternally following the same orbit as if it were tied to the iron handle of a water-well.

They carried him back to his birth in Atlantis, a beautiful rich island providing in great abundance all the commodities of the world. It was a land with an exquisite civilization and great power but its king had become possessed by vanity, ambition and arrogance, and had decided to conquer Attica and Egypt.

Lord Life had been strongly opposed of the expedition but was only a nineteen-year-old officer at the time. The attack on Attica was intense and violent but the skilfully trained Athenians, with their great knowledge of the art of war, led the kingdoms of Attica to victory over the army of Atlantis.

There were countless dead bodies. Many other Atlanteans, including Lord Life, were captured. He was forced to become an oarsman on the Athenian king's galley. The years passed and while enslaved he heard that Atlantis had sunk. All of its people, including his family, had been lost beneath the ocean's deep dark waters.

One night they were returning from the island of Dilos, where the Athenian king had gone to offer sacrifices and worship the God Apollo. There was a fair favourable wind filling the sails, giving the oarsmen some respite from their toil. Suddenly the wind decided to blow hard into the sea. Enraged, the sea began to resist with foamed hands. The harder the wind blew, the more the sea pushed back in fury. The travellers watched the peaceful seascape transforming into wild and hostile waves.

The night was dipped in darkness, covered by black opaque clouds. The mighty foes, wind and water, collided in their wrath like bulls, throwing lightning and thunder from their nostrils like bursts of cannon fire. Rain pelted down on the galley before turning into hailstones as large as eggs. Before the sailors could bring them down, the sails were shredded to rags despite their leather bracings.

Within moments the ship was covered with the balls of white ice. The vessel swirled uncontrollably in the heart of the storm. Waves like mountains thrust it to their peaks, then plunged it down into abysmal darkness. The galley staggered drunkenly, making sick those on board as they struggled to hold on.

The sea had become a maniac killer, beating the defenceless passengers mercilessly with its waves. Both the king and the captain were at the stern, grasping the ship's bridge and barely protecting themselves from the blows of the hailstones. The king kept shouting to his crew to cut the ropes and free the enslaved oarsmen. With difficulty, all the slaves from Atlantis, Lord Life among them, were freed.

Whips of crimson lightning fell continuously from the sky, their fire extinguished by the raging waters. One of them hit the galley's single mast, collapsing it onto the ship like a felled tree, crushing two sailors and the captain.

Lord Life saw that part of the mast had fallen onto the king's legs. He struggled towards the trapped man, holding on to the gunwale with grim determination. The king moaned in pain, clasping his broken leg. The ship too roared with agony, as if its own bones were breaking as it was thrust onto a sharp reef.

Lord Life realized that nothing would now save the vessel from sinking. He grabbed an axe and hacked off two pieces of wood, lashing them together to make something like a stretcher and a life-raft. He tied the king onto it, shouting to the sailors to jump ship.

The men from Atlantis, traditional islanders as they were, swam like dolphins. They plunged into the waves of hell, followed by the rest of the crew. As the galley heeled over and started sinking, Lord Life lifted the Athenian king with the help of some loyal sailors, and they found themselves in the water. He wrapped a rope round his arm and held its end tightly, so that he would not drift away from the stretcher.

Other men from Atlantis had seen his struggle and came to help Lord Life in his effort to save the injured king from drowning.

Their struggle lasted many hours but eventually they reached the shore and, when daybreak came, they realized that they were in South Evoia. All the Atlantean slaves were safe, as well as most of the crew and the king. Grateful for his life, the king of Athens gave the slaves back their freedom, right there on the sands, and Lord Life decided to stay and live there, since he no longer had a homeland to go back to. Later, he met Hercules, Theseus and many other heroes and impressed the Olympian Mythical Gods. Before the Earth's destruction, they asked him to live among them in the First Parallel Dimension.

Many years later, another soul was born in that dimension. They met in Chaos. A chance in a trillion!

"*Somewhere in space there is someone awaiting us. It is the same person for whom, we are waiting. The remaining half of the apple, as the Chinese saying goes. Two entities loving each other before they even met in life*", Lord Life thought.

As he walked on, his memories continued to unfold. He remembered how the love between Danae and him was born and grew. The special feeling of the first heartbeats. He never made any attempt to conceal his great love – what would have been the point?

All the Gods liked her. Eros told Lord Life that he had chosen well, saying he, Eros, was sure that they suited each other. Lord Life believed him because Eros was the greatest expert in

Creation on that subject. The question was whether she would want him too.

Lord Life spoke to Danae, filling her heart with love: *"I've been waiting for you for my whole life. I didn't know where you would come from or what you would look like."*

He told her to think things over carefully and also to ask Eros's opinion. All this had happened shortly before the Gods left for the Second Parallel Dimension.

They delayed getting married. And when the wedding took place they decided not to have a child at once because Lord Life had already been given the leadership of Utopia and had many extra duties. Then, a hundred and twenty Earth years ago, he knew what it meant to be a father.

His thoughts were jumping from one thing to another, like a bird seeking seeds. What to recall first after so many years together? For a long time they had lived on Earth. Danae could not adjust easily, because she had been born and raised in the Land of the White Sun. How right Eros had been! She was a perfect mother; a fearless fighter, and a good, wise companion. Now she was dead. He would never remarry, but sleep at night with his memories.

With each painful step Lord Life felt himself ageing. When a young Orizon from the previous intake of trainees had asked him how old he was, he had replied: *'My heart is only twenty; that's how I've felt ever since I was fifty.'* Now he felt his heart becoming a thousand years old.

The sun had risen by the time Lord Life's band reached the Fortress. The guards in the watchtowers saw them coming from afar, baffled by their attire and the two stretchers. As the battered group drew closer they recognized Lord Life and Leiko.

The trumpets sounded, the gate opened and several guards ran out to meet their leader. It didn't take them long to grasp the magnitude of the disaster.

Lord Life still refused to let the stretcher be taken from him and the children clung on just as tightly.

"Take the Cyclopes to the hospital and call Doctor Afterland to try to save him," Lord Life ordered the guards.

Princess Felicia heard the trumpets and thought that an attack had begun. She mounted her horse and galloped towards the Gate. She saw the procession from afar and recognized her father. Lord Life continued walking, proud and unbending, staring straight ahead as his daughter approached.

Felicia knew what had happened just by her father's expression. She fought to control her feelings as she took the stretcher handles from Lee. She looked at her mother's peaceful face and then at her father's ramrod-straight back. She cast her gaze up to the sky and then back to her mother's closed eyes and silent lips.

With each step the group took, the crowd around them grew. The procession headed towards the theatre. By the time they arrived, everyone in the Fortress was there. Only the sentries remained at their posts. Leiko and Bull walked beside the stretcher, flanking the princess. Everybody walked lightly and in step, barely making a sound. Nobody spoke. Even the birds stopped singing, flocking together and flying in formation over the crowd and the dead queen, their eyes fixed upon Lady Danae as they too paid homage. There were thousands of them, like a multicoloured cloud mantling the mournful sun. A deathly silence reigned, and as the procession moved along the path the trees lowered their branches. The wind in their leaves held its breath.

The words of Pegasus came back to Rebecca: *"You must be tough and prepared to endure."*

But he was dead now too, killed by mean-spirited bullies. Rebecca knew that the mean of spirit were those who caused the greatest harm. She had become aware of the meaning of Evil and what power it possessed. She vowed that she would fight its forces for as long as she lived.

What had Pegasus ever done to deserve this? He did not take part in war; he took no initiatives, he had no authority or power to make decisions. Why had they killed him? If they had killed her it would have been justified, but why Pegasus? Now Rebecca understood why Lord Life had wept for Pegasus and the horses although he had borne up against the death of Lady Danae, whom he surely adored.

She tried to compare and judge the two leaders without bias: Turgoth and Lord Life. Both of them were outstanding. There was no equal to them. Both had been trapped by the unjust, superficial and dangerous decision of the Mythical Gods. Both were brave and were prepared to sacrifice their lives and their families for the sake of their people. They freely offered their love to the Enemy if they deemed it necessary. One of them was a tough yet sensitive child of the desert, the sky and Nature. He favoured knowledge and reflection and was a profound anatomist of life with brand new ideas and controversial codes of his own. He was a banner-bearer for the young, an enemy full of experience and wisdom. Inelegant but true. The other, in spite of being wise, was against too much examination of the way things were. He had the calm strength of a great leader, full of remarkable sensitivity. He was a down-to-earth pragmatist, but also a strong supporter of simple things. He was a conciliatory planner, brimming with love and humanity.

The group entered the theatre. They went to the horrified Wise Tree and laid the stretcher in front of it. After a while Felicia left for the three-dimensional broadcasting station to make the following announcement:

"People of Utopia. At midnight, the house of Lord Life underwent a cowardly attack by the forces of Evil. Twenty Cyclopes and twenty Porths killed Pegasus and the other horses, then surrounded Leiko's house and set fire to it in order to burn him alive. Luckily, Leiko was out with the trainee Orizons.

"Then they surrounded the house of my father and mother and set fire to it, intending to burn alive my parents and the young trainees whom they believed to be asleep inside.

"A fierce fight broke out and lasted for quite some time. The forces of Good were victorious. The twelve Cyclopes and six Porths that survived retreated.

"We have brought back a seriously wounded Cyclopes and he is being operated on at this moment in hospital.

"The trainee Orizons, Leiko and Lord Life are safe. Only the trainee Sergei has a slight injury, to his arm.

"Lady Danae fell in battle, fighting against the forces of Evil. She has been brought here to the Fortress, where she will remain until six in the evening. As of now, we are in a state of war. Since the forces of Evil have violated the rules, there is a risk that they may attack not only the Fortress but also your houses. For this reason, as from today all minors and non-combatants will move to our special buildings in the Fortress. There will be patrols and observers posted at strategic spots. As soon as they see something suspicious they will warn any warriors who happen to be outside the Fortress at that time to immediately evacuate their houses and farms.

"We will arrange for all the necessary equipment and supplies, so that the Fortress is fully stocked for at least three months with everything we may need. Our hospital will also be in a state of readiness day and night in case of emergencies.

"Lord Life has sent messengers to Turgoth requesting a meeting for talks on neutral ground. By this evening we shall have Turgoth's answer and will inform you at once. Thank you for listening."

After the announcement the princess went back to the theatre. Field Marshal Foster, Claudia and Hunter were already there and offered their condolences. At six, Lord Life and Princess Felicia picked up the stretcher and carried it home. Only Leiko and Bull followed them.

Lord Life dug a grave under a tall, lush palm tree that Danae herself had planted. Taking her in his arms, he kissed her tenderly and laid her down in the grave. Then he covered her with earth, creating a low mound. He watered it and sowed some seeds that Bull gave him. Finally, he thrust Lady Danae's sword deep into the ground at the head of the grave.

"Leiko," Lord Life said later, when they were all sitting in the house. "I want you to go back to the farm. Take some volunteers and carriages. Then come back, bringing all the livestock with you, and take the animals to one of the empty fields of Utopia, wherever you choose to make your home."

Turgoth agreed to the meeting. It was to take place at a spot approximately halfway between Utopia and Beast. Next day, Lord Life and Bull set out for the meeting place with five hundred armed Orizons, two hundred Amazons and two hundred Centaurs.

The two leaders arrived at almost the same time. But as Lord Life drew up with his mighty force he saw that Turgoth had only one Cyclopes, one Porth and one Sharkan general in his entourage. He was surprised and embarrassed that Turgoth had come practically unarmed while he had brought so many troops with him.

While still at some distance, he ordered everyone else to stop and proceeded with just Bull by his side.

"What's this, Lord Life?" Turgoth mocked. "Did you need to bring a whole army with you?"

Trying to cover his awkwardness, Lord Life spoke sternly. "What would you have me do, Turgoth? You've violated rules that nobody has dared to break for thousands of years. You've gone back on all our agreements. You attacked a young girl. Then you sent the Gorgons to kill children. And then you tried to burn us all alive. So I guessed that you might be setting a trap again today. I have every reason to be suspicious. You know perfectly well that I don't put my own life first, just as I know that you don't put yours first either. But, like you, I am responsible for my people, so I came prepared. I am deeply disappointed in you for having deceived me so wickedly that night when I came to your house looking for Rebecca. We in the Land of the White Sun have never been hypocrites and liars, regardless of which side we were on. I never expected that of you, nor any of these other things."

Lord Life's words stung like a whip. Turgoth bowed his head in shame.

Turgoth's face plainly revealed his sadness. "First of all, I want to offer you my condolences on the death of your wife. I know how you must be feeling because I went through the same thing once myself. I also want to apologize for the matter of Rebecca. What you say is right, but once I'd set things in motion I couldn't go back or I'd have betrayed my people.

"There has been a tremendous reaction among the people of Beast and I fear a mutiny, especially among the Porths who have enticed the Cyclopes onto their side.

"My leadership is questioned. I wanted to resign from my duties, but since I'm the only immortal Sharkan in Beast not everyone accepted it; the Sharkans in particular objected. So, as the leader of these people, I must do my duty."

"Look, Turgoth," said Lord Life, "are the rules and the agreements that we made thousands of years ago still in force? I need to know that you won't attack non-combatants or do anything against our laws again. You must give me your word that you'll put a stop to all this."

"Lord Life," Turgoth said apologetically, "you know I'm not underhand and I don't care about my own skin, but I cannot give you my word. I'm not in total control of the situation. A rebellion might break out. There are factions who oppose our treaties and they affect our decisions.

"Ever since we lost four generals and one was crippled, they all felt they had to do something to maintain their authority and morale. For them it wasn't a pretext but a need. Now they feel somewhat appeased by the death of Lady Danae."

"All right," said Lord Life. "I respect you for telling me this and I thank you for speaking in such a straightforward manner. You should know that we have a Cyclopes with a serious head wound. We've had him operated on. If he survives, I'll send him to you as soon as he can be moved. I bid you farewell."

He turned his horse and left. Bull followed him. Turgoth watched them pensively, feeling ashamed and confused. But at the same time he also felt the power of the indignation that had been smouldering inside him for centuries at the profound injustice of the Flame. It felt as if the burden of responsibility towards his people was crushing him.

The next day Rebecca met Bull, Princess Felicia and Lord Life. She told them everything about the incident with the Gorgons, making it clear that there was a traitor in Utopia. The worst thing was that the traitor had to be a high-ranking official, since he had known the exact location of the meeting place, something that had been known to very few.

Lord Life briefed Rebecca about his meeting with Turgoth and she became lost in thought, trying to predict Turgoth's next move. That evening, she visited the Wise Tree.

The tree stroked her hair with its branches.

"I caught a glimpse of you the day before yesterday," it said. "I was hoping that you'd come by yesterday, at least."

"I've been very confused and troubled. A few days ago I made a friend. Although we spoke very little he immediately found a special place in my heart. He was so sensitive, and had profound thoughts and interesting views. He loved children, just like you do, and he told me that I had to be tough and prepared to bear difficulties."

The Wise Tree felt an army of jealous worms burrowing into its insides, eating everything they found.

"So that's why she didn't come," it thought. *"She's made another friend."*

The Tree could see that Rebecca was an exceptional creature, and it did not want her to have anyone else to share her thoughts with. It was afraid that she might spend more time with the new friend and forget her old friend, the Tree, never coming to read books to it or teach it how to read. It restrained itself, hid its thoughts and said nothing. It was the first time it had ever felt jealous, but it was also the first time it had made such a good friend.

"We shouldn't be jealous," it thought. *"It isn't right. For thousands of years I've been advising everyone not to be jealous and here I am not following my own advice."*

It willed the worms of jealousy to leave it in peace.

"Alas, my dear friend," Rebecca said, her eyes brimming with tears, "the evil ones have murdered Pegasus. They killed a defenceless innocent horse. Can you believe it?"

"What a pity," said the Tree, a little hastily.

"I'm going to Earth the day after tomorrow."

"When are we going to read books?" the Tree asked timidly, anxious about all these changes.

"Next summer, when I return to continue with my training. I'm going now. I'm very upset. I'll come to say goodbye tomorrow. Good night."

"Good night," said the Wise Tree in a broken voice. It noticed that its bark was covered with sweat.

The following day, Rebecca visited the hospital. The Cyclopes had shown great progress after Doctor Afterland and Rashid's grandfather had performed the operation. Rashid's grandfather had been an expert in head surgery for thousands of years, performing miraculous operations since the time of the Pharaohs.

Even though the Cyclopes's condition was grave, he recovered consciousness the following day. The doctors' prognosis was that the worst was over and the Cyclopes would make a full recovery.

The Cyclopes was puzzled when he heard Rebecca's knock because, apart from the doctors and the princess, no one else had visited him. He was reading *Gulliver's Travels*.

"May I come in?" asked Rebecca.

"Of course. What a pleasant surprise!"

"I'm going back to Earth tomorrow and I've come to see how you are."

"I'm feeling well. If you're leaving, you must be one of the trainee Orizons. You must have been there. What's your name?"

"Rebecca. Yes, I was there and I really wanted to kill you."

"I too wanted to kill – you and your comrades, in my case – but not any more. Will you do me a favour? Can you ask the princess to let me stay? I'll bring my wife and two children and live here with you. I'll fight on your side."

"Why do you want to do that?"

"Because Lord Life saved my life."

"Turgoth saved my life, too. Does that mean I should go to Beast and fight against my people?"

The Cyclopes's mouth gaped open and his one eye looked as if it might pop from its socket.

"Did Turgoth save your life? If he did, then you have a great obligation to him. It's one thing for a friend or an ally to save your life and something else for an enemy to do so. You must consider that. But my case must be the only one of its kind in the world. I killed Lord Life's wife. I told him so and yet he saved my life. Please help me stay. You are an important person. From what I've heard you're held in high esteem. If you put in a good word for me they may let me stay."

"What's your name?"

"Rondo," the Cyclopes said proudly.

"Can you tell me, Rondo, how you knew that the plan involving the Gorgons had failed and that you would have to attack us at Lord Life's house?"

"Rebecca, changing camps doesn't mean I'm willing to turn

traitor," the Cyclopes said angrily. " I don't want you to intervene or say anything about me. Is that why you came to see me? You may leave now. Please go!"

"I didn't mean to offend you. I'm sorry. I got carried away. I won't try to justify myself. You see, I sense a traitor in our midst and I must seek him out. Goodbye!"

Rebecca left, sorry that she had insulted the Cyclopes and feeling perplexed. *"How is it possible that the ones who refuse to turn traitor are on the side of Evil, and those who betray their comrades are on the side of Good?"*

In the evening she went to say goodbye to the Wise Tree. She embraced and kissed it.

"I'll think about you. I'll tell the moon about you," she said.

"Have a good journey. I'll be waiting for you," replied the Wise Tree, watching sadly and lovingly as Rebecca walked away.

The Tree had never felt so confused. Had the seething mass of jealous worms disappeared because it had sent them away, or had they left by themselves as soon as they had heard that Pegasus had been killed?

ADJUSTMENT

When Rebecca returned to Earth the sky was overcast. She had been looking forward to seeing the moon but clouds obscured it for the next couple of nights, as if punishing her for not having appreciated what she had had for so many years.

Despite the strength that she gained from the Flame, adjustment was not easy. The Earth seemed a gentle place, its tranquil surface concealing the depth of the problems below. There seemed an inconceivable distance between the bloodshed at Lord Life's house and the mist shrouding the countryside around London.

On her first day back home Rebecca walked familiar routes, passing the school she had attended when she was little and other places that brought back memories. Just after noon, she headed towards the woods where her schoolmates used to play. It had been a hideaway of the magical carefree years. That was where the first stirrings had begun: the secret loves of the classroom and the neighbourhood, fighting for a share of her emotions with the demands of classes, games and playmates.

Such anxiety for a sign!

The search, and the child's interpretation of a glance, a smile, a conversation, a movement. Do you take courage or lose what you haven't even got?

'He looked at me …' 'He smiled at me …' 'She spoke to me …'

Doubt – loss of appetite. The drawing from a secret admirer on the pencil case rousing the imagination. The love letter from a mysterious stranger with the writing deliberately disguised.

The colourful, blossoming flowers of hope smell so sweetly! We water, tend and take care of them. We'll never allow them to wither, as long as we live. Above all, we will never cut them!

The triumphant entrance into adolescence. Flirtation. Kissing! The bell ringing happily. Anxiously and inexpertly, we assume the roles of men and women. Important years. Decisive ones.

Autumn was advancing once again, bringing pale sunshine and beneficial rains, mischievous winds and monotonous fog. Despite man's intrusions, the season would distribute its bounty as it knew best. Once again, it would do its duty with care until it handed Nature over to the sturdy arms of winter.

Rebecca traipsed among the trees in the damp wood, trampling the fallen leaves. A slight breeze made them rustle. More kept falling, drifting in the air. Those that still clung to the branches fluttered like multi-coloured fans. The dreamlike colour of the leaves lent enchantment to the golden trees and to the earth around them. She held out her hands with open palms and a leaf on its first and last journey fell into their warm, tender nest.

"You die beautiful, strong and proud because you enhance Nature with your extraordinary beauty. And you're happy because you served your purpose while you lived," Rebecca whispered to it lovingly, taking it home to press between the pages of a book.

The wind turned stronger, as if it was trying to blow away autumn's depression from the forest. Suddenly, Rebecca thought that the trees looked like giant birds trying to take off and fly. The branches looked like their wings and their leaves like feathers.

The next morning Rebecca set off for London, walking through the streets and riding upstairs on the city's red double-decker buses, revelling in the lush greenness of the parks and the stillness of the Thames, the city's main artery that gave it rhythm and life. Along its banks glass skyscrapers had sprouted like parasites. Despite them, Rebecca had never seen London looking so beautiful.

Each building had its own character and charm, not only housing people but also reflecting the great intellectual inheritance and exquisite taste of centuries. The effect was spoiled only by the presence of cars, as in so many great cities. Seeing children sitting on the steps outside their front doors Rebecca thought how much happier they would be without the vile vehicles that polluted the atmosphere and sapped human health.

When she shut out the cars, the asphalted streets and the commotion from her consciousness, the infinite seductiveness of the city shone through. All around her she imagined only pedestrians, horses and carriages, as in the Land of the White Sun.

Rebecca stayed in the city until late at night, absorbing its ambience with the deepest relish.

Rebecca still couldn't get used to the idea that she was immortal. The sense of eternity filled her with awe. When she had learned a few months earlier that she would never fall ill, she had been overjoyed. She'd heard from others how much they and their families suffered from various ailments, even those that didn't last long. It was something unknown to her. She'd never even caught a common cold.

She had also witnessed the great misery of those with serious illnesses and had seen how their close relatives suffered along with them.

From an early age Rebecca had realized that people were alive and healthy by chance. Incurable diseases always lurked within the human body. They would suddenly awake from their lethargy and develop to weaken or even kill people. Bacteria and viruses were constantly on the prowl, invaders trying to enter the body and destroy it. Constant vigilance and luck both played their parts. A chance encounter, close or otherwise, with another human being might prove to be a death sentence.

Rebecca became aware of the anxiety and uncertainty that many people went through when they went for medical check-ups. When a check-up began, Moira, the goddess of Fate, flipped a coin. If the coin fell heads up, the outcome would be good. Tails up meant that the X-rays or the biopsy would point to death.

Rebecca would never have to face such distress, never have to worry whether she had a serious illness. The Flame had made her invincible. Yet she saw the injustice in it too. She remembered a fellow pupil, Oscar, from when they were both eleven. He was an only child, and a very healthy one who rarely caught even seasonal colds. He was tall, strong and a star at gymnastics and basketball. One day he had stopped coming to school. Then they heard that he was in hospital. The diagnosis was acute leukaemia. He died within eight days and the whole school had attended the funeral. His mother was about thirty years old and her hair had turned as white as snow. They said that on the first night, when she had been told the diagnosis, she had stayed at the hospital. By morning her hair had gone completely grey. The nurses had never seen anything like it. It had changed colour by the hour. They couldn't believe their eyes. In her despair she couldn't understand why they were looking at her so strangely. In the morning she went to the bathroom to wash her face and in the mirror came face to face with a white-haired stranger. Oscar's father had lost all his hair within two days although he was only in his thirties. Rebecca later found out that he went into a state of depression and entered a special clinic. The mother, with female fortitude, bore up better.

In Rebecca's opinion, everyone should have the Flame and never fall ill. It ought not to be the sole privilege of the Orizons.

She had grown into a pretty girl just like her mother, except that her eyes were brown while her relatives' were blue, grey or green. She was now about five feet seven inches tall and beautifully proportioned. The gymnastics that she had done when she'd been younger had helped build a shapely figure. Her long brown hair fell in soft waves. The beauty that radiated from her face rose from deep within her and anyone who looked at her sensed it. Her full lips and serious eyes gave her a compelling look of maturity. And when she smiled her whole face filled with a wondrous light and warmth that soothed the souls of all who looked on her.

Rebecca was satisfied with the thought that she would never grow old and that the face she saw in the mirror would remain as it was for ever. She would never have any wrinkles and her strength would never fail. Yet the idea of living for ever – unless of course she was killed – was something that she found hard to absorb.

Her parents wanted her to tell them in detail exactly what

had happened at Lord Life's house and in particular about Danae's death. But when they saw that she was not ready to talk about it they respected her silence.

That night the wind began to roar angrily and the clouds ran in terror to hide. Some of them were so scared that they began to cry tears of rain. Rebecca sat on the veranda again, waiting impatiently just as she had done the two previous nights. Eventually the sky cleared and the moon appeared, washed clean and bright.

It was as if it had preened and prepared itself especially to meet her and she felt a much-needed solace within her soul. She felt herself growing serene. In two days the moon would be full.

"I'm sorry it took me all these years to appreciate you," Rebecca said. "When I became aware of your absence I realized that I needed you deeply. Our brief parting showed me how indispensable you are to me and how much I love you. Forgive me."

As she looked at the moon, she saw that its expression was one of love and understanding. A warm, sweet smile spread over its face. It didn't bear grudges.

She spent the following two nights with it. On the second night the moon was full and she talked to it about the Wise Tree.

The following day Rebecca felt able to tell her parents in detail what had happened. She talked to them about the issue of the traitor and her failure so far to discover who it was.

"Rebecca, you can be absolutely sure that an Orizon would never turn traitor," her father assured her. "Even if one wanted to, the energy of the Flame would never let them."

They told her not to worry about her readjustment to Earth.

It was natural to feel confused after such a sudden change. They too had gone through that phase. But of course in her case it had been harder because she had endured shocking events and experienced intense adventures.

Before the start of school Rebecca painted two pictures. One of them showed the theatre, the Wise Tree, the hill and the Flame with the Sphinx. Above the Tree and to the right she painted the moon. Their gazes met and from their facial expressions it seemed as though they were engaged in a lively conversation.

The second painting was larger and depicted Lord Life and Turgoth on the shores of the lake. There were swans, flamingos, ducks and other birds on the water and in front of the two leaders was an altar bearing the Flame of the White Sun. The lord and the king had raised their wine cups in their left hands while they clasped each other's right one in a warm handshake. They were both smiling. Around them Orizons and Sharkans were celebrating in perfect harmony, playing music, singing, dancing and clinking their cups together.

Rebecca was looking forward to the first day back at school. She had missed her classmates and teachers. All of them talked of their holidays but she couldn't say anything. What *could* she say? That she'd had a good time? That she hadn't had a good time? She wasn't so sure herself.

As she returned to her daily routine on Earth, she cut back on the hours that she spent on school sports. Her physical education teachers couldn't understand why, when she had such great talent, she did not want to improve her performance. The only thing she practised systematically was kung fu.

Out of school Rebecca dedicated many hours to practising her dagger throwing. She wanted to make good progress by the following summer, so that Bull would teach her more of his secrets.

She began intensively rereading excerpts from the philosophers and scholars. Every word, every phrase was an intellectual and spiritual treasure: a precious legacy for all generations. The store of her knowledge was growing by the day. She had a lot of discussions with her father, whose own studies had included politics and economics.

During the Christmas holidays Rebecca returned to Kenya. Thomas told her that he had sometimes seen the lion near the grave. They reached the burial site a little before noon and pitched their tents close by. Rebecca suggested that they stay there for forty-eight hours at the most and that they should leave if the lion did not appear.

She went alone to the spot, taking with her some water and smoked meat. The dead lioness and cubs had indeed been well covered and grass was already growing on their grave. A few stones had been used to form the shapes of three hearts. She sat down and waited patiently.

After about four hours Rebecca heard the lion's roar. She rose and saw it running in the distance. She ran towards it and they met, rolling together on the ground in an embrace. The face of the King of the Jungle showed that he was the happiest lion in the world. They walked together towards the place where they had first met, next to the grave.

Rebecca offered him water, then drank some herself. She talked to him all the time and he growled happily. When they'd eaten she lay down and rested her head on his belly, just as she had done before.

"I've been working on what I promised you," she told him.

"But it's still in the early stages. I'm in contact with many people who love you and want to help. I think we'll succeed in getting significant improvements that will eventually lead to a ban on the use of animals in circuses.

"And please, I beg you not to go on living alone. You must strive to keep your species alive. Next time I come, I'd love to have you introduce me to your companions."

As the sun struck the mountaintops in the west, the peaks burst into a vivid glow that spread across the sky. The land and the lakes and the wildlife of Kenya basked in the incredible colours, while the humans were distracted by other concerns. The sunset bathed everything in the area: the trees, the low foliage, the grave, Rebecca and the lion. They looked like film stars – directed by the God of the Jungle – lit by the mighty spotlight that shimmered a hazy red from the heat and humidity. A herd of giraffes with their peculiar, dancing gait walked slowly, their long necks arched and proud, through the scene. They enjoyed the sundown quite unafraid, as if they knew that the fierce lion – their worst enemy – was absorbed in his companion and would not pounce on them. Indeed, today the lion looked at them indifferently. He usually felt jealous of them because they were the tallest animals and were closer to the heavens and to the Creator than himself, even though he was the King of the Jungle. He believed they could talk to God. In his opinion, they were friends with Him and that was why they always danced so haughtily.

"I have to go because the others are waiting for me," Rebecca said. "I intend to see as much as I can of your beautiful country. But before I go I want you to meet my grandparents and a friend of ours from the Masai tribe who takes care of your kind. They all love you and are interested in you."

She stood up, turned to where the others were waiting and waved, signalling to them to come over. They had already bundled up the tents and they began walking towards her. The lion had been lying down but, as soon as they approached, he rose like a perfect host.

One by one, as Rebecca introduced them to the lion, they stroked him. He accepted their caresses gladly and raised his right foreleg in a formal gesture of greeting. Waves of love spread between them. Maybe that was how God had created Nature and how humans had lived with animals in the beginning.

When they returned to their jeep the lion followed them and remained watching until they left.

"I'll be back," Rebecca called out. "Wait for me."

During the following days they visited Masai villages and met Thomas's parents. Everywhere they went they were welcomed with delight, and dances were staged in their honour. Rebecca became acquainted with the problems of those proud people, their way of life, habits and customs. She also visited several other tribes.

They met a team of archaeologists whose leader was an old acquaintance of Rebecca's grandfather.

"That team has spent many years searching for fossils in Africa," her grandfather told her when they left. "They claim human life began here. I don't argue with them. They've dedicated their lives and have often spent their own money to satisfy their scientific curiosity.

"You see, Rebecca, they want to prove that man descended from the apes rather than as is recounted in mythology and religious texts. From time to time they discover something. But what they claim is questioned by other scientists. Every discovery triggers new questions, speculation and dead ends. The archaeologists make a tremendous scientific effort that yields no firm results.

"I respect their work but I don't believe that it benefits humankind. Nothing that they assert will ever be fully accepted because people have an inner need to believe in something from which they can seek spiritual aid. Instead of looking for fossils, the archaeologists should help people and animals and stop them from becoming fossils themselves."

In the summer Rebecca returned to the Land of the White Sun, which was still in a state of war. The children and noncombatants were still living inside the Fortress. Day and night, sentries with trumpets were on guard at various posts, far from Utopia. Any sentry who spotted anything suspicious would blow his trumpet. On hearing it, the next in line would blow his, so that within two minutes the alarm would spread throughout Utopia. Those working on their farms would then return to the Fortress immediately.

At night they all slept in designated buildings that had been allotted to individual families. These places were not as comfortable as the people's own homes but at least they were safe.

The Cyclopes had made a full recovery and had returned to the kingdom of Beast. Lord Life refused to allow him to live permanently in Utopia. Though he had saved the Cyclopes's life, he could not bear the daily sight of the one who had killed his wife. The Cyclopes, after thanking Lord Life for his help and kindness, promised never to fight against Utopia again, his heart having been touched by Lord Life's forgiveness.

"I will never be ungrateful. The ancient ones used to say that ingratitude is the worst sin. I promise that I'll never forget."

On the first night after her return Rebecca took the painting she had brought with her to the Wise Tree.

"I painted this on Earth so that I could have you and the moon together for company," she explained. "We'll hang it on one of your branches so you can talk to it at night. See how beautiful the moon is and how friendly? I've talked to it a lot about you and it knows you well. You can keep each other company."

The Wise Tree trembled with excitement. They chose the right branch together and Rebecca hung up her painting of the bright and peaceful companion.

The young Orizons' training routine was as tough as before, but they all made good progress. Rebecca excelled in the use of the sword. Only Field Marshal Foster could take her on and even he lost his sword a few times while Rebecca never did.

"Do you remember my telling you on your first day of training that some of you may become better than me?" he asked. "Well, here's the proof! Needless to say, I have never let my sword slip from my hand on purpose. After Princess Felicia, whom I trained some years ago, Rebecca is the best sword-fighter I have ever come across."

Foster looked deep into Rebecca's eyes.

"A good teacher is always very happy when his students surpass him, because then he is achieving his goal."

He looked at each of them in turn.

"You have all made great progress with the sword. I also hear that you've made excellent headway with the bow and arrow, the spear and the javelin. Congratulations to all of you!"

One day, when Rebecca was practising dagger throwing with Bull, the Minotaur said to her:

"You mustn't harbour suspicions about Foster. While you were away, I had a talk with Lord Life, who insisted that we shouldn't hunt for the traitor among the Orizons. It's impossible that it should be one of them because they all have the Flame inside them."

"My father told me the same thing and since then I no longer suspect him."

Bull taught Rebecca that someone's neck was most effective target for the dagger. A strike there was almost always fatal, but there was a greater risk of missing because the target was small. The chest and the belly were easier marks, but the result was not always lethal.

Their daily confinement within the Fortress enabled the fifteen children to get to know each other better. Almost every night they got together, singing, dancing and talking for hours on end. Every new circle of trainees formed their own bonds but this group had been brought even closer by their previous shared experiences.

They spoke about serious matters but they also told jokes and played games. The greatest tease and practical joker in the group was José. He brimmed with life, love and warmth. His jokes flowed out in a torrent, making the youngsters laugh themselves silly, as if they were tickling one another.

Rebecca needed laughter and whenever she had the chance she would let herself go. Besides, laughter is the music of life. In her view, Carlos was actually the one with the deepest and brightest sense of humour. Besides making her laugh and relax, he raised issues from which useful lessons could be learned. The incredible duo, José and Carlos, never left anyone in peace.

The person they teased most of all was Bill, whom they had nicknamed 'Cowboy'. No one used his real name any more. But Cowboy-Bill was far wiser than his years, as indeed they all were. He took the others' teasing good-naturedly and was the first to burst out into uproarious laughter. His unpredictable self-satire often left them speechless with mirth and he was also capable of great seriousness. Everyone remembered that he had been the first to attack Stheno, armed with nothing more than his sword.

"It's very difficult to help people," he said one day. "Those who aren't happy won't readily accept the happiness of others. Those who are ill are jealous of other people's good health, and those who are penniless envy the wealth of others. Here there are no rich or poor people but on Earth people make such comparisons all the time. How can we deal with this situation? How can we make people cast their jealousy aside when these disparities exist? How can we do anything when there are at the same time sick people and healthy people?"

The young folk were maturing rapidly because of the burdens they shouldered. During the past school year they had come to realize the great problems spreading through every country on Earth.

Carlos reminded them how Lord Life had said that they should be optimistic like fishermen.

He told them that in Paris he had met some Orizons from the previous group of trainees. "They were a mix just like us, but from France, Germany, Italy, Switzerland, Portugal, Austria, Hungary, Poland, Denmark, Holland, Sweden, Finland, Norway and Iceland. I felt exhilarated after meeting them. They attack problems and do amazing work. They are restless, like bees. Due to the Flame they're like different minerals from the same mine and they're very optimistic and highly coordinated. Along with their studies they're actively involved in projects and are producing results. Their band comprised twenty Orizons from various parts of the Earth. They too are a close-knit group like us, sharing the same dreams."

Carlos's Spanish temperament warmed the group with an invisible fire. It was as if he always had a brazier beside him from which he would pick out glowing embers of good feeling. He shared them generously with the children, who opened their hearts to receive them gladly.

"It's so important to make our dreams come true. It's even more important, though in a less happy way, if we don't. But we mustn't allow others to *bury* our dreams, and most of all we must never bury them ourselves. Dreams prod our life and they urge to a gallop, even sometimes to run amok."

Carlos was keen to see bullfighting stopped. He couldn't bear to watch the matador with his murderous sword, like the Angel of Death with its scythe, killing the defenceless victim. He couldn't understand the spectators' delighted cries whenever the bull was tormented, tortured and wounded. And most of all he was indignant at the ecstatic frenzy of the crowd when the bull finally fell to the ground. The sickening culmination of this ghastly drama was the way in which the triumphant murderer became a rich and famous 'hero'.

Sergei was a sensitive boy with high ideals and concerns, a realist who also cherished dreams and hopes, envisaging a country that would be different in the best possible way and willing to fight to achieve it.

The traditional but sincere politeness of Lee tied in with his simplicity. Cloaked in the mystical veil of the Orient, he concealed within himself many mysteries. From the very first moment he had given the key that unlocked them to the other children, who explored and discovered the beautiful world that existed in the depths of Lee's soul.

Louise was very concerned about the way that people chose to entertain themselves in the modern world.

"Television," she said, "is the cheapest and most popular form of entertainment. A fixture in people's living rooms, kitchens and bedrooms; a permanent companion, dominating the family. It transfixes, entices, seduces, misleads and dominates ...

"It's filled with images of fairy-tale houses, fabulous riches, handsome men, sexy women wearing sensational dresses and jewels, and with tycoons, aristocrats and action heroes as role models. Melodramatic love stories, torrid affairs and deep hostilities penetrate people's hearts and subconscious minds. Few resist. Anything that is worthwhile or useful must struggle to survive.

"Violence spreads into children's bedrooms and blood spatters their pillows and their tender hearts. Vampires, ghosts, witches, people possessed by evil spirits, hardened criminals and demented murderers float around their rooms and hide beneath their beds. Perverts want to get under the bedcovers and trainee wizards rouse children's imaginations, leading them along the wrong paths in search of hollow worlds.

"Yet the astonishing, enthralling, magnificent and magical art of cinema can, if its practitioners wish, transport people to higher realms, raising them above the dross and chaos."

Everyone agreed with Louise's views. She was a great speaker.

Samantha, who was beautiful and full of love, could also become very aggressive towards Evil.

Sweet-natured Tamina was brave and patient.

Pedro talked of his dreams of Orizon power rushing like a whirlwind to sweep away Evil.

Jabal hated the fact that his country lived on oil. Rather than use the cliché 'black gold' he called it 'black death.'

Rashid the Egyptian was a very thoughtful and responsible person, ready to face any kind of adventure ahead. He was like a volcano ready to explode, but he always found a way to spread his lava fire around till it cooled in the sea. Although he laughed when they were joking, his heart was crying, due to the misfortunes of humankind. He loved all his companions and felt as though they were his brothers. He often sang and although his voice wasn't melodic it had a special charm, because it was warm and conveyed his longing for Earth's resurrection. "We need to cross the borders and fight. We have the foundations, but we still must spill our sweat and even our blood, if that is to help", he was saying.

Lovable Tiki was furious about the derogatory names that so-called civilized people use when they talk about Native Americans, Aborigines, Australians, Asians, Africans and other people of colour.

José, spontaneous and impulsive, actively fought for the preservation of traditions, family ties and mutual respect within the family unit.

"People often forget that their parents are the ones who brought them into the world and raised them," he explained. "Just as their parents tolerated their complaints when they were young, so children should in their turn tolerate any difficult behaviour or complaining by their parents.

"Children should understand that life is a cycle. Their parents washed them and changed their dirty clothes when they were young. So, if the need arises and the parents are old and ailing, the children should wash and change them and not abandon them to their fate. When people grow old, they become like children again and need similar loving care."

During the nights, when the young Orizons all got together, he often lit his heart's torch and shared its warm light with the others.

Abu was like a time bomb, ready to explode at any minute. But when he did explode it was only love that he radiated. He was very bitter about the ecological devastation of the planet and of Africa in particular.

Almost every night, Rebecca visited the Wise Tree and read books to it.

"Do you see this book?" she asked on her first night back. "It's small but it contains thousands of pictures, events, thoughts and feelings. Countless heroes who are asleep inside it are eagerly waiting for us to wake them. As soon as we open the book and begin reading they'll stand in line, waiting their turn to leap out."

"This book seems like magic to me," said the Wise Tree. "I thought books must be huge since they contain so many things. It's tiny: does it really do all the things you said?"

"All you have to do is open it. It may stay in a bookcase for many years, forgotten. But the characters are still inside and as we read they come alive and enter our hearts and minds. People in love show us their happiness. Those who are unhappy want us to share their pain. Through books, you can live as many lives as you want. As you read, you leave your own life behind and enter others with the characters. You see them up close as a member of their own family would. Then, if you wish, you can combine what you experienced while you were reading with your own knowledge and awareness of life. In a few hours you can live a whole lifetime and, as you read over the years, it is as though you've lived a thousand lives."

"Do all books have this magical effect?"

"All novels and fairy tales and plenty of historical accounts."

"I can't wait to start, to see what's hidden inside."

"This book is a masterpiece that describes the war between Good and Evil. It unfolds in an imaginary land. I'm sure you'll like it. Let's begin."

While Rebecca was reading, the Tree frequently interrupted her with questions. From time to time it moved its branches or trunk, showing that it wanted to help the forces of Good win the battle that Rebecca was reading about.

As it listened to Rebecca, it could see the hero on his horse leaping out of the pages, brandishing his sword, vanquishing his foes. Whenever the forces of Good won it would shout for joy.

Rebecca also spent time every day teaching the Tree to read and write. She had brought suitable books for the early stages. The Tree learned easily and each day when she asked questions it showed that it had understood the previous day's lesson well. It studied hard, using two branches to hold the books while turning the pages with their leaves. Sometimes, when the pages got stuck together and turned over two or more at a time, the Tree followed Rebecca's advice and moistened its leaves, as a person would lick a finger. Time passed and the day of the return to Earth drew closer.

Day after day, night after night, the people of Utopia expected an attack. There were times when some of them said: "Whatever happens, the sooner the better." Never in the long history of the Land of the White Sun had there been such an atmosphere of tension and suspense.

Rebecca had now turned sixteen. She felt that the time had come for her to put the Wise Tree's advice into practice and she started beginning by getting to know herself better. She would try to see her faults as clearly and as objectively as possible, and decide what to improve and what to correct, even though she believed that the basic elements of character didn't change.

She wanted to put down strong foundations inside herself her so that her inner world would not collapse. Then she would begin to build on them. She realized that the Wise Tree of Knowledge had been right when it had said that the greatest and most significant achievements are easily toppled if their underpinning is not strong. She was thinking that, even if their substructures are well built, when high attainments crumble, as well as possibly killing or injuring you as they fall they create a lot of debris – on which you may have to walk for the rest of your life. However strong your feet may be, walking and balancing on mounds of rubble is hard.

Rebecca also always remembered the Tree's words: '*There is no victory or defeat without struggle.*' She believed that it was hard to fail but it was even worse never to have made the attempt.

Regardless of the Flame and her obligation to fight until Evil was defeated, as Rebecca grew and matured she had to define her limits. She recalled a Chinese proverb that advised people to demand much of themselves and to expect little from others. A failure could mean stepping closer to success.

The more she studied the more she realized that Turgoth's and Bull's words were true. History had been distorted and was still being distorted every day. The written history of each nation differed at many points from writer to writer and from one book to another. The truth had been twisted.

Teachers were forced to teach a preordained account of history, which often included monstrous inaccuracies. Books that contained unpalatable truths did not stay in circulation for long; they were withdrawn or burned. The greatest crime of that kind was the torching of three thousand volumes in the library of Alexandria. That cut the thread of history even though some other sources remained. Rebecca believed that the overt or covert burning or other types of removal from public access of books, songs, plays and films by any kind of junta suppressed freedom of thought, speech and all other forms of expression.

History created counterfeit heroes and imaginary acts of heroism for entire nations. It obliterated real heroes if they proved threatening or annoying to those in power. It was difficult to tell who had helped Good prevail. A person whom one group of people saw as a good leader, politician or hero was seen by others as a traitor, opportunist and criminal.

Rebecca felt sure that a leader didn't need a throne or an office. A leader needed strong legs, good ears, the eyes of a hawk, the nose of a bloodhound and a strong neck and shoulders to pull the yoke alongside the people when necessary. A leader did not need eiderdowns and soft pillows, but strong bones so as to be able to sleep on cobblestones. He had to live with the people and not in isolation.

A leader had to steep himself in his people's daily problems and needs.

She disapproved of "charitable" donations by people like Al Capone. The gangster had made a fortune from corruption and drugs and had then donated part of his bloodstained profits for the construction of churches. She was opposed to all fundraising activities, begging, sponsorship and ostentatious acts of charity that were done to get something – usually an honour of some kind – in return. Her belief was that anyone who wanted to do good should do so anonymously.

Rebecca did not approve of those who became the leaders of

charities just to show the world that they cared about the poor, unfortunate and sick. They organized charity events and fund-raisers to project an image that promoted their own self-serving aims. True concern should not be shouted from the rooftops. Otherwise it was like stealing a blind man's dog and cane, then helping him to cross a busy road so as to be seen doing good deeds.

Rebecca discussed her views with her parents. They never voiced a specific viewpoint, allowing her to make up her own mind and choose which opinions to form. They answered all her questions, giving her plain facts and many-sided explanations so that she could draw the final conclusions herself.

One evening her father said to her: "Even though you're young you have a great deal of knowledge and wisdom. But you lack the experience to use them properly. You'll gain experience in time, as you are ground between the millstones of life.

"Like all human beings, we Orizons are not like fruit, grain or vegetables that have a specific time-span in which they grow and mature. For us the process is slow and takes years, so we have to be patient. Otherwise it's like pulling at the stem of a plant to make it grow faster. Sometimes sudden events speed up the process. Talent is nurtured in solitude, while character is formed in the full flow of human life. 'Because they have the Flame, Orizons usually mature faster, but it still takes time. Metal must first be placed in the furnace and become malleable before anything can be made from it.

"The important thing, Rebecca, is to know your strengths; to plan and proceed according to your objectives. If you are not killed, you have a whole eternity in front of you and will be able to offer much to humanity. So you must neither rush things nor neglect to take action.

"Always remember that the truth hurts and that as a result

most people don't like to look at it. They refuse to separate lies and useless information from what is true and useful. That's where you need discrimination and skill.

"I congratulate everyone else who seeks and speaks the truth."

Rebecca discovered every day that lies prevailed everywhere, not just among leaders but also among the ordinary people who did not want to learn the truth, although the words of truth are simple. They regarded it with fear, or were indifferent and pushed it away. They felt the need to gloss over everything and that was what all the "experts" were happy to do for them, promising a good time, prosperity and a solution to all their problems. That was what people wanted to hear so that was what they were told.

The only thing that people cared about was for the political party they supported to be in power. Then everything was perfect. But if the other side was in power, everything was wrong. Fanaticism blinds!

Rebecca believed the bloody revolutions that had taken place in the name of democracy had brought only misery, bitterness and disappointment to anyone not in power. She thought that revolutions did not break out to help some non-existent Democracy, but rather to help dictatorships change hands.

She talked with left-wing schoolmates and university students. What they said seemed good.

"I'm probably left wing," she thought.

Then she would talk with right-wing schoolmates and university students. Their ideas seemed good too.

"I'm probably right wing too," she would think again.

THE ORIZONS OF EARTH

It was the Christmas holiday and Rebecca's father Julius looked as though something was troubling him deeply. One evening, when all three of the family were at home, he told his wife and daughter that he had information about a planned terrorist attack, which was likely to cost the lives of five thousand victims.

"The Orizons are using every possible means to verify the information," he said.

There had already been a number of terrorist attacks and the death toll for each one had often been high, but there had been nothing on this scale yet. A few days later, Julius told them that he and some other Orizons were going to the Land of the White Sun to meet Lord Life. They now had specific information.

According to their sources, the attack was planned for New Year's Eve and would be targeted on a cruise ship. More than five thousand passengers and crew would be on board. The terrorists would blow up the ship in front of the world's media, so that all would witness the appalling sacrifice.

The problem facing the Orizons was that if the information reached government secret service the informants would be revealed and multiple blind attacks would follow. The only option was for them to foil the attack by stealth themselves.

Upon his return from the Land of the White Sun, Julius told Rebecca that besides themselves the families of Cowboy Bill, Pedro, José, Louise, Susan, Rashid and Jabal would all be taking part in the operation.

Each family would have a designated role to play and they would all act together at the right moment.

There could be no definitive final plan of action because they did not know the details of the terrorists' movements. None of the Orizons underestimated the danger of the operation. It was certain that the terrorists would be well organized. They were willing to die and take all the ship's passengers along with them.

"Lord Life told us to ask the eight children of the involved families whether they want to join us or not," Julius told Rebecca. "The decision is yours. It will be extremely dangerous. On the other hand, it gives you a chance to participate in one of the missions that the Orizons often have to undertake on Earth."

"I want to be part of it," Rebecca assured him. "I want to help as much as I can."

The eight families met three days before the cruise was scheduled to start. All the children had agreed to take part. Rashid's father, Samal Maher, was the mission leader with Jabal's father, Fued Hamam, as his second in command.

None of them could work out how the attackers planned to bring explosives on board, since security searches were so thorough that no one could sneak a pin onto a cruise ship. The engine room of this particular ship had steel-plated doors, with combination locks like those used on the flight decks of airliners. Would they seize a submarine and attack the ship with torpedoes? But that would almost certainly leave many survivors.

The *Myrtilla*, the newest and most luxurious cruise ship in the world, was scheduled to set sail on the evening of Wednesday, 26 December. The ship was truly gigantic, a floating multistorey city.

It was a seven-day cruise and the *Myrtilla* was due back on the morning of 2 January. The attack was probably scheduled for just after midnight on New Year's Eve, on the return leg.

Some suggested that the attack might take place later on the morning of New Year's Day, so that TV crews could get better footage of the explosion. Another source said that the terrorists were not planning to give any warnings: they would just send a public message stating their cause a few seconds before detonation.

The Orizons would board the ship in family groups, carrying passports in which only their first names were genuine. They were divided into four teams of two families, each two-family pair allotted to one of the four different passenger classes. They were already studying the personal records of the crew members: when they had been employed, details of their past lives – and whether there were any indications that some among them might undertake a terrorist mission.

No one to start with was rated any higher or lower a risk than anyone else. For the Orizons, *every* passenger and crew member was a suspect.

Once the cruise had started, the families would only meet during excursions on land when the *Myrtilla* stopped at various islands. There they could exchange views. While on board each team would appear to be two friendly families eating dinner together and keeping each other company.

Julius Newton was disguised to look like an old man in a special wheelchair. He carried documents showing him to be a disabled ex-serviceman who'd been wounded in the Falklands and who had a pacemaker and so was not allowed to go through metal detectors. Eight pistols with silencers and spare ammunition clips, along with Rebecca's two daggers, were well hidden in the customized wheelchair. The seat was made in such a way that even X-rays would not detect the weapons.

They were all provided with thin gloves to wear inside their cabins so that they would leave fake fingerprints.

Once they were on board, the Newtons kept company with Susan and her parents, Kate and Robin Caben. Although the voyage was magnificent and each island they visited was gorgeous, the Orizons couldn't enjoy the cruise. Every waking moment was spent puzzling over how the terrorists could attack, where they would hide the explosives and how they would get them on board in the first place.

As planned, when the Orizons visited the first island they each bought some bows that looked like traditional handicraft items from a shop that sold handmade wooden artefacts. They showed them off proudly to anyone who was interested, making it seem as though they had bought souvenirs.

On the next island they bought arrows – without arrowheads – that resembled long bird-feathers, and at the last island they obtained arrowheads.

The twenty-four Orizons were now armed with weapons that they had all been trained to use very effectively. Now they were a small army.

During those six days, Rebecca had the chance to get to know Susan better as they talked for hours about the enormous responsibilities that they had assumed, as well as the possible outcomes of their mission. They communicated so well that Rebecca knew what Susan was going to say even before she had finished a sentence. She felt as if she was plucking petals off a daisy and could guess the outcome a few petals before the end.

Susan wanted to study physics in order to help the planet, especially in dealing with the problem of environmental pollution. She also believed that the largest crisis facing humanity was drug abuse and the corruption of youth. She couldn't bear to see children with cigarettes in their mouths, alcoholic drinks in their glasses or pockets full of drugs.

She wondered how the drug problem could be tackled when great writers, pop idols and famous scientists claimed that they wrote, performed or worked better under the influence of drugs. How could they get the message across to young people when actors, singers, artists and even athletes, adored by thousands, were drug addicts too?

"I knew a beautiful, rich and educated girl whose dealer threatened to deprive her of her fix unless she could lure a certain rich young man into drugs," Susan said one evening as they were sitting together on the deck. "She had to flirt with him and pretend to be in love. After some time she managed to move in with him. The next step, of course, was to get him into the drug world.

"One day, as I was on my way home from school, she started sending me text messages on my mobile. She sent one message after another, for hours on end. I began copying them. I have them here, because I often read them."

She took a few pages from the pocket of her jeans and unfolded them.

"Read it," she said. Rebecca began to read.

Today, it's very windy and the rain is freezing. I'm in a park. The damp sparrows are nestling among the foliage. Dazed by the blasts of the north wind, they are barely clinging on.

You can keep out the cold with clothes, a roof, a fire and blankets, but nothing keeps out the damp. It's got through my skin and my bones and into my marrow. I'm soaked through.

As descendants of Adam and Eve, we are all cousins. Why do we harm each other? I've harmed the one I embrace. I led him astray, wrecked him, like a sly iceberg that sinks an unsuspecting ship. Everyone is vulnerable to such attacks.

We need a new, simple view on life. A dog, a horse and a hen have the same rights. Peace, humanity, love, brotherhood, equality, justice, kindness and freedom are all essential values that hardly exist!

Manufactured gods and saints are impotent and useless. They seem tough, but they are cowards. Even humans try more than they do! It is time for them to drop their masks ...

Politics and religion have been transformed to ugly decorated puppets, without will or power.

Most politicians are vain, arrogant, opportunistic, grasping liars. Many of them are criminals.

In the gladiatorial stadiums, people are watching in silent agony ... As they got smarter, they at least stopped screaming.

The hypocritical emperors turn their icy empty sight all round, like a periscope ...

The murderous thumb turns down and demands death. The blood flows in the arena.

Bombs drop in the slave markets and destroy innocent children!

Kamikaze terrorists blow themselves to pieces, together with their defenceless innocent victims.

The barricades are built with wooden boxes, stones and mattresses, while the defenders fight with sticks, Molotov cocktails and slingshots against missiles. They are waiting for them to come. They want them! They need them, so that they'll feel useful and become heroes.

Around the neck of the proud war hero they hang a small steel circle with a nice little ribbon attached, because he managed to kill many enemies and helped conquer the barricades of straw and the useless, so-called strategic hills, or because he supposedly saved others who were more cowardly.

If, however, the hero lies dead under the ground, the tin medal, this brilliant evil invention, is delivered to the devastated mother, so that she'll feel proud and hand over the rest of her children to be sacrificed too.

And so more pointless history is getting written, so that people will be celebrating victory against the barricades.

Fairy tales can't provide peace to the soul, nor can they mirror dreams. Besides, there is no fairy tale more real than the illusions of life that crush destiny.

People have no warm nest. At best they go into their shells, which are more fragile than those of snails.

Both rich and homeless cry at the same time, asking for mercy.

Quantity destroys quality.

Alas, for everyone there is always a useless cause.

I'm in hell and you came for me to save me and get me out. You're a special friend, Susan, and I love you.

Your eyes are always filled with Love. Never before have I witnessed so much love. You're like good lyrics that don't need to be set to music. On their own they are rhapsody, tragedy, comedy, musical, songs, thus they are poetry, and poetry can't be taught or learned. The same is true for love.

Thanks for standing by me. But it's too late because I've done great harm to another person. If it wasn't for that, you would have saved me for sure.

We can escape from everybody. Never, though, from ourselves! Because ... the most important things ... are those which we hide.

Virtue means ethics, said the ancient philosophers. But we should be ethical because we want to be and not out of fear!

Ethics is a personal value, with many different angles.

It's not wise to focus ethics around sex, feelings and rules that society forces on you, killing truth, Nature, purity.

They called resisting Nature ethical, but that collapsed. When one tries to overcome Nature, one will come to a tragic end.

They fill us with their useless and meaningless theories, which can't be applied ... And so we keep talking of things we don't understand ...

The visible side of the moon isn't good enough for us; we want to explore the invisible side too.

With the tip of my tongue, I slowly, carefully lick my upper lip from one end to the other, as if I were putting on lipstick. Then ... from that side back to the beginning. Now I bite my lower lip tenderly, like a mother, so that it won't complain.

We bring down the curtain. The audience weeps or laughs, without applauding.

I looked deep into the world. That's why I got disappointed. I wasn't at all ready.

The birds train their wings before they dare to fly. Alas, I hadn't learned to watch the skies, to caress the lakes or listen to the seas and rivers.

We are looking for a better world. Where is it hidden? How are we going to discover it?

Useful metals do not grow by themselves. First we must dig and hurt the Earth. Then we must burrow like rats to extract them.

It is difficult to become a human, and even harder to remain one.

With brainwashing they can turn people into fanatical zombies.

Demons dressed like priests strike the bells with passion, while inquisitors destroy the angels' feathers ...

Preachers of truth have sealed their mouths with plaster!

How can you tell innocent from guilty? They look so much alike.

Although there is a wind, the clouds decided to walk the earth with me, so a thick fog has fallen ...

The sparrows are still hanging on there. They've made it.

I'm walking wearily beneath the trees on the slippery grass ...

Moments don't exist ... they get united with Nothingness!

The rare feeling of completeness, the extraordinary Tension in an atmosphere of Assimilation ... The agitated Peace ... The lost Courage ...

There is no extra courage in the colourless sky for me to steal.

I began to blow out the stars, one by one ... With the last blow, my breath had ended and the sky turned black ...

The toys are lost! Have they stolen them? Have they hidden them or sold them? Who knows? But the new ones are expensive to buy.

Life laughs only when kids laugh.

Laugh ... laugh and cry!

The sea, the rivers and the lakes are full of signs warning: ATTENTION, DEEP WATER! HE WHO FALLS GETS DROWNED ... Well, he who falls gets saved, say I ...

How do parents feel when they lose their child?

Why should we scare the others, since we know what fear is like?

When we climb up, we must try our best. Every move we take needs immediate thought and action. Where to put the nail and tie the rope? Where to place our boots to keep secure and be safe to continue climbing?

The endless gap is waiting with its mouth open, pulling like a whirlpool.

Even though I know the outcome I am experimenting on myself, like Doctor Jekyll.

It's like fishing in the mountains, or cutting wood for the fire from the sea. I put society onto the surgeon's table but I don't have the tools to operate.

I am now looking at my calf ... Flesh, veins, blood will all disappear and all that'll remain will be bones. My soul shall sleep for ever, together with a skeleton!

I can feel the beginning of Death ... He is coming for me, riding his black horse in this timeless moment.

Drops of rain are giving me farewell kisses ...

Rebecca put down the piece of paper and gazed at Susan.

"I didn't like the way the message trailed off so I rang her immediately," Susan said. "She'd turned off the phone. It was her last message. The police found her dead beneath the trees, with the syringes. She had taken a fatal overdose. There are many such cases. How can they be dealt with? The underworld is mighty and ruthless."

On another occasion Susan told Rebecca:

"As I read, compare, ask, search, think and try to discover the truth, it almost drives me crazy. How can we put the Earth in order? So what if we are immortal? How does that help? This is an utterly mad, incomprehensible world.

"Something else that has concerned me for years, Rebecca, is the way that soldiers' mothers plead with God that their children will be safe, win the war and return home quickly. That means they will probably have to kill their enemies. Yet the mothers of the soldiers on the opposite side pray for the same thing. Who is God to listen to? To whose mother will He grant a favour? Especially when both sides share the same religion and believe in the same God."

The two girls had endless discussions as the cruise ship continued on its way without mishap.

New Year's Eve arrived and the Orizons had no idea what was going to happen. Everyone was tense.

Julius had given pistols to the rest of the men, most of whom had served as agents in the secret services of their countries. They were all excellent marksmen. Now that there was no likelihood of their being searched they all carried their guns, ready for action.

Under her loose-fitting blouse Rebecca wore a belt that held her two daggers. The bows and arrows were in bags inside the Orizons' cabins. The arrowheads were laced with a substance that instantly rendered unconscious anyone whose skin they pierced.

They set sail at six in the evening from their most recent port of call and were soon on the open sea.

After dinner, the New Year's Eve celebration began. The Orizons were scattered around the decks and other strategic points. Julius, in his wheelchair, and Rebecca were close to the bridge, while Ernest, another Orizon comrade, walked back and forth outside the radio room.

They communicated with each other using micro-transmitters in their ears and on their chests. Each of them always knew where the others were.

Midnight came and the New Year began. Everyone exchanged kisses and good wishes. Old acquaintances and complete strangers embraced while the Orizons remained alert and ready.

Fireworks lit up the sky and the passengers rushed out on deck to watch. They danced, laughed, drank and sang. For most of them it was the trip of a lifetime, a dream come true. None of them suspected that the bloodthirsty beast of terrorism was preparing to pounce.

The Orizons all felt the attack was imminent. But when, and how? Gradually the celebration wound down and the passengers – sated, giddy and content – went to bed. Soon there was no one left outside the cabins.

The Orizons didn't know what to do. Should they wait up or get some sleep?

At twenty to three the ship changed course. The Orizons on deck noticed at once and contacted the others.

Rebecca pushed Julius's wheelchair towards the wheelhouse. There were two uniformed men inside as well as the helmsman. They were obviously taken aback to see the old man and his daughter at that hour of the morning.

"My name's Jefferson," Julius said. "I'm sorry to come here uninvited but, as a former captain, I was surprised by the change of course."

It was true that for a while he had worked as the captain of a merchant vessel while following up a drug trafficking case. The two uniformed men relaxed visibly in the presence of a fellow officer.

"The name's Michael Carty," the older one said, extending his hand. "I'm the first mate. Patrick is the second mate and our helmsman is called Nick. We've changed course slightly but we're still moving towards our destination. There's been a fire on a small cruise ship about three miles to port and there's no other ship close by. There are twenty-three passengers, including seven small children, plus the crew on the vessel in distress."

Julius frowned. *"The operation has begun,"* he thought. *"It must be a trap."*

He kept talking to the officers, knowing that all the Orizons could hear him.

They gave Julius a pair of binoculars but he couldn't see from the wheelchair. "How long will it take us to reach them?" he asked.

"About ten minutes," replied Patrick.

"Has the captain been informed?"

"Yes. He'll be here as soon as we get close to them."

"Were you informed by the port authorities or by the ship itself?"

"By both the ship and the Barbados port authority. The ship had sailed from there and was on its way to San Juan like us. But their New Year celebrations started a fire," said Carty.

"Are they in the lifeboats?"

"They only have one small boat, which is carrying the children and a few women. The rest are jumping overboard. Only the captain and the crew have stayed aboard, trying to put out the fire," replied Carty.

The Orizons were now on deck and they could see the burning boat in the distance.

"It may be a trap," said Hamam over his micro-transmitter and the others agreed.

The order was given for them to get their bags with the bows and arrows, assembling again on deck in small groups. Maher directed the Orizon women to patrol the cabin corridors, looking for anything suspicious.

The captain came to the bridge. The others told him that Mr Jefferson was a retired captain who had happened to be there when they'd changed course. The captain shook hands with Julius.

"Pleased to meet you, Mr Jefferson," he said.

The burning ship could be seen clearly now. They could make out figures jumping into the sea. The captain gave the order to stop engines and lower the *Myrtilla's* big motor boat to save those who were swimming.

It didn't look staged. The ship was actually ablaze and looked totally incapacitated. Several people were struggling with the waves. Cries for help came from all around. As the motor boat sped to the swimmers the lifeboat carrying the women and children reached the *Myrtilla.* The captain ordered the entrance door leading to the reception area to be opened and the gangway to be lowered to receive the terrified survivors.

"What nationality are the shipwrecked passengers?" asked Julius.

"They're all American citizens but the ship is Jamaican," replied the captain.

Everything looked genuine.

"We'll stay on alert." Maher said.

The *Myrtilla* kept a safe distance from the flaming ship. A man, clearly a very strong swimmer, was following the lifeboat. From time to time he would hold on to the stern and catch his breath. There was obviously no room for him in the boat. As the boat reached the gangway four crewmen helped the women and children to climb the steps. There were eight women and seven children, two of them just babies held in their mothers' arms.

They were followed by the man who had been swimming. Some of the children were frightened and crying. All those rescued were dark-skinned. The women were quite young and wore long, loose dresses. The two carrying the babies put them down gently – and pulled out automatic weapons from under their garments. The others followed their lead. One woman had two guns and threw one to the man who had swum behind them.

"Nobody moves. Don't make a sound," the man commanded in perfect English.

One woman locked the crewmen in a reception-area office while the rest of the team ran to the lift. They seemed to know the ship well and pressed the button for the bridge. When they emerged, they ran straight for the wheelhouse.

"Freeze!" the man shouted, his clothes dripping with water. "You, captain, come to the radio room with us."

Two of the women stayed on the bridge while two more went with their leader to the communication centre. They didn't have to ask the way. The radio operator jumped up, terrified, as they burst in.

"Send out a general signal that you've rescued us all," the man ordered. "Say you've picked us up and you're on your way to your destination. If you make the slightest mistake, you'll die."

The signal was sent exactly as ordered. Then the man and the women bound the radio operator's feet before searching the desk drawers and the rest of the office for weapons. The leader left the two women behind and went back to the reception area with the captain.

The motor boat with the supposed survivors from the stricken ship was on its way back. As soon as they too were on board, the terrorists locked up the two crew members from the motor boat with the others. The sound of another engine was heard in the dark and a large black speedboat approached, running without lights. There was only one man on board as it approached the *Myrtilla's* gangway; there the men who had been picked out of the sea unloaded a number of sacks, taking them aboard. Finally, one of them straightened, secured the speedboat's steering wheel so that it would keep the craft on a straight course, lit a fuse attached to a cluster of explosives, jammed the throttle down and jumped overboard as the speedboat roared back into the blackness of the night. A couple of minutes later it blew up in a mighty explosion.

The man who had set it off climbed onto the ship with the help of the others and the gangway was raised. In the reception area there were now eight men, four women, seven children and the captain. Their leader took the captain up to the bridge again.

Julius kept his right hand, which he'd been holding awkwardly so that it looked crippled, inside the big pocket of his wide jacket. He was keeping his finger on his gun's trigger. He pretended to look confused and afraid. The terrorist leader ordered the captain to set sail and follow the *Myrtilla's* intended course, according to schedule.

"Soon we'll have distributed our explosives," he told them. "When they go off, they won't just sink this ship – they will blow it and everyone on board to smithereens.

"When day breaks, we'll send a message all over the world that we've hijacked this ship. We'll tell them that we're a group of eight families: eight couples with our seven children who will all die in the name of Allah, for our great cause and our war against the criminals who have been victimizing our people for hundreds of years. The whole world must understand that we are determined to win, so that our people can live in freedom."

Rebecca recognized the message. The terrorist was one of those leaders who believed that they served their cause by killing innocent people.

The captain said nothing. He felt guilty for having fallen into such a trap: while trying to save lives he had condemned his crew and his passengers to death. He didn't care about himself. He was an old British sea dog! He had been at sea since he was a boy and had long ago lost the ability to feel fear.

All over the ship, the Orizons listened over their radio links and waited for their orders. Maher, their leader, did not know how many of the suicide bombers were armed or what kind of weapons they had. Julius wondered how he could warn everyone that the terrorists had automatic weapons.

Rebecca looked the terrorist leader in the eye and said icily: "I respect your struggle and your people's cause. You may be right to feel so angry, but you're certainly wrong to put so many innocent people to death. It can never be right to kill the children of your own people.

"What you're doing is cowardly. Regardless of whether you think you're going to be in Allah's paradise eternally, your children won't follow you there."

The leader looked at her, startled. "How dare you talk to me like that? Why are you here, anyway?"

"We came to watch your rescue. As your captive, I have the right to talk, and so do your fellow fighters, who are now in prison. They must speak and express their opinions. You've come here carrying automatic weapons, ready to kill. You've captured five thousand innocent and unsuspecting people in order to send them to their deaths. Armed warriors against unarmed civilians:

experienced, fearless, strong and trained soldiers against people who know nothing of guns and fighting. Do you really think you are brave and fair?"

The listening Orizons all heard Rebecca mention the automatic weapons.

One of the women was glaring at Rebecca with hatred, pointing her gun at her, making small circular motions with its muzzle as if she couldn't wait to riddle the young girl with bullets. Rebecca felt the woman's stare piercing her like a dagger of ice.

"Are you Jewish?" the woman asked, her voice full of hatred.

"No, I'm not. But if I were, what would it matter? If some Jews committed crimes, would I be at fault?

"Is this the kind of reasoning by which you, the so-called righteous ones, wish to win? You are so blinded by fanaticism that you can't see properly those who incite you to kill. You give those who wish to harm you the opportunity to do so. They use you! Then they'll give you the crumbs you're asking for and everything will be settled. What will *not* be settled are the murders and the unjust sacrifices.

"The struggle will never be won by acts of retaliation – they only spill blood in vain. You too are victims of satanic propaganda."

"Where are you from and what is your name?" the leader demanded.

"I was born in England and my name is Rebecca."

"What did I tell you? She's a Jew. She has a Jewish name," snarled the woman. Her eyes were wild and it looked as if she would soon be unable to stop herself pulling the trigger of her gun.

"I'm not a Jew. Many Christians bear my name. The same is true for most of the Jewish names mentioned in the Bible."

"You may not be a Jew but you *are* English," the man said. "Your leaders govern the world along with the Americans. In reality it's your country that dictates US policies."

"English women hang diamonds around their necks while we hang weapons around ours. They wear expensive rings on their fingers while we wear the ring of a grenade pin. You English must all die ..." spat the woman.

Before she could finish her tirade the captain charged at her, willing to sacrifice himself to compensate for his error of judgement.

The woman fired her gun and bullets riddled the captain's his body as it fell on top of her, bringing her down with him. The other two officers and the helmsman instinctively rushed to their captain but were shot down by the leader and the other woman.

Without removing his hand from his pocket, Julius pulled the trigger of his pistol twice and in two seconds each of the two terrorists had a bullet hole in the middle of their forehead. Before the woman who'd killed the captain managed to get up from under the corpse she met the same fate.

Julius spoke through the micro-transmitter to the others. "We're in the wheelhouse. There were two women and their leader here. They all had automatic weapons. They're dead, and so are the captain, two officers and a sailor. There must be thirteen terrorists left, not counting the children. Two women armed with guns are probably in the radio room and the rest are planting explosives. I don't know how many weapons are still left or if the terrorists have any support among the passengers. Rebecca and I are going to the radio room. I still have nine bullets left and a spare clip."

Maher ordered the children to remain at their posts on the

two decks by the swimming pools. They were to take cover out of the line of fire and use arrows to shoot down any terrorists they saw, if they were sure there was no danger of being injured or killed themselves. Even if the arrows did not kill outright, the treated arrowheads would knock out anyone they hit.

The children ran to their posts and took cover. The eight Orizon women remained in the corridors by the cabins, keeping the area under surveillance. They were to act according to the circumstances.

The remaining seven Orizons who had pistols concealed them as planned under plaster casts on supposedly broken wrists. Then they went to the lower decks to find and eliminate the terrorists planting explosives. Everybody moved like lightning to follow their instructions.

Rebecca pushed the wheelchair towards the radio room as Julius covered the bullet holes in his jacket pocket with his left hand. As Rebecca opened the door to the radio room and pushed the wheelchair inside, Julius lolled his head to one side as if seriously ill. The two women in the room looked disconcerted.

"What are you doing here?" one of them demanded.

"My father is very ill and we can't find the doctor. The on-board communications are not working. We want to ask his doctor in London what to do."

"You're going to die anyway," retorted the woman.

Through half-opened eyes, Julius saw that the women were not about to fire their weapons. The radio operator was already dead, his body riddled with bullets. He lay on the floor, his feet still tied together. Julius fired twice and the two women met the same fate as the others.

Julius and Rebecca decided to go down to the reception area.

Julius looked at his watch. Fourteen minutes had passed since the moment when the invaders had first reached the wheelhouse.

"The two women in the radio room are dead. We've hidden their automatic weapons. They'd killed the operator. Rebecca and I are going towards the reception area," he informed the others.

"OK, Julius," Maher responded. "We're going down to the engine room and the hold."

The seven gun-toting Orizons looked as if their right wrists were broken. At the tip of each plaster mould was a concealed pistol and the Orizons had their fingers on the triggers. The identical casts would not raise any suspicions because those wearing them were widely scattered through the ship.

As Julius and Rebecca took the lift down Julius changed his ammunition clip so that he had twelve bullets in the magazine of his pistol once more. When they arrived, they found four women with automatic weapons and seven children, two of them babes in arms. One of the women was seated in an armchair. She had put her gun down to breast-feed her child. When they saw Rebecca and Julius, the three other women raised their weapons and advanced towards them.

"What do you want here?" asked one woman.

Julius had once more assumed the expression of a gravely sick person. His left hand was again over the bullet holes in the pocket of his jacket.

Rebecca told them that they were trying to locate the doctor and couldn't find him. She got no sympathy.

"OK, OK, we're going," murmured Julius in a weak voice.

The women relaxed slightly and lowered their guns. In three seconds all three of them were dead. Julius looked at the one with the child. Although he'd turned his gun towards her he stopped, unable to kill a breastfeeding woman.

She didn't instantly comprehend what had happened to her comrades; she hadn't heard the shots because of the silencer on Julius's gun but even in her confused state of mind she realized that the crippled man was the cause of her friends falling.

She threw the baby onto the seat beside her, grabbed her automatic weapon and started firing. Rebecca dived to the left of the wheelchair while simultaneously hurling a throwing knife. Julius was already shot through with bullets by the time the dagger pierced the woman's throat. She turned her weapon on Rebecca, firing one last burst. But Rebecca had already rolled across the floor, almost reaching the row of seats where the woman had been feeding her baby a few moments before.

As Rebecca rolled she pulled out the other knife and prepared to throw it. But already the woman had dropped her gun and was clutching her throat with both hands. Her eyes were bulging.

Rebecca looked at her father. He was slumped over in his wheelchair. His clothes were soaked with gore, his face mutilated, skin, cheeks, nose and bones all crushed and torn.

As she rose she looked again at the woman, who had fallen face down. Blood was spurting from her carotid artery. Rebecca approached her father. His smashed mouth was hanging open. His one remaining eye stared out from the other world, completely still. Teeth, gum flesh and pieces of bone from his shattered jaws lay on his tongue.

Tears streamed from Rebecca's eyes. She couldn't understand how the Orizons could claim that they didn't cry when they were in pain. She was sobbing uncontrollably.

With her left hand she stroked Julius's hair and head. In

her right hand she was still holding the dagger by the tip of its blade. She bent down and kissed her father's forehead where it wasn't injured and disfigured, forcing herself to stop weeping.

Four of the children were bending over the three women whom Julius had killed. They hadn't heard the silenced shots and could not understand why their mothers were lying motionless on the floor. They cried as they hugged and shook the women, falling over their bodies. Rebecca noticed that no child had gone to the woman she had killed. She probably had only the baby that she had been breastfeeding.

One child stood alone, frozen to the spot, terrified. The baby that had been breastfeeding a short while ago was on the seats crying loudly, maybe because its mother hadn't finished feeding it and it was still hungry. Another baby on the floor was sucking its thumb.

Rebecca watched the four children get up off the dead bodies and rush at her father, pounding on his body with their fists, their hands becoming covered in blood. One of them kept kicking Julius's legs. They were crying and screaming but she couldn't understand what they were saying. They'd realized who had killed their mothers.

Rebecca froze as she watched the great injustice unfold. Her father had loved everything – animals and plants – and he had adored all people. He'd dedicated his life to the good of the human race. He'd fought to provide these children, who were now kicking him, with freedom and happiness without hunger or war. He hadn't cared about money or material comforts. He had kept his distance from political parties and all other falsities. He hadn't cared for glory. Many people on Earth fought and sacrificed themselves only for glory and medals, yet nobody would ever know about her father's sacrifice, no book would ever mention it. What the Orizons did on Earth would never become known.

"Are the children right to strike him because he killed their mothers?" Rebecca wondered.

She remembered him telling her:

"Children don't wear masks. They are innocent, spontaneous and candid."

Were they perhaps justified in hitting him?

He'd the right to kill because he was acting in self-defence and was also fighting to save the people on board. Good sometimes had to act in order to save lives.

How many heroes had been in a similar position? They sacrificed their lives for others and in the end were humiliated, sent to prison or executed. No recognition whatsoever. The hero was seen as a murderer. Would Rebecca also meet this kind of treatment one day?

Her father had told her that it was a common occurrence on Earth for those who fought for what they believed to be right and just to be rewarded with torture and death for what they saw as their virtuous efforts.

Was it really worth it to fight for all the things she valued, considering how those small and innocent children were treating her dead father?

She took a deep breath, her eyes burning.

"Rebecca speaking. Julius Newton is dead. Four more female terrorists have been killed so there are none of their women left alive. I'm in the reception area, awaiting orders."

For a few seconds, no answer came. It seemed that news of her father's death had left them speechless.

Then she heard a voice.

"Ernest here. I'm near the engine room. I've killed a terrorist who was carrying explosives and was armed with a sub-machine gun. I'm moving further down."

"There are six terrorists left who must all be in the hull. Be careful not to hit any explosives," Maher said. "Rebecca – now that you have no armed protection, leave your father there and go up on the deck with the rest of the children."

"I have my daggers, sir."

"Your orders are to go up on deck," Maher repeated.

"There are seven children here. Two are babies and the others are five to six years old. They're upset."

"This is Robin. I'm in the third hold. I've killed one man and I'm going to keep searching," Susan's father interrupted.

"My wife and Fued's wife are to go to the reception room to take care of the terrorists' children," their leader instructed. "As soon as they arrive, Rebecca will leave to join the rest of the Orizon children upstairs."

"This is Fued. I've killed a terrorist in the first hold, and I'm continuing my search".

Rebecca went up to the female terrorist whom she'd killed, pulled her dagger from the dead woman's throat, wiped it clean and put it back in its sheath. She moved her father's body into a corner and waited.

Fued's wife arrived first and began to take care of the children. She spoke the same language as them and she tried to calm them down, but they could still see their mothers' lifeless bodies.

Rebecca took the lift up to the deck. By the time she got there two more terrorists had been killed. She reached the first deck and stepped outside. In her mind confusion reigned. Her immortal father was dead. It was the worst nightmare that a child could endure: the death of a parent. The only greater pain for a human was that of a parent losing their child.

When the Orizon children spotted her, four of them ran from their hiding places. She shouted at them to go back to their safe posts and then she went over to Susan. Orders were orders and they had to be obeyed to the letter. The four children returned to their positions.

Susan didn't say anything, nor did she attempt to embrace or console Rebecca. Her eyes said it all, though, and Rebecca sat beside her in silence.

They received the news that two more terrorists had been killed. Soon afterwards they were told that the last terrorist was dead.

"The two Orizon women in the reception area are to lock the terrorists' children in a room and then all the women are to go to meeting point B. We'll continue searching for another five minutes in case we're mistaken and there are any more terrorists.

"We'll move the dead terrorists along with any weapons and the explosives to the reception area. Then we'll dump our weapons and the rest of our equipment in the sea in line with the instructions. Wait for us at point B. Hamam and Ernest are to keep their weapons and meet me in the reception area."

Soon the Orizons had disposed of everything. The time was three-thirty – less than an hour since they had first noticed the ship's change of course.

The group leader had taken Julius's pistol, removed the silencer, wiped the fingerprints clean and placed it in the captain's hand. Hamam and Ernest helped move the two dead officers to the reception area. They removed some bullets from their three pistols, took off the silencers, wiped off the fingerprints and put a pistol in each officer's hand. Then they put the last pistol in the radio operator's hand, after first untying his feet. They left four automatic weapons in the reception area, two in the radio room, and three at the wheelhouse. Finally they threw the others, along with the explosives, into the sea.

When the Orizons had all assembled, Maher said: "Our aim is still to cover up the big attack. The way things are, it will look as if pirates tried to seize the ship. But the heroic captain, first and second mates and radio operator managed, with great courage and self-sacrifice, to kill them and save the passengers and the ship.

"It will also seem that the helmsman and a retired, disabled ex-serviceman, a Falklands veteran who just happened to be in the reception area by himself, were killed. We must be careful to wipe off all our fingerprints and do everything else that we planned. At this moment the ship is sailing without a captain. When our wives were in the reception area downstairs they realized that some of the crew must have been locked in one of the offices there. They're probably the sailors who went to rescue the alleged shipwreck survivors. When they're set free – something that we'll make look as if it happened by chance – the event will become known because the crew will wake up the other radio operators who will broadcast the news.

"The passengers noticed nothing because the bridge, the communication centre and the reception area are far from the cabins and so the automatic weapons weren't heard. We're not going to get together again. Go back to the way we were during the rest of the voyage, as if we were just small groups of friends. Now is not the time to talk about the Orizon or Julius. Adriana and Rebecca must take care of the removal of his body from the ship, without the rest of us getting involved. Now let's all go back to our cabins."

Maher and his wife then went down to the reception area

and broke down the door. There was uproar at first but the sailors soon came out and saw the gruesome sight.

Everything went as Maher had predicted and in the next few minutes the whole world learned that pirates had used a feigned shipwreck to try and take over a cruise liner. The pirates had brought along their seven children, whom experienced crew members were looking after.

The following day the *Myrtilla* reached port.

Ernest gave directions so that no TV crews or reporters should come to the ship. The police did not conduct an investigation either.

When one of the top operatives of the foremost ultra-secret civil service department gave orders, no one asked for details or explanations. Only the Orizons knew the truth. So it was, in effect, as if no one at all knew.

LOMANI

Julius's body was taken first to London and later that same night to the Land of the White Sun, travelling in a special body bag that Bull and Doctor Afterland had brought with them. Adriana and Rebecca accompanied him. He was buried at the house where he had been born.

The following night Rebecca and her mother returned to Earth and the day after that there was a staged burial of Julius attended by a few close friends.

Sharp nails seemed to be tearing Rebecca's insides to pieces. She felt a clamp tightening around her throat till she could hardly swallow or breathe. Sounds echoed in her ears and her eyes gazed without seeing, as if she had been hypnotized. Two hammers were continuously pounding on her temples. Stormy waves from her mind battered at every cell in her body. Even the Flame couldn't help her overcome the trauma of her sudden loss.

Rebecca had always wondered how she would feel if she suddenly lost one of her parents, particularly when it had happened to some classmates and she had observed the reactions of the bereaved children. She had tried to put herself in their position and understand what they were feeling. At the time, she'd no idea that her parents were immortal and ran no risk of dying suddenly except by accident.

Now she had suffered that painful loss and she couldn't take it in. She wondered how people endured such a terrible blow. She wondered if losing a parent during adolescence might hurt more than it would have done in childhood. And when you are grown up, have your own family and your own children and feel the immense love for them that a parent feels, then perhaps the pain of losing a parent yourself is not so overwhelming and tragic.

The holidays were over but Rebecca was not in the mood to return to school. She preferred to paint, to spend her time close to Nature. She felt the need to visit Africa again. She believed that being with animals would help her cope better with the unending pain she felt inside. But that wasn't possible, so she plucked up what was left of her courage and forced herself to get on with her classes.

She watched her sad, silent mother, trying to get inside her head and understand how she was feeling. She didn't want Adriana to suffer even half of what she herself was enduring. They both avoided talking about it. Each one of them tried to face their dramatic loss on their own.

Rebecca kept seeing visions of her father in the house, as if everything that had happened on board the *Myrtilla* had been no more than a bad dream. Every night she crept into the study where he had often worked until late at night. He would raise his head, open his arms wide and swivel his chair around, signalling to her to run and give him a hug. She missed such tender moments and would sit in the empty study and reminisce. She could sometimes convince herself that she could see him again, holding out his arms, inviting her into his fatherly embrace, and she would touch the armchair where he used to rest his back.

She realized, as did her mother, that it was too painful to continue living in that house, full of so many memories. It was like a cold tomb with Julius's phantom floating around it. They discussed moving but it wasn't easy to move to another home when the nearby forest was so convenient for the spaceship to land. They began searching, just in case they found another house in the same area.

Rebecca worked on nothing apart from her school projects, playing music, painting, meditating and talking to the moon. She couldn't think about getting organized to tackle Earth's problems. She put all that out of her mind.

She had believed completely in the cause when she'd received the Flame.

She'd been shocked by the way the little children of the terrorists had behaved towards her dead father. To them it was of no consequence why he had killed their mothers, whether he was justified, and how many lives he had saved by his sacrifice. They didn't understand that he was the reason they were alive, or that their mothers would have been killed anyway, along with them, when the ship blew up.

It felt like the Flame inside Rebecca had bound her with strong ties to the struggle for Good. However much those ties were stretched, they wouldn't break, but she feared that they could be severed instantly with a pair of scissors. And scissors could easily be found.

Her father had said that she would gradually gain experience as she was ground between the millstones of life. The death of Lady Danae and the cruel murder of Pegasus had transformed her into a windmill ready to grind any trace of Evil to nothingness. But her father's loss had ripped the mill's sails and broken its support beams. Rebecca felt the fierce icy wind rage through the bare struts and the tattered cloth. The power of the wind was wasted and the sails wouldn't turn. If Rebecca had felt like a ship with torn sails she could have taken up the oars to get it moving. But a windmill could not move by any other means.

The loss of her father was a reason to push other things aside. She isolated them, locked them in a box inside her so that she didn't have to think about them. Her changing priorities surprised even herself, like red-hot lava solidifying into black rock as soon as it is spewed forth from a volcano. She constantly felt tremors as strong as earthquakes and had to struggle not to collapse. In her desperation she was nonetheless aware of her school obligations and the scheduled completion of her training in the Land of the White Sun: two burdens that she could not bear. She felt like a traitor.

Lord Life came to visit Rebecca and her mother. Rebecca scarcely recognized him. He'd shaved off his beard and was wearing a suit and a tie. But she instantly recognized his eyes, which radiated the same special light, and his voice, which was still calm, measured and decisive.

He told them that although Utopia was in a state of war he'd decided to stay on Earth for some time. He trusted Princess Felicia implicitly and knew that she could manage without his help, even during another war against Turgoth.

"She's been doing so for more than a hundred years," he said.

Rebecca was startled to learn that Felicia was over a century old when she didn't look a day over thirty.

The summer holidays came round again and Rebecca returned to the Land of the White Sun, despite her concerns about leaving her mother on her own for such a long time. She resumed her training along with the others but everybody could see that she was no longer as eager or lively. She attended her lessons as usual, but something was missing; something was on her mind. She avoided conversations and kept to herself. The other children excused her withdrawn behaviour, attributing it to the death of her father. But there were other things worrying Rebecca as well. She felt sure that solutions could be found to stop the wars in the Land of the White Sun.

Even though the situation on Earth was grave, she firmly believed that it should be easy to stop the conflict in the Land of the White Sun and that they could all then live together in brotherly harmony. The scene that she had painted on her canvas could come true. All it needed was for everyone to realize they had to leave the past behind and forget the blood that had been spilled. They could all share the Flame amicably and together turn their efforts to making Good prevail on Earth. It was a waste for even a single life to be lost in the Lomani. She couldn't understand how the Orizons could work so hard on the great problems of the Earth and leave unsolved what she saw as a simple issue that caused war and death in their own land. The forces of Good claimed a monopoly on goodness while committing a great injustice. Rebecca thought how the same thing happened on Earth. Before a country had worked out its own problems and ensured the prosperity of its own people it would send its army and politicians to resolve the problems of other states. They set off like Gods, omniscient and arrogant, to solve major problems abroad when they were in no position to deal with simple matters in their own lands.

Such nations would sometimes gain financially and politically by their intervention. But how could the Orizons, who had no vested interest in interfering on Earth, possibly justify such intrusion? She thought that they should first settle the simple matter of the Flame and only then attempt to deal with the enormous problems on Earth.

Rebecca discussed her ideas with the Wise Tree and it agreed with her. It was her chief supporter in Utopia. She told it everything she was feeling. That was the only issue she was in the mood to tackle and she struggled to find a solution. She felt her heart beating again and her powers returning.

Despite becoming a little restless, cooped up behind the walls of the Fortress, the citizens of Utopia still looked happy and seemed to have adjusted to the situation. They had become like beings with no will of their own, brought up to obey orders and to be killed, if need be, in order to keep the Flame. They didn't seem concerned that they might die, as long as the Flame was not taken from them.

They were joking and making fun of Death, as if they and he were old buddies, as if they expected to enjoy their own funeral parties. It was the schizophrenia that Turgoth had talked about.

All of their immortal lives they'd been taught that it was their duty. War ran in their veins from the day they were born, taking root in their minds from the moment they acquired consciousness. They identified with it, as much the victims of propaganda as anyone on Earth. So to them everything seemed natural.

The second person to whom Rebecca revealed her thoughts was Bull the Minotaur. He agreed with her too. So then there were three of them who shared a philosophy that was still in its infancy. Rebecca planned to talk to Princess Felicia as well, to listen to her opinions and then expand on her own controversial ideas. She was trying to find the right password. Time was passing but her instinct did not guide her to start that discussion.

She could understand that her ideas were a kind of action too. An effort to influence. A revolution that nobody could kill or confine.

The young Orizons' training was almost over. They had all performed extremely well and had become warriors, ready for action. A celebration was to take place at the theatre, where Princess Felicia would speak to them. All the residents gathered together once more in the late afternoon.

"About two years ago, you learned that you had a purpose," Felicia told the children. "You began training and decided to receive the Flame of the White Sun and become immortal Orizons. You've trained hard: it's been a lot of work, but the results are excellent. Before you have turned eighteen you are ready to defend the Flame and fight for Good to prevail on Earth. During this time you've had some dramatic adventures, but you have all survived and grown stronger. Today's celebration marks the conclusion of your training. Now you have ten days to rest and then you'll return to Earth. If war breaks out and your presence is needed here, you're to come at once. Lord Life will guide your activities on Earth. He has decided to stay there for a while so as to coordinate better the struggle against Evil. Congratulations to all of you. Now, let's have fun. Even when times are difficult, Orizons know how to have a good time and be happy. But before our party begins Field Marshal Foster will announce which military corps you belong to."

As she was listening to the princess, Rebecca decided to ask for a hearing the following day to explain her ideas about why the war should stop. She would tell Felicia that she wasn't claiming to be smarter than everyone else, but that to her mind and heart there was a strange contradiction. It was a huge lie, like those found everywhere on Earth. There the Orizons were trying to put a stop to lies that caused pain and misery when they had not solved their own most fundamental problem. She would argue that there were no winners in wars, only in sporting events. In the words of Benjamin Franklin: '*There was never a good war or a bad peace.*'

Field Marshal Foster rose and stood next to the princess. "Heartfelt congratulations from me as well. I'm going to announce the generals' final decision about which corps each of you will join. They're the ones that you yourselves have agreed on, as you've become aware of your own aptitudes. Carlos, Bill, Abu and Pedro have been assigned to General Hunter's unit. Louise, Susan, Tiki, Lee and José have been assigned to General Claudia's unit, while Rebecca, Samantha, Tamina, Jabal, Rashid and Sergei have been assigned to mine.

"Tomorrow your generals will give you more details about which section you must go to and what you must do in case of war. But for now, have a good time."

Felicia gave the signal for the musicians to play and the party began. As they danced and sang they heard trumpets sounding over the noise of the music. Confused, they looked up and saw Calphie the Sphinx flying over Highlow and then vanishing. The music stopped and a murmur of unease rippled through the crowd. They couldn't believe their eyes. It had been thousands of years since the Sphinxes had flown; and they never went to each other's lands. What was Calphie doing there?

The Sphinx rose up again and flew towards the armoury, hurling herself against its roof, caving it in and crumbling the walls to rubble with repeated blows. In just a few minutes it was in ruins.

Satisfied with her destruction there, Calphie charged at the Gate, which had been closed as soon as the trumpets had sounded, and fell against it heavily, striking it with her hindquarters. The Gate held. Lifting off, she flew around the outer side and fell on it again with all her might. The Gate shook and cracks appeared in it. Calphie continued to strike it and the cracks widened until the thick wood eventually splintered. It was only then that the Sphinx flew away.

Princess Felicia gave orders for the trumpeters to sound the alarm that they were under attack and for three hundred Centaurs armed with spears to cover the open Gate.

She told the generals to meet at her house to evaluate the situation and she asked Bull to go to Highlow to find out what had happened. As soon as the staff officers had assembled, the war council began. Everyone was sure that Turgoth was going to attack.

Soon Bull returned in a state of agitation. "Calphie's destroyed all three of our spaceships – just smashed them against one another. All their landing legs are broken. It'll take ages to repair them. The Sharkans have cut us off. We can't bring in reinforcements from Earth or even fetch Lord Life. We're completely isolated!" He slumped despairingly into an armchair, pulling at his short horns as though he wanted to uproot them like carrots. They all remained silent and thoughtful as other officers began to arrive and report on the situation.

So far the armies of Beast were nowhere in sight. This gave the people of Utopia a little time to get better organized and recover from the enemy Sphinx's sudden attack. Soon a report came that all the troops were in position as directed and the Gate had been reinforced. The trumpets heralded the approach of a horseman.

"The Sphinx is coming again," he yelled as he ran into the house.

"Everybody outside," ordered Princess Felicia.

They dashed into the courtyard in time to see Calphie charging the three-dimensional projection station, reducing it to rubble. Then she headed for Felicia's house. They watched in awe as the winged monster dropped onto the roof of the house, caving it in. She lifted off again, picked up speed and repeated the attack until the whole roof came crashing down into the house, bringing most of the walls with it.

Nobody knew what to do as they watched the demolition. Bull's house was the next to be destroyed before Calphie flew away once more, leaving behind her ruined buildings and a shaken people.

The princess gave instructions that whenever the enemy Sphinx appeared non-combatants and children were to evacuate all the buildings. She designated the hospital as a makeshift headquarters, hoping that Turgoth would at least respect and spare that building.

As the sun set, Felicia, Afterland, Bull, Leiko and the generals were in conference in the hospital. They decided that experts should go to Highlow to assess the damage done to the spaceships and that the workshop should start making the spare parts needed for repairs as soon as possible. They also decided to have the Gate fixed without delay.

"These attacks are catastrophic," Field Marshal Foster said. "They've selected their targets well. By knocking out Highlow and the three-dimensional projection station, they've cut off all communication with Earth. We can't even tell them what's happening here. The demolition of the Gate and the armoury were strategic blows, while the houses were demolished to undermine our morale.

"We can't fight back against the Sharkans' Sphinx; she's invulnerable to arrows and spears. She strikes like a saboteur. Turgoth has broken the rules again by bringing Calphie into the war. He also failed to give us any warning. I'm sure that the attacks will continue as long as we're unable to respond."

He looked at each of them in turn, ending with Felicia.

"In my opinion there's only one way to put the struggle back on equal terms. We must bring Glory into battle. Princess, you must give her the order to be on standby and as soon as the trumpets signal that Calphie is attacking Glory must intercept her before she reaches the Fortress."

Bull obviously had reservations. He didn't like the idea of Glory leaving the Flame unprotected. But when he thought it over, he had to admit that Foster was right. There was no other way of dealing with the situation. He himself would guard the Flame if Glory could be persuaded to go.

The princess was silent and thoughtful when an agitated messenger arrived, his eyes blazing.

"Princess, they've cut off our water supply! They must have closed off the points where the water enters the aqueduct at Mount Thunder. It's something we hadn't foreseen and there are no reserves."

Everybody froze. There were about ten thousand people in the Fortress, including children and non-combatants, Amazons and Centaurs, and there were at least as many horses and other animals. Turgoth had put them at a disadvantage yet again. They had no wells from which to collect water, and it was not the rainy season.

Felicia ordered Doctor Afterland to start a drilling project in the hope of finding enough water to meet their basic needs – otherwise their horses would die of thirst in a few days. In a month or so the besieged city's human population would be in trouble. She issued a directive to everyone to drink fruit juice sparingly in order to eke out available stocks.

The trumpets sounded as night fell. The armies of Beast were on the march and were about three hours from Utopia.

The princess decided to go to Glory at once with Leiko, Bull, Foster, Claudia and Hunter. They found her sitting before the altar of the Flame, looking deeply worried.

The Princess looked her in the eye. "Glory, have you seen the terrible disaster Calphie has brought on us?"

"I have, princess. She's caused great harm. If the Gods hear of it, they'll punish her for disobeying their commands."

"Glory, it's certain that she'll continue her attacks and destroy us. You're the only way we have of dealing with her. There is no other solution. The minute the trumpets sound a warning that she's coming, you must fly out and stop her."

"Princess, I won't leave my post. I have orders from the Gods to guard the Flame and protect it from any attack. Let Calphie dare come here and you'll see what happens to her."

"I know that those are your orders and you definitely must protect the Flame. But if Calphie's attacks continue, she'll annihilate us. The powers of Evil will get in and seize the Flame. So if you want to defend it you must do as I say. If the armies of Beast conquer Utopia, it will be too late."

"I'm not leaving my post unless the Gods order me to. Let the powers of Evil come to take the Flame and they'll bitterly regret it. I can kill them all. I'm sure of that."

Seeing that they couldn't make her change her mind, Felicia's group left without having accomplished anything. Night covered the Fortress like a funeral pall. It dragged past as if drawn by weary cattle. Everyone was awake, awaiting the enemy's next move. Uncertainty about what might happen spread like a contagion. After thousands of years, the foe had unexpectedly turned cunning, striking slyly like a snake.

In the Fortress's workshop several scientists were already trying to build the spare parts for the spaceships. Rebecca's grandfather was among them.

At dawn the Princess received a full report. It appeared that Turgoth had laid siege to Utopia. He had camped about two-thirds of a mile away from the Fortress walls. Many enemy troops were in Domus Forest, where they could not be counted with any accuracy. Reports confirmed, however, that it was the first time so many forces of Evil had gathered against them.

It seemed that Turgoth was not planning to start the attack straight away, otherwise he would not have set up camp. Presumably he aimed to weaken the forces of Utopia by laying siege to the Fortress and depriving its inhabitants of water before making his attack. The trumpets sounded as soon as the sun rose.

The Sphinx Calphie reappeared. This time she attacked Utopia's workshop and demolished it, although everyone managed to get out in time. The workshop was where weapons and other articles were made from crystal, metal and wood: everything required by the country. Its destruction was the hardest blow yet.

Princess Felicia and her generals began to lose heart. They knew that being cut off from Earth and also from the Second Parallel Dimension where the Mythical Gods dwelled could radically change the future of the Land of the White Sun and of the Orizons who lived on Earth.

The princess summoned all the scientists and engineers who worked on energy, spaceships and other projects. Sixty Orizons, forty-four men and sixteen women, gathered outside the hospital. Tony Newton was among them. All of them were obviously upset.

"None of you is to take part in any battle," Felicia said. "As soon as darkness falls, Field Marshal Foster's forces will break through the weakest point of the enemy lines. They'll help you to escape and you'll go to Mount Thunder where you'll stay until the war is over. Whoever wins, you must live. Take as many tools as you can carry. Your first priority is to survive and eventually to repair the spaceships or to build a new one. You must, without fail, go to Earth and find Lord Life, who will then decide what is to be done. I don't know how long it will take. You'll learn the outcome of the war from observers that you will send at intervals. Nobody must know your whereabouts. It goes without saying that you must not, under any circumstances whatsoever, disobey these orders and abandon the crucial mission assigned to you.

"I appoint Tony Newton your leader and he'll name deputies to replace him in case anything happens to him. Your escape route will be carefully planned. Until then, you're to split up into five groups designated by Newton so that if something unexpected occurs you won't all be hit at once. Make sure that each group includes people with a range of skills so that if one group is attacked the other groups won't be left without the necessary specialists. Each group will have a leader appointed by Tony Newton. Any future communication between the Land of the White Sun and Earth and the Second Parallel Dimension depends on you. Those of you who have children or spouses can take them with you. Bid farewell to your other relatives. As of now you are a separate community whose sole purpose is to survive and reconnect the Land of the White Sun with Earth and the Mythical Gods. I wish you all the very best."

It wasn't long before the trumpets announced the approach of Calphie the Sphinx once more. This time she hit the stables.

Most of the horses were out, being ridden by Orizons preparing for war, but there were still some inside.

Doctor Afterland told the princess that they were digging for water at fifty different points in the Fortress, so far without success. Bull the Minotaur told Felicia that he wanted to go in person to Glory the Sphinx to try and make her change her mind. Since they were both Mythical creatures they might be able to communicate better. Felicia agreed and Bull left the hospital.

At that moment Rebecca arrived astride a bay horse. "Bull," she said, "We fifteen young Orizons of Earth don't know where to go or whom to fight. We don't know what's going on. Nobody had time to give us directions. The children are waiting at the theatre for me to brief them."

"That's where I'm going now. Felicia is inside with Leiko. You'd better go in and agree on what you should do. The situation is very bad. Nobody expected this and Utopia is not prepared to face a war without the rules. If I don't persuade that blasted old Sphinx of ours to fight, we're doomed. Turgoth isn't following the rules at all. That's why we're at a disadvantage. It's very unfair. What he's doing is unheard of; it's led to an imbalance of power."

"Haven't we, Bull, been unfair for the thousands of years that we've been using the Flame? Not only are we immortal but we're also stronger than they are, better warriors and we don't need injections of courage when we fight. And, as you well know, courage gives power to mind, spirit and body.

"Because of the Flame within us we don't know the meaning of fear. However brave the Sharkans may be, whenever they hear the drums of war they also hear the pounding of their own hearts. The adrenalin rises, the suspense of an impending threat overwhelms them and the trembling of anticipatory dread causes their teeth to rattle. It makes their mouths go dry, their breath falter, their hands sweat, their legs buckle, their bodies turn numb and their minds grow confused. That's what happens to every soldier in the world, even to heroes, before they go into combat. They know very well that all it would take would be a bullet or an arrow and they would see and hear no more. But Orizons breathe freely and their hearts never flutter. Not only are they not concerned about the battle, they eagerly seek it out as if it were some kind of child's game. There's no adrenalin because the Flame has vaporized it."

Bull said nothing. He knew that Rebecca was right, just as Turgoth might also be. He was sure that if Turgoth did not win this war he would kill himself. He remembered the king's words on Mount Thunder.

"I'm leaving now," Bull said. "This isn't the right time for such a serious discussion. You must go and find your grandparents and kiss them goodbye."

"Bull, make sure that you appeal to Glory's pride. Tell her that Calphie will go down in history if she's the reason Utopia falls and Beast succeeds in taking the Flame. Make it clear to her that the Gods do not meddle in such matters. They allow us to take the initiative and settle them. Find a way to flatter her feminine self-esteem. Sorry, Bull. I'm too young to advise you, but I think what I say might help."

Once Bull had gone, Rebecca went into the hospital and found Felicia. She explained the problem that she and the other children had.

"Tell them all to come here," Felicia said. " Leiko will take you under his wing."

The fifteen children soon arrived and Leiko gave them instructions. After a while Bull returned.

"Glory has promised me that as soon as Calphie shows up, she will deal with her."

"How did you manage it, my dear Bull?" Felicia asked.

"It was easy, princess. I appealed to her vanity," said Bull, smiling enigmatically.

Two hours later the trumpets sounded again and everyone left the buildings. To their surprise they saw their own Sphinx in the sky.

"Let's go to the watchtower to see what happens," suggested Felicia.

Bull, Leiko and the children mounted their horses and galloped with her to the Gate.

After circling above Utopia to boost the morale of the people, Glory spotted Calphie approaching from Domus Forest and flew towards her. They met in the sky between the forces of Beast and the Fortress.

"Where are you going, Calphie?" Glory growled. "Haven't you done enough damage for no reason? Why have you become involved? This is not your job."

"I agreed with Turgoth to attack because I've been treated unfairly and my patience is exhausted. As you know, I come from Syria and there weren't enough Mythical Gods coming from there, Gods who would have taken my side. Whereas you come from Egypt and have many compatriot Gods ready to take your side, all of whom are also skilled in the arts of persuasion and public relations and have connections with the higher-standing deities. That's why, when the Gods voted on which one of us would become the Guardian of the Flame, you won."

"The Gods are never unjust, and now you have treacherously demolished half of Utopia. You have left me no choice but to kill you," roared Glory, instantly rushing against Calphie before she had time to prepare herself, wounding her on the left wing. Lashing out in a clumsy defence, Calphie managed to slash Glory's neck.

Never in the history of the Universe had such a ferocious battle been fought between such mighty foes. They were the strongest mythical creatures in the world. In ancient times both had defeated whole armies on their own and now they faced each other with no hope of any mercy being shown on either side.

Both camps watched from the ground. The people of Utopia knew that their future security depended on the outcome of this duel, while the forces of Beast knew that Calphie's survival was vital to their final victory. A large part of their plan of attack was based on the tremendous damage she was capable of inflicting upon Utopia before it had time to react.

The Sphinxes rose high in the air and fell repeatedly against each other at great speed, colliding side to side, back to back, head to head, like giant airborne battering rams.

The collisions were so violent that their mighty bodies shuddered with each impact. For hours they battered against one another, each time drawing back without any visible result, preparing themselves for their next assault. They were both supernaturally powerful creatures, almost invulnerable, and their chances of victory were equal. No one could predict which of the two would falter first. If it had not been a battle to the death but a simple competition, the match would certainly have ended in a draw, both sides eventually exhausted by the strength of their opponent.

Then Calphie, with a clever manoeuvre, managed to get astride Glory's back, almost immobilizing her wings.

She clamped Glory's head with her two powerful lion's forelegs and squeezed tightly, pulling backwards in an attempt to snap her opponent's neck.

However hard she shook and twisted, Glory couldn't free herself from Calphie's grip. Inch by inch her head was forced further and further back, bending her spine towards breaking point. Then Calphie moved one of her legs from Glory's head to her throat, sinking her nails in deep in an attempt to strangle her and sap her strength.

Blood bubbled and welled up on Glory's throat. She was struggling for breath. Her vision blurred and things began to grow dark around her. Death was closing in.

Summoning the last remnants of her strength, Glory spun onto her back, dragging Calphie with her. Still flying, but upside down now, Calphie's own weight forced her to loosen her grip on Glory who grabbed her chance and pulled away to gather her strength. After regaining their balance they charged at each other again, meeting with an explosion of noise so loud that it could be heard throughout the land, and locking together. Both exhausted, they spiralled downwards, disengaging just before they hit the ground. Almost simultaneously they both rose again to their feet.

"Let's take a breather," Glory suggested, wiping the blood that dripped from her neck.

"OK," Calphie agreed as she examined her damaged wing, which was throbbing with pain. She was losing blood from the place where her flank connected with it.

"Don't think, Glory, that I've turned evil,' she said. "We were never wicked. Back on Earth we always fought on the side of Justice and we achieved wonders in helping our countries. We should be satisfied because the rest of our kind in Greece and in Asia were not chosen by the Gods and were lost in the destruction along with everybody else. We are both survivors."

The warriors on both sides stared anxiously up into the skies, waiting for the battle to start again or for a victor to rise up. They were unable to work out why both the Sphinxes had landed, why they'd stopped their fighting – unless one of them was dead.

"If both of us were not good," Calphie went on, "the Gods wouldn't have chosen us and brought us here to escape the destruction."

"That's right. But now you're on the side of Evil and your underhand attack makes you wicked and I'll have to kill you ..."

Before finishing her words Glory rose on her hind legs and fell on Calphie, who instantly rose on her hind legs too, lifting Glory with her.

Now they looked like wrestlers, each trying to overthrow the other, towering over the surrounding forest as they reared up and fell back together. Few among even the most long-lived of the spectators had ever seen such a sight. They'd each grabbed their opponent by the shoulders, their nails piercing the other's flesh. Moving their grips to each other's back and middle, they used all their weight and strength to push, both trying to force their opponent to lose her footing and fall. Their wings were spread and moved slowly. They were sweating profusely as the hours passed.

The scratches on both of them multiplied and deepened. During all this time they kept trying to kick each other but neither could reach. During one such effort Glory lost her balance and fell on her back, bringing Calphie down on top of her.

Glory had landed awkwardly, her wings taking the brunt of the fall. The pain took her breath away as she struggled desperately to be free, afraid that if the wings had sustained any serious damage she wouldn't be able to fly. She kept trying to flip her opponent over far enough to free them and ease the pain. Calphie made a clumsy move, trying to ease her own wounded wing, and Glory seized the opportunity to hit her with her left foreleg, straight in the face, smashing her nose and making her swollen lips bleed. Shocked, Calphie let Glory go and covered her face with her paws.

Anxious to find out if her wings were still working, Glory took off and flew. There was no pain and she breathed easily again. A few moments later Calphie rose into the sky behind her, despite her damaged wing. She kept losing blood from her side near the wing as well as from her nose. As the duel continued in the sky once more the watchers held their breath. The balance of the fight shifted constantly. There was still no way of predicting who would be victorious.

Little by little the Sphinxes' fatigue was beginning to show as their blows became weaker and their moves slower. Calphie's body had sustained more wounds from Glory's wings and claws but Glory had an ugly cut across her throat, which was gushing blood at a terrible rate. Their exhaustion was as much due to loss of blood as to the length of the battle.

Neither of them had much strength left and both knew that they had to put an end to the fight as soon as possible. In their desperation they became fiercer. Their attacks grew even more savage and they got more careless. Calphie could see that the wound in Glory's neck was gaping wider and she struck it again without taking precautions to protect herself. The claws of Glory's two hind legs ripped into her belly. But Glory's luck was no better. Calphie's claws had widened the gash in her neck and her throat flesh now hung in shreds, blood spurting out like a fountain. Her vision dimmed again and everything swirled around her. The sky and the land alternated in rapid succession. The ground came up too fast for her to be able to take evasive action and hit her hard.

As Glory lay dying she wondered why all this had to happen.

She felt the urge to die close to the Flame. Gathering her last remaining shreds of strength, she managed to stand, knowing that she could no longer fly. She turned towards the Gate. With her right foreleg she pushed back the shredded flesh at her throat and took a few staggering steps.

"I'm going to guard the Flame ..." she shouted with all her remaining strength. "Have no fear ... No one can take it away ..."

Thinking about the Flame redoubled Glory's courage and hope, but after just a few steps she sank down and remained motionless.

All Utopia froze. They saw all their hopes evaporate as Calphie flew slowly away. As they watched in despair, she too began to lose altitude and plummeted down into the trees below. They could see that, even if she wasn't dead, she was severely injured. The fall had been too steep to survive.

Their morale rose anew. The guardian of the Flame might be lost, but Calphie's death meant that they could still win. Suddenly they were no longer afraid of the powers of Evil. But at the same time they were upset by Glory's death. She had sacrificed her life to save Utopia and put the warring sides back on an equal footing.

Returning to the hospital, the princess gave orders to have Glory the Sphinx buried and to cancel the departure of the sixty Orizon specialists. That lifted everyone's spirits even more. The experts would continue working day and night to get spare parts made for the spaceships. Now their most pressing problem was the loss of their water supply. As the day wore on, the sun grew hot and the lack of water was becoming uncomfortable; the horses were thirsty. The news from Doctor Afterland was not encouraging.

Field Marshal Foster suggested that they be patient until the evening and then launch a massive attack at night to clear a way through the forces of Evil beside the lake, find where the water had been cut off and try to reconnect the supply.

Bull believed that such a course was too risky because Turgoth would expect it and would protect the place well. Felicia decided to let everybody recover until morning from the Sphinx's attacks. All the fighters were to sleep in shifts, even on the battlements, so they would be rested and in good shape.

"Tomorrow morning we'll decide what action to take," she concluded.

Foster didn't agree but he had to obey. The warriors of Utopia were impatient. Their morale was now high and they couldn't forgive Turgoth's treachery. They wanted to attack their foes and defeat them once and for all.

When day came, a message was delivered to Felicia from Turgoth on parchment. She sent for the generals, Afterland, Bull and Leiko, and read it to them.

Princess Felicia,

I know that Lord Life is absent on a visit to Earth. I have also calculated the damage that our Sphinx caused before she kicked the bucket. We have cut off your water supply and it will be tough for you to repair the damage. We have strong forces stationed in the area where the damage is and you are bound to fail if you try to take it back. You'll suffer and mourn for ever.

I suggest we reach a compromise at long last; I suggest we share the Flame and put an end to our fighting. This time we are committed to either win or fight to the last man and die in the process. I swear! There can be no other solution. Our chances of losing are negligible. But even if you win your losses will be devastating and the Land will be left a wasteland.

Thousands of years of anger have accumulated inside my people, who feel like citizens of a lower world. It is unjust of you to call us evil and yourselves good. It warps your values, making them counterfeit and unable to stand up to close inspection.

Our Land is like a ship gone mad, the oarsmen so drunk that half of them row forwards and the other half backwards. All their labours are in vain. The ship can't move, it can only turn round and round, like a top.

It's time to re-evaluate the situation, use our common sense and reach the only solution possible. This is not against the decrees of the Gods. They, in their laziness, gave superficial guidelines without detailed instructions and without paying any attention to the ramifications. As usual, they had no interest in the results of their decision.

The dispute between us over who has the right to the Flame leaves them indifferent. But we should live in amity. We are not beasts with bloodthirsty instincts. The only reason we fight to the death is over the injustice of the Flame.

You show it off as if it belongs to you exclusively and we watch from afar, starving. The showcase for your goodness cracked on the very first day you talked the Gods into giving you the Flame. You serve it to yourselves and you grow drunk on the power. You, princess, put yourself forward as the shepherdess who takes good care of her flock, while we are depicted as rapacious wolves, attacking the innocent sheep.

I want us to live in peace together as we did in the past. Our division today is due to human imperfections that are inherent in all of us, whether we have the Flame or not.

After reconciling our peoples we can combine our forces and implement meaningful programmes that will rouse people on Earth from their inertia; help them get rid of the debris accumulated inside them, fight against corruption and put a brake on everything that leads to the planet's destruction. The Earth will not be saved by half measures but with bold initiatives that can turn things upside down. We will put incorruptible and competent people in all the key positions, people who will give no quarter to any lawbreakers. Ignoramuses won't be able to reach and hold high positions of authority. New laws will leave no loopholes that allow opportunists, cheats and warmongers to survive. We shall pursue and destroy the drug lords to the very last one.

Actually, princess, what we should do to the people who start the wars is hang them by the feet after cutting out their tongues. Then we should break the hands of all those who pollute and destroy the planet. As for the ones who take advantage of the petrol, robbing people, we should make them take a bath in it and throw in a lighted match to burn them alive. We should then go on to stuff the mouths of drug dealers with cocaine and inject them with massive doses of their own heroin, after first kicking their backsides.

Once things are settled on Earth we will implement the programmes we have been adhering to in our Land, helping Earth's people rebuild their lives on a sound basis.

I will wait twenty hours for your reply. Then, if I have no word from you, I will attack. I do not want you to suffer from the lack of water. I do not want to see the children die first, followed by the adults. It would be better to fight it out. What will be, will be.

I have cut off your water supply to shake you up, to force you to come to your senses, even at the last moment.

Turgoth

As soon as Felicia finished reading, Claudia stood up. "What a nerve he's got," she shouted indignantly. "The boaster, asking us to surrender! As if we would!"

Everyone's opinions differed. The letter showed that Turgoth wasn't bluffing and that he felt both strong and determined. He pretended he wanted to avoid bloodshed. It was certain that if his forces stood firm and their lines were not breached by a counter-attack, then the people of Utopia would soon die of thirst. Yet he declared that he would not go to that extreme but would attack instead. Turgoth appeared to be truly smooth-tongued.

Some thought his letter was nonsense and said they should ignore it, while others said it contained a message that they should all listen to.

"Whatever Turgoth says in this letter," Felicia said, "however many arguments he has, we have no choice but to fight. The Mythical Gods gave us the Flame subject to our obeying certain commands and we must defend it for ever. A lot of blood has been shed over many years so that we could keep it and we mustn't forget that."

Bull had been breathing as heavily as a rumbling volcano

ever since the princess had started reading. "I agree with what you say, princess," he growled, his eyes flashing like the pulsing fire of a flame-thrower. "But I'm mystified. How can Turgoth possibly know that Lord Life is away? Is he some kind of oracle, like Pythia? Even though oracles went out of business ages ago, he knew all about Rebecca's indecisiveness and the children's itinerary; now he knows about Lord Life's absence. It's as though we sent someone to shout about it all over Beast. How can this be? Why aren't we troubled by these signs of treachery?"

He spoke as if there were nails in his mouth and his tongue was a hammer beating them into everyone's heart, including his own.

"Why are you bringing all this up now, Bull?" grumbled Foster. "We're facing a major crisis and all you can talk about is treachery."

Bull raised his voice too, obviously upset. "Does it anger you when I think aloud, Field Marshal? Shouldn't I point it out? I didn't accuse anyone. I simply stated a fact. Do you not think we should be concerned?"

Foster rose from his seat and paced up and down with his head bowed. He looked bewildered, like a naughty child being reprimanded. A shadow passed fleetingly over his features, then settled. The angles of his face looked tauter. His brow creased and his lips pressed tightly together. The commander looked like a veteran soldier being led to face a firing squad.

"I'm sorry, Bull," he said quietly. "You're right. Indeed, how could Turgoth possibly know that Lord Life is away? And how did he know in such detail the route of the children during the exercise? Very few of us knew those facts."

Nobody spoke and the atmosphere grew heavy. General Hunter snorted in exasperation. Foster resumed his seat and suggested that they should organize a vigorous attack, break through the enemy lines and find out where the water-supply system had been damaged. He would use a large contingent of Centaurs in a square formation and his own horsemen. Then archers would take up position along the whole pipeline to protect it from further sabotage.

The princess gave her consent. Four hundred Centaurs with spears and five hundred Orizon horsemen with swords got ready. Two hundred Amazons would be standing by, ready to charge as soon as the enemy lines were breached.

They launched the attack before noon at the point where the pipeline led to Mount Thunder.

Hunter's spear-bearing Centaurs marched as a single body until they reached the enemy. They held large shields of light crystal that protected them from the crowns of their heads to the ground. They could see clearly through the tough transparent crystal. They held their spears upright and their shields almost interlocked so that not even an arrow could squeeze between them.

The left side of the square formation faced left and moved sideways to the right. The right side of the square faced right and walked sideways to the left. One hundred Centaurs at the front of the square marched forward in normal fashion, but slowly, so that the Centaurs on the sides of the square, who walked sideways and thus much slower, could keep up with them. Even though it was natural for Centaurs to walk sideways and backwards, the units had done intensive training in that kind of marching.

Another hundred Centaurs at the rear of the square walked forward normally. But as soon as problems arose, they could swivel and walk backwards, thus shielding the square on all sides, rendering it impregnable. It looked like a huge crystal box, a Mythological beast slowly advancing on its target. So far it had never suffered any losses because it was in effect an armoured unit.

Inside the square marched the fearsome blue-and-white-uniformed Orizon warriors of Field Marshal Foster, ready with their swords to crush any resistance. They too had always reached enemy lines without sustaining a single injury because the Centaurs' shields protected them.

Once they were a few yards from the enemy, two sides of the square would fan out, aligning themselves with the front row and launching a savage attack at the gallop. The Centaurs in the back row observed the battle and provided reinforcements as need.

Hundreds of Roman-style chariots, pulled by two steeds and driven by Sharkans, charged from the enemy lines. Each chariot had a long thick shaft extending about six yards in front of the horses. It was Turgoth's new invention.

The attackers rushed at the shields of the Centaurs like a hurricane and breached the formation. Then the Sharkans, with their reins in their left hands and swords in their right, fell upon them without mercy.

While Foster's troops were trying to recover from their surprise and fend off the attackers, thousands of black-clad Sharkans on horseback surrounded the formation and forced their way inside the square, past the scattered Centaurs.

The warriors of Utopia were unable to break through the lines of the besiegers. Their protective formation had been breached and they found themselves surrounded. Their losses were massive. Field Marshal Foster fought like a lion, as always. Most of the warriors were his pupils and they too fought fiercely and bravely. But the Sharkans outnumbered them at least five-fold and fought with similar courage and skill.

After the break-up of their lines the Centaurs fought like wild beasts but their losses were great too. General Foster soon realized they were fighting on unequal terms. He saw that the situation was out of control and their casualties were growing by the minute. He commanded his forces to lower their weapons and ordered a retreat.

He didn't know what orders Turgoth had given and whether the king's troops would honour the rules that had hitherto applied when one side decided to cease combat. To his relief, as soon as the soldiers of Utopia lowered their weapons the forces of Beast stopped fighting. Turgoth had complied with the rules.

The forces of Utopia collected their dead and wounded and slowly turned back to the Fortress. Foster led them with his head hung low. It was the first time in the history of Utopia that they had been defeated in battle and brought almost to the point of surrender. Those on the watchtower at the Gate and on the battlements could not believe their eyes. The Centaurs posted in front of the Gate to protect it parted, making way for the defeated army to pass. The soldiers of Utopia were all ashamed. They would rather have been killed. They could not understand why General Foster had issued such a command and stopped the battle.

But Foster was certain that not one of them would have been left standing. That had never been a good strategy. When there was no hope of victory you never sacrificed even a single life, much less a whole battalion, unless it was for some good reason, as in the Battle of Thermopylae where King Leonidas and his three hundred Spartans deliberately sacrificed themselves.

A dead hero is no help at all, while a defeated survivor can become a living hero. That was the Field Marshal's philosophy. Nobody could accuse him of cowardice. He had distinguished himself in that battle as in all the ones that had gone before. He had encouraged and helped those who were in trouble. He hadn't stopped fighting for an instant. His life had been constantly in danger. A major tactic of every army was to make great efforts to kill the enemy's leader in order to lower the troops' morale and eliminate the strong, experienced fighter who could direct the battle. Because of that Foster had faced the most direct attacks. Whoever killed him would instantly have become a hero.

The hospital filled up with casualties. There had been more than a hundred deaths. Foster still could not believe the resistance he'd encountered. The powers of Evil had undergone a transformation.

"I've been fighting the warriors of Evil for many years," he said at the next meeting. "It's the first time I've come up against such strength, training and determination. Our losses are great and I am solely responsible for our defeat. It's the first time in my life that I've felt so bad–"

Princess Felicia interrupted him. "Such things happen, Field Marshal Foster. We cannot always win. Even if we had broken through their lines and fixed the pipes our forces would have been scattered and vulnerable. Of course we would have had time to collect some water, but the whole operation was fraught with difficulty. The point is that we tried and we are not going to lament–"

Before she could finish her sentence the trumpets sounded a new attack. They all rushed outside and ran to the Gate watchtower.

Turgoth had launched a massive attack on the Centaurs who

were lined up outside the Gate, guarding the opening in the wrecked entrance. Once again the attack came from the special chariots with the protruding shafts. In a few minutes the Centaur unit had been obliterated, their crystal shields unable to withstand the chariots' onslaught. The archers on the battlements could not fire in case they killed the Centaurs once the Sharkans were among them.

General Foster ordered the reinforcement of the Centaurs by two hundred Orizon horsemen with swords and shields. The battle grew fiercer. The forces of Utopia put up strong resistance for a while but gradually they began to fall back again. Their losses were tremendous and the pressure of the attack grew more and more intense.

Felicia surveyed the battleground. She saw that the forces of Good were being lost outside the walls to no purpose. Their resistance could not halt the attack. She told Foster, Claudia and Hunter that they had to withdraw into the Fortress, shut the Gate with makeshift barriers and face the siege from within the walls.

Although that would be the second consecutive defeat on the same day, they realized there was no other solution. There were so many dead and wounded, and it would be hard to retrieve them while combat continued since the fighting would not cease until the last Utopian warrior had entered the Fortress.

The trumpets sounded the retreat. Blood and bodies lay everywhere. The forces of Evil had sustained casualties too, but not in great numbers. A second victory in a single day had lifted their spirits and strengthened their ardour.

Once Turgoth realized that his forces had become easy targets for the archers up on the battlements they returned in triumph to their base. The Gate was sealed with the makeshift barricade. To wooden beams and carriages were added piles of sacks stuffed with earth and stones. The forces of Good now felt truly besieged.

Once more, they took stock of the situation. More than one hundred Utopian soldiers had died and another hundred had been wounded in the last battle, huge losses when added to those from the previous defeat.

Princess Felicia and her staff returned to the hospital and began to discuss the new predicament. Before they'd had time to draw breath and decide on the next move, the sound of the trumpets warned them of a new attack.

A large unit of Porths and Cyclopes, protected by enormous specially designed shields, were advancing on the Fortress. When they reached the Gate they began to pound the makeshift barricades with mighty tree trunks.

Felicia ordered the Utopian forces to execute Defence Plan A and commanded a thousand warriors to get ready to position themselves at the places inside the Gate designated by the plan. They were to trap the attackers by suddenly pulling the barricade away and permitting the Porths and the Cyclopes to enter the Fortress. They would then barricade the entrance once more, trapping the invaders inside. Then they would fall upon and overpower them. At the same time they would reinforce the defences of that section of the battlements. Felicia ordered large cauldrons of boiling oil to be readied for use. Boiling oil had been abolished as a means of defence hundreds of years earlier by mutual agreement, because it caused many casualties with serious burns and those who didn't die on the spot spent the rest of their lives in agony. However, Turgoth's violation of the rules had made Felicia decide to resurrect that cruel but effective tactic.

When Felicia had given them their orders, Foster, Claudia

and Hunter left. She told Bull to stay with the children and instructed Leiko to go with her and be prepared for a battle with the Cyclopes. Leiko took his club as well as his sword.

The children could tell that something was about to happen. They asked Bull whether they should go with the princess.

"We're to stay here. Those are our orders," replied Bull.

"But when are we going to fight?" asked Sergei.

"You'll fight too when the time comes. Though I hope it never does," said Bull.

By the time Felicia and Leiko reached the Gate the defence troops had already been deployed according to Plan A. The forces of Utopia had devised the plan many years earlier in case of an invasion through the main Gate. They had practised it regularly during military exercises and knew precisely what to do. The archers took up their positions. As soon as the enemy came through the Gate arrows would rain down upon them. Some five hundred Amazons and archers were ready to deal out death to whoever entered. At the same time the Centaurs would throw their javelins. At the right moment the shower of arrows and javelins would cease. The Centaurs would instantly seize their spears and attack with Foster's army from six directions.

Felicia ordered the defenders to release the Gate in such a way as to make the attackers think that it had not been done on purpose but that they had succeeded in breaking through the barricade.

As soon as some thousand warriors of a Beast contingent made up of only Porths and Cyclopes had got inside, Felicia would order the boiling oil and burning torches to be flung from the watchtower as a back-up to the arrows and javelins thrown from the battlements. At the same time they would barricade the Gate again.

The attackers burst in like victors, believing that they'd seized the Fortress. But they were caught unawares. They were easy targets for the highly trained Amazons and Centaurs who unleashed a blizzard of arrows and javelins at them. Their cries of victory turned into screams of pain.

The invaders felt like trapped animals. They didn't know where to take cover or how to protect themselves. The entrance area of the Gate was laid out in such a way that they were sitting targets.

The invasion ground to a halt under the boiling oil that the Orizons kept pouring and the torrent of arrows and javelins flung from the battlements. The burning torches ignited the boiling oil and blazing bodies ran like living candles until they fell writhing on the ground.

The area in front of the Fortress Gate had become an inferno. Aloft on the battlements were two groups of warriors. One threw arrows and javelins at the attackers outside the Fortress while the other aimed at the invaders trapped inside. General Foster estimated that already about three hundred Cyclopes and Porths were either dead or seriously injured. He ordered the archers and the javelin throwers to stop. Orizon horsemen and the Centaurs carrying spears charged at the enemy from six different directions. Felicia, Leiko, Hunter and Foster himself joined them.

The battle was ferocious as they wrought vengeance on the invaders. The bodies of Porths and Cyclopes fell as if mown down by an invisible scythe. Beheaded bodies became strange moving geysers, spraying blood as their hearts continued to pump.

Severed heads stared up with bulging eyes at the trunks on which they had stood for so many years as they stumbled a few steps, holding swords or clubs, before collapsing. They opened their mouths as if surprised at how easily they had been separated. The bodies, heads, hearts and brains were dying separate deaths.

Princess Felicia seemed invincible. She sowed fear, panic and death around her. Countless were those struck dead by her frenzied sword. Foster, Leiko and Hunter fought like demigods. Leiko's club cracked open many a Cyclopes's skull. He was like a hurricane spreading destruction. Within a few minutes more than five hundred Cyclopes and Porths lay dead from the terrible counter-attack. They were ready to surrender and began to throw their weapons to the ground.

Foster saw them surrender and ordered his forces to stop. About two hundred remaining Cyclopes and Porths bowed their heads and ceased combat.

The enemy trumpets were heard sounding another attack. Felicia, Leiko and the generals rushed to the battlements. The incredible sight in front of them filled them with foreboding. Gigantic wooden siege machines, each drawn by six horses, were surrounding the Fortress. The horses came to a halt at a safe distance from the archers on the walls. Behind each machine there were about fifty Sharkans, a few Porths and some Cyclopes. The defenders stared at them, dumbstruck. There must have been more than a hundred machines surrounding the Fortress. They were slightly taller than the battlements and their tops were wooden boxes, each one filled with more attackers. On the back of each machine was a ladder for the warriors to climb. The siege machines could come right up against the walls without taking any casualties because they were completely covered in wooden protrusions to deflect arrows and javelins: monstrous wooden creatures!

In the past ladders had been used to scale the walls in a

siege, and they had been easy enough to deal with. But with those military engines all the forces of Beast would be able to invade the Castle in minutes.

Field Marshal Foster wondered why the Cyclopes and the Porths had attacked the Gate when Beast had such equipment at its disposal. He couldn't have known that their leaders had insisted, asking Turgoth to allow them alone to attack and seize the Fortress by the Gate. They had believed they could do it and thus expunge the shame of their humiliating defeat at Lord Life's house.

The forces of Beast released the horses and yokes, disconnecting the siege machines. The machines seemed to stare menacingly at the Fortress, like dragons ready to lunge. The warriors began pushing them slowly closer until they were about three hundred yards away.

Felicia and the others raced down from the battlements.

"Would you take twenty Centaurs," Foster asked Leiko, "lead the prisoners into a school building, remove their weapons, lock them inside and watch over them? Otherwise, if the enemy get inside the Fortress they could all join forces."

"Send orders for plenty of troops to cover Highlow," Felicia told Foster, "and tell them to protect the spaceships at all costs. Let the sixty experts know that they are not to take part in the battle. Even if we're defeated, they'll still be indispensable. You and Hunter go along the whole left flank. Order everyone to leave the battlements and tell our fighters to assume their positions in the Fortress and to prepare to face the invader according to Plan A. It's pointless to fight on the battlements. There's no way we can stop those siege engines. We'll let the enemy think there's no resistance and when we have them between our fighters and the wall we'll strike."

She ordered the trumpets to sound the signal to put Plan A into effect, mounted her horse and set off towards the right side of the Fortress. Everywhere she went she issued orders and boosted the morale of the besieged warriors, telling them that they'd already won by implementing the first part of the plan and completely destroying a whole army of Porths and Cyclopes.

The people of Utopia had mixed feelings. They had the inexhaustible reserves of courage and great strength needed to put the invaders to rout and protect their Flame, but to allow the enemy inside without putting up any resistance did not sit well with them. It confused them. It felt like allowing bandits to ransack and desecrate their homes. When the siege machines touched the walls they crushed the hearts of those besieged.

THE FLAME OF THE WHITE SUN

It was the first time in thousands of years that the inhabitants of Utopia had seen black-clad Sharkans on the walls of the Fortress. Lined up along the battlements, the intruders looked like a mournful lace pattern sewn onto the venerable fortifications that the people of Utopia, their fathers and forefathers had built with their own hands and had always considered impregnable. They felt as if body-snatchers were ready to steal their Flame.

As they stood concealed and ready to attack, most of them wept for their imminent capture. They knew, however, that Princess Felicia would never have given such an order if it were not in the interests of their homeland. Those who had seen the approaching siege machines understood it well. It was impossible to stop them or to face such an all-out organized attack on the battlements.

In terms of tactics, that was the way it had to be. Besides, they had prepared Plan A and had trained frequently to deal with such a situation.

The invaders wondered why they had encountered no resistance. They descended from the battlements uttering war cries, thinking that they were already victors and that the people of Utopia had surrendered. As soon as they touched the ground, the same surprise awaited them. They were trapped between the walls and the defenders' tactical zone. Arrows and javelins swiftly reduced their numbers. The enemy leaders soon realized what was happening. The difference between the fighting abilities and mental capacity of the Sharkans and those of the Porths and Cyclopes, however, was wide.

The Sharkans saw that if they remained where they were they would all meet their deaths. There were more than eight thousand of them. They far outnumbered the defenders, who had already suffered considerable losses, so most of the units regrouped and counter-attacked. The Orizons were forced to stop shooting arrows and throwing javelins and fight with their swords and spears.

Fierce clashes ensued. The enemy's numerical superiority put the forces of Utopia at a severe disadvantage. The situation was becoming critical for the defenders. They did, however, have the advantage of fighting on horseback, while the enemy was on foot.

Princess Felicia was everywhere. Amid the pandemonium of battle she ran, shouted, gave orders and encouraged the Orizon warriors. Wherever she went she spread death. The defending troops saw how their princess was fighting and took heart. The balance began to even out again and now the enemy was once more sustaining serious losses.

A messenger found the princess in the thick of battle and told her that Bull wanted her urgently. Felicia went immediately to the hospital and found Bull and the children waiting for her in the courtyard.

"Felicia," said Bull, his voice full of anxiety, "we've been informed that Turgoth and many Sharkans have got through the Gate and are heading towards the theatre and the Flame. Part of the zone in front of the Gate fell just a short while ago. Then our forces retreated to their fall-back position but they weren't able to stand their ground. Sharkans kept pouring in and our troops could no longer hold them back. Eventually Turgoth entered, followed by a large carriage. I didn't know what to do, so I sent for you."

"Where's Foster?" asked Felicia.

"I've no idea," replied Bull.

Felicia realized that it had been some time since she had last seen Foster. She had not spotted him in the battle. Her mind raced. She had to make some decisions. Suddenly a group of Orizon horsemen appeared, leading a horse carrying the Field Marshal's body. They all rushed over, lifting him off the horse and laying him down. An arrow was sticking out of his throat.

"Someone call the doctor," exclaimed the Princess.

Bull left at a run and returned with Doctor Afterland. The doctor leaned over the body and examined it.

"There's nothing we can do. He's dead," he said and everyone froze.

"Where did you find him?" the princess asked the Orizons.

"On the main road, near the theatre," they replied.

"There are five of you. I want you to go and find thirty Orizons each and return here as soon as possible," Felicia ordered. They all left immediately.

Felicia turned to Bull. "What's happened to the warriors defending the Gate?"

"I don't know, princess. From what I've heard, Claudia was the only leader left there before they retreated. I don't understand how our forces were scattered and how the Sharkans and then Turgoth got inside so easily."

Princess Felicia paced up and down restlessly, deep in thought. She stopped and looked at the children.

"Are you ready to defend our Flame? Fate has ordained that you will play an important part in your first battle. We've pinned the enemy down at all points within the Fortress apart from the area around the Gate. The Sharkans must have reached the Flame by now. They intend to steal it. But we'll overpower them *and* their leader."

Everyone looked at her, impressed. She was no longer the calm, peaceful princess they knew. She had been transformed into a magnificent leader. She radiated power, decisiveness, optimism, faith and confidence. Her radiance was supernatural.

The children looked at Rebecca as though urging her to speak for them. She realized it.

"We're here, Princess," Rebecca said, "for that purpose. During our training our instructors toiled, as did we, to prepare for moments such as these. But while we know that the battle is raging and blood is being shed we sit here doing nothing.

"We may not be completely prepared for Lomani but we'll do what we can to protect Utopia and the Flame from the invaders."

"The time has come when we need all our troops," the princess told them. "Get on your horses. As soon as the others arrive we'll set out for the theatre."

Once a hundred and fifty Orizons had assembled they set off for the theatre together at a gallop. When they got there they saw a fierce battle unfolding outside. Other Orizon troops had already become aware that the Sharkans were moving towards the Flame and had rushed over to stop them at any cost.

"It shouldn't be difficult for us to rout them," Felicia told Bull. "Keep the children at a distance. Don't intervene unless you have to."

She spurred her horse into a canter and ploughed into the

heart of the battle, followed by the other Orizons. The children stood with Bull a short distance away. It was the first time they had seen the Princess fight. It was hard to believe that anyone, even an Orizon such as Felicia, could fight like that. They couldn't keep count of her sword strokes. She kept shifting her position, one place at one moment and another at the next.

Rebecca thought there could never have been a better warrior in the history of the Universe. No poet, historian or writer could ever adequately describe the unique Felicia. Even the kindest and most tender-hearted people in the world would certainly wish to watch her battles – in spite of the bloodshed – just to see her fight. She had become one with her horse. The enemy couldn't encircle her or get close enough to impede her. She attacked unceasingly, at the speed of lightning, anywhere, anyhow, any time she wished, constantly showing panic around her. Each and every movement of her sword spelled one word only: death!

The latest reinforcements and the active participation of the Princess undermined the morale of the enemy. Heads fell, rolling like balls. Bodies tumbled from horses one after another, headless, without brains or senses. Some still crawled instinctively, searching for their lost heads, before finally falling motionless.

Felicia stepped back a little from the battle and shouted, "Bull, take the children and ride into the theatre."

She turned towards the fighting warriors with her sword held high.

"Fifty Orizons follow me inside," she yelled.

The children and Bull raced after her on horseback, together with many Orizons. They dashed into the theatre but stopped dead in their tracks. To the right and left were one hundred Sharkans, lined up on horses. Between them walked Turgoth and Claudia, carrying the large plate with the Flame on it. As soon as they saw Felicia and the others, they stopped and set the Flame down.

Felicia, Bull and Rebecca dismounted while the rest of the Orizons remained on horseback. Turgoth drew out his sword and Claudia took her bow from around her neck and plucked an arrow from her quiver, placing it in the bow and drawing back the string, ready to shoot. A sardonic smile spread across her face.

"You've lost, Felicia," she said triumphantly. "Turgoth and I are getting married and we're going to rule the Land of the White Sun. That imbecile Foster didn't want me. I showed him my love for so many years but he scorned me. My body was alight with a fire that burned away at me. But flames aren't all red; they can be blue as well, and poisonous. So my great love turned into hatred. Sometimes we hate without knowing it, and we're surprised when we realize it.

"You can build more solidly on hate. Hate lasts and grows. The foundations of love are weak. They easily topple and love departs, fading like footprints in the sand that are easily erased by waves. When I killed Foster today he looked at me, his eyes goggling in astonishment. He said, as he lay dying '*You … you?*' 'Yes! Me!,' I answered him. He couldn't understand how an Amazon feels when she's drawn by her feelings but is then rejected and scorned.

"I tampered with the power supply in my house. I called him over, pretending that I wanted him to fix it. And he did. But then I damaged it even more and scolded him, saying that it was his fault. I insulted him and forced him to bring Newton. That paved the way for Rebecca's abduction. Turgoth and I met frequently. We used to meet by the lake in the evening and make our plans. No one can stop us."

As Claudia finished speaking she released her bowstring and let her arrow fly, carrying death with it.

"Now it's *your* turn to die," she crowed. As the arrow pierced Felicia's neck, Bull was already throwing his first dagger. A split second later it was plunging into Claudia's throat.

The princess grabbed the arrow and snapped. Then her knees buckled and she fell, her forehead hitting the ground hard. She slumped onto her side.

Claudia was already dead.

Turgoth looked first at Felicia, then at Claudia and then back again. His face was expressionless. They all watched, frozen to the spot. It had all been so rapid that even the seasoned Orizon and Sharkan warriors had not taken it in immediately.

Rebecca approached Turgoth and looked him straight in the eye.

"So, King Turgoth, did you confuse your duty with romance? Would you have married a traitor and a murderer? She betrayed her homeland. She murdered the field marshal and the princess before your very eyes. We've learned not to strike from behind or treacherously, while we're still talking, but that's what *she* did."

"I told you, Rebecca: I will never remarry. Claudia impressed me as a woman but I never gave her any reason to believe that our relationship would end in marriage. We agreed on the matter of the Flame and about the injustice done to us. What are we to do now?"

Turgoth was telling the truth. He had never promised to marry Claudia. But he did not wish to contradict further any woman, especially one who was dead. Claudia had felt the need to restore her pride after Foster's rejection of her.

"Take your warriors and go back to your kingdom," Rebecca

said. "I give you my word that we'll find the best and most just of solutions. I'm sure you believe me. I only want you to give me a little more time."

"I believe you, Rebecca, but this cannot be. I'll be seen as a traitor. I've prepared for this day for three whole years. I changed our tactics. We toughened up! We trained methodically and with strict discipline, just like Spartans. I've held the Flame in my hands again, after thousands of years. I must finish what I've begun or I must perish.

"We could have found a solution but Princess Felicia didn't want us to. I sent her a long letter offering excellent terms. She gave no answer but attacked instead. Now we're in control and we're leaving, taking the Flame as a trophy."

"You're not going anywhere with the Flame, King Turgoth. Only over our dead bodies! We're determined. You're not in control of anything. You just think you are. In reality things are quite different. Your forces are pinned down and we're going to kill them all. The Orizons are never defeated when they fight for the Flame. Take your troops and leave," Rebecca said. Then she walked over to the fallen princess.

She had wanted to run to her the moment Felicia had been hit, but duty had dictated that her first priority was to save the Flame. Everyone watched in amazement, seeing before them a teenage girl who had the air of a great leader. She knelt and touched Felicia lightly, then lowered her head over hers.

"Bull," she said, "the princess is alive. Get her to hospital at once."

Bull had been watching Rebecca carefully, ready to intervene, which was why he had not rushed to Felicia's side. He felt terrible because he had not protected her. He had acted an instant too late. He did not want to repeat the same mistake with Rebecca. He too had thought that the princess was already dead.

He didn't question Rebecca's orders, as that would have belittled her in front of the others. He lifted the princess up in his arms and left. Nobody followed him. They all wanted to see what would happen next.

Rebecca approached Turgoth again and drew her sword.

"I predicted this, Rebecca," he said. "I witnessed this very scene up on Mount Thunder: the two of us duelling in front of the Flame. I was afraid this would happen and here we are. Fate has ordained it. We Egyptians believe in Fate." He looked at her affectionately. "I don't want to kill you. We'll take the Flame and go. It's too late now."

Rebecca looked into Turgoth's eyes and saw the confusion there. She wanted him to be clear about what he was doing before their duel began. "We must get this over with, King Turgoth: you have no right to betray your people."

Turgoth understood. He pulled out his sword and the great duel began. He was taller than Rebecca and had longer arms, which gave him a great advantage. From the first blow Rebecca realized that it was going to be a tough fight for her. She strained to repel Turgoth's attacks, continually on the defensive. It was obvious that the king wanted to put a swift end to the fight.

She kept looking him in the eye as she dodged his dangerous blows with increasing difficulty, but he did not look at her at all. Maybe, she thought, he was thinking of the Flame, his people, the sick children and premature deaths, and that was why he was fighting so fiercely.

Rebecca soon realized that Turgoth was an even better swordsman than Foster had been. She also knew that the future of Utopia and her people's access to the Flame now depended on the skills of her hand and her sword. But her hand was smaller and less experienced than the hand of the king.

The clash of the swords roused the warriors and raised their hopes. The urgings of the spectators, their shouts and body language as they stood in their stirrups showed that in their minds and souls each Orizon was fighting against Turgoth and each Sharkan against Rebecca. Their anxiety communicated itself to their horses, making them neigh and stamp their hooves on the grass as they flinched nervously from side to side.

The king's blows were fiercely aggressive and Rebecca could do no more than defend herself and hope for a chance to attack. So every Sharkan felt that they were on the offensive while every Orizon was on the defence.

Turgoth never used any specific method or rhythm when fighting, so his opponent could never anticipate his next move. Arm, hand and sword moved like a piston, an engine, a scythe, intent on taking off the young Orizon's head. At times his sword swept past the left of her head three times in a row and at others it feinted left, right and then four times on the left and twice on the right. Always the target was her neck. As Rebecca parried his blows right and left, Turgoth suddenly raised his sword and brought it fiercely down like an axe, trying to split her head in half as he would a log. With lightning speed she held the blade of her sword with her hand and kept it over her head to deflect the fatal blow.

She needed great speed and steady hands, something she and the rest of the Orizon fighters had practised a lot. But she knew that practice was one thing and reality another when she faced such an opponent.

Because she was retreating all the time, trying to avoid the deadly blows, Rebecca stumbled on something and fell heavily, finding herself lying on her back on top of Claudia's body. The fall left her neck and head exposed, as well as everything below her crystal breastplate. She had become an easy target as she lay sprawled on the dead Amazon's body. Turgoth had his chance to cut off her head and send her straight to the next world. It would take only a second. As the deadly weapon arched downwards towards Rebecca's neck, a hopeless gasp escaped every Orizon's lips.

But the king had acted just one second too late. Rebecca twisted her agile body and with an incredibly quick kung fu movement she leaped back up as Turgoth's sword ripped into the grass of the theatre instead of into her.

Turgoth stood in front of her again. Their stares met for the first time since the beginning of the fight. Now he did not look confused. Yet there was something showing in the depths f his eyes. But what was it?

Their swords clashed again: the hard, unbreakable treated crystal produced sparks.

All the time Rebecca's quick mind kept working:

"Why did Turgoth attack a second late? Did he spare my life once more? If so, why is he attacking so fiercely? Why is every blow so well thought out, so strong and skilful that I have great difficulty deflecting it?"

She was completely convinced that his every blow was aimed at her with deadly intent. Was Turgoth so sure that she would be able to parry his strokes however dangerous they were? What new twist was this? It reminded her of the time at his palace when he had left her next to her sword, giving her the chance to kill him and escape.

But if she had made the slightest mistake so far, if she had been even a tenth of a second too late to counter a blow, her head would have been separated from her body.

Suddenly Rebecca became aware of a piercing pain in her shoulder. She wondered if it had been there since she had got up, but her thoughts and the imminent danger had allowed her no space to pay it any attention.

Then she recalled that when she had fallen she'd landed on something hard. It must have been Claudia's quiver.

The pain grew and became unbearable. It travelled along Rebecca's nerves and reached her wrist and fingers. Her arm was slowly becoming numb, growing heavy and difficult to move. But to lose any strength or speed would mean her death.

Drops of sweat appeared on her brow and her teeth ached painfully from being kept so tightly clenched in concentration. The king must not see that she was in pain and vulnerable or he would use it to his advantage. She must continue to fight at the same furious pace.

Rebecca feared that if Turgoth saw her sweating he would realize she had a serious problem and he would increase his efforts to bring the fight to a speedy conclusion. He might have already realized it, since he was such an experienced fighter.

The questions returned: *"Why was he a second late? Was he taken by surprise or did he spare my life one more time?"*

Soon Rebecca would be too weak and slow to be able to deflect Turgoth's fast and deadly thrusts. There was a danger that her sword might even drop from her hand, struck by one of his mighty blows.

Turgoth hammered at her mercilessly, going repeatedly for her head. Each second brought at least two potentially fatal blows from Turgoth and two painful and laborious defensive movements from her.

Rebecca knew that to gain any advantage she had to go onto the attack and try to hit him before her strength finally left her. Only in attacking and taking the initiative was there any hope of surviving.

She thought that, since Turgoth had been on the offensive all that time, he wouldn't be expecting her to counter-attack. Unwittingly, she had lulled him into a false sense of security and overconfidence, which she might be able to turn to her advantage. His constant attacks made him vulnerable at two points and she had to take advantage of them. He was not wearing a breastplate – just like Foster, Bull and Leiko – while all the rest of them always wore one during battle.

Rebecca pretended to retreat, taking three uninterrupted steps backwards, luring Turgoth towards her. Then she stopped abruptly. Turgoth raised his sword. She did not counter-attack at this point but bent her knees at the moment his sword finished its trajectory, passing so close over her head that it barely missed her hair. The hissing sound it made as it cut through the air sounded like Death's breath. If she had been a tenth of a second late, or miscalculated by a few centimetres, his sword would have cut a slice off the top of her head.

She took a great risk by not defending herself against the blow, but she had no other choice. Now her sword was left free, something that Turgoth didn't expect since she'd had no chance to attempt even one attack blow so far.

But now things had changed.

At last! Now Rebecca had her sword ready and the unsuspecting Turgoth was surprised to feel it plunge deep into his unprotected chest.

It was the Sharkans' turn now to let out a cry of despair. Nobody in the theatre could believe their eyes. They stood stock still as if they'd been turned to stone by the Gorgons. The fierce combat was over. In the Orizons' eyes good had triumphed, while for the Sharkans injustice had prevailed yet again.

The Orizons did not know whether Felicia was alive or not. But if she were dead a new leader had just been born. Rebecca had emerged like a great shining hope from the dark night that had engulfed state Utopia.

The Sharkans also understood that the creature confronting them was someone exceptional. The experienced warriors recognized that the duel had been tough: Turgoth had tried to kill Rebecca many times but her great talent and unusually swift reflexes had saved her.

Rebecca gently pulled her sword from Turgoth's body. He fell heavily to his knees, as though worshipping a new and almighty Goddess. He thrust his own sword into the ground with both hands and all the strength left in him and looked at her, slowly opening his mouth as if to say something. His right hand released its grip on the sword and his fingers formed a curious shape, as though blessing her. His eyes looked like vigil lights running out of oil, their wicks guttering.

"... seek the truth ... play chess ... stop the wars ... you look very much like ..." he whispered.

Turgoth was back in the Sahara, kneeling in the oasis. Haruma was dancing for him, making the melodious cries of the desert that were known only to the Bedouin. Frenzied musicians beat drums and blew pipes, making a sound like the wind of the Sahara. The starlight and the flames lit up Haruma's face and her almond-shaped eyes shone strangely, enticing him. Turgoth tried to leap up and dance too, but his legs would not lift him and he could not understand why. Suddenly Haruma was holding a sword instead of a tambourine.

From the night of the oasis Turgoth was transported to the friendly sunshine of his village. He could hear the cicadas as he sat up on a branch of the leafiest tree by the shore of his favourite lake. He looked down at its twin, planted upside down and inviting him, rustling its leaves. As he dived, his body dragged his sword down with him. It pressed against his chest. Then ... at last ... for the first time ... he found fish in the thick branches and colourful foliage. But he didn't manage to talk with them and fulfil his childhood dream.

Rebecca didn't watch Turgoth die, but she heard what he said. The only thing that she couldn't understand was what he meant by "*you look very much like*". It felt strange to see drops of blood from the man who had stirred her so deeply dripping from her sword. Without wiping the blade, she returned it to its scabbard, as if placing a holy relic in a crypt. At that moment she decided never to use the weapon again and never to clean it.

In the silence Rebecca's strong, decisive, calm voice rang out. "Go away. Take your whole army and go back to your homeland. I promise you that I'll do my best to solve the problem of the Flame so that we may live together in peace.

"Fighting is still going on in different parts of the Fortress. The forces of Utopia have the upper hand and our victory is assured. Two Sharkans come with me and we'll let everyone know the war is over.

"You've brought a carriage to take away the Flame. It's waiting outside the theatre. Use it to carry your great leader to his house. Bury him with full honours and remember him always. He was not only a rare commander and an exceptional leader of his people and army, he was a spiritual leader too: a thinker and a gifted visionary with a creative mind. He was honest, moral, free, incorruptible, unyielding, stubborn ..."

At that point it seemed to many of them that Rebecca's voice broke and her eyes clouded over. But she recovered and went on, addressing the Orizons now.

"We'll move the Flame back to its place at once. The young Orizons who came with me will stay on the hill to guard it until all the forces of Beast have withdrawn. And all of you other Orizons must stay here in case something unexpected happens. I'm going with the two Sharkans."

The rest of the Sharkans walked away with their heads bowed. As they stepped outside the theatre, they realized that the fighting there had already stopped and their fellow warriors had surrendered. They set off with Rebecca to the places where the battle was still raging.

In many other parts of the Fortress the invaders had already surrendered. But where the fighting still continued Rebecca shouted out to them to stop, while the Sharkans with her told their warriors that Turgoth was dead and the Lomani was over.

When all combat had ended and the forces of Beast were slowly withdrawing, Rebecca went to the hospital. Felicia was in the operating theatre and Bull was waiting outside.

"She was still alive when I brought her in. One of her carotid arteries was torn and she was losing a lot of blood. They gave her a transfusion and now they're operating. It may take hours. The minute the blood transfusion was done I went over to the theatre but you'd already taken care of everything. So I came back here. The operation is very tricky but the doctor said there's a good chance of success. The most serious problem is that part of her brain was starved of blood for quite some time."

"Soon all the forces of Beast should have left the Fortress," Rebecca told Bull. "I gave directions that when they've removed their wounded and dead they're to push the siege engines back from the walls and burn them. One never knows. A new leader may arise suddenly and bring the Sharkans back here.

"As soon as the doctor has finished we must decide what to do. I don't know who's been appointed to take over in such cases, until Felicia gets better or Lord Life returns."

"The orders are that if something happens to Felicia Doctor Afterland will take over and if something happens to him Foster would take charge. After Foster, it would be me. If something happens to all of us the oldest Orizon would take charge and then they would elect a new leader. That's the hierarchy."

"So, as soon as the operation ends, Afterland must assume his duties."

"There are many wounded," said Bull. "But he'll find time to resolve the matter."

Meanwhile, Leiko arrived panting. He had just heard about Felicia and his look was filled with panic.

"Tell me what's going on, because I'm going out of my mind. I've heard such confused reports. How is she? Is she alive?"

Felicia's operation lasted several hours. Afterwards they assembled in the theatre and Doctor Afterland gave them instructions. The Orizon experts had to keep working until they had repaired one of the three spaceships and the communication station. Whoever wanted to could go home to get some sleep. The following day they would all get to work to repair the damage. One team would immediately tackle the problem of restoring the water supply.

They made a count of the dead and severely wounded. There were three hundred and seventy dead and two hundred and fifty injured. It was the first time that Lomani had resulted in so many casualties for the people of Utopia.

Leiko stayed at the hospital, following Felicia's progress after Doctor Afterland told him that her condition was serious.

"The first seven days are extremely difficult. The seventh is the hardest of all. If she survives that, she has a good chance of recovering completely. We'll give her the Flame every morning, which may help her even more. As from tomorrow morning, you can go into her room and sit with her."

Leiko entered Felicia's room at the crack of dawn. She looked calm, as if she were asleep. Her throat was wrapped in bandages. After he had sat and watched her for some time, he went outside and asked for papyrus sheets, a quill pen and some ink.

Leiko went back and sat next to her. Then he unfolded the papyrus and began to write:

FIRST DAY

Dearest Felicia,

Since you cannot hear me, I'm going to write to you and you can read it all when you wake up.

I won't write only about what's happening in Utopia but also about what's been going on inside me for a hundred years.

Some of these things you may have guessed, some you know already and some you may never even have thought of.

Which is our best guide: our reason or our heart? Reason may err, because it is all cold calculation and judgement. The heart is full of instinct, emotions and waves of love.

Nobody can blame me for falling in love with you. I lived with your parents for thousands of years. I stayed with them because I loved them and most of all because I respected them; not because of you or because I knew that you would be born and find your way into my heart.

A hundred and twenty years ago, you arrived. You were a great joy to your household but also a serious worry for your wise parents, concerned about what you would choose.

You grew up and we were all so proud.

You stood out from the beginning and showed early that you were a born leader. Your father, having received the approval of the Gods, put his trust in you and let you rule. Everybody trusted you.

We moved away to a new house, living in isolation so that Lord Life could think in peace and quiet about the problems of the Earth and seek solutions. You had assumed responsibility for everything here and you managed very well.

From time to time you came and visited us. When you left I was filled with sadness. I missed you. I thought of you by day and I dreamed of you by night. You had pitched your tent in my heart. That's how I knew that I'd fallen in love with you. When I realized it I was alarmed. I felt ashamed. I didn't want to be-

lieve it. I hoped I was wrong but with each passing day I grew more certain. I was upset about it.

It had never crossed my mind that a day would come when you'd find your way into my heart and enslave it.

I trembled when I told your father for the first time. I wanted him to know how I felt, to ease my conscience. I couldn't conceal from him the fire that was growing inside me.

"Lord Life," I said, "I believe we should respect every kind of heartfelt expression. Our behaviour should never harbour hypocrisy, double-dealing or ulterior motives.

"Yet we often fear the result of speaking openly. Not only because we bare our innermost thoughts, feelings, ideas and beliefs, but more because we fear the reactions we may encounter.

"So we're often forced to live in silence, insincerity and lies. I could never do such a thing. That's why I'm telling you what's happening to me."

Then I told him the secret of my heart.

Lord Life smiled. He patted me on the back in a fatherly way. He stroked my head and ruffled my hair.

"Nobody can take away your dignity or your honour, Leiko," he said. "You only lose them if you want to. It's up to you. They won't leave you if you hold on to them tightly, no matter what people say or what they accuse you of.

"Don't worry about what's happening to you, and

pay no attention to what other people might say. No one should lead his life thinking like that. Women are the most serious matter in men's lives, Leiko, and also the most indispensable. You're very unlucky. You've fallen in love with a wild creature whom you will not easily tame. Let's see how you go about it, and whether you succeed in the end. Try hard and don't give up easily. Now I value you even more highly."

A great weight was lifted off me and I felt very satisfied with your father's attitude.

It's important to be appreciated for your true worth, whatever it is, by the ones you hold in esteem. All of us possess some worth, however small. We all have certain virtues from the day we are born, perhaps created in the womb, as well as those we acquire throughout our lifetimes. It is helpful if these virtues can withstand the pressures of time, attrition, trials and tribulations, lasting, if possible, till the end of our lives.

Victor Hugo advised those who loved and suffered to love more. That's what I did, but love became infinite and imperishable. When I realized how much I love you, I got scared.

Although I suffered I didn't tell you anything about it for three whole years. Each time I saw you, you dazzled me. When the sun dazzles us we shut our eyes. Our eyelids are the curtains that God has given us for our protection. I often shut them when I looked at you, but then I missed your beauty. I'd open them again but the brilliance would burn me. I sought a middle solution: neither to burn nor to lose you from my sight. I succeeded in seeing you only with my heart and mind. But then my mind was going mad and my heart was choking.

Then I found the solution. I half closed my eyes and peered out though my eyelashes, as if I was behind prison bars.

I made up my mind and spoke to you. I don't remember what I told you. I didn't know what I was saying. When I stopped you looked at me tenderly, like a mother looking at a naughty child, although I was older than you by several thousand years. You took me by the hand and we went towards the river. We walked and talked … and talked. We sat on the bank. The river played the music and our hearts sang.

"It's very important to learn how to listen to the sounds of Nature but also to the whispers of silence," you said.

I agreed, since apart from the written and spoken word there is also the language of silence, and I knew that you had been influenced by this first stage of initiation into the philosophy of Pythagoras.

We looked at our faces in the water. As the river flowed I felt that it was sweeping us along too, at times towards the waterfall to be broken on the rocks and at other times towards the lake to find peace. I didn't want us to be swept away by it. I wanted us to leave.

"Shall we go to the springs?" I asked you.

You got up silently. You took my hand again and pulled me towards the hill.

It was the beginning of April. Reaching over the spring was an almond tree in blossom. I cut a sprig and gave it to you. And you looked at me … and looked at me … Then you embraced me and burned me with the hot coals of your lips.

"If you can wait, do so. I have many things to do and many obligations to fulfil," you said and ran off, holding the twig.

Almost a hundred years have gone by since then and I'm still waiting. Every time I see you, your eyes tell me: "Wait."

I know that you wouldn't tell me to wait if you didn't love me. And every year, at the beginning of April, I visit the spring. I cut a twig from our almond tree and bring it to you.

The tree with its blossoms betrothed us; that's why I love it so.

SECOND DAY

Today one of the spaceships was repaired and Bull departed with two Orizons. They travelled to Earth to bring back your father. The Orizons had to go to contact those on Earth, because we had no means of communication yet to keep them informed.

Everything is going well here. The Gate will be ready today and the communication station in a couple of days. The water is back and all the animals have quenched their thirst. When people aren't working at repairing the damage they go home. Life is getting back to normal. I hope your father will come tomorrow.

This morning Doctor Afterland gave you the Flame again for some time. When he left, I began to sing to you without lyrics or music. I used only my heart and my mind.

I used to do that a lot when I was missing you.

But in the pain of your absence I had the flowers that you had planted in my heart the moment you embraced me. Their scent was strong and beautiful. Their aroma ran through my veins and spread to my every cell.

I was intoxicated by the perfume of the flowers united to the harmony of Nature's sounds.

They became the fortitude, patience and most of all the hope that gave me the strength and the courage to wait.

THIRD DAY

Today Lord Life returned from Earth. As soon as Bull brought him to Highlow he came to visit you. He sat with you for hours, talking with Afterland about your condition.

Rebecca wanted us to have a meeting. Your father, Afterland, Bull, Hunter and I were present.

Rebecca talked for some time. I was astounded by what she said to Lord Life and the rest of us.

I'll write down as accurately as I can the things that impressed me most.

"My lord, the people here are one family, governed by two worthy leaders who are sensible, experienced, brave, virtuous and, up to a point, honest. But even though they couldn't find a solution to their family problems, they both wanted to work for the Good of the Earth. You, Lord Life, have succeeded in doing this for many years and you truly do your best for its Good. Turgoth was not able to do anything, although he was concerned about it too.

"Was he really evil, or was it circumstances that made him seem so? If he had become evil, could it have happened because he felt so unfairly treated?

"But while you did not use knowledge and wisdom to solve the straightforward problems of the Land of the White Sun, you wanted to solve the enormous problems of the Earth. To me, it looks like adding salt to the ocean.

"It is incomprehensible that you did not sort out such an easy problem that has brought about death and misery for thousands of years, whereas you were preoccupied with other, more complex and difficult issues.

"Innocent, multicoloured wild flowers sprout on the

battlefields. However, their pure roots, about which you spoke so impressively, my lord, stand in soil drenched with wasted blood. If we smell the flowers we'll sense the indelible odour of death. And if we listen mindfully to the birds flying in the area we'll realize they don't sing, they wail mourning verses, trying to make us sober up and see reason.

"I'm not trying to be smart or preach to you, who are older and wiser. I'm too young for that. I apologize for being so forward. But I simply cannot understand this situation. There are serious contradictions. I have the Flame inside me and I must fight for the Good of Earth. Yet, at the same time, I must also kill the citizens of Beast. I've already killed at least two, and I'm not sure how many I killed at your house. But I don't feel that I can go on doing it in the future. It all clashes with the love, goodness and justice that we Orizons have to teach on Earth. I feel terribly confused. Again, I'm sorry, but some things must be cleared up. This is not the appropriate time for it, I know. Especially at this moment when your only daughter is hovering between life and death and Utopia is in a state of emergency. But I'll be waiting for you to discuss things and answer my questions whenever you can.

"I believe, Lord Life, that after your intercession, if the Mythical Gods think it over carefully, they may change their unbending minds and our land may become peaceful again.

"Let's not forget that in the hour of need even the Gods are swayed. The Gods became angry because of your quarrels and they discriminated against one side. They may now correct their mistake.

"Lord Life, it is not right for authority to abolish justice. It's no good counting justly and then sharing unjustly. Concerning basic values there can be no discord."

My darling, we all listened to Rebecca entranced. We were dumbfounded by the strength of her views.

Lord Life looked at her and listened to her carefully. He said nothing except that he would think about it and talk it over with her again.

Rebecca has an iron nerve and a sharp mind. Some of her words hurtled at us as if sent by a catapult. At the same time, her soul is as tender and sensitive as a boll opening up on a cotton plant.

Her questions made me think, too. I think she's right. Blood is shed to no purpose here. Her question about who is ultimately good and who is bad has become embedded in me like a thorn, tormenting me.

FOURTH DAY

Lord Life left for the Second Parallel Dimension. He's gone to inform the Mythical Gods and discuss things with them.

Our communication with Earth has been re-established.

Everyone's working hard to put everything back in order.

Today I was thinking that during one of your visits you once told me:

"Leaders must have a calm, sensitive, indestructible and crystal-clear conscience that can withstand time, harsh criticism and every kind of attack, using as a shield only the truth, selflessness, a clear mind and strong nerves. Moral virtue and absolute dedication are the basic, essential talents that leaders need in order to serve their people worthily.

"Good parents are not necessarily good leaders and good leaders are not good parents. And both are so important. Probably the most significant responsibilities in life are accountability for the fate of the people you rule and the conscientiousness to bring up a child properly and be as close to it as necessary. Both take up all your time and totally absorb you. That makes them incompatible.

"If, in spite of all that, you want to wait for me, do so."

When you left, I had a long talk with my heart. I realized it was taking you a long time to reach a decision and I had to be patient.

I climbed the highest palm tree. I watched you as you went off into the distance. I stayed there for many hours. You were so far away, so far from my touch and yet so close and so much inside me.

I looked around. All the palm trees had your name carved on them. The one I was sitting on had my name too, carved next to yours.

My love for you was brimming over and I kept sending it to you in turbulent waves. I've never asked you if your heart felt them splashing against it.

FIFTH DAY

Lord Life is back. He came and sat with you again for several hours.

I left you alone with him and when he left I returned.

Today I'm going to reveal to you two more secrets.

You often asked me what the small leather pouch that I've hung round my neck for so many years contained.

I told you it was a lucky charm that was very dear to me. You wanted to see what was inside it but I wouldn't let you.

Your hair is inside it. For years I used to collect the hairs from your pillows each time you left your father's house.

It kept me company. I kept taking it out of the pouch, stroking it and putting it back again.

I remember when you used to come to the lake and we went swimming. You would emerge from the water and then fly. The water dripped off you as it does from the feathers of swans.

I couldn't fly, as I am not an Orizon. I would take the small boat and pull on the oars keenly as if they were its wings. In the middle of the lake I'd wave my hands for you to land there. You'd come and we'd go for a romantic row. I used to tell you that every night while you slept I would sit by your side. I'd listen to your breaths and count them. I'd cover you up if your blankets slipped when you tossed and turned. I'd try to guess your dreams from the sweet expression on your face. Then, when you awoke in the morning, as I fed you, you would recount, with your mouth still full, the dreams that you'd during the night. Then, when you went to do good for our Land and its people, I'd sleep for a while and have the same dreams you'd told me about.

I used to tell you all that, and you'd laugh. But again your eyes would tell me: "Wait!"

From the moment you told me to wait, the loss I felt because of your absence became even more intense.

The songbirds would only sing lonely songs and would not change their repertoire. The soul, multicoloured and fragile like a glass bowl, needed to replenish itself with the fragrant essence of love, be it a drop at a time.

The tranquillity of the countryside with its special

sounds, the trees that turned the winds into a melodic symphony, the frost and the rain, all of it cleared my mind and let thought emerge to contemplate, remember, weigh up, filter, search and finally write, dipping the pen into the hasty blood of the heart.

First I composed a piece of music that I called 'Melody of the Wood', and then I wrote lyrics for it.

Poetry requires proper respect. That's why verse may only be written with a feathered pen and real ink under quivering candlelight. Then it acquires an infectious sensitivity and sprouts a sweet, solemn fragrance, like a mystagogue.

My mind was like a beehive and my memories constantly buzzed. I began writing my memoirs. Thousands of years of life. What to write first and what to leave out. I had seen a lot on Earth. I had countless dusty, embalmed memories. In addition, I had read and heard a lot while I was here.

I started by writing about my childhood. I wanted to be like my father: I wanted to perform heroic feats too. But he and Theseus had killed all the monsters and evildoers and settled the serious matters. There was nothing left for me to do. I didn't even face the Hercules dilemma concerning whether to follow the path of virtue or that of evil.

Luckily I caught the thunderbolt in the Forest of Mysteries. Later I strangled some snakes to keep up the family tradition.

The hero must fight against great evil powers. He'll either win or die. In each case he still will be a hero, especially when he volunteers to struggle, and doesn't do it because others force him.

I was interested in posthumous fame, but when I grew up I realized it was a vain, human weakness.

I wrote about my experiences as a child. How the child of a hero sees life, then how an adolescent, a young man and later an adult sees it. I described the constant suspense and uncertainty. How hu mankind was held in scant regard during what were supposedly epic years. Wars, massacres, deprivation of liberty, trafficking in humans, forced labour. At the same time, the pleasures of the rulers and the wretchedness of their subjects was a permanent, unchanging reality. High-living kings were succeeded by arrogant war-loving emperors and bloodthirsty thieving dictators. I observed all that as a solitary sojourner.

I tried to portray the struggle of a man searching for the definition of social dignity, in order to stand upright in the world: the spiritual misery, the worn-out dreams, the broken hopes, the stale ideals and the dark paths of the soul. My writings were a lament for what happens in life. I cannot bear another defeat for fading humankind.

I was angered by historical distortions and chronological inaccuracies that I myself had noticed, as well as those revealed from the information brought by the

Orizons who went to and from Earth. I was trying to restore the truth as much as possible.

Alas, the labours of around one hundred Earth years, the essence of my soul, were burned when the Cyclopes and Porths set fire to my house.

Some nights, while looking at the stars, I wrote about love, friends and passion; the strength, depth and extent of those feelings. I believe that the frontiers between them are fine, fragile and ruled in broken lines over which you can cross from one feeling to another without violating borders. You go in and out – seeking, acquiring experience and doing things that are right and wrong. You feel happy, suffer pain, enjoy yourself, risk yourself and have regrets; you feel weak, powerful, large and small. They call you honourable, dishonourable, friendly, unfriendly, brave, treacherous, dishonest and honest; an atheist, a sinner and a believer. You agree with some of that, you disagree with the rest. Then you change. You don't agree any more with what you thought before, and vice versa. The same goes for other people. They may go back on their views or modify them, either for the better or making them even more outrageous.

A great deal has been said about love. Most important for me are those words: "The greatest sin, for which there is no forgiveness, is to murder love in a human soul."

Much has been said about friendship too, but I single out one wonderful piece of advice: "We should not let grass grow on the path of friendship." To which I add: Above all, if you can help it, don't allow the multi-coloured flowers of love to grow in it.

Naturally the most that has been written has been about love.

One evening of majestic silence a star came in through the window and looked at me. How the room glowed!

It told me you had sent it to give me a kiss. Then it sat on my desk and said:

"It is the first time in eternity that this has happened to me. I've seen billions of lovers, but nobody has ever asked me to do anything like this. That's why I escaped at once and came to meet you and at the same time carry out the mission of the one for whom I'm doing this favour. Now I want you to describe your feelings for her."

"Thank you for the kiss," I answered in amazement. "But I can't do you that favour, because he who can recount his love loves little. And I cannot!"

"I understand you," said the star happily. "I hope you never can!"

So, when it comes to love, I choose those words that I told the star.

SIXTH DAY

Today I have some very pleasant news.

Lord Life gathered us all together at the theatre. He talked for some time. He mentioned some of the things that Rebecca had pointed out.

He told us that the Mythical Gods had decided that the Flame was to be shared by all the inhabitants of the Land. When Sharkan children are born, we will give them the Flame, if their parents so wish, and the children will decide whether they want to receive it again at the age of fifteen, just like the Orizon children.

"There's been too much bloodshed," Lord Life told us. "It began thousands of years ago because we squabbled and allowed jealousy, envy and evil to take root. We often do wrong without being aware of it. We let other sentiments overshadow love, which is the most precious thing of all as well as that which brings happiness.

"As from this day, only love will reign over the Land of the White Sun. It is within our power, and the Flame will help us put it into practice for all eternity.

"The Mythical Gods have forgiven all our mistakes and united us once more. The fair wind of reconciliation has started blowing.

"Making friends with an enemy has greater value than acquiring countless new lifelong friends.

"We are all children of the Great Creator and have the same rights."

I expected much opposition from the Orizons, but they all seemed to understand. There were many representatives from Beast present. How they celebrated!

There were hugs ... kisses ... We who had been killing each other seven days ago were like brothers and sisters.

In the end, Rebecca did it. That girl, who has just turned seventeen, succeeded in persuading Lord Life and he in turn convinced the Gods.

Another piece of good news is that Lord Life met your mother in the Elysian Fields. The Mythical Gods valued the fact that for thousands of years she had proved herself to be a true leader. She fought on the side of Good and dedicated herself to the service of the people and her family. She is in the Elysian Fields with my father and other heroes and demigods.

He also met Julius there. The Gods deemed that he too had devoted his life to working for Good and had sacrificed himself for it. Rebecca is very happy and pleased with that turn of events. She thanked Lord Life for bringing her the good news.

The big surprise was that Turgoth was present too when the Gods made their decision. He looked incredibly satisfied. He felt justified.

Just now, as I was sitting here writing to you, you smiled. Who knows where you are, or what you can see. Maybe you're reading my mind.

SEVENTH DAY

This morning I came early with Doctor Afterland.

He said that today is the most crucial day. He gave you the Flame again for quite some time.

Then he checked your arms and legs as well as your palms and the soles of your feet.

He was silent and expressionless. I couldn't draw any conclusion but I didn't dare ask, either.

Rebecca came to see you for the first time. She knelt beside your bed. She talked to you in a low voice, almost in a whisper. She cupped one of your hands in both of hers. She kissed it and covered it with her tears. Then she left.

Her behaviour affected me so much that I cried out:

"Don't go away yet, my beloved. You still have so much to give. We all need you. I'll break down if you leave.

"If a sapling bends over, we use a prop to help it stay up straight, spread its roots and stand firm once more. But if an old plane tree bends over, then it's finished. How can you prop it up? How can you keep it straight?

"That's how I feel. If you leave me, I'll collapse."

As soon as I uttered these words, you opened your eyes for the first time and you looked at me for what seemed like an age.

Could you see me or not? Who knows?

I was beside myself with joy. I wanted to run and fetch the doctor to witness the miracle but my legs wouldn't carry me and I didn't want to leave your side. You might have said something.

But, my dearest, as you looked at me, your eyes were sad, so very sad.

I waited, in case you moved your lips or smiled as you did yesterday. But after a while you closed your eyes again and sank back to the place where you have been for the last seven days.

Two doves came to your window, representing all Nature. They looked in, cooing and conversing, wishing you a speedy recovery. Then they flew and sat on the branch of the tree opposite. They looked happy.

I went back to writing.

Yesterday when I left your side I rode to our spring. The water murmured sorrowfully, as if in a funeral lament. The sun was setting sullenly in mournful colours.

I was astonished. A branch on our almond tree was in blossom, even though it was out of season.

It was as though it was waiting for me to give it to you as a present. I have it here, in the vase beside your bed.

When I got back I slept and had a fateful dream: you had recovered at last and told me it was time for us to marry. You were even anxious to see what kind of children we would have. It would be the first time that an Orizon would wed a son of Hercules.

I felt optimistic that the union would produce a fine race.

Our wedding took place in the Garden of the White Roses. A soft breeze played around the blue silk wedding gown that Lady Life had sewn for you when you came of age. You looked superb. For the first time in my life I wore a waistcoat. It was blue too, but made of leather.

Everybody showered us with rose petals. The harps began to play the wedding march.

We knelt down. Lord Life walked towards us, slowly and majestically. He came close and put the Flame round our tightly clasped hands.

Then he handed it to Bull and he placed his hands on our heads.

"Let the Flame bind you for ever," he said, touched.

We rose, kissed his hand and then he embraced us both.

Everybody was there: your mother, Lady Danae, my father Hercules, Field Marshal Foster and Julius Newton. Rebecca wouldn't leave her father's side.

The musicians started playing the waltz of the Land of the White Sun.

We danced. You were fantastic and I was the happiest man in the world. Then I danced with your mother and you danced with Hercules.

Rebecca danced only with her father. She was absorbed in him and wouldn't leave him for a minute.

The dream was so vivid that it seemed real.

Did you perchance have the same dream too?